By the Sea

ALSO BY ABDULRAZAK GURNAH

Memory of Departure

Pilgrims Way

Dottie

Paradise

Admiring Silence

Desertion

The Last Gift

Gravel Heart

Afterlives

By the Sea

Abdulrazak Gurnah

Riverhead Books | New York | 2023

RIVERHEAD BOOKS
An imprint of Penguin Random House LLC
penguinrandomhouse.com

First published in hardcover in Great Britain by
Bloomsbury Publishing, London, in 2001
Copyright © 2001 by Abdulrazak Gurnah
First United States edition published in hardcover by
The New Press, New York, in 2001
First Riverhead trade paperback edition published 2023

Library of Congress Cataloging-in-Publication Data

Names: Gurnah, Abdulrazak, 1948– author.
Title: By the sea / Abdulrazak Gurnah.
Description: Paperback. | New York : Riverhead Books, 2023. |
First published in Great Britain by Bloomsbury Publishing 2001.
Identifiers: LCCN 2022043947 (print) | LCCN 2022043948 (ebook) |
ISBN 9780593541999 (paperback) | ISBN 9780593542002 (ebook)
Subjects: LCGFT: Novels.
Classification: LCC PR9399.9.G87 B95 2023 (print) |
LCC PR9399.9.G87 (ebook) | DDC 823/.92—dc23/eng/20220912
LC record available at https://lccn.loc.gov/2022043947
LC ebook record available at https://lccn.loc.gov/2022043948

Hardcover edition ISBN: 9780593716540

Printed in the United States of America
1st Printing

BOOK DESIGN BY LUCIA BERNARD

For Denise

By *the* Sea

1.

Relics

She said she'll call later, and sometimes when she says that she does. Rachel. She sent me a card because I don't have a telephone in the flat, I refuse to have one. In the card she said that I should call her if her coming was a problem, but I haven't. I have no urge to do so. It's late now, so I don't suppose she'll be coming after all, not today.

Though, in the card she did say today after six. Maybe it was only one of those gestures that was complete when it was made, to say that she had thought of me, in the sure expectation that I would take comfort from that, which I do. It doesn't matter, just that I don't want her turning up in the deep hours of the night, shattering its pregnant silences with a racket of explanations and regrets, and blurting out plans to take away more of the remaining hours of darkness.

I marvel how the hours of darkness have come to be so precious to me, how night silences have turned out so full of mumbles and whispers when before they had been so terrifyingly still, so tense with the uncanny noiselessness that hovered above words. As if coming to live here has shut one narrow door and opened another into a widening concourse. In the darkness I lose a sense of space, and in this nowhere I feel myself more solidly, and hear the play of voices more clearly, as if they were happening for the first time. Sometimes I hear music in the distance, played in the open and coming to me as a muted whisper. I long for night each arid day, even though I dread the darkness and its limitless chambers and shifting shadows. Sometimes I think it is my fate to live in the wreckage and confusion of crumbling houses.

It is difficult to know with precision how things became as they have, to be able to say with some assurance that first it was this and it then led to that and the other, and now here we are. The moments slip through my fingers. Even as I recount them to myself, I can hear echoes of what I am suppressing, of something I've forgotten to remember, which then makes the telling so difficult when I don't wish it to be. But it is possible to say something, and I have an urge to give this account, to give an accounting of the minor dramas I have witnessed and played a part in, and whose endings and beginnings stretch away from me. I don't think it's a noble urge. What I mean is, I don't know a great truth which I ache to impart, nor have I lived an exemplary experience which will illuminate our conditions and our times. Though I have lived, I have lived. It is so different here that it seems as if one life has ended and I am now living another one. So perhaps I should say of myself that once I lived another life elsewhere, but now it is over. Yet I know that the earlier one teems and pulses in rude good health behind me and before me. I have time on my hands, I am in the hands of time, so I might as well account for myself. Sooner or later we have to attend to that.

I live in a small town by the sea, as I have all my life, though for most of it, it was by a warm green ocean a long way from here. Now I live the half-life of a stranger, glimpsing interiors through the television screen and guessing at the tireless alarms that afflict people I see in my strolls. I have no inkling of their plight, though I keep my eyes open and observe what I can, but I fear that I recognize little of what I see. It is not that they are mysterious, but that their strangeness disarms me. I have so little understanding of the striving that seems to accompany their most ordinary acts. They seem consumed and distracted, their eyes smarting as they tug against turmoils incomprehensible to me. Perhaps I exaggerate, or cannot resist dwelling on my difference from them, cannot resist the drama of our contrastedness. Perhaps they are only straining against the cold wind that blows in from the murky ocean, and I am trying too hard to make sense of the sight. It is not easy, after all these years, to learn not to see, to learn discretion about the meaning of what I think I see. I am fascinated by their faces. They jeer at me. I think they do.

The streets make me tense and nervous, and sometimes even in my locked-in flat I find myself unable to sleep or sit at ease because of the rustlings and whisperings that agitate the lower air. The upper air is always full of agitation because God and his angels live there and debate high policy, and flush out treachery and rebellion. They do not welcome casual listeners or informers or self-servers, and have the fate of the universe to darken their brows and whiten their hair. As a precaution, the angels release a corrosive shower every now and then to deter mischievous eavesdroppers with a threat of deforming wounds. The middle air is the arena for contention, where the clerks and the anteroom afreets and the wordy jinns and flabby serpents writhe and flap and fume as they strain for the counsels of their betters. Ack ack, did you hear what he said? What can it mean? In the murk of the lower air is where you'll find the venomless time-servers and the fantasists who'll believe anything and defer to everything, the gullible and the spiritless throngs that crowd and pollute the narrowing spaces where they congregate, and that's where you'll find me. Nowhere else suits me quite as well. Perhaps I should say nowhere else *suited* me quite as well. That is where you would have found me when I was in my prime and pomp, for since coming here I have not been able to ignore the misgivings and the agitation I feel in the airs and lanes of this town. Not everywhere, though. I mean I do not feel this agitation everywhere and at every time. Furniture shops in the morning are silent, expansive places, and I stroll in them in some equanimity, troubled only by the tiny particles of artificial fiber which fill the air and which corrode the lining of my nostrils and bronchials, and which in the end drive me away for a while.

I found the furniture shops by chance, in the early days when they first moved me here, though I have always had an interest in furniture. At the very least, it weighs us down and keeps us on the ground, and prevents us from clambering up trees and howling naked as the terror of our useless lives overcomes us. It keeps us from wandering aimlessly in pathless wildernesses, plotting cannibalism in forest clearings and dripping caves. I speak for myself, even though I presume to include the unspeaking in my banal wisdom. Anyway, the refugee people found this flat for me and brought me here from the lodging where I had been staying, from Celia's bed-and-breakfast house. The journey from there was brief but full of twists and turns through short streets with lines of similar houses. It made me feel as if I was being taken to a place of hiding. Except that the streets were so silent and so straight, it could have been a part of that other town I once lived in. No, it couldn't. It was too clean, and bright and open. Too silent. The streets were too wide, the lampposts too regular, the roadside curbs still whole, everything in working order. Not that that town I lived in before was excessively filthy and dark, but its streets twisted in upon themselves, curling tightly on the corrupt detritus of fermented intimacies. No, it couldn't be part of that town, but there was something alike in it, because it made me feel hemmed in and observed. So as soon as they left me, I went out, to see where I was and to see if I could find the sea. That was how I found the small village of furniture shops round the corner from here, six of them, each as large as a warehouse, and arranged in a square marked out with car-parking spaces. It was called Middle Square Park. Most mornings it is quiet and empty there, and I stroll among the beds and the sofas until the fibers drive me away. I enter a different store every day, and after the first or second time, the assistants no longer make eye contact. I wander between the sofas and the dining tables, and the beds and the sideboards, lounging on an item for a few seconds, trying out the machinery, checking the price, comparing the fabric of this to that one. Needless to say, some of the furniture is ugly and overdecorated, but some of it is delicate and ingenious, and in these warehouses I feel for a while a kind of content and the possibility of mercy and absolution.

I am a refugee, an asylum seeker. These are not simple words, even if habit of hearing them makes them seem so. I arrived at Gatwick Airport in the late afternoon of November 23 last year. It is a familiar minor climax in our stories, leaving what we know and arriving in strange places, carrying little bits of jumbled luggage and suppressing secret and garbled ambitions. For some, as for me, it was the first journey by air, and the first arrival in a place so monumental as an airport, though I have traveled by sea and by land, and in my imagination. I walked slowly through what felt like coldly lit and silent empty tunnels, though now on reflection I know I walked past rows of seats and large glass windows, and signs and instructions. Tunnels, the streaming darkness outside lashing with fine rain and the light inside drawing me in. What we know constantly reels us in to our ignorance, makes us see the world as if we were still squatting in that shallow tepid pool which we had known since childhood terrors. I walked slowly, surprised at every anxious turn that an instruction awaited to tell me where to go. I walked slowly so that I would not miss a turning or misread a sign, so that I would not attract attention too early by getting into a flutter of confusion. They took me away at the passport desk. "Passport," the man said, after I had been standing in front of him for a moment too long, waiting to be found out, to be arrested. His face looked stern, even though the blankness in his eyes was intended to give nothing away. I had been told not to say anything, to pretend I could not speak any English. I was not sure why, but I knew I would do as I was told because the advice had a crafty ring to it, the kind of resourceful ruse the powerless would know. They will ask you your name and your father's name, and what good you had done in your life: say nothing. When he said *Passport* a second time, I handed it over, wincing in anticipation of abuse and threats. I was used to officials who glared and spluttered at you for the smallest mishap, who toyed with you and humiliated you for the sheer pleasure of wielding their hallowed authority. So I expected the immigration hamal behind his little podium to register something, to snarl or shake his head, to look up slowly and stare at me with the blaze of assurance with which the fortunate regard the supplicant. But he looked up from leafing through my joke document with a look of suppressed joy in his eyes, like a fisherman who has just felt a tug on the line. No entry visa. Then he picked up his phone and spoke into it for a moment. Smiling openly now, he asked me to wait on one side.

I stood with my eyes lowered, so I did not see the approach of the man who took me away for questioning. He called me by name and smiled as I looked up, a friendly worldly smile which said with some assurance, Why don't you come with me so we can sort out this little problem? As he strode briskly ahead of me, I saw that he was overweight and looked unhealthy, and by the time we reached an interview room, he was breathing heavily and tugging at his shirt. He sat in a chair and immediately shifted uncomfortably in it, and I thought of him as someone sweatily trapped in a form he disliked. It made me fear that his distemper would indispose him toward me but then he smiled again, and was soft-spoken and polite. We were in a small windowless room with a hard floor, with a table between us and a bench running

7

along one wall. It was lit with hard fluorescent strips which made the pewter-colored walls close in out of the corners of my eyes. He told me his name was Kevin Edelman, pointing to the badge he wore on his jacket. May God give you health, Kevin Edelman. He smiled again, smiling a lot, perhaps because he could see my nervousness despite my best efforts and wished to reassure me, or perhaps in his work it was unavoidable that he should take pleasure at the discomfort of those who came before him. He had a pad of yellow paper in front of him, and he wrote in it for a moment or two, taking down the name from my joke passport before he spoke to me.

"May I see your ticket, please?"

Ticket, oh yes.

"I see you have baggage," he said, pointing.

"Your baggage identification tag."

I played dumb. You might know *ticket* without speaking English, but *baggage identification tag* seemed advanced.

"I'll have the baggage collected for you," he said, keeping the ticket beside his notepad. Then he smiled again, interrupting himself from saying more on the subject. A long face, a bit fleshy in the temples, especially then as he smiled.

Perhaps he was only smiling in anticipation of the mixed pleasure of picking through my baggage, and the assurance that what he saw there would tell him what he needed to know, with or without my assistance. I imagine there would be some pleasure in such scrutiny, like looking into a room before it has been prepared for viewing, before its truthful ordinariness has been transformed into a kind of spectacle. I imagine there would be pleasure too in having an assured grasp of the secret codes that reveal what people seek to hide, a hermeneutics of baggage that is like following an archaeological trail or examining lines on a shipping map. I kept quiet, matching my breathing to his, so that I should feel the approach of annoyance in him. Reason for seeking entry into the United Kingdom? Are you a tourist? On holiday? Any funds? Do you have any money, sir? Traveler's checks? Sterling? Dollars? Do you know anybody who can offer a guarantee? Any contact address? Was there someone you were hoping to stay with while you were in the United Kingdom? Oh, bloody hell, bloody stupid hell. Do you have family in the UK? Do you speak any English, sir? I am afraid your documents are not in order, sir, and I will have to refuse you permission to enter. Unless you can tell me something about your circumstances. Do you have any documentation that might help me understand your circumstances? Papers, do you have any papers?

He left the room, and I sat calmly and still, suppressing a sigh of relief, and counted backward from 145, which was where I had got to while he was talking to me. I restrained myself from leaning forward to inspect his pad, in case he had seen through my dumb silence, but I suspected someone would be peering at me through a spyhole, watching for just such an incriminating move. It must have been the drama of the moment that made me think that. As if anyone could have cared whether I was picking my nose or secreting diamonds up my bowel. Sooner or later they would get to know all they needed to know. They had machines for all that. I had been warned. And their officials had been trained at great expense to see through the lies people like me told, and in addition they had great and frequent experience.

So I sat still and counted quietly, shutting my eyes now and then to suggest distress, reflection and a trace of resignation. Do with me what you will, O Kevin.

He returned with the small green cloth bag I had brought as my luggage, and put the bag on the bench. "Would you mind opening this please," he said. I looked agitated and uncomprehending, I hoped, and waited for him to elaborate. He glared at me and pointed at the bag, so with smiles of relief and understanding, and placating nods, I got up to unzip the bag. He took one item out at a time, laying each one carefully on the bench, as if he was unpacking clothing of some delicacy: two shirts, one blue, one yellow, both faded, three white T-shirts, one pair of brown trousers, three pairs of underpants, two pairs of socks, one kanzu, two sarunis, a towel and a small wooden casket. He sighed when he came to the last item, turning it round in his hand with interest and then sniffing it. "Mahogany?" he asked. I said nothing, of course, touched for the moment by the paltry mementos of a life spread out on the bench in that airless room. It was not my life that lay spread there, just what I had selected as signals of a story I hoped to convey. Kevin Edelman opened the casket and started with surprise at its contents. Perhaps he expected jewelry or something valuable. Drugs. "What's this?" he asked, then carefully sniffed the open casket. It was hardly necessary, as the little room had filled with glorious perfume as soon as he opened the box. "Incense," he said. "It is, isn't it?" He shut the casket and put it down on the bench, his tired eyes sparkling with amusement. Interesting booty from the reeking heat of some bazaar. I sat down on the chair as he instructed me, and waited while he went back to the bench with his pad and noted down the grubby items he had laid out there.

He went on writing for a moment longer after he came back to the table, having now filled two or three pages of his notepad, then he put his pen down and leaned back, wincing slightly as the back of the chair bit into his weary shoulder blades. He looked pleased with himself, almost cheerful. I could see he was about to pronounce sentence, and I could not suppress a surge of depression and panic. "Mr. Shaaban, I don't know you or know anything about the reasons that brought you here, or the expenses you incurred and all that. So I am sorry for what I now have to do, but I'm afraid I'm going to have to refuse you entry into the United Kingdom. You don't have a valid entry visa, you have no funds and you have no one who can offer a guarantee for you. I don't suppose you can understand what I am saying, but I have to tell you this anyway before I stamp your passport. Once I stamp your passport as having been refused entry, it means that next time you attempt to enter the United Kingdom you will automatically be turned away, unless your papers are in order, of course. Did you understand what I just said? No, I didn't think so. I'm sorry about this, but we have to go through these formalities nonetheless. We'll try and find someone who speaks your language so that they can explain it all to you later. In the meantime, we will be putting you on the next available flight back to the destination you came from and on the airline that brought you here." With that he leafed through my passport, looking for a clean page, and then picked up the little stamp he had placed on the table when he first came back.

"Refugee," I said. "Asylum."

He looked up, and I dropped my eyes. His were angry. "So you do speak English," he said. "Mr. Shaaban, you've been taking the piss."

"Refugee," I repeated. "Asylum." I glanced up as I said this, and started to say it a third time, but Kevin Edelman interrupted me. His face had gone slightly darker and his breathing had changed, had become less easy to match. He breathed deeply twice, making a visible effort to control himself when what he would really have liked to do was to pull a lever and have the floor beneath me open into an airy and bottomless drop. I know, I have wished the same myself on many occasions in my earlier life.

"Mr. Shaaban, do you speak English?" he asked, his voice mellowing again, but this time more sweaty than oily, officially soft-spoken now, laboring. Maybe I do, maybe I don't. I was catching up with his breathing again.

"Refugee," I said, pointing at my chest. "Asylum."

He grinned at me as if I was persecuting him, giving me a long look which I returned this time, smiling back. He sighed wearily, then he shook his head slowly and chuckled, perhaps amused by my uncomprehending smile. His manner made me feel that I was a tiresome and stupid prisoner he was interrogating, who had just momentarily frustrated him in some petty wordplay. I reminded myself, needlessly, to watch out for a surprise attack. Needlessly because his options were many and I had only one: to make sure that Kevin Edelman did not become angry and contemplate something brutal. It must have been the tiny room and the duplicitous courtesy with which he was speaking to me that made me feel I was a prisoner, when both he and

I knew that I was trying to get in and he was trying to keep me out. Wearily, he leafed through my passport, and I felt again that I was a tiresome nuisance, causing reasonable people needless trouble and inconvenience. Then he left me in the room again while he went to consult and check.

I knew he would find that the British government had decided, for reasons which are still not completely clear to me even now, that people who came from where I did were eligible for asylum if they claimed that their lives were in danger. The British wanted to make the point to an international audience that it regarded our government as dangerous to its own citizens, something both they and everyone else has known for a long time. But times had changed, and now every puffed-up member of the *international community* had to show that it was taking no more nonsense from the unruly and eternally bickering rabble that teem in those parched savannas. Enough was enough. What did our government do that was worse than the evils it had done before? It rigged an election, falsifying the figures in front of *international observers*, whereas before it had only jailed, raped, killed or otherwise degraded its citizens. For this delinquent behavior, the British government granted asylum to anyone who claimed their life was in danger. It was a cheap way of showing stern disapproval, and there weren't too many of us, being only a small island of relatively poor people only a few of whom would be able to find the fare. Several dozen young people did manage to raise the fare, forcing parents and relatives to give up their secret hoards or borrow, and sure enough when they arrived in London they were admitted as asylum seekers in fear of their lives. I too was in fear of my life, had been for years, though only recently had my fear reached the proportions of crisis. So when I heard that the youngsters were allowed in I decided to make the journey myself.

So I knew that Kevin Edelman would return in a few minutes with a different stamp in his hand and that I would then be on my way to detention or some other place to stay. Unless the British government had changed its mind while I was airborne, had decided that the joke had gone on for too long. Which it hadn't, because Kevin Edelman returned after a few minutes looking wry and amused, also defeated. I could see that he would not after all be putting me back on the plane to where I had come from, that other place where the oppressed manage to survive. For that I was relieved.

"Mr. Shaaban, why do you want to do this, a man of your age?" he said, sitting down clumsily and looking sad and furrowed with concern, then leaning against the back of the chair and working his shoulders slowly. "How much danger is your life really in? Do you realize what you're doing? Whoever persuaded you to do this is not doing you any favors, let me tell you that. You don't even speak the language, and you probably never will. It's very rare for old people to learn a new language. Did you know that? It may take years to sort out your application, and then you may be sent back, anyway. No one will give you a job. You'll be lonely and miserable and poor, and when you fall ill there'll be no one here to look after you. Why didn't you stay in your own country, where you could grow old in peace? This is a young man's game, this asylum business, because it is really just looking for jobs and prosperity in Europe and all that, isn't it?

There is nothing moral in it, just greed. No fear of life and safety, just greed. Mr. Shaaban, a man of your age should know better."

At what age are you supposed not to be afraid for your life? Or not to want to live without fear? How did he know that my life was in any less danger than those young men they let in? And why was it immoral to want to live better and in safety? Why was that greed or a game? I was touched by his concern though, and wished I could break my silence and tell him not to worry. I was not born yesterday, I knew how to look after myself. Please stamp that passport, kind sir, and send me away to some safe place of detention. I dropped my eyes in case their alertness should reveal that I understood him.

"Mr. Shaaban, look at yourself, and look at these things you've brought with you," he said, visibly frustrated, holding out his arm toward my worldly possessions. "This is all you'll have if you stay here. What do you think you'll find here? Let me tell you something. My parents were refugees, from Romania. I would tell you about that if we had more time, but what I mean is, I know something about uprooting yourself and going to live somewhere else. I know about the hardships of being alien and poor, because that is what they went through when they came here, and I know about the rewards. But my parents are European, they have a right, they're part of the family. Mr. Shaaban, look at yourself. It saddens me to say this to you, because you won't understand it and I wish you bloody well did. People like you come pouring in here without any thought of the damage they cause. You don't belong here, you don't value any of the things we value, you haven't paid for them through generations, and we don't want you here. We'll make life hard for you, make you suffer indignities, perhaps even commit violence on you. Mr. Shaaban, why do you want to do this?"

That this too too solid flesh should melt, thaw and resolve itself into a dew. It had been easy to match my breathing to his as he spoke, until the very end, because for most of the time his voice was calm and ordinary as if he was only reciting regulations. Edelman, was that a German name? Or a Jewish name? Or a made-up name? Into a dew, jew, juju. Anyway, the name of the owner of Europe, who knew its values and had paid for them through generations. But the whole world had paid for Europe's values already, even if a lot of the time it just paid and paid and didn't get to enjoy them. Think of me as one of those objects that Europe took away with her. I thought of saying something like this, but of course I didn't. I was an asylum seeker, in Europe for the first time, in an airport for the first time, though not for the first time under interrogation. I knew the meaning of silence, the danger of words. So I only thought this to myself. Do you remember that endless catalog of objects that were taken away to Europe because they were too fragile and delicate to be left in the clumsy and careless hands of natives? I am fragile and precious too, a sacred work, too delicate to be left in the hands of natives, so now you'd better take me too. I joke, I joke.

As for indignity and violence, I would just have to take my chances on them—though there weren't many places you could go to avoid the first, and the second could come at you out of nowhere. As for someone to look after you when you are old and poorly, better not to put too much hope in that solace. O Kevin, may the rudder of your life stay ever true and may hail never catch you in the open. May you not lose patience with this suppliant, and may you be kind enough to press that stamp in my joke passport and let me sniff the values of Europe's generations, alhamdulillah. My bladder is in urgent need of relief. I didn't even dare say that last, though it was true at the time. Silence imposes unexpected discomforts on you.

He went on talking, frowning and shaking his head, but I stopped listening. It's something I taught myself to do over the years, to win a little respite from the blaring lies I had to endure in my earlier life. Instead I stared dumbly at my passport, reminding Kevin Edelman that this one had got away, so could he put an end to the sport and inscribe. He stopped suddenly, frustrated in his good intention to persuade me to get back on the plane and leave Europe to its rightful owners, and riffled through my passport with the other stamp, the good stamp, held between the fingers of his hand. Then he remembered something, and it made him smile. He went back to my bag and took out the casket. As he had done before, he opened it and sniffed. "What is this?" he asked, his emphasis sterner, frowning at me. "What is this, Mr. Shaaban? Is it incense?" He held the casket out toward me, then took a deep sniff and held it out again. "What is it?" he asked placatingly. "It smells familiar. It's a kind of incense, isn't it?"

Perhaps he *was* Jewish. I stared back dumbly, then dropped my eyes. I could have told him it was udi, and we could then have had a pleasant conversation about how it was he remembered the perfume, some ceremony in his youth perhaps when his parents still expected him to participate in prayers and holy days, but then he wouldn't have stamped my passport, would have wanted

17

to know exactly how my life was in danger in my little bit of parched savanna, might even have had me sent back on the plane in shackles for pretending not to speak English. So I didn't tell him that it was ud-al-qamari of the best quality, all that remained of a consignment I had acquired more than thirty years ago, and which I could not bear to leave behind when I set out on this journey into a new life. When I looked up again I saw that he would steal it from me. "We'll have to have this tested," he said, smiling, waiting a long time to see if I understood and then bringing the casket back to the table with him. He put it down beside him, next to his yellow pad, tugged at his shirt to make himself more comfortable, and went on writing.

Ud-al-qamari: its fragrance comes back to me at odd times, unexpectedly, like a fragment of a voice or the memory of my beloved's arm on my neck. Every Idd I used to prepare an incense burner and walk around my house with it, waving clouds of perfume into its deepest corners, pacing the labors it had taken me to possess such beautiful things, rejoicing in the pleasure they brought to me and to my loved ones—incense burner in one hand and a brass dish filled with ud in the other. Aloe wood, ud-al-qamari, the wood of the moon. That was what I thought the words meant, but the man I obtained my consignment from explained that the translation was really a corruption of qimari, Khmer, Cambodia, because that was one of the few places in the whole world where the right kind of aloe wood was to be found. The ud was a resin which only an aloe tree infected by fungus produced. A healthy aloe tree was useless, but the infected one produced this beautiful fragrance. Another little irony by you-know-Who.

The man I obtained the ud-al-qamari from was a Persian trader from Bahrain who had come to our part of the world with the musim, the winds of the monsoons, he and thousands of other traders from Arabia, the Gulf, India and Sind, and the Horn of Africa. They had been doing this every year for at least a thousand years. In the last months of the year, the winds blow steadily across the Indian Ocean toward the coast of Africa, where the currents obligingly provide a channel to harbor. Then in the early months of the new year, the winds turn around and blow in the opposite direction, ready to speed the traders home. It was all as if intended to be exactly thus, that the winds and currents would only reach the stretch of coast from southern Somalia to Sofala, at the northern end of what has become known as the Mozambique Channel. South of this stretch, the currents turned evil and cold, and ships that strayed beyond there were never heard of again. South of Sofala was an impenetrable sea of strange mists, and whirlpools a mile wide, and giant luminescent stingrays rising to the surface in the dead of night and monstrous squids obscuring the horizon.

For centuries, intrepid traders and sailors, most of them barbarous and poor no doubt, made the annual journey to that stretch of coast on the eastern side of the continent, which had cusped so long ago to receive the musim winds. They brought with them their goods and their God and their way of looking at the world, their stories and their songs and prayers, and just a glimpse of the learning which was the jewel of their endeavors. And they brought their hungers and greeds, their fantasies and lies and hatreds, leaving some among their numbers behind for whole lifetimes and taking what they could buy, trade or snatch away with them, including people they bought or kidnapped and sold into labor and degradation in their own lands. After all that time, the people who lived on that coast hardly knew who they were, but knew enough to cling to what made them different from those they despised, among themselves as well as among the outlying progeny of the human race in the interior of the continent.

Then the Portuguese, rounding the continent, burst so unexpectedly and so disastrously from that unknown and impenetrable sea, and put paid to medieval geography with their seaborne cannons. They wreaked their religion-crazed havoc on islands, harbors and cities, exulting over their cruelty to the inhabitants they plundered. Then the Omanis came to remove them and take charge in the name of the true God, and brought with them Indian money, with the British close behind, and close behind them the Germans and the French and whoever else had the wherewithal.

New maps were made, complete maps, so that every inch was accounted for, and everyone now knew who they were, or at least who they belonged to. Those maps, how they transformed everything. And so it came to pass that in time those scattered little towns by the sea along the African coast found themselves part of huge territories stretching for hundreds of miles into the interior, teeming with people they had thought beneath them, and who when the time came promptly returned the favor. Among the many deprivations inflicted on those towns by the sea was the prohibition of the musim trade. The last months of the year would no longer see crowds of sailing ships lying plank to plank in the harbor, the sea between them glistening with slicks of their waste, or the streets thronged with Somalis or Suri Arabs or Sindis, buying and selling and breaking into incomprehensible fights, and at night camping in the open spaces, singing cheerful songs and brewing tea, or stretched out on the ground in their grimy rags, shouting raucous ribaldries at each other. In the first year or two after that, the streets and the open spaces were silent with their absences in those late months of the year, especially when we felt the lack of the things they used to bring with them, ghee and gum, cloths and crudely hammered trinkets, livestock and salted fish, dates, tobacco, perfume, rose water, incense and handfuls of all manner of wondrous things. We missed the ill-kempt gaiety they filled the town with. But soon we mostly forgot them as they became unimaginable to the new lives we led in those early years after independence. In any case, perhaps they would not have gone on coming for much longer. Who would choose to come hundreds of miles across the sea to sell us cloth and tobacco when they could live a life of luxury in the rich states of the Gulf?

This is the story of the trader I obtained the ud from. I'll tell it this way, because I no longer know who may be listening. His name was Hussein, a Persian from Bahrain, as he was quick to remind anyone who mistook him for an Arab or an Indian. He was among the more affluent traders, dressed in the light cream embroidered kanzu of the Persian Gulf and always clean and perfumed and faultlessly courteous, which was not the case with all the traders who came with the musim. His courtesy was like a gift, like a kind of talent, an elaboration of forms and manners into something abstract and poetic. His business was perfume and incense, and to tell the truth that combination of courtesy, affluence and unguents made him seem slippery and dissembling. For some reason he befriended me. I don't mean that I had no idea why he befriended me, but Hussein was not the kind of man to announce such things, and I am afraid of seeming immodest by speculating. I fear I might end up flattering myself, and make Hussein's subtle cultivation of our acquaintance into something crude.

This was the musim of 1960 and I had just recently set up in business, openly. For some four years before then I had been doing a little business on the side, along with my job as an administrative officer in the Directorate of the Financial Secretary. But the British were nervous of employees of their administration running a private business as well, especially if they were anything to do with financial services, and since opportunities came my way, I was forced to take them clandestinely while I was accumulating some capital. Then in 1958 my father died, and left me enough to turn to business as my livelihood. A life of business is a cruel one, merciless, preying, open to misunderstanding and gossip. I did not know that when I started out. Then my stepmother died soon after. I buried both of them with all due regard and observances, as I shall recount in its place, despite malicious muttering to the contrary. When I met Hussein, I was thirty-one years old, recently bereaved of my father and soon after that my stepmother, living alone in a comfortable house and envied by many for the good fortune that had befallen me.

Tongues were wagging mischievously about me, which in the kind of little place I lived in was an unmistakable sign of growing power, I thought. In my vanity, I lost sight of the looming malice around me.

Years before, the British authorities had been good enough to pick me out of the ruck of native schoolboys eager for more of their kind of education, though I don't think we all knew what it was we were eager for. It was learning, something we revered and were instructed to revere by the teaching of the Prophet, but there was glamour in this kind of learning, something to do with being alive to the modern world. I think also we secretly admired the British, for their audacity in being there, such a long way from home, calling the shots with such an appearance of assurance, and for knowing so much about how to do the things that mattered: curing diseases, flying airplanes, making movies. Perhaps *admired* is too uncomplicated a way of describing what I think we felt, for it was closer to conceding to their command over our material lives, conceding in the mind as well as in the concrete, succumbing to their blazing self-assurance. In their books I read unflattering accounts of my history, and because they were unflattering, they seemed truer than the stories we told ourselves. I read about the diseases that tormented us, about the future that lay before us, about the world we lived in and our place in it. It was as if they had remade us, and in ways that we no longer had any recourse but to accept, so complete and well-fitting was the story they told about us. I don't suppose the story was told cynically, because I think they believed it too. It was how they understood us and how they understood themselves, and there was little in the overwhelming reality we lived with that allowed us to argue, not while the story had novelty and went unchallenged. The stories we knew about ourselves before they took charge of us seemed medieval and fanciful, sacred and secret myths that were liturgical metaphors and rites of adherence, a different category of knowledge which, despite our assertive observance, could not contest with theirs. So that is how it seems when I think back to the way I was as a child, with no recourse to irony or knowledge of the fuller story of the multitudinous world. And at school there was little or no time for those other stories, just an orderly accumulation of the real knowledge they brought to us, in books they made available to us, in a language they taught us.

But they left too many spaces unattended to, could not in the nature of things do anything about them, so in time gaping holes began to appear in the story. It began to fray and unravel under assault, and a grumbling retreat was unavoidable. Though that was not the end of stories. There was still Suez to come, and the inhumanities of the Congo and Uganda, and other bitter bloodlettings in small places. Then it would seem that the British had been doing us nothing but good compared to the brutalities we could visit on ourselves. Their good, though, was steeped in irony. They told us about the nobility of resisting tyranny in the classroom and then applied a curfew after sunset, or sent pamphleteers for independence to prison for sedition. Never mind, they did drain the creeks, and improve the sewage system and bring vaccines and the radio. Their departure seemed so sudden in the end, precipitate and somehow petulant.

Anyway, they picked me out of the ruck of other eager students, along with three others that year who won scholarships to Makerere University College in Kampala, a different place then from what it has since become. I was eighteen years old, and now I think how fortunate I was in having had my eyes opened to a different way of looking at the world and to see how we looked from that angle. Puny and ragged.

Hussein. The year 1960 was a blessed musim: calm steady winds, dozens of richly loaded ships sailing safely into harbor, none lost at sea, none forced back. The harvests were good that year too, the trade was brisk and there were almost none of the high-spirited fights between ships' companies that sometimes broke out between the uncouth sailors. It was Hussein's third musim, and he came to the new furniture store I had opened to look at some of the things I had there. It was not really a *new* store, but my father's halwa shop converted, repainted and relit to sell furniture and other beautiful things. Despite all efforts, the smell of hot ghee still lingered in the store, and at times of despondency it seemed no different from the dingy dark cave from where my father sold halwa in small saucers. But I knew it was different, that my despondency was just an affliction of the glooms and faintheartedness, and that such dispirited moments were unavoidable. I tried thus to be wise. I knew the store looked smart and expensive, and the objects I displayed in there spoke for themselves. I have always had an interest in furniture. Furniture and maps. Beautiful, intricate things. I employed two cabinetmakers and installed them in a shed at the back of the store, and they built items on order: wardrobes, sofas, beds, that sort of thing. They did these things well, to designs they were familiar with and with wood they knew how to work. The real money, though, and where my passion for the business lay, was in acquiring auction lots of house contents and then picking out the valuables and the antiques. A small sandalwood cabinet made in Cochin or Trivandrum brought in a great deal more, pleasure and lucre, than a shedful of new oily monstrosities in mahogany and trinkety glass panels, which also in any case fetched a small profit from customers and traders who bought such things from me. If any restoration work was necessary I did it myself—guesswork mostly at first, but my customers knew even less about it than I did, so no harm was done.

My customers? For the antiques and the exquisites, they were European tourists and the resident British colonials. We were a day stop for the Castle Line cruise ships from South Africa to Europe and back. There were other lines as well, but the Castle was a regular twice-a-week call, one going up, the other going down. The tourists disembarked, were taken in hand by accredited guides, who (for a commission) brought many of them to my shop by and by. They were my best and most welcome customers, though I also did a little trade with resident colonial officials, and the one or two consular officials of other colonial nations, the French and the Dutch to be precise. Once the British Resident, the Ruler of the Waves himself, sent an agent to look over a mirror in a silver-studded Malacca frame made in the last century. The price was beyond him, unfortunately. The underling he had sent curled his red lips and stroked his fair hair with distracted distaste when I mentioned the price, as if I was asking too much, but I guessed it was just beyond him. He stomped up and down a few times, puffing his hot cheeks and saying *outrageous, outrageous* to himself, waiting for me to defer to the Admiral's right to choose his price, but I smiled attentively and stopped listening. Anyone who knew Malacca would have seen that it was not worth a penny less.

It was not that my countrymen were incapable of seeing the beauty of these things. I arranged the most beautiful of them as exhibits in the store, and people came in to look at them and admire. But they would not, could not, pay the prices I was asking for them. They did not have the same obsessive need of them that my European customers had—to acquire the world's beautiful things so they could take them home and possess them, as tokens of their cultivation and open-mindedness, as trophies of their worldliness and their conquest of the multitudinous parched savannas. At a different time, the British Resident's underling would not have been deterred by the price of the silver-studded Malacca mirror, especially after I told him that there were only a few of them left in the world. He would have taken it at his price, or no price at all, as a right of conquest, as a reflection of our comparative worth in the scheme of things. It was something like that that Kevin Edelman had done with my casket of ud-al-qamari. It's not that I don't understand the desire.

I recognized Hussein when he walked into the store, a tall unmistakable man with a look of the world about him. When he came into the store my head filled with words: Persia, Bahrain, Basra, Harun al-Rashid, Sindbad and more. I was not acquainted with him, but I had seen him in the streets and in the mosque. I even knew his name, because people spoke of him as the trader who the year before had taken lodgings with Rajab Shaaban Mahmud, the Public Works Department clerk, a man I had had some delicate dealings with in the past. He wasn't staying with him in 1960, some falling-out with a hint of scandal in it as rumor had it, but he was living in the area, and was known for his generosity. When I heard about his generosity, I knew that the usual malingerers would have already touched him for handouts, those shameless whiners whom our way of doing things allows to make a life out of weakness and abjection. He spoke to me in Arabic, offering courteous salutations, asking after my health, wishing me prosperity in my business, perhaps a little oversalted by and by. I apologized for my Arabic, which was scratchy at best, and spoke to him in Kiswahili. He smiled ruefully, saying, *Ah suahil. Ninaweza kidogo tu.* I can do little, little only. Then, surprisingly, he spoke to me in English. It was surprising because the traders and the sailors who came during the musim were an uncouth and rough-hewn riffraff, although this is not to say they did not have a decorous integrity of their own. Of course Hussein did not look or act like that, but still, English meant school, and people who went to school did not become sailors and musim traders who traveled in cramped and squalid dhows in the grimy company of loudmouth, brawn and thick ear.

He sat in the chair I offered him, stroking his jet mustache and smiling, waiting for me to invite him to state his business. He had heard about my shop, he said, and that I had many beautiful things there. He was looking for a gift for a friend, something delicate and attractive.

"For the family of a friend," he said.

I understood from this that he wanted a gift for a woman, perhaps the wife of a business friend or perhaps not. I showed him round and he was taken first by a slim ebony box which when I acquired it made me think it would have housed an assassin's dagger. Then he paused over a round teak cabinet engraved with a design of arched doorways and wheels. But I had already seen his eyes wandering toward a low table on three delicately bowed legs, made of ebony so highly polished that it glowed tremulously even from a distance. Before he got there he looked a long time at a set of green fluted goblets on a silver tray, running a finger round the gilded rim and sighing. "Beautiful," he murmured. "Exquisite."

"And this," he said, when we arrived at the ebony table I now knew he coveted.

"This little thing?" I asked. He smiled politely when I named the price, and then nodded. We went back to our chairs to begin a pleasurable and courteous exchange of views on the matter. After a while, when it became clear we were too far apart to agree, Hussein dropped the subject and began to talk about something else, I can't remember now. That was how we became friends, in that casual exchange of opinion over that beautiful table, and in the enjoyable appreciation of the little courtesies we extended to each other. Perhaps also there was some pleasure in speaking to each other in English. At some point during the day, Hussein would be sure to step into the store, look to see that *my table*, as he called it, was still there, and then settle down for a chat. Sometimes someone else would be there, passing the time of day, delivering and collecting news, doing a bit of business, the convivial routine of small-town life. Then Hussein would sit back and do his best to follow the conversation. There was nothing portentous about these conversations, but Hussein listened attentively, appealing to me for help if there was something he particularly cared not to miss. It was part of his talent for courtesy, and sometimes because he did not want to miss a delicious twist to a bit of gossip. But if there was no one else in the shop, he leaned back in the chair with his right ankle tucked under his left thigh, made himself a fat roll-up and talked.

This was his third musim in Africa. His family had no business this way before that, trading mostly further east. His grandfather Jaafar Musa was a merchant of legend. He had lived most of his life in Malaya and Siam, going there as a boy apprentice to another Persian merchant known to his father. Persian and Arab merchants had been trading in Malaya for centuries, and merchants from Hadhramut took the message of Islam there in the seventh century, in the same generation as the Prophet's revelations in Makka. There were also merchants from India and China, and all these people worked and competed in the way of trade. But the word of Islam spread over Malaya, to the extent of the creation of Muslim states and empire. Even though the Portuguese and the Dutch came to conquer and take charge in their characteristic ways from the 1500s, it was not until the British swaggered in in the 1850s that the power of the Muslim Malay states was finally made null. All this had a bearing on Hussein's story.

From the very beginning of his time in Malaya, the endeavors of Hussein's grandfather Jaafar Musa were blessed, and he made his fortune while still a young man. In his prime he was dealing in all kinds of business and running several ships all across the Asian seas. This great prosperity coincided with the time when

Europeans, especially the British, were taking a firmer grip on the world. In the far east trade, in the 1880s, they were squeezing everyone else out in the name of a higher civilization. They wanted the opium, the rubber, the tin, the timber, the spices, and they wanted it all without any interference from anyone else, native, muslim or worshipper of a thousand demons, and especially not from merchants who were from territories outside their authority. There was every reason to imagine that they would have their way here as they had everywhere else. So Jaafar, looking to defer the moment somewhat, employed Europeans to captain his ships and to work as clerks in his office. By some guile or other, he managed to make it seem that his European employees were running him, that he was the dupe of his resourceful retainers, without whom the business would collapse. To casual appearance it was a European company, but in reality Jaafar Musa stayed in his old timber room at the back of the office counting the blessing of God on his enterprise and plotting new ventures. His ships traded as far south as Sulawesi and as far east as the country of the Qimari, the Khmers, and as far west as Bahrain, and anything else in between was also fine. Quietly, he watched the blustering European companies going bankrupt and the dashing captains and crews of their ships turn into suicides and wharf rats. Not all of them went bankrupt, of course, but an encouraging number did, and after a while it became impossible not to notice that Jaafar Musa was becoming one of the richest merchants in Malaya, despite the steamboats, the repeating rifles and the Malay sultans lining up to capitulate to the new world order.

It was a moment of great peril for him, something he understood very well. The British were interfering everywhere they could, energetically penetrating the orderly shambles of native government, asking searching questions, writing reports, cleaning up, imposing consuls and residents and customs regulations, creating order by taking charge of everything that looked as if it would deliver a penny or two. And here was this rich Persian merchant, this Arab as the British insisted on describing him, whom rumor and speculation made far richer than he really was, and whom envy transformed into a legendary and merciless intriguer, a despot, a slaver, a keeper of a harem, a sodomizer of little boys, craftily controlling trade which should be in more deserving hands. There was talk of investigating his business methods or even the possibility of criminal proceedings against him for kidnap and murder. No one said this in front of Jaafar Musa, but he knew this was the loose talk of the Europeans and he understood how much they wanted it to be true. He saw something in the eyes of the Europeans who worked for him that made him suspect that they found it harder than ever now not to sneer at him, even though their manner was still obsequious and correct.

Jaafar Musa had a son and two daughters, all of them born in Malaya to his late beloved, Mariam Kufah, may God have mercy on her soul. The daughters Zeynab and Aziza were honorably married by the time of these events and living in Bombay and Shiraz with their husbands, both of whom came from families distantly related to Jaafar. That was how it had been for decades, perhaps centuries. However far people traveled for trade, they received news and sent news, and when it was time to marry their sons and daughters there was always an honorable option available to them. So it had been with Jaafar's daughters, as it no longer is in our time. Jaafar Musa's instinct was to begin a careful and disguised withdrawal out of Malaya before the greed of the British became something impossible to resist. He would transfer the business to Bombay and Shiraz in his daughters' names and put his sons-in-law in charge while events ran their course and the moment came when he and his son could leave with as much as possible intact.

His son Reza disagreed. For years he had fretted at his father's subterfuge of having Europeans appear to be running his business, at the high-handed disregard with which he thought these employees were treating both his father and him. "If they now want war, let's give them war," he said to his father. They should dispense with the arrogant dogs and employ Malays and Indians and Arabs and then do as cutthroat trade as they could. Jaafar Musa, who had been doing cutthroat trade all his adult life, was alarmed and distressed by his son's anger. These are not village sultans we are talking about, but the rulers of the world. He cajoled him, talked to him about the hardheaded realities of their circumstances, in the end insisted with him. Reza dutifully desisted but was not persuaded, was still seething at the injustice.

In the year 1899 Jaafar Musa suffered a stroke. He was walking on the wide upstairs veranda of his house, on his way to the afternoon walk he always took round his beautiful garden, when it seemed as if someone hit him a powerful blow in his diaphragm. His heart burst. The gardener, Abdulrazak, who always watered the beds in late afternoon and who in any case waited until the master appeared to commend and instruct him, and who in his mind thought of these exchanges as the climax of his working day, was at that moment picking jasmine for his wife, with half an eye on the veranda which opened out from the merchant's bedroom. So he saw Jaafar Musa curl over and fall to the side and stood transfixed for a moment at the sight of the world's end. The gardener ran upstairs, screaming for help, slipping and grazing his shins and leaving muddy footprints on the polished teak staircase. He clutched the merchant in his arms, rocking him as if he were a child, and screaming out for someone to come and help them. No one came. There was no one to come at that time of day and on this side of the house. This was the merchant's garden terrace, where in time gone by he sat with his beloved Mariam Kufah through the early hours of the evening, talking with her or listening to her recite, and where sometimes their daughters, when they lived here before their mother's death, joined them in song and laughter and conversation. When Reza was younger, he sat with them too. After their departure, no one came to this part of the house except the gardener, not at that time of day. So it was that Jaafar Musa, the legendary Arab cutthroat trader, died in the arms of his gardener, Abdulrazak, whose face was covered with tears and snot and blood from sinews which had burst in his grief.

E ven as he led the huge funeral procession, my father Reza was planning changes," Hussein said. "It was hopeless, and he lost the business as my grandfather predicted. He got rid of his European employees as soon as he could, sometime in 1900, but then he couldn't get anyone to accept a job with him, not a senior job. They were too scared of the British. By then all the sultans had signed the British paper, accepting protectorate. My father Reza had to pay big compensation, very big, to all the captains and managers he had got rid of, and all the companies that had been waiting for consignments and deliveries. They made him pay in court. Insurers refused to give him cover. Customs, they searched everything, delayed everything, accused him of bribery. It was probably true. He probably thought that was what they wanted. He was in his twenties and he thought he was as good as anyone, but he wasn't. Not as good as the Europeans, anyway. So slowly like that they strangled him and the business went to ruin. He could not get credit even from local sources, let alone the high-and-mighty British. After 1910 all Malaya was theirs, even Johor and the northern states, and in that ten years the great company my grandfather had so cunningly built was just a little thing, although still not in debt. It was an obsession of my father, to avoid debt. In the end he was forced to consider selling the house and its beautiful garden. The gardener, he kept the garden beautiful all this time. And then, when the house was for sale, all those stories about my grandfather started again, slaver, criminal, and so on. Only this time they added that he fucked the gardener, pardon my language, which was why he was found dead in his arms. It was time for my father to go, to get away from the ugliness of people who skinned their faces with such shamelessness."

That was how Reza told the story to him, Hussein, and sometimes to others who wanted to know about his time in Malaya, but it wasn't something he liked to talk about. It made him angry to tell it, and sometimes the injustice of it made him tearful. It was not a good story to tell, especially not to a son, and especially not to merchants, who were the people Reza associated with in Bahrain. He had lost the fortune his father had so diligently accumulated, and in such a far-off place. Jaafar Musa had done what every merchant dreamed of. He had fulfilled the romance of the trader who sets off to a distant destination with his worldly goods and finds prosperity and respect. Reza's loss was the nightmare of that dream, that after a lifetime of cunning and sacrifice, the son would lose it all. That was what I thought too when Hussein told me. I even predicted to myself, as soon as Reza entered the story, that he would lose everything. Well, he did not lose everything. He retrieved enough from the wreck to start another business in Bahrain, importing perfume and incense and cloth from Siam and Malaya and places further to the east. Bahrain was ruled by the British too, as was so much of the known world, but their government there was a ramshackle affair. To them it was just a place from where they could launch attacks on their enemies and refuel their ships. And the Persian and Arab and Indian merchants who had been operating out of Bahrain for centuries were too wily to be browbeaten by lordly disdain. Before they found oil there in the 1930s, there wasn't much to fight over anyway apart from the import trade—no tin or rubber or gold or any of those commodities that could be gouged out of the earth to be taken to Europe as loot.

Sometimes Reza dealt in rare wood when there was a demand for it, when an Agha was building himself a new mansion and his carpenters needed teak for the staircase or mahogany for his bedrooms. Or when a dealer for some Syrian sultan or Russian baron or German banker was buying up supplies for a palace in which he could sit and gloat over his good fortune. I imagine these transactions, though Hussein did mention doing business with a dealer for a Russian baron who had established himself in Mashhad, in preparation for the Tsar's takeover of Persia, which he thought was imminent. I forget what it was Hussein said he dealt in. Perhaps he didn't say. Reza even left a rump of the business in Malaya to act as agents for acquiring supplies, and to look after whatever little property still remained in his hands.

Anyway, the move to Bahrain was blessed too, just as his father had been in Malaya, though not in quite the same spectacular fashion. The war against the Turks did him no harm, only good, bringing business along with the thousands of the odious English and Indian armies passing through on their way to the battles in Iraq. (Poor Iraq, it seems the British have been fighting there for one reason or another so often in this century.) And soon after the war, in 1918, he married and was blessed with three daughters before Hussein arrived. People came and went from his shop all day, always sure of a welcome whether they had come to buy or sell or sit and chat in the atmosphere of heady scents. His children milled around the shop, spoiled and praised by everyone, accepting such adoration with precocious composure.

"He loved his children," Hussein said, his eyes glinting with water at the memory. "And they loved him. He was very . . . emotional about it, and it seems he wanted everyone else to love them too."

When Hussein was ten years old, Reza decided to make a trip to Malaya, to wind up what bits of business still remained there, and to see the old places again, and to show everyone who cared to know that things had not turned out all bad for him. He took

Hussein with him as testimony of the good fortune that had befallen him, but also so that he would see the big world and begin
to learn how to cope in it. They spent four months traveling—
the sea voyage, doing business, seeing the sights, visiting and
staying with friends.

"Wait, wait," I said to Hussein. "Let me fetch a map. I want
you to show me all these places. I want to see where they are."

They even went to Bangkok, where Reza had lived for some
months as a teenager, living with his father's agent there in the
days before their affairs went bad. It was a calm, beautiful port
town then, with canals and riverside boulevards, not the teeming
behemoth it became later. People from all over the world congregated there: Chinese, Indians, Arabs, Europeans. To Hussein
it was an incredible journey, an unbelievable journey, and images
of that time have stayed with him all his life. And even though he
only told them to me as stories, they've stayed with me too ever
since. To this day I imagine a walk he described across the courtyard of a temple on the royal island, I imagine the austere tran-
quility he described, and the overwhelming authority of the
temple dome. I have seen a photograph of the temple since coming here, but it revealed nothing of the beauty that Hussein
described.

In Bangkok his father purchased a consignment of the best
quality ud-al-qamari from Cambodia for a good price, and had it
shipped to Bahrain on the same boat that they took back. It was
he, Hussein's father, who explained that ud-al-qamari, the wood
of the moon, was a corruption of ud-al-qimari, the wood of the
Khmers. The Japanese war started soon after they returned to
Bahrain, and there was no ud to be had for another seven or

eight years, so Reza made a healthy profit for years on that consignment.

"I still have some," Hussein said, smiling to see how the story of the journey and the ud had so excited and captivated me. It was at this point that I realized that crafty Hussein was still bargaining for that ebony table. He glanced at it briefly and gave me a friendly knowing look.

"Do you have some with you?" I asked.

So the next time he came he brought a small mahogany casket with the most beautiful ud-al-qamari it has ever been my good fortune to inhale. With the help of the coffee seller across the road from my shop, who contributed some pieces of glowing charcoal, Hussein prepared an incense burner and perfumed the air we breathed. People walking along the street stopped in their tracks and came to sit by the glowing scent. The coffee seller crossed the road and stood on the steps, saying, "Mashaallah, mashaallah, that is beautiful, Allah karim. May I bring you some coffee, maulana?" His gratitude did not extend to me because I had ruined his life. As everyone knows you can't eat halwa without a cup of coffee in your hand, so when I stopped the halwa business I also cut his throat, as he put it. I assassinated him. But now even he entered the store and sat breathing the same scented air as the rest of us. I thought I could catch the odor of the fantasy of those distant places in the dense body of that perfume, although that was only because Hussein had bound the two things together for me with his stories, and I had surrendered to both so completely.

Of course I let Hussein have the ebony table, in the end.

"Tell me one thing," I said to him in the process of our negotiations, smiling and making it possible for him to turn the matter into a joke if he chose to. "Why do you want this table so much? Is it for someone special?"

He smiled evasively, drooping his eyelids theatrically, playing the rogue. "It's a delicate matter," he said.

I knew, everyone knew, that he was wooing the beautiful son of Rajab Shaaban Mahmud, the Public Works Department clerk, at whose house he had lodged on an earlier trip, and where he was still a visitor. I will tell the story this way, for all the blemishes in the telling, because I no longer know who may be listening. In any case, the rumor was that Hussein was wooing the beautiful son of Rajab Shaaban Mahmud, the Public Works Department clerk. For all I knew he had already corrupted that glowing youth, but I could not imagine that the ebony table would be of any interest to him. It was more likely that the rumored gifts of money and silk cloth would be appropriate to the seduction of the vanity of such a youth. Young people caught up in the stews of their passions have no sense of the beauty of *things*. Perhaps the table was a gift to Rajab Shaaban Mahmud himself, a token of courtesy to him as a way of saying that because he wished to seduce the son, this did not mean that he did not esteem the father. A bribe. Or perhaps the cunning Persian trader was playing an even more complicated game, really stalking Rajab Shaaban Mahmud's beautiful wife Asha by pretending to be after the son. She was indeed a beautiful woman, and I had found her courteous and self-respecting in the very brief acquaintance I had with her up to that time. As it concerned the matter of Hussein, though, she was rumored to have been game for a fling or two in the past and was still willing, according to those who had the gift for pronouncing on such matters. These are difficult things to know, and miserable matters to talk about, but they are the currency of daily commerce in a small town and it would be false not to speak about them. Nevertheless, it makes me uncomfortable to do so. And now I feel foolish and dissembling for protesting so much. Perhaps it was all a tease for Hussein, at least at first, occupying the long months of the musim after he had disposed of his merchandise and was waiting for the winds to change for the return journey. None of it was my affair, though in such a small place it was impossible not to know about such things.

We agreed that Hussein would pay me half my asking price for the table in cash, and for the rest he would give me a twenty-pound packet of the ud-al-qamari. He was generous, or I was better at bargaining than I thought I was. He gave me the casket as a gift, the casket Kevin Edelman plundered from me, and with it the last of the ud-al-qamari Hussein and his father bought in Bangkok in the year before the war, the casket which I had brought with me as all the luggage from a life departed, the provisions of my afterlife.

Kevin Edelman, the bawab of Europe, and the gatekeeper to the orchards in the family courtyard, the same gate which had released the hordes that went out to consume the world and to which we have come sliming up to beg admittance. Refugee. Asylum seeker. Mercy.

But the arrangement we made over the little ebony table wasn't the end of my dealings with Hussein. It was a bad year for the return winds of the musim, coming so late and fitfully at first. In any case Hussein overextended himself in his dealings, perhaps out of boredom or playfulness. As I got to know him a little better I came to understand that so much of what he did was playful and mischievous, and when the mischief led to a little havoc and rancor, his laughter thickened with unkind glee. At those moments I thought I caught glimpses of something cruel in him underneath the courtesies and the gleeful chuckles, a sternness or cynicism that was uncomplicated and assured. I thought I could imagine him killing or causing someone unbearable pain if he felt it necessary to protect what he valued. Whereas I can't think there is anything that valuable. Anyway, I could imagine him trading out of boredom, just for something to do, inching toward ruin. It doesn't sound like good business, but then he was a Persian who traded in incense and perfume, gliding with his stories and his courtesies only just out of reach of the tangles that made us so ordinary. Who is to know whether doing things in style seemed to him a better reason for making decisions than ensuring that there was a lamb curry to eat every day?

He underestimated the cost of style, which also doesn't sound like good business, and approached me for a sizable loan, and I was fortunate to be able to extend it to him. Business had been good, which is to say that my customers had been foolish enough to pay my prices and the carpenters had not thought to ask for an increase in their payment, or I had managed whatever came my way with wily efficiency and prudent husbandry. Whatever it was I did, I was in the gloatingly happy position to lend Hussein the money he needed. Such loans used to be frequent between traders, especially traders across the ocean, although no one would dream of doing it these days, now that everyone is scrabbling for the merest coppers. In those days . . . Such sad words for a man of my age, and, after everything that has happened, such useless words. Then, someone borrowed money from you here, went to trade somewhere else, then repaid the loan to an associate of yours at yet another place. The associate purchased what merchandise you required and shipped it to you. Everyone got a cut, and honor and trust prevailed between merchants, marriage contracts were agreed, families became closer, and business prospered. Now and then there was drama and intrigue as something went wrong, and scandal threatened, but obligations and self-respect prevented a descent into chaos, and if worse came to worst, scholars of law and scholars of religion, who might be the same personages, would be called in to arbitrate. Although even by then things had changed in the few decades of British rule, and when worse did come to worst, it was more likely that a Gujarati lawyer would be consulted, some Shah & Shah or Patel & Sons, rather than the qadhi, a good and gentle man at that time unlike the ranters who came after him.

In any case, I was new in business and had no associates of the kind I have described, no one who would be obliged to care for my money as if it were his own. Such associates were relations or the work of a lifetime, cultivated and then inherited, generation after generation, life after life, obligation by obligation, inescapable and impossible to terminate. So I had to ask Hussein for something to hold against the loan.

"Without doubt," he said, relieved and smiling. It made me

wonder whether he was in greater difficulties than he had told me. "I made that mistake once myself in Bombay. Only a trivial sum, I'm glad to say, but I never saw an anna of it back."

"Bombay," I said. "Is there no end to your adventures? What were you doing there?"

"I was sent to school there. My aunt asked for me. My aunt Zeynab, you remember her. She asked for me so I could go to school," Hussein said, sneering gently and raising his eyebrows at his aunt's earnestness. "I learned a great deal in Bombay, a city of many wrongs. I also learned the language of our conquerors, may God give them strength."

I ignored that last remark, taking it to be another of his provocative ironies. Anyway, Hussein had brought a surprising document with him, which all along he had intended as security for the loan. It showed that in the previous year he had lent Rajab Shaaban Mahmud, his landlord at that time, the exact sum of money he wished to borrow from me, and that by that agreement Rajab Shaaban Mahmud undertook to pay back the money not less than twelve months later. The penalty for failure to pay was the loss of Rajab Shaaban Mahmud's house and all its contents. It was sworn to and witnessed in front of the qadhi.

"Why don't you just get your money off him?" I asked, though I had a very good idea why not. Rajab Shaaban Mahmud was a Public Works Department clerk, who had a love for the forbidden drink, the devil's brew, and on the evidence of the document was a complete fool. He had inherited the house from his aunt Bi Sara only the previous year, otherwise he had little else to his name. Why agree to the loss of the house as penalty? The very roof over his head. It was not much of a house, but enough to keep shame at bay and provide a roof over the heads of his loved ones. Where was he going to find the money to pay that loan back? Hussein must have known that all along, and must have lent him the money to put him under a crushing obligation for some reason. And if there was any truth to the rumors of his seduction of the son, then that reason was the gratification of what was beginning to look like a playfully malicious desire.

"I don't intend to press for payment," Hussein said, no doubt guessing my thoughts. "If you agree, I intend to have the document made over to you, for you to hold as security until I come back next year. Then I will repay you and you'll return the document to me."

I wish I had refused the plan, because after the havoc he wreaked on Rajab Shaaban Mahmud's household at the end of that musim, I didn't think it likely that he would come back. Though I could not be sure what a reckless and proud Persian merchant might do, what jinns and demons he had as his playmates, what dishonors and indignities he could bear without embarrassment. In the eight months or so until the next musim, I considered the options available to me and waited, but sure enough, Hussein did not come back. He sent a letter with another trader, with greetings and apologies, pressure of business elsewhere, and may God bless all your enterprises until we meet again, which, inshaallah, will be in the year after. He also sent a gift, a map. It was a mariner's map of South Asia. It belonged to his grandfather Jaafar Musa, he said in his letter, and it didn't look as if it had been used very much. He found it in his father's papers and thought I might like to have it. The gift made me smile. He remembered how much I liked maps. Such a fine map.

The money could wait until next year, and I still had the note on the house. Business was good, alhamdulillah. I talked to myself in this way, but could not quite still the anxieties the affair filled me with.

I speak to maps. And sometimes they say something back to me. This is not as strange as it sounds, nor is it an unheard-of thing. Before maps the world was limitless. It was maps that gave it shape and made it seem like territory, like something that could be possessed, not just laid waste to and plundered. Maps made places on the edges of the imagination seem graspable and placable. And later when it became necessary, geography became biology in order to construct a hierarchy in which to place the people who lived in their inaccessibility and primitiveness in other places on the map.

The first map I saw, though I must have seen others in innocence before that, was one a teacher showed us when we were seven years old. I was seven anyway, even if I can't say for certain about the ages of the multitude which shared this experience with me. There or thereabouts, anyway. For some reason, you had to be *below* a certain age before you could begin school. I have never properly considered the oddness of this before and it is only now as I think it that I realize its strangeness. If you were over a certain age, it was as if you had gone over the point beyond which you could be instructed, like a coconut that had overripened and become undrinkable, or cloves that had been left too long on the tree and had swollen into seeds. And even now as I think of it I can't come up with an explanation for this stern exclusion. The British brought us school, and brought the rules to make school work. If the rules said you had to be six and no older than six to be allowed to start school, that was how it would be. Not that the schools had things their own way, because parents shaved off however many years it was necessary to have their children allowed in. Birth certificate? They were poor, ignorant people and never bothered to obtain one. Which was why they wanted their son to go to school, so he wouldn't end up a beast like them.

In our own lives, everyone had been going to chuoni for generations. Chuoni, that was where we went to learn the aliph-be-te so we could read the Koran and listen to the miraculous events that befell the Prophet throughout his lifetime, sala-llahu-wa-ale. And whenever there was time to spare, or the heat was too great to concentrate on the nimbly curling letters on the page, we listened to stories of the hair-raising tortures that awaited some of us after death. Nobody bothered with age in chuoni. You started more or less as soon as you were toilet-trained and stayed there until you could read the Koran from beginning to end, or until you found the nerve to escape, or until the teachers could no longer bear to have you around, or your parents refused to pay the miserable pittance which was the teacher's fee. Most people had made their escape by the age of thirteen or so. But at school you started when you were six and progressed as well as you could, year after year, all of you the same age together. There were always stragglers, those who had been required to repeat a year, one or two in every class who lived with their shame throughout their school life. For the rest of us, we were all the same age, on paper. You could never be sure how old classmates really were, and as we grew a little older, some developed mustaches at a tender age and some disappeared for a few days and returned with eyes alight with secret knowledge, followed by whispered rumors of quiet weddings in the countryside. We did tend to marry early in those days. I don't know what happened in girls' schools and wish now that I did. Perhaps the girls would have just disappeared from school, there one day, gone the next, and everyone would have guessed they had been married. Married off, married by, done to. I try to imagine what that would have felt like. I imagine myself a woman, feeble with unuttered justification, unutterable. I imagine myself defeated.

But I was talking about the first map I saw. I was seven when the teacher showed it to us, even if I can't say for certain the ages of the other boys in the class. Seven is a propitious number, and I have been here for seven months, though that is not why I cling to that number for the moment of my first map. I know I was seven because it was my second year at school, and I have the integrity of the British Empire to bear me out, since I would have been six the year I started, as the rules required. The teacher introduced his subject in a dramatic fashion. He held up a hen's egg between thumb and forefinger. "Who can tell me how to make this egg stand up on its end?" That was how he introduced Christopher Columbus to us. It was a fabulous and unrepeatable moment, as if I too had stumbled across an unimagined and unexpected continent. It was the moment at the start of a story. As his story developed, he began to draw a map on the blackboard with a piece of white chalk: the coast of northwest Europe, the Iberian peninsula, southern Europe, the land of Shams, Syria and Palestine, the coast of North Africa which then bulged out and tucked in and then slid down to the Cape of Good Hope. As he drew, he spoke, naming places, sometimes in full, sometimes in passing. Sinuously north to the jut of the Ruvuma delta, the cusp of our stretch of coast, the Horn of Africa, then the Red Sea coast to Suez, the Arabian peninsula, the Persian Gulf, India, the Malay peninsula and then all the way to China. He stopped there and smiled, having drawn half the known world in one continuous line with his piece of chalk. He put a dot halfway down the east coast of Africa and said, "This is where we are, a long way from China."

Then he put a dot in the north Mediterranean and said, "This is where Christopher Columbus was, and he wanted to go to China, but by following a route in the opposite direction." I don't remember much of what he told us about the adventures of greedy Cristóbal, so many other stories have silted up over that innocent moment, but I remember that he said that Columbus set out on his voyage the same year as the fall of Granada and the expulsion of Muslims from Andalus. These names too were new to me, as were so many of the others, but he said them with such reverence and longing—the fall of Granada and the expulsion of Muslims from Andalus—that I have never lost the moment. I see him now, a short plump man, dressed in a kanzu, kofia and a faded brown jacket, his face pitted with smallpox scars yet composed into a look of forbearance and tolerance. And I remember the fluency with which he created an image of the world for us, my first map.

The egg? This was the story. The sailors on Columbus's ships had never sailed west into the Atlantic, nobody had. For all anyone knew, the ocean suddenly ended and its waters fell into a gigantic chasm and then traveled through caverns and gorges under the earth to a depthless pool infested with monsters and devils. Then also the journey was long and difficult, the ocean empty, no glimpse of Cathay however sharp-eyed the lookout. So the rabble grumbled and plotted. We want to go home. In the end Columbus confronted them, holding a hen's egg between thumb and forefinger. Which of you can make this egg stand on its end? he asked. None of them could, of course. They were only sailors, doomed to play superstitious bit parts in such high drama, and grumble and cook up improbable plots. Columbus gently cracked the end of the egg—the teacher demonstrated with his own egg—and then stood it on the quarter-deck rail. I am not sure now whether the moral was that in order to eat an egg you have to crack it, and therefore in order to find Cathay you have to put up with suffering, or whether it was just to demonstrate that Columbus was a great deal cleverer than the sailors and was therefore more likely to be right about the most sensible course of action. In any case, the sailors immediately gave up any thought of insurrection and sailed on in search of the Grand Khan. As I would have done when I was seven. The teacher carefully put his hard-boiled egg down on his desk for later consumption.

We never had that teacher again, although he was a regular teacher at the school. Our class teacher was absent that day and he was looking after us for the morning. At the end of the morning we trooped out to go back to our class, and when I peeped in later to see the world he had shown us, the map had been wiped off the board.

Hussein would not have known about this, would have had

no idea how it was that maps began to speak to me, but he knew how I loved looking at them and collecting them, and he sent me his grandfather's old map to placate me because he owed me money. I laughed with pleasure when the gift arrived, but I was also almost certain that I would not see Hussein again. Why would he want to come our way to sell bits and pieces of sandal-wood and rose water when he could be trading in Rangoon and Shiraz and other such far-flung places in the great world, places hard to reach and therefore beautiful because of that?

2.

She didn't come. Sometimes she doesn't, even when she says she will. She comes to me when it suits her, or so it seems, which is not always how I would prefer things to be. Get a telephone then, she tells me, but I prefer not to. I have never had a telephone and I refuse to burden myself with one now. When she does come, she makes it seem that her every day is a hectic dance between duties that she has to leave incomplete. It suits her, the hecticness. It makes her glow with a restless energy as she weaves between deferred moments. It gives her eyes an elusive depth as if they secrete a concealed point of convergence, a hidden place or instant which is their true focus. Not here, not this moment, true life is racing somewhere else. Her name is Rachel. She told me that the first day I met her when she came to visit me at the detention center. "I'm a legal adviser with the refugee organization that has taken on your case. My name is Rachel Howard," she said, smiling, offering her hand, pleased to meet you.

And my name is Rajab Shaaban. It is not my real name, but a name I borrowed for the occasion of this lifesaving trip. It belonged to someone I knew for many years. Shaaban is also the name of the eighth month of the year, the month of division, when the destinies of the coming year are fixed and the sins of the truly penitent are absolved. It precedes the month of Ramadhan, the month of the great heat, the month of fasting. Rajab is the month which precedes both, the seventh month, the revered month. It was during Rajab that the night of the Miraj occurred, when the Prophet was taken through the seven heavens to the Presence of God. How we loved that story when we were young. On the night of the 27th of Rajab, the Prophet was sleeping when the Angel Jibreel woke him and made him mount the winged beast Burakh, who took him through the sky to al-Quds, Jerusalem. There, in the ruins of the Temple Mount, he prayed with Abraham, Moses and Jesus and then ascended in their company to the Lote Tree of the Uttermost Limit, sidrat al-muntaha, which was the nearest that any being could approach the Almighty. The Prophet received God's injunction that Muslims were to pray fifty times in a day. On his way back, Moses advised him to return and haggle. He had been in the business a lot longer than the Prophet, and guessed that God would probably come down a bit. The Almighty came down to five times a day. In the telling of the story, a great sigh would issue from the congregation at this point. Imagine praying fifty times every single day. Then the Prophet returned to al-Quds and mounted the beast Burakh again, who flew him back to Makka before morning. There he had to face the inevitable carping and doubting from the benighted jahals of that town, but to the believers the miracle of the Miraj is an event of joyous celebration. Rajab preceded Shaaban which preceded Ramadhan, three holy months.

Though God had only commanded that we fast during Ramadhan, the pious fasted throughout the three months. That was
the holy joke my namesake's parents played on him, calling him
Rajab when his father's name was Shaaban, like calling him July
when his father's name was August, and no doubt they had a
good chuckle but he paid for it, the name. As I would have done,
if my parents had really given me that name.

I didn't say any of this to Rachel Howard when she came to
see me at the detention center. I didn't say anything. To call it a
detention center is to be melodramatic. There were no locked
gates or armed guards, not even a uniform in sight. It was an encampment in the countryside, which was run by a private company. There were three large structures that looked like sheds or
warehouses, where they gave us a place to sleep and fed us. It was
cold. The wind howled and wailed outside, gusting at times as if
it would lift the whole building and hurl it away. I felt as if the
blood in my veins had stopped flowing, had turned into sharp-
edged crystals which bit into my inner flesh. When I stopped
moving my limbs went numb. We slept in two of the buildings,
twelve in one and ten in the other, our sleeping spaces parti-
tioned with boards but without doors. Each building had a toilet
and a shower, and a separate tap labeled "Drinking Water." I
wondered about that, and whether it meant I should use the
shower with circumspection, whether the water was safe. We ate
in the third building, food delivered to us in a van in large square
metal containers. It was served to us by a middle-aged Englishman of crumpled and gloomy appearance, not a specimen I
had met yet in my travels at that point, but which I have seen in
large numbers since. In fact many of the people I met in those

early months surprised me in appearance. They seemed so unlike the straight-backed, unsmiling variety I remembered from years ago. Our Englishman was called Harold, and he served our food as well as cleaned the showers and the toilets in his own fashion. Another man sat in an office in a small building which also contained a public telephone, a dispensary and a consulting room. He usually went home at night, whereas Harold slept in the building where we had our meals and seemed to be nearby at all times. There was yet another man who came to relieve Harold for a night or two, but he only came once while I was there, and kept himself out of the way, avoiding us. Harold provoked endless teasing from the detainees, which he lugubriously ignored, ticking his tasks off silently, as if consulting a list in his head. He must have seen many others like us passing through, whereas to us he was our first Englishman at such close quarters.

The sheds that accommodated us could once just as easily have contained sacks of cereals or bags of cement or some other valuable commodity that needed to be kept secure and out of the rain. Now they contained us, a casual and valueless nuisance that had to be kept in restraint. The man in the office took away our money and our papers, and told us we could take a walk in the countryside if we needed exercise, so long as we stayed within sight of the camp, in case we got lost. "If you got lost, there'd be no one to come and find you," he said, "and it gets cold out there at night, and some of you lads aren't used to that." It would get colder, I had known that all along. Napoleon's retreat from Moscow was not until February or March, and everything was frozen then. General Winter at the head of the Russian offensive. I arrived in November, three months before February, and it was already unbearably cold with months of deepening winter still ahead of us. It would get colder.

There were twenty-two men in the camp. The twelve in our building were four Algerians, three Ethiopians, two Iranian brothers just out of their teens, who clung to each other and whispered and sobbed in the night before they fell asleep in the same bed, a Sudanese and an Angolan, who was the dynamo and live wire of our establishment, bursting with advice, with jokes, with politics, with deals, with the righteousness of UNITA's cause in the war. No Nigerians here, the Angolan told us. Too many of them in detention and they're too much trouble, so they have to be kept under lock and key in an old castle in the frozen north, away from human habitation. Too many of them in the world altogether. His name was Alfonso, and he had a deep and unrelenting antipathy to Nigerians, which he did not explain but which illuminated every day of his life, it seemed. He had been in the camp, the barracks as he preferred to call it, for several weeks. He refused to be moved, saying he needed the seclusion and the rural air to finish the book he was writing. If he went and mingled with the English in the streets and spent all his evenings in their pubs watching football on TV, he would lose the edge of his recollections and there would be no point to anything he had done. He liked it there in the barracks among his rootless brethren, thank you. The detainees in the other building were all from south Asia, from India and Sri Lanka, and perhaps people of Indian origin from elsewhere. I don't know. They conducted their affairs separately from us, sat together as a group during meals, and seemed to have a language with which to speak to one another which was not comprehensible to the rest of us.

It was to the small building, which contained a dispensary, an office and some kind of consulting room, that I was summoned to meet Rachel Howard.

"I understand you don't speak any English," she said, consulting her papers and then smiling at me with an intense burst of goodwill, ardently requiring me to understand her despite my apparent lack of the language. It was early days, and I was not ready to be questioned and documented, and perhaps to be moved somewhere else. I had been in the camp two days and I liked it there despite the numbed feelings in my legs. I liked the spongy greenness of the countryside, which looked as if it had some give in it. I liked the drift of muffled rumbles and crashes in the sodden air, which made me slightly apprehensive at first because I thought they were the distant pounding of the sea but which I guessed only much later to have been the noise of traffic on a big road nearby. I enjoyed Alfonso and his anarchic joy, the Ethiopians and their fragile silences, policing some secret understanding between themselves, the Algerians and their mannered courtesies, their chortling mockery of each other, their endless whisperings, the Sudanese, serious and intimidated, and the two Iranian boys deep in their fertile miseries. I did not feel ready to be rescued yet from these only just visible lives.

They shuffled themselves to make room for me, calling me shebe, Agha, old man, mister. What's brought you all this way so far from God and your loved ones, ya habibi? Don't you know the damp climate and the cold could damage someone with bones as fragile and ancient as your own? That is what I imagined them saying, because none of us apart from Alfonso spoke English to each other, and Alfonso didn't seem to care who listened to him or who understood him, waving his arms about, acting out his comedies, ignoring what sometimes felt to me like the unkind laughter of the others, especially the scornful Algerians. I suspected they thought themselves nobler than this loquacious Black man who carried himself with such confidence. Alfonso rattled on regardless, as if nothing could ever hurt him or molest him, as if he had no control over the mean little demons that kept him chattering so frantically.

I, on the other hand, was still not sure why the man who had sold me the ticket had advised that I did not speak English, or when it would be wise to admit that I did. And I was also unsure if the ignorance of English of my fellow camp-dwellers was similarly strategic, if they knew the reason for pretending not to speak it or if they too were acting on canny advice from another ticket seller from elsewhere. Perhaps they feared that the one reckless English speaker among us was some kind of informer, a thought that had occurred to me too, and they were sitting skut sakit until the danger was past. We were all fleeing places where authority required full submission and groveling fear, and since this was not enforceable without daily floggings and public beheadings, its servants, its police and army and security apparatus carried out repeated acts of petty malice to demonstrate the jeopardy of reckless insurrection. How could I guess the manner of infringement that would infuriate the doorkeepers of this estate? I did not wish to get caught out through lack of a proper exercise of cunning and find myself transferred to an old castle in the freezing north, or worse still, find myself on the plane making the return journey. It was altogether too soon to give up the deception, even though I would have enjoyed the drama of startling Rachel Howard's ardent smile from its attractive perch. Instead I shook my head and shrugged slowly, unaggressively, and smiled a helpless foreigner smile at her.

Her hair was black and curly, worn in a style that was deliberately unruly and tangled. It gave her appearance a touch of gaiety and youth, and made her look dark and a little foreign, both of which were no doubt intended. She frowned at her papers, leaning forward, while I sat silently in front of her. Then she looked up and smiled, and I thought that would be it until she could bring back an interpreter. She nodded vigorously to reassure me and then grabbed her hair with both hands and pulled it off her face. "Now what?" she said, holding on to her hair with both hands and giving me a long look. I couldn't tell whether she was familiar with this ruse of not speaking English and wished to let me know that she was, or whether the look of cunning on her face was relish for a deepening intrigue. She stood up and walked away from the table, and turned to look back at me. I saw then that she had not really seen me, that the crafty look was turned inward on the ways and means at her disposal. She was neither tall nor strongly built, but her movements had a supple assurance which suggested physical strength. Compact shoulders, probably a regular swimmer. "We'll have to have you moved somewhere where you can have classes. Get you out of this detention center, anyway. I don't think that will be too hard, because of your age, you see. That's the first thing we've got to do, arrange for you to be moved to the care of our area authority."

She frowned, still not seeing me, perhaps unsure what she should do next, unable to tell me in words what she was planning for me, concerned to make me feel that she was caring and that she was efficient. But she was not seeing me yet, she was looking inward. I guessed she was the same age as my daughter, midthirties, the same age as my daughter would have been. It seems absurd to call her mine. She didn't live long, she died. Rachel Howard came back to the table and sat down opposite me. I raised my eyes to hers, to let her know that I was there, and she did not become perturbed but sat silently taking me in. Then she reached out and put her hand on my arm. "Sixty-five, that's a fine age to run away from home," she said, smiling. "What could you have been thinking of?"

I liked that she had made me think of my daughter, and that the thought had come not as a recollection of blame or pain but as a small pleasure amidst so much that was exotic and strange. Raiiya, that was what I called her, an ordinary citizen, a common indigene. Her mother thought the name a provocation, and certain to be an embarrassment to her when she grew up, so she called her Ruqiya after the Prophet's daughter with Khadija, his first wife and his benefactor. But she did not live long, she died. Rahmatullah alaiha.

"We'll have to see if we can find an interpreter," Rachel Howard said, nodding encouragingly because I had spoken those last two words aloud, invoking God's mercy on her soul when it was God and his angels who took her away before she could even become a citizen, and then took her mother away too, may God have mercy on her soul, while I neither knew nor was there.

"Don't you understand *any* English? Never mind, we'll get you to school when we get you out of here. I think it's hard to learn when you're a certain age," she said, smiling again at the thought of my age. "Never mind, we'll get you out of here first of all. You'll like it there, where we're going. It's a small town by the sea. In a few days. We'll find you a bed-and-breakfast and get you fixed up with Social Security and all that. Then we'll find an interpreter. Do you have any relatives or friends? Oh I really hope so. It's hard enough as it is, but at your age."

A small town by the sea. Yes, I'll like that, I thought. In a few days.

They took me to a bed-and-breakfast first, Rachel and a man called Jeff who drove the car they came to pick me up in. He was much younger than Rachel, tall, big-boned with reddish hair and an exaggeratedly serious voice. I imagined he laughed loudly and ate heartily when he did not feel he had to play a part. I sat in the back seat with the little bag that Kevin Edelman had rummaged in beside me, now missing the casket of ud-al-qamari which he had stolen from me, but containing a camp towel that Alfonso had shoved into it at the last moment. "You must always keep yourself clean," he said, his eyes shining with a kind of helplessness. "Baba, do you hear me? Whatever they do to you, keep yourself clean." I was nervous about the towel, in case someone searched me before I left. I had seen people beaten until they sobbed for pilfering much less, a bar of soap or an empty Coke bottle. There, not here, in my earlier life, my before life. But no one searched my bag. The man who sat in the office escorted me to the car and waited patiently while I shook hands and shared smiles with all the others. Maasalama, they said, go with peace. Kwaheri, I said, may good times befall you. Rachel and Jeff were elated at my delivery, discussing between them the rules and the laws they had bettered, naming officials and the government minister whose cynical and expedient ruling they had outwitted, comparing my triumphant release to the cases of others for whom decision was still pending. Perhaps no one told them about the high policy that considered my life at risk at the hands of my own government, or perhaps they did not think that would be enough to enable my admission, or perhaps, despite the indignantly superior moral gesture of allowing people from my country asylum, someone had started to count the cost of admitting a man of my age to the United Kingdom: too old to work in a hospital, too old to produce a future England cricketer, too old for anything much except Social Security, assisted housing and a subsidized cremation. But they did it, they got me in, and as I sat in the car I felt mean that I had felt a touch of mockery for their excited self-congratulation, and sorry that I had to continue to pretend that I could not understand them or say how quaveringly grateful I was to them.

The bed-and-breakfast was an old dark house in a quiet street off a main road. The woman who ran it was called Celia—Celia has agreed to take him, we should get there just in time for one of her teas, no thank you, she's weird isn't she, but really kind—and as we stood in front of the open door, ringing the bell, she shouted for us to come upstairs. The entrance hall was small and gloomy, the floor covered with a worn rug in which fragments of red were still visible in the threadbare gray. The stairs, just a few steps, made a sharp turn to the right and then another sharp turn to the right again, a good position to defend. The intruder, who more likely than not will be right-handed, will have no space to swing a weapon and will also be vulnerable from a well-swung stick or a bucket of hot oil or whatever. Celia was sitting in the living room, reading a magazine in front of a muted television. It was the smell that struck me first, something both new and familiar, which now with experience I can describe. At that time it made me think of damp chicken shit in an enclosed space, as in houses where people allowed chickens to roost in stairwells or on ledges, in houses not unlike this one, with those sharp turns in the stairs, where as a child I had at times been frightened out of my wits by the angry clucking of a chicken I had disturbed as I groped up the stairs in the dark. Now I know that it's not the smell of chicken shit but of old dusty closed rooms: upholstery that had soaked up fluid detritus over decades, faded and worn rugs that clung to tangles of human hair and animal fur and crumbs and seeds, the reek of old fires and soot, the stale miasma that the bundles of cloth and bags in corners of the room gave off. In one side of the room were three birdcages on brass stands with creatures in them that looked more or less alive, at least to judge by the bits of food around the cages.

Celia herself was a tall, well-built woman with long thin hair which she hennaed. She rose to her feet as we entered and ushered us in, bustled us in. "Sit down and have some tea," she said, her voice loud and bullying despite the laughter in it. "Cold out there, isn't it? There's some tea in the pot, come nearer the fire, there're some cups on the table there. Sit down. Hello, nice to have you here. This is Michael, Mick. Say hello to our new guest, Mick."

She pointed to a man who looked older than her, perhaps in his seventies, and was occupying the chair opposite hers. He glanced kindly at me and then returned to staring at his hands. As I was to find out, Mick did little more than stare at his hands and smile kindly at everybody, and when he was told to do so, he looked at something on the television or drank his tea or even spoke briefly on some matter on which his opinion was invited, saying yes or no or couldn't be better, and then retired to the bed he shared with Celia. "And this is Ibrahim and that is Georgy." Celia gestured toward the two young men sitting at the large table further into the room. Ibrahim was wearing a green shirt marbled with blue over a black T-shirt, and Georgy, the darker of the two, was wearing a brown zipped leather jacket. They both waved casually, and I saw in their eyes what I had not seen in either Celia's or Mick's, a wariness, a bit of swagger, a flash of malice. I would have known without being told, they were strangers here. They greeted Rachel and Jeff by name and offered them beaming cheeky grins, ready for a bit of banter if any was in the offing. I was wary, perhaps worse. Young men on the make, greedy, too obvious in their hungers, desperate, perhaps merciless, I didn't know, but I was wary. Those carefully tended mustaches.

"Ibrahim is from Kosovo, running away from those terrible, terrible Serbs and their bloodlust," Celia said, glancing at me. "I think you'll be all right, won't you, Ibrahim? Yes of course you will. His family has been dispersed all over the place, he's been shot at, chased in the streets. Dreadful. And this is Georgy darling. Georgy is a Roma from the Czech Republic. He's been here ages. They keep trying to send him back but he's got something wrong up top"—Celia tapped her right temple—"and the doctors make a fuss, so the Immigration leave him alone for a while. They beat him up so badly over there. Damaged him. Baseball bats to the face and that sort of thing. Despicable behavior, just because he is Roma. Those Serbs . . ."

"Czechs," Rachel corrected.

"Czechs then," Celia conceded tetchily. "I still don't know why people can't tolerate each other, I honestly really don't. We didn't discriminate against them when we helped them during the war. We didn't say you are Czech and that one is Roma, so we'll help you but we won't help that one. We helped everybody. So far the Home Office people can't bring themselves to force Georgy back. They keep trying to make him say that it wasn't that bad, and even that he wasn't really beaten up at all. I think they will send him back in the end though, poor old Georgy darling."

"No, there's still a chance," Rachel protested. "We're doing everything we can. We're fighting really hard for him. How're the lessons going, Georgy?"

Georgy nodded, following the exchange with molten eyes, a picture of abjection and humbled dignity, a tragic body whose life depended on sustaining the enthusiasm of people who were debating its outcome.

"And these are the budgies Antigone, Cassandra and Helen," Celia said, glancing at me and then waving toward the birdcages one by one. "I can't remember which is which anymore, but they don't seem to mind. Oh well, you've met everyone now. Come and sit down near the fire and have some tea. You must be freezing."

"Mr. Shaaban doesn't speak any English, Celia," Rachel said apologetically.

Celia glanced at me and I saw disbelief, a kind of shock in her eyes, and I felt as if she had seen through me. She even shook her head a little and turned down her mouth as she looked at me, a little bit displeased at the turn of events. My heart had been sub-siding gently from the moment we entered the overcrowded liv-ing room, made anxious by the thought of the squalor of the bed I would be expected to sleep in later. Celia's suspicions made it sink deeper. I had never met English people like Celia and Mick before, she with her fussy and random motherliness, and the sexual undertone in her movements that was too explicit to miss, he with his appearance of kindly decrepitude. Apart from gloomy and crumpled Harold and the silent man in the office of the detention center and, of course, Kevin Edelman, the English I had dealt with before had mostly been customers at my furni-ture shop or tourists, and, at a distance, the senior officers of the Directorate in the time I worked for the government. They were all superior, prosperous, easy to offend and a little too rude to like. Self-important and puffed up in every gesture, as if at all moments they were on the alert to display scorn and sternness. I could not imagine what they were like among themselves, but I could not imagine them differently from the way I saw them. I say mostly they were like that because I except two of my teach-ers at Makerere College, who managed some of the above but were also gentle and courteous and enthusiastic at other times.

And since arriving in England I had been dealing with officials and functionaries, nobody who could actually see me, people under stress of their own work and with a lifetime of stories and descriptions about beggars like me. Celia had seen me, it felt like that. Her sharp look was a kind of recognition, and one which I had no desire for. I couldn't think why right away.

"Well, we'll have to get along with sign language and noises, then," Celia said irritably. "Don't worry, Rachel, darling, we're quite used to that here. Aren't we, Mick? He used to speak something once, you know. Mick, what language was it you used to speak? Malay, wasn't it? Malay. Mick, was it Malay? Does Mr. . . . ?"

"Shaaban," said Rachel, frowning a little while still keeping a small smile on her face, her hands running restlessly, once, over the front of her trousers. It made me worry even more that she was so eager to leave.

"Shaaban, Shaaban, Shaaban," Celia practiced. "Does Mr. Shaaban speak Malay? I expect not." Celia went to the door of the living room and shouted *Susan* twice, and then came back to her chair. "We'll get Susan to bring some tea. Shaaban, Shaaban."

Susan turned out to be a woman of Celia's age, small and round-faced with a harried and jumpy manner, which was only too easy to understand in someone who worked for a loud, self-assured bully like Celia. She did the cooking and cleaned the house while Celia did the office work, as she put it. Rachel and Jeff left a few minutes after Susan was called, declining the offer of tea. And when Susan returned with a plate of toasted bread, a saucepan of baked beans and another plate of sliced tinned ham it was easy to see why. We all sat around the big dining table and had our tea. I pointed to the sliced ham and shook my head at Celia.

"Pig," Ibrahim said, grinning from ear to ear, and turning to share the joke with Georgy. "Muslim man, he don't eat pig, he don't piss alcohol. Clean clean clean, wash wash wash. Black man."

Georgy laughed out loud at *Black man*. I don't know if it was the thought of a *Black* man who was a Muslim that made him laugh, or the comedy of a dark-skinned man in a frenzy of *clean clean clean*, *wash wash wash*, or if they were sharing a private joke. Later I understood that Georgy laughed at everything Ibrahim said. They both looked at me with taunting, grinning stares and I was at a loss to understand their malice. Perhaps their circumstances and their anxieties had made them acrid and mocking, and the lies and the subterfuges that had been necessary to sustain the first story of their oppression had made them cynical about the true extent of their suffering and that of others who professed the same condition as them. How could they know that I had not been witness or victim to degradations and violence that would have at least required their humane silence? Nobody had swung a baseball bat into my face, but how could they know, and how could they know that I had not witnessed even worse? After whatever horrors they had been through, how could they stop knowing that such horrors can happen to anyone?

Mick ate his baked beans with a spoon while Celia sipped her tea and talked unhurriedly, without any fear of interruption. She talked about the budgies, about other guests who had stayed with them and had then become friends, about the refugee organization—they are such lovely people—about the demonstrations in the town against asylum seekers, about exaggerated newspaper reports, about how little she understood the changes that had taken place in the world. Ibrahim lit a cigarette after a few bites of toast, and pulled the overflowing ashtray nearer so that it was alongside his plate, like a special side dish all of his own, a condiment to toast and beans and ham.

"There's a church down this street, St. Peter's, that's where we used to go. That was our church," Celia said, casually waving the cigarette smoke away. "It's a club or a café or something of that sort now. A disco. We weren't specially religious or anything like that, but we went to church on the big days. Now it's a club or a café. It's wrong for a Christian country not to care for its churches. I bet you won't see a temple in Mr. Naashab's country being turned into a bar or something. I never go in there, though I think the boys do, don't you? What else can they do? They're just stuck here, not allowed to work or find a place of their own. Poor Ibrahim has had to send his wife and daughter to London to stay with his brother's family because they won't let the little girl go to school here. The parents protest, you see. They don't want them in their schools, they say. It's dreadful. Anyway, the boys go into that bar sometimes, but I never do. I couldn't, it would feel wrong after having gone in there so many times before for services and prayers. There used to be a painter who lived down this road, a proper painter, not a house painter. My mother told me about him, although I think I can picture him myself. He had his studio in the big downstairs room at the front of the house. You could see him from the street, standing in front of an easel with his smock on. Big beard and a belly, well-known now, I think. There weren't any foreigners then, when I was growing up, just the odd French traveler, not real foreigners. Or we didn't meet any, anyway, did we, Mick? Not until the Italian prisoners after the war. You weren't here until then, Mick, were you? I forgot that. You couldn't have met any before then, anyway, could you? Mick was in Malaya. Now foreigners are everywhere, with all these terrible things happening in their countries. It didn't use to be like this. I don't know the rights and wrongs of it, but we can't just turn them away, can we? We can't just say go back to your horrible country and get hurt, we're too busy with our own lives. If we can help them, I think we should. Be tolerant. I can't understand these people who demonstrate in the streets saying whatever about asylum seekers. And these National Front marches, I can't bear those fascists. It didn't use to be that there were so many in the country, but what can we do? We can't send them back to those horrible places. I don't know what we can do."

I listened with my head down, and the others listened in silence. From the measured and unhurried way Celia was talking, I began to fear that she would just continue until she was exhausted, way beyond midnight. I made a sign that I wanted to go to bed and Celia raised her eyebrows in a put-upon way, as if I had asked for something difficult. It was only just after six o'clock but I wanted to get away from that oppressive room and its duplicities and dissemblings, its smells, its atmosphere of neglect and cruelty, its paltriness. I wanted to sit alone in the dark and count the bones in my head.

Celia showed me upstairs, another right turn and then another, to a small overcrowded room, in one corner of which was a bed covered with what looked like an old maroon rug.

"I've been living in this house for nearly sixty years, Mr. Bashat," she said, standing in the doorway with one hand on the frame, smiling at the achievement. She was going to tell me the story of the house, and how her mother, who used to arrange the flowers at St. Peter's, had been secretly in love with an artist hothead who ran off in despair one stormy night because she would not enter into anything improper, and now returned to bang on the windowpanes looking for her love. No. "Sixty-odd years, and still hale of mind and limb or however they say it, unlike poor old Mick. Though he enjoys his life all right, old Mick. The Japanese did that to him. He came back like that and I took him in. These things you see in the room, they all have meaning for me, every one of them. Please be careful with them. The bathroom is the room next to you. We all use it, so please keep it neat. Otherwise you've met everyone and I wish you would speak English soon so we can have a proper chat. Oh, and Ibrahim and Georgy darling sleep upstairs."

She turned away with a look of dislike, her eyes sharp with suppressed irritation. What now? What have I done to her? "Breakfast is served between eight and ten," she said a little haughtily, half turning back. "We would appreciate it if you would be punctual. I lock the front door at ten o'clock at night, so I'm afraid that if you're out after that you'll have to ring the bell until someone comes to let you in. Good evening, Mr. Showness."

The rug on the bed puffed up a thin cloud of dust when I pulled it back. The bedsheets looked and smelled as if they had been slept in before. There were spots of blood on the pillow-case. The bed had the same smell as the upholstery downstairs: old vomit and semen and spilled tea. I dared not even sit on it out of an irrational fear of contamination, not just fear of disease but of some inner pollution. I tried the elegant-looking settee—elegant in its lines and shape—but the upholstery was in the same rancid state as the rug on the bed. The bathroom was caked: the sink was spotted with what looked like vegetable mat-ter, the tub had developed a dark shadowy skin and the toilet was an impenetrably opaque black hole. I gagged but had no choice, aware all the time that for all I knew something lived in that dark murk and that it had teeth that might be tempted by the weight of my manly endowments. They do acquire a kind of nobility at a certain age. English was going to be forced out of me the next day when Rachel came to collect me for what she called my debriefing. I hadn't come all this way to perish out of carelessness. I spent the evening going through Celia's valuable memories with a mixture of the old pleasure and equally old re-grets, pricing and assessing them as if they were part of a house lot I had acquired at auction. There was nothing much on the table: a ship in a bottle, some trinkety jewelry, photographs in clumsy frames, a biscuit tin with a picture of a man in the uni-form of a naval captain at the center of a garland of fruits and nuts from all over the Empire, containing a variety of odds and ends, buttons, badges, feathers. I wondered later that I had felt no interest in these objects, even in my own mind, that I did not even speculate on how they were precious to Celia, never even thought to imagine her life with them.

On the wall was a large gilt mirror, too large for that dark little room, but the gilt was in good condition and the mirror needed only a touch of repair. That would have brought in a penny or two. In that gloomy light, my reflection in the mirror looked like a creature suspended in a rising haze, the circle of light from the shade hanging like an open noose on my shoulders. I slept on the floor by the table, with the towel Alfonso had forced on me under my head. I knew there was little chance of sleep, what with the hard matted carpet on which I lay and the gnawing hunger in my belly. Late in the night I heard the unmistakable thumping rhythm of lovemaking and wondered whether it was Celia mounting Mick or whether it was the boys in the midst of high-spirited japes.

Rachel did not come the next morning. I used the bathroom with my eyes shut, touching what I had to touch with my fingertips. Then I opened the curtains and sat on the floor of my room, with Alfonso's towel spread under me. My room was at the back of the house, overlooking an untended garden made gloomy by large bushes and trees. The rain was running down the windowpanes. I had not been able to wash myself properly after the big ablution, especially as the beans had given me the runs as they always did. I cleaned myself as well as I could with the paper, but as I sat there on the floor I felt as if a stain was spreading under me. The house was silent, everyone still in bed. Later, when I heard the steps on the stairs and the sound of cups and plates, I felt too unnerved by Celia's look of dislike to venture out. I would wait for Rachel on Alfonso's magic carpet, safe from disregard. But Rachel didn't come, and sitting on the floor of that dusty overcrowded room, unable to think about anything else except my worthlessness, demoralized me so much that I went downstairs.

Mick was sitting at his station in front of the muted television, a dirty knife and plate in his lap. Celia was at the dining table, a newspaper open in front of her. She looked up when I came in, and then leaned back in the chair and grinned. She was still in her dressing gown, not too tightly gathered together, and even from where I was, I could see that that was all she was wearing. "Good morning, Mr. Showboat. You had a nice lie-in, didn't you?" she said, jovially waving me over to the table. "I'm sure it did you good. I hope you were warm enough. Pour yourself some tea, go on. Oh, I forgot. Tea, slurp slurp. Pour, go on." She mimed the slurping and the pouring, and then grinned at me again. "Or would you like Mummy to pour it for you?"

I poured myself some tea and went to sit near Mick, watching the muted television with him, but keeping a corner of my eye, I am ashamed to confess, on Celia reading her newspaper at the table. The dressing gown reached just below her knees, and since she rocked her body slightly from side to side as she read, it opened a chink now and then between her legs. At one point she reached down absentmindedly and rubbed the inside of her thigh. I heard Mick chuckle beside me, but when I glanced at him his eyes were on the television. I turned myself more fully round, so I should not be made a fool of. We sat like this for an endless age, Mick and I staring at the muted television, waiting for Rachel, afraid to move, not knowing where to go, what to do, while Celia rustled the pages of the newspaper and sighed now and then. As she finished the paper and folded it up, she said, "Well, you seem to be getting on very well there, you two. The boys have missed breakfast again. You know, they sleep till all hours of the day, Mr. Showboat. Like kids. Poor boys, what else can they do, though? They might as well sleep till teatime. Save on lunch. We don't provide lunch, Mr. Showboat. Just breakfast daily, and tea by arrangement except on Thursday, today. Susan's day off. Oh, I hope you don't mind me calling you Mr. Showboat. It's just my way of remembering your name. I hope you won't be offended. Mick, Mick, I'll just go and make myself decent. Mick doesn't like me to stay in my dressing gown all morning like this when there are guests around. He gets jealous. You'll get used to our ways, Mr. Showboat. I should think you'll be staying with us for a while, most asylum seekers do. We've made some wonderful friends, from everywhere. Only you'll have to learn some English, Mr. Showboat. It's a strain having you look at me like that, and not even know what you're thinking."

I ran away to Alfonso's towel, and once on it I felt as if I was in an invisible place. I stayed on it all afternoon, cursing the ticket seller who had deprived me of the power to speak and protest, and cursing Rachel and Jeff for having stolen me away from the detention center where I was among people whose lives were deepening me, only to bring me to this dungeon with its twisting stairways and its eccentric bawabs from whom I sensed danger and neglect. I had had no food all day, which is not such a terrible deprivation at my age, except that it did not concern anyone. No one was concerned whether I ate or not, whether I was well or ill, whether I rejoiced or grieved. I heard the boys getting up and later running downstairs like a couple of barking baboons, to be greeted by Celia's raucous laughter and flirtatious admonitions. Those two young champions of justice and human rights had delivered me to a zoo and then gone to see their friends and colleagues to boast about how many ministers they had outwitted to get an old man out of the nasty detention center and the fascist clutches of the state, and how now he was in the merciful hands of kind Celia and her playmates. Rachel, I conjure thee in the name of the Almighty.

Later in the afternoon I began to feel ailing and delirious and decided that the time had come to say Ya Latif, O Gentle, O Gracious. We had performed the prayer together when we were in prison, at times of illness and anxiety, and it is best done that way, as a congregation and on behalf of the one who is ailing and distressed. But there was no one there to perform it for me, and I hoped I would not offend the form by saying it for myself.

I went to the bathroom and performed the udhu in preparation for prayer, washing my hands, my face, my arms and my feet. Then I returned to Alfonso's towel and began. First the statement of the intention to perform Ya Latif, then seeking refuge in God from Satan, the stoned one. Then bismillah, *In the name of God who is merciful and compassionate.* After that, al-Ikhlas three times: *Say God is one, is eternal. He is without child, and without father. No one is equal to him.* Then the latifun: *Gentle is God toward his servants. He gives to whom He will. He is Invincible, the Almighty.* Then the prayer on the Prophet, a beautiful-sounding prayer:

> *A salatu wa salamu alayka ya sayyidi ya habiba-Llah,*
> *A salatu wa salamu alayka ya sayyidi ya nabiya-Llah,*
> *A salatu wa salamu alayka ya sayyidi ya rasula-Llah,*
>
> *Blessing and peace upon you, o beloved of God,*
> *Blessing and peace upon you, o prophet of God,*
> *Blessing and peace upon you, o messenger of God.*

Then speaking the words *Ya Latif*, without rush or haste, turning the head to the right and then turning it to the left, for a thousand times.

It was already dark by the time I was finished, much comforted, and I was beginning to wonder if I should go downstairs to beg for more slurp-slurp and whatever crumbs were available, or whether I should go out and walk in a straight line for half an hour, when I heard Celia coming up the stairs. Some instinct told me she was coming for me, and I stood up from my towel so as not to have her find me there. She knocked loudly, demanding admission, and entered without further ado. It was not possible to lock the door. "You certainly like your sleep, Mr. Showboat," she said cheerfully, groping for the light switch. "Rachel just sent a message for you. Ibrahim called round at the office and Rachel said to tell you— But that's silly. She must've forgotten you don't speak English. Oh well, never mind. You don't know there's a message so you won't worry that you didn't get it. You've made yourself cozy in here, I see."

"Rachel," I said, and heard my voice croaking pathetically like a wheedling beggar. My voice was hoarse from praying in a whisper for so long.

"Yes, Rachel sent a message, my darling. Everything's all right, don't worry about a thing, Mr. Showboat. Why don't you come downstairs and watch television with your friend Mick? You two were getting on so well this morning. Come on, you've been stuck up here all day. It's not good for you. Come, come and join us," she said, opening her right arm out and swinging her hips slightly, once.

I followed her downstairs, wishing I could reach out and

shake her until Rachel's message fell out of her. Oblivious as before, she was talking over her shoulder, half turning once to glance at me under her eyebrows. "Here he is," she announced to the world of monkeys as we entered the living room. Mick gave me a benign smile, Georgy grinned and waved, Ibrahim gave me a mock salute. The boys were playing cards. "Go on, sit in your chair," Celia said, pointing to what was now my place beside Mick. Rachel, in the name of the One and Only, make haste.

"Rachel," I said, looking at Ibrahim.

"Raschel," he said, mocking, grinning at me. "She say you are too old. No good. Black man." And the two of them laughed, exchanging sparkling looks over those naughty words. "She want young man."

"I don't know," Celia said, gurgling like a baby. "Mr. Showboat looks like he's got a bit of life in him." That set them off again. Black man, Mr. Showboat, wash wash wash, clean clean clean. I felt I should have wanted to know about Ibrahim and Georgy, to listen, to show sympathy, to hear about the horrors and the ambitions that had made them make the journey they had, but I did not. They did not want me to know. I suspected they did not think me worthy of their tragedies. It made me think of Alfonso and the Algerians, and how they had treated his brand of desperado confidence as a kind of presumption on his part, because in their eyes he was a Black man, a lesser son of Adam than them, capable only of a subservient rage and an unreflecting resilience.

When they finished their card game, they got up to leave, and then for some reason Ibrahim took pity on me. Standing at the door of the living room, he said, "Raschel, she come later." Then he smiled round the room, pleased with his kindness. When the two young men were by the front door, Ibrahim called Celia out, and she got up with a smile to go out to them. There was laughter and sounds of a struggle and then silence. Mick and I sat in our own silence, staring at the muted screen. After some minutes, the front door banged and Celia returned, her eyes sparkling. She sat in the chair opposite Mick and picked up her magazine. Raschel, she come later. But she didn't.

I stayed in the living room for as long as I could bear it, in the hope that a piece of bread or a cup of slurp-slurp would make an appearance, but nothing did. It was Susan's day off. In the end, nearly comatose with boredom and hunger, I crawled back up-stairs, sharp right and sharp right again. I was too tired to care about the filthy bed, and the night was getting cold. I got into bed without changing my clothes, though I folded Alfonso's towel and kept it draped over the back of a chair. I did so out of gratitude to Alfonso, and as a gesture of respect for his instinct for self-preservation, but also because I felt I had not been able to live up to his injunction to preserve dignity. Whatever they do, keep yourself clean. I had not been able to, and I lay down in a dirty bed in clothes that felt soiled because my body was un-clean. It was the end of my first day of freedom, and I fell asleep without a moment's delay.

She came in the middle of the morning. I had thought of go-ing out for a half-hour walk in a straight line, so that I would be able to find my way back without complications, but I feared that I would miss her and would have to wait for days before an-other visitation. I felt paralyzed. So when she arrived, looking attractive in a maroon suit and smiling with an air of cheerful busyness, can't stop for long, I was sitting beside Mick in front of the muted TV while Celia was somewhere at the back berating Susan about economy and waste.

"You look settled in, Mr. Shaaban," Rachel said. I growled in return, but not that it made any difference. She was already talking to Mick, who had a benign, indulgent smile steadily glowing. Celia came in and took charge of things, saying how comfortable I was in the house, how I was already friends with the boys, and I really got on with Mick, we just sat there all day watching TV together like two Sams in a milk-pond. I think that's what she said though I may have got it wrong: I was unfamiliar with the expression. "He mopes a bit at times," Celia said. "But I think that's because he doesn't understand everything we say. Do you, Mr. Showboat? That's what I call him. It's our nickname for him. He doesn't mind, I've asked him."

It took a while to work out that Rachel had come to take me to their office for my promised debriefing, that I didn't need to bring my bag with me because I would be staying with Celia and Mick for the time being, and that we would be walking to the office. Rachel strode off and I followed as well as I could. Now and then she slowed and apologized, saying it wasn't far. It was my first walk through English streets. I had imagined more bustle and rush, and that somehow things would look newer and brighter. Something in the streets reminded me of Celia's house, faded and grubby and cramped, and we passed many older people walking slowly and young people shouldering their way through with raised voices. But something else inside me made me walk on a little pocket of joy, as if I had slipped the chains of my life and now roamed in another. It was the beginning of the feeling which would grow on me, that my previous life had ended and I was starting a new one, and that now that earlier life was closed off forever. I imagine it like this: that to get here I had wriggled through a passage that closed in behind me. Too many *A Thousand and One Nights* stories when I was younger perhaps, that image of the passage. It was just a conceit, but the feeling of the end of a life comes back to me even though I know that the previous one still pulses within me.

The office was a house between a vegetable shop and a pub, although I did not know at the time that that was what it was called. A tavern. I would have liked to have known. I was struck most of all by the picture of a military personage from a previous age, dressed in bright colors and wearing plumes in his hat, which swung above the door of this establishment. The Royal Dragoon. Rachel took me to an interview room off the main office where two of her colleagues were sitting at their desks. One of them was Jeff and he smiled mechanically at me as I walked past, ducking his head as if he feared that I might stop and talk to him, keep him from the important work he was doing. I suppose I was no longer the prized refugee rescued from the jaws of the state. I was now a case. Rachel took off the jacket of her suit and put it on the back of her chair. Then she spread her papers on the table and sat down, facing the door. She smiled at me, looking pleased with herself. It puzzled me for a moment, but I suppose she was just enjoying her work and her life. I sat opposite her, facing the window with a view of a brick wall.

"Mr. Shaaban, I'm sorry I didn't come for you earlier . . . but we have been very busy. A ferry ship from Le Havre with 110 Roma people from Romania on board arrived yesterday, all asylum seekers. The immigration authorities wanted to send them all back and we argued that some of them should be permitted entry. They were all sent back, you may wish to know, though I suspect they'll be making the crossing to another port in a few days. Anyway, I thought we would get further if we had an interpreter," she said, making a comical face. "But I'm afraid . . . It's not hopeless, because someone I approached returned my call this morning. He seems willing to do it, but I'll confirm and let you know. Here we are anyway, and I don't know how we're going to get anything done, but I thought you might be worrying. Or thinking we'd abandoned you."

"I don't think I need an interpreter," I said. I was silently gleeful as I said this, of course. Even when you get to my age you can't resist such petty triumphs, and at that moment my glee was no different from that I had felt as a child or the hundreds of other times later when I had been sensationally and unexpectedly knowledgeable. I no longer cared what injury the ticket seller had been trying to save me from with his canny advice, and I was beginning to think that his canniness was something to do with the paranoia of the powerless. Having to bear the indignities of Celia's house in silence had made me reckless, and I needed the sweetness of that triumphant moment to lift me from my confinement there. And it was clear that someone had to take charge of my new life, before Celia and Mick and the boys soured it with the squalor of their petty-minded existence. And both Rachel and Jeff were too busy with the heady battles they were fighting within their secure citadels to do that. And that left to so many neglectful hands I would be pawed and pushed and pulled and left to linger in mute humiliation while I became an instrument of other people's contented stories. And I was perishing with hunger. Rachel stared at me with a look of stunned disgust.

"I see," she said, the smile gone. "What does this mean? Why did you say you couldn't speak any English?"

"I didn't say," I said.

"All right, why didn't you reply when you were spoken to in English?" she asked after a moment, rephrasing her question with adroit lawyer precision, her voice a little sharper with exasperation.

"I preferred not to," I said, glancing at the brick wall through the window opposite me.

"What!" she exclaimed, now unashamedly irritated.

So then I knew she did not know the story "Bartleby the Scrivener." The brick wall made me think of it as soon as I walked into the room, and I was certain that when I started to speak I would find a way to say that sentence, to see if the wall had made her think of it too. A beautiful story.

"Do you know how much trouble we went through trying to find an interpreter?" she asked, once again sneering with disgust. "We didn't even know what language you spoke. We've found someone at the University of London who is an expert on your area, and he's willing to help. He's willing to give up his time to come down here and help you. And now after you've put everybody to a lot of trouble, you tell me that you could speak English all along. Could you at least explain to me . . . ?" She pushed unruly curls of hair off her face, which was now scowling and hot with annoyance, and pulled her notepad toward her, ready to write down whatever I might say and hold it against me in evidence.

"I'm sorry," I said.

An expert in my *area*, someone who has written books about me no doubt, who knows all about me, more than I know about myself. He will have visited all the places of interest and significance in my *area*, and will know their historical and cultural context when I will be certain never to have seen them and will only have heard vague myths and popular tales about them. He will have slipped in and out of my *area* for decades, studying me and noting me down, explaining me and summarizing me, and I would have been unaware of his busy existence.

"When I bought my ticket, I was advised not to admit to speaking English when I arrived here," I said. "I didn't know why, but I thought I would wait and see. I'm not wiser now, but I thought I had better speak. Everything was becoming complicated and uncomfortable at Celia's house, so I thought I'd better speak before I created an impossible situation. Even though I would've preferred not to."

I couldn't resist slipping it in again, just in case she hadn't heard it the first time, but there was no reaction. I saw that she was struggling with herself, when perhaps what she might have wanted to do was to storm out of the room and go and find Jeff and complain about my annoying pretense. But she didn't, and though her eyes still sparked with grievance, I saw that the angry flush was subsiding. It made me concerned for her, that she was so mortified over such a small matter, such a petty ruse, what to

her should have appeared as little more than a pointless deception. She did not have to listen in silence while stories were told
about her, only ring a couple of organizations to see if they had
an interpreter for a client who spoke a language she could not
name and was too ignorant of the cultural geography of the
world to make a guess. It was not even ignorance, but an assurance that in the scheme of things it did not matter very much
what language I spoke, since my needs and desires could be predicted, and sooner or later I would learn to make myself intelligible. Or sooner or later she would find an expert who would
make me intelligible. But I was concerned for her, so I told her
the story of my deception and the small discomforts it had led to,
and told it in a way that made me comical and at last made her
smile again. Now that I could speak, she was ready to hear about
my plea for asylum. I told her frankly about the story I had heard
that we would be granted asylum if we claimed that we feared
for our lives under our government, and how I decided to become a refugee. She nodded, they had already found that out
from the coordinating office of refugee organizations. Then,
back on my side again and bristling with efficiency and her own
cleverness, she told me that she would need some more details to
prepare a plea, that she had fixed an appointment for me with
Social Security, had been in touch with the housing department
and there was a chance of a small flat quite soon, though there
were still some formalities. She had registered me with a GP especially for someone of my age, and had arranged for me to receive some emergency clothing more suitable for the climate
than the rags I had brought with me. She had also fixed for me

to begin classes in English at Refugee Helpline at the local college. "Though that will not be necessary now," she said with a sparkling, forgiving smile.

"I must remember to call the man from the university and tell him we don't need him anymore," she said, making a put-upon face.

"I'm sorry to have put you to so much trouble," I said. "And to have troubled an expert on my area from the University of London. Please extend my apologies to him."

She waved my apologies away and consulted her notes. "Latif Mahmud. That's his name. I'll call him later and say that we won't be needing him after all." Rachel busied herself with her papers for a moment, putting everything in order, bringing our interview to an end. It was a shock to hear that name. I reflected on the name and the man it referred to, a man whose story I knew. Part of his story I knew very well, only too well, but that was when he was a son and a youth, and called by a different name. The story of the rest of his life, his real life, I knew only as rumor. I could not suppress a feeling of anxiety and apprehension as I thought of him, that after having come such a long way I should have come so close to him. So he was the expert on our area! Mashaallah, that was something, not a stranger who came to summarize us, but one of our own. It made me regret that I had broken my silence when I did.

"Latif Mahmud, how wonderful," I said.

"You know him," Rachel said, delighted.

"A little," I said. "When he was very young."

"I think I mentioned your name in the message I left on his

answering machine," Rachel said happily. "I'm almost sure I did. So if you knew each other, he'll probably be getting in touch. Oh that's incredible. And I thought you were going to be all on your own and unable to speak to anybody, when all the time you were just . . . grinning behind that gloomy composure. I understand, it wasn't meant personally. But tell me, why did you decide to become a refugee? Tell me that. Your life wasn't really at risk, was it? From what you told me, you only thought of leaving . . ."

"My life has been at risk for a long time," I said. "It is only now that the Government of Her Majesty the Queen of England has recognized it and has offered me sanctuary. It is only a worthless life now, but it still matters to me. Perhaps it was always worthless though it mattered even more before."

"What do you do for a living, Mr. Shaaban?" she asked, no doubt intrigued by the somber drift of my words. I had tried to speak calmly, even softly, avoiding any suggestion of rancor or bitterness, but even as I spoke I could feel the heaviness of the words between us in that brightly lit room.

"In the last few years I have been doing nothing very much, selling bananas and tomatoes and packets of sugar. In the years before that I had been a trader, a man of business. In between I spent many years in jail, a prisoner of the state." Poor Rachel, she sat stunned in front of me, caught out by the brutality of my reply. "But all will be well now," I continued, running out as I began. "Here by the sea. In the little flat."

"I've got to go now," she said, looking calmly back at me, and I thought that perhaps I had been wrong to think she looked stunned. "I'd love to hear some more about that. Well, I will hear some more about that." A friendly smile came on her face, amused, though not unkindly. It made me regret the self-pity that had made me speak so brutally.

Latif Mahmud. I thought I'd hear some more from him too, if she told him my name. I thought he would come to find out about me and to tell me the story of all that had happened to him since all those years ago.

For now I sit in a house that Rachel and the council found for me, a house whose language and whose noises are foreign to me, but I feel safe in it. At times. At other times, I feel that it is too late now, that this has now become a time of melodrama. And at these times I find fear in the stealthy passage of time, as if all along I have been standing still, loitering in one place while everything had slid past, at times going about its business, at other times jeeringly convulsed in silent laughter at all the numbed and abandoned cosmos like me. At those times I feel defeated by the overbearing weight of the nuances that place and describe everything I might say, as if a place already exists for them and a meaning has already been given to them before I utter them. I feel that I am an involuntary instrument of another's design, a figure in a story told by someone else. Not I. Can an I ever speak of itself without making itself heroic, without making itself seem hemmed in, arguing against an unarguable, rancoring with an implacable?

3.

Latif

Someone called me a grinning blackamoor in the street, speaking out of a different time. A grinning blackamoor. Picture the sight. I was striding along from the tube to work, hurrying a little because I like the drama of stepping out of the station in that purposeful and directed way a mandatory destination gives you. But I was also hurrying out of habitual anxiety that I might be late. I look at my watch often, though I didn't have one on that morning. The strap rotted on me some months ago and I hadn't got round to getting a new one. The result was I worried even more without one than if I had one, imagining myself late when I might be perfectly OK. I don't know why that is, that worrying about time. It feels unhealthy. Though I worry quite a bit anyway, and I hate to be late, having to rush and bustle and disappoint and apologize.

So there I was, striding to work, worrying a little but not unduly, my mind churning with the usual crap, work, unspoken regrets, neglected duties, walking along the north side of Bedford Square from Tottenham Court Road toward Malet Street. I swerved a little to avoid a man I had expected to make a little room as we approached each other on the pavement. I did not really notice his approach, just registered it and prepared to lean out of the way. As it turned out, he didn't make room, so I had to lean away in a slightly more exaggerated way than I had assumed I'd have to. I suppose I made a meal of it, raising my shoulders and taking a little sidestep, as in some of those silly ballroom dances we used to try and learn out of books when we were teenagers back in nativity. Then as I was almost past, I heard him hiss—sssssssssss—a strange, menacing and medieval sound if you're not used to it, as I wasn't. Without looking round I was instantaneously looking back in my mind at the man I had walked past without noticing. Then, when I looked properly, I saw that he was an older man in a heavy and expensive black coat, not tall, shoulders slightly hunched. Hiss, hissing out of another time. And then he said, "You grinning blackamoor."

I didn't even know I was grinning, but I did grin after that as I turned to look at the clever one. He looked like one of those tucked-in Englishmen you see in 1950s British movies, a banker or civil servant of that cinematic era, racked by a moral dilemma he cannot resolve, stern and jowly, strolling on, now that we had passed, with the deliberate clop-clop of the doomed hero. You gwinnin blackamoor. But not to mock, he might be in the midst of a crisis and contemplating self-annihilation, and his hiss of loathing was really a cry for help disguised in that bookish abuse. Such a strange word, blackamoor, that *a* between black and moor bothered me at once, and habit or training made me start thinking about when it came into use, whether it was in use in ordinary parole, to the extent that people wandered down the street and accosted a strolling darkie with it, or whether it was a literary reinvention as a way of constructing the speech of an earlier time. I looked it up in my *Concise Oxford Dictionary* as soon as I got in my office, and got very little for it: Negro, black + moor. You can do better than that. So I looked up black, and quailed: blackhearted, blackbrowed, blacklist, blackguard, blackmail, Black Maria, black market, black sheep. Entry after entry like that, so that by the time I finished reading through them all I felt despicable and disheartened, smeared by the torrent of vituperation. Of course I knew about the construction of black as other, as wicked, as beast, as some evil dark place in the innermost being of even the most skinless civilized European, but I had not expected to see so much black black black on a page like that. Stumbling on it so unprepared was a bigger shock than being called you gwinning blackamoor by a man who looked like a disgruntled, dated movie persona. It made me feel hated, suddenly weak with a kind of terror at such associations. This is the house I live in, I thought, a language which barks at and scorns me behind every third corner.

I didn't dare look up Moor after that. But later in the afternoon, after the last of my three classes that day, my busiest day of the week, I went to the library and looked up blackamoor in the *OED*, the big mama herself. There it was, the word has been in print since 1501, and since then has slipped from the pen of such worthies of English letters as the humane Sidney, the incomparable W. Shakespeare, the prudent Pepys and a host of other, minor luminaries. It lifted my spirits. It made me feel that I had

been present in all those strenuous ages, not forgotten, not root-
ing and snorting in a jungle swamp or swinging naked from tree
to tree, but right there, grinning through the canon for centuries.

When I got back to my office I rang up the refugee council.
Or perhaps that was another day. Some while back
someone had left a message on my office answering machine to
ask if I could help translate in the case of an old man who had
just arrived from Zanzibar as an asylum seeker and could speak
no English. The speaker said she had been told that I understood the language they spoke there. I suppressed the dread I
always felt when I was required to meet someone from nativity.
Would they tell me, or think to themselves, how English I had
become, how different, how out of touch? As if it was either here
or there whether I had or not, as if it proved something uncomplicated about alienation, as if I was no longer myself but a self-
treacherous pretense of myself, a processed stooge. And I also
suppressed my irritation with the suggestion that the language
they spoke *out there* was unnamable or unknown, when more
people spoke Kiswahili than spoke Greek or Danish or Swedish
or Dutch, or probably all of them together. Maybe.

I had done this kind of thing for refugee organizations before, and would have been happy to do it again, but the next
message on the answering machine canceled the first request. I
took down the number anyway, and pinned it on the board
above my desk, where it joined several other bits of paper pinned
there because they were potential sources of something or the
other: an idea, a poem, a sense of engagement, busyness. It's

hard work keeping yourself on the up and up in the business I am in. Several weeks later—no, months later, sometime during the following term . . . on the day the doomed hero of British 1950s movies called me a grinning blackamoor or on another day . . . on a day late in the spring—I rang the number to find out what had happened to the old man asylum seeker. Perhaps being called names in the streets made me wish for a kind of solidarity. That was how it began.

I abhor poems. I read them and teach them and abhor them. I even write some. I teach them to students (of course not my own bits of offal, for God's sake) and squeeze what I can out of them, make them laconic where they are verbose and posturing, wise and prophetic where they are clumsily speculative. They say nothing so elaborately, they reveal nothing, they lead to nothing. Worse than wallpaper or a notice outside the departmental secretary's office. Give me a lucid bit of prose any day.

I t was such a relief that second message on the answering machine, to say that I didn't, after all, have to do penance for my treacherous absence from nativity. I took down the number because I didn't believe the second message. I thought they would still come back for me, and pinned the number on the board to remind myself, to keep myself on the alert, ready for the blow when it came, rather than dozy and dopy and relaxed and then churned up when it arrived. Then in the end I rang, after all those weeks, all those months, to check if I was safe. The man I spoke to said brusquely that he knew nothing about me or a call made to me. I started the conversation by giving my name, out of politeness, not because I expected him to recognize it. What! You mean you've never heard of me? I was brusque back, indicating I was a member of the tribe, or at least familiar with the strange courtesies of anonymous telephone conversations, and after that we had a friendly and chatty exchange. "Oh, yes, the old man. That was a while back, a long time ago, but I remember him. It must have been Rachel who rang you. She's taken him on. He's all right now, I think. A strange one, it appeared he could speak English all along but he preferred not to." The way the man inflected *preferred* made it sound as if he was quoting.

"Preferred. Like Bartleby," I said, always eager to show off, to confirm my credentials as a teacher of literature.

"I'll get Rachel to give you a call," he said, so I assumed he didn't know the story.

"Oh no, there's no need. I was just interested."

"It'll be no problem," he said, his voice beaming causal good-will, playing on the same side, dancing to the same cha-cha-cha tune, us refugee redeemers in our holy frocks.

"Oh that would be very kind," I said. "I'd love to know what happened to him. She has my office number but I'll give it to you, anyway." I didn't want to hear from her. I really just wanted to know if I was in the clear. "There's an answering machine so any time is fine."

She called within minutes, or the next day.

"Rachel Howard," she said, busy and distracted, perhaps reading something as she spoke to me. I tried to picture the voice:

young, trying hard to stay slim, a little sweaty under the armpits from all the tension and straining.

"I was calling about that old man you rang me about a while back, apparently a long while back, the one you said needed a translator, the one from Zanzibar. You left a message on my answering machine. I wondered how he was, if everything worked out."

"Yes, thank you," she said. "He's fine, settled into a flat and looking after himself really well. He's fine, quite self-sufficient, really. Did I tell you he's sixty-five years old? A bit old to be running away from home, but there you are. He doesn't think so. Thank you for calling to ask about him. I'll tell him."

"That's very kind of you," I said, preparing my exit, beginning to shift the weight on my elbow so I could put the phone down, rounding my lips for goodbye and thank you.

"He'll be pleased you called," she said gaily. "He told me you two know each other."

"Do we?" I asked. Too late, that sinking feeling. "What's his name?"

"I thought I left his name in the message. I'm sorry," she said. "I mentioned your name to him and he said he knew you. I wondered whether you might want to get in touch. I was sure I left his name." Implying that I might be a potential afternoon visitor to read the old absconder a story now and then, sing him a qasida to put him in touch with the plangent melodies of his abandoned self.

"His name is Mr. Shaaban. Mr. Rajab Shaaban," she said, her voice rising a little, either through excitement or because she was concentrating on saying the name right. She should have pronounced the *j* in Rajab as a harder sound and it should have been Shaaban with a long *a*. "Do you recognize it? Does it mean anything to you?"

"No," I said.

"Oh, what a pity. Oh dear, he'll be disappointed. I'll tell him you called, anyway."

I am a grinning blackamoor. *You* are a grinning blackamoor. *He* is a grinning blackamoor. *She* is a grinning blackamoor. *We* are grinning blackamoors. *They* are grinning blackamoors. It's not clear about that *a*, why it has survived in blackamoor when it has been dropped in other black combinations. A conundrum of the first order, beyond the accumulated wisdom of the *OED*. A vague memory comes back to me of a film I saw as a teenager about Viking ships in the Mediterranean and at some stage an encounter with a Black sultan of a North African kingdom. The sultan lounges on his right elbow, his torso gleaming beautiful naked black, grinning. Does one of the Viking rapists call him a grinning blackamoor before wiping that grin off with his broad blade? I think it was the incomparable Sidney Poitier who played the part of the sultan, and the still of that pose made it to the cover of *Ebony* magazine. I swear it, it's all coming back, and the film was called *The Long Ships*, and the Viking pillager did say you grinning blackamoor. As far below the reality as a blackamoor is unlike the sun.

Those are pearls that were his eyes. Rajab Shaaban was my father's name. Someone had picked up his name and brought him back to life. Or perhaps it was someone who had as much right to the name as my father did. The name of my father is not sacred.

He worried about being late even more than I did, my father. He was a complete nuisance about it. And he worried about other people's lateness as much as he did about his own. He made me realize just how much of our lives was spent in waiting, waiting for someone, waiting to go and meet someone, waiting for the muadhin to make the call to prayers, waiting for the new moon to appear at the beginning of Ramadhan, waiting for it to appear again at the end of Ramadhan, waiting for a ship to dock, waiting for an office to open. For my father all this waiting was agony, impossible to ignore, and so I learned to dread delay because of the anguish it put him through. Yet with many other things he was so casual, very nearly to the point of negligence. He had so much cruelty in his life that I hesitate to judge him harshly, but he was negligent. That was how he lost my brother Hassan and how he lost the house when he should have known better, and nothing that came after that gave him content. I don't know how he lost my mother, exactly.

It took me a long time to understand that my mother despised my father. I don't even think I *understood* that until much later. I don't think I would have known to use that word to describe how she was with him until I was in my twenties and a long way from home. But at some stage I grasped it, in things I overheard, in the tone of voice she used with him, in the way she lived her life. I never heard the story of the beginning of this disdain because they never talked about it to me. I don't suppose parents talk about such things until the same misfortune befalls their own children, and then they only talk because they think they've overcome them.

My brother Hassan never mentioned it either, although on almost everything else he was the fount of wisdom and secret knowledge, the spirited source and tablet of the law. There was nothing Hassan did not know about or did not have an elaborate and detailed theory about. Mostly he just slipped into an explanation or a description without any appearance of effort, but now and then he required a few seconds before he began to invent and elaborate. I remember once he recited Brutus's speech over the corpse of Julius Caesar to me. For some reason he was required to learn it by heart by the English teacher. I mean the teacher of English at school, who was as English as you and I, who came to work in a kanzu and kofia, and who was a pious Muslim and ardent Anglophile without contradiction or anxiety. He loved for his students to learn passages from great works by heart, and recite them day after day, one after the other, class after class, nice work if you can get it. Then he would sit at the back of the class with his eyes shut and a little smile on his face and listen to them recite from *Julius Caesar* or from Kipling or from "La Belle Dame sans Merci." Hassan thought it a waste of time, like doing cross-country races or attending the Saturday-morning Inter-Schools debate ("This house believes that a woman's place is in the home"), but the teacher carried a short leather strap in his pocket and used it on those who had not shown enough diligence in learning their lines. And I think Hassan really quite liked knowing those powerful lines.

At the culmination of his efforts with *Julius Caesar*, he declaimed the result to me as we sat on the shallow steps outside the house, him holding his arm cocked across his chest like a senator from ancient Rome and with his chin lifted and angled in a sagacious pose.

> Romans, countrymen and lovers! hear me for my cause; and be silent that you may hear: believe me for mine honor; and have respect to mine honor that you may believe: censure me in your wisdom; and awake your senses that you may the better judge.

And although he explained who Julius Caesar was and what was done to him, and who Mark Antony and Brutus, and who the Romans were and who Shakespeare, the speech made little impact at the time (I was about nine or ten) except for the opening lines which reminded me of the greeting politicians made in the rallies that were happening two or three times a week in those years. That and the line *I have the same dagger for myself*, because I liked the sound of *dagger*.

> With this I depart,—that, as I slew my best lover for the good of Rome, I have the same dagger for myself, when it shall please my country to need my death.

What is a dagger? I asked Hassan. And for some reason he stumbled. It's a glass of whiskey, he said uncertainly. I had no specific idea what that was, although I knew it was drink and haram. Then Hassan hit his stride and told me all about the meaning of whiskey in Roman culture and how Brutus was saying that he was intending to have one if the crowd did not like his speech. And I have the same dagger for myself if you don't like what I say. That was one of his bad moments, and there were many more of the same, but there were other moments when his touch was exhilarating. Then he spoke of jinns and ancient kingdoms, of the tragic life of Frankenstein's monster, and of the midnight sun on the North Pole, where the poor monster drifted despairingly on floating ice, of the grandeur of Muslim Spain and of the awesome sternness of Nazi Germany. So much flowed from him with effortless lucidity and with the gleam of conviction that made you certain that what he was saying was true. Never a word that I remember, though, about the disdain with which my mother acted toward our Ba, or why our Ba, who could be fierce enough if you were late for something, never protested.

Hassan was six years older than me, and in the early years of my life he was the source of everything I desired. He gave me love and reassurance when he knew I needed them. He gave them in his own way, with rough words and hurtful blows at times. He explained the meaning of things I encountered and which made me anxious or uncertain. Whenever he let me, I followed him around like a pet while he extemporized the straight-faced invention that was winning him a reputation for wit and mischief. Often he explained for the sheer pleasure of exercising authority over the incommensurable, making a case against the ceaseless contingencies that are on the point of crushing us, refusing his mute place in the scheme of things, speculating and blustering as if silence would drown him, blah-blah with sparkling smiles and mild obscenities that grew less mild with each passing year. He was my existential warrior, my desperado, yes, I loved him like a brother, like a father, like a beloved. Others cast covetous eyes on the grace of his glowing youth. I know they did. Then, in the end, which was not long in coming, he swaggered defiantly over the horizon, and now he is lost to me.

As is my mother, as are all of them. My mother was beautiful. Her name was Asha, after the third wife of the Prophet, who was married to him when she was six years old. In the afternoon, when my mother was dressed to go out, her eyes glowing and lined with kohl, her lips gleaming like wet blood, I looked at her with pride and a kind of fear. I did not fear her, not much, not often, only when she lost her temper about some petty stupidity on my part, so I must have feared for her. I didn't think *that* at the time I was nine. I just feared as I looked at her, and felt pride that she was my mother, that her smile was so bright and deep, so complicated. I just feared as she stood by the door in the heavy cloud of the perfume she wore, her clothes steeped in incense. Then she went to call on friends and neighbors, and did not return until the middle of the evening. On some of those afternoons she met men. My mother took lovers. She slept with other men. Not professionally, not in numbers. Perhaps only one or two. I don't know. For fun or perhaps for other reasons. An affair here and an affair there. I think. Though later she accumulated rich gifts whose sources were never mentioned. I found out as I grew older, as events gradually became clear to me, as I began to understand the meaning of things I had seen, and because people at school made fun of me, and sometimes girls in the street shouted mocking innuendos at me. But I knew before then, I just didn't know for sure what I knew. And that perfume she wore has always made me think of bedrooms and intrigue, and a ripe kind of shame. In later years, in the years after independence, she became indiscreet, and then it was impossible not to know. The taunts in the streets stopped then, as she lived her transgressions openly, or perhaps because I was older and my tormentors were older, or because of what had happened to Hassan or because of all the other things that had happened to all of us. Or because one of her lovers became powerful. In any case, for reasons I will never know for sure, no comments about her were made in my presence in those later years.

In the year I was nine, and Hassan was fifteen, and my mother groomed herself for her afternoon sorties among friends and lovers, my father Rajab Shaaban Mahmud worked as a clerk in the Public Works Department. Some people called him bin Mahmud, after his grandfather, my great-grandfather, who was well-remembered for something I've forgotten. No, that's not true, I know very well what he was remembered for: for high-level probity and for a pious soul. Something useless in itself, and probably useless to him, but which made him and everyone else feel more human. My father was not pious, not yet, not in that year. He drank, which according to the way we lived made him a shameful failure. And although he was discreet, there was no way of hiding such things. Sometimes I'd wake up out of sleep and I'd know that he was home because of the smell of alcohol in the house. It was a four-roomed house, and Hassan and I had our own room which we bolted shut when we went to sleep, but the smell still woke me from sleep. He must have reeked like that to everyone in the streets. Once or twice, no more than twice that I can remember, he went too far and had to be helped home, silent and weeping. I imagine it was shame. He didn't speak for days after those two times, creeping about with eyes downcast, walking with the softest of footfalls.

My father was a clerk in the Public Works Department. I don't know what he did there. Every morning, he left home at seven in the morning dressed in a clean white shirt and light-brown trousers and leather sandals, and walked the few minutes to the PWD depots. I don't suppose he was ever late. At five minutes to one o'clock, the siren went to announce the end of the morning and my father came home to lunch. He always looked tired and unhappy when he came home, as if the work dispirited him, or the walk home in the sun wore him out, or something was sucking the vigor out of him. He never neglected to look for Hassan and me when he came home, calling for us by name if we were nowhere in sight. Then he would stroke our heads with a small, sad triumphant grin on his face and go and have his shower before lunch. I never minded the ritual, and I don't think Hassan did that much, even though as he grew older he found it hard not to make a face of scorn and turn his head away as my father attempted to stroke his face. I tried hard not to, but at times I found it impossible to resist grinning back.

During the musim of that year when I was nine and Hassan was fifteen, a man came to stay with us. We were told to call him Uncle Hussein. My father met him at the café and they got talking, and it seemed that they got on so well that they became excited and firm friends. That was how I would have understood it as a child, though probably they met several times and talked on many occasions before they became good friends. He came to eat a meal with us one Friday, a rare event for us, whose only visitors were women friends and relatives of my mother. I could never tell the difference between my mother's friends and relatives, as they all addressed me as if they had a share in me and took similar liberties with me. When Uncle Hussein came for the meal on that Friday afternoon he was still *my good friend*, said like that in English. That was how my father addressed him. My father could read the Koran fluently but could not make conversation in Arabic, and Uncle Hussein only had a few words of Kiswahili, so they spoke to each other in English. *My good friend* did not become our uncle until he moved in. He was a tall man, dressed in a kanzu that was the color of light honey, and embroidered in silver thread in the style of the merchants from the Gulf. He subsided to the rug on the floor in an effortless fluid movement, a lustrous cowrie-shell grin on his face. Let me describe the house we grinning blackamoors lived in. It will relieve the strain the memory of Uncle Hussein makes me feel.

The house was on two floors. There were three rooms upstairs where we lived, one room for Hassan and me and one room for my parents. The third room was for receiving visitors, listening to the radio, sitting, a sitting room. There was a small terrace, part of which was covered and was where my mother cooked, and part of which was open and was where we hung our washing. The upstairs was a small space when we were all there, familiar and friendly, intimate to me even as I recall it now. There was one large room downstairs just by the front door and a small enclosed courtyard beyond that, from where the open stairs ascended. The courtyard was open to the skies and was overlooked by the upstairs terrace. It was always silent and cool in the courtyard, and when it rained hard the concrete floor filled with water and made a shallow pool to slide and splash in. The large room downstairs was for receiving male visitors who were strangers to the family, on the days of Idd or Maulid Nabi, or at a death or marriage. That was why it was near the front door, so that covetous male eyes would not penetrate to the tender pulse of family intimacy. It was the kind of room we did not usually have much use for as my father did not invite male exotica to our house, nor did he have open house during Idd and Maulid Nabi as some people did. I imagine it was used for the women's wake and readings after the death of my father's mother, but I was only three years old then and have no memory of the event.

It was usually kept locked, with the windows shuttered, and used as a place of temporary storage, but there was little enough to store and for some reason my father liked it kept clean and uncluttered, as if on any day he would open it to a public function he was planning. There was a rug rolled up along one wall, to protect it from whatever little light got through the shutters, and there was a bed with wooden slats at one end of the room. A straw mat covered the slats. It was an ascetic room, but it had a pungency that made me think of the musim, dhows rocking in the harbor and sailors smelling of dried fish and sunbaked skin and ocean spray. It made me think of parched and stony places, of sailor grime and sweat-stained rags.

My father called the rolled-up rug a Bokharra and was concerned for it. Every year during Ramadhan, we unrolled it in the courtyard and beat the dust out of it with sticks before rolling it up again and covering it with a canvas cloth. Otherwise the room was locked and mostly empty aside from a few sacks and boxes and a carved wooden trunk with a brass padlock on it. Once when I was alone in the house, I became frantic about finding the key to that room. I searched in my mother's wardrobe, her favorite hiding place for anything valuable or secret, behind medicine bottles, in the jewelry drawer of the almirah, under doormats, on the shelves above the windows, in empty flower vases, in the pockets of trousers, and I never doubted that I would find it in the end. It was not as if there was anything valuable in there or something dangerous.

When I did find the key, it was inserted in a tiny crack above the doorframe, and I only managed to see it by putting a chair on top of the built-up bench just inside the front door of the house. The room was dark and cool as always, but this time there were two large clay jars in there, probably being stored for a relative or a friend, or a relative of a friend or a friend of a relative. The jars made me think of stories of jinns rising out of them, of young women abducted in them, of the young prince having himself conveyed in one to his beloved's chamber. I knew stories like that: a fisherman low on luck and desperate for a good catch snares a jar in his net. At first he is overjoyed thinking that his luck has changed at last, and instead of dragging in old debris he had a thrashing great marlin in there. But as he pulls and drags and feels the dead weight of what he is pulling and dragging, he suspects that at best there is some stinking dead thing in his net, a donkey or a dog. It turns out to be a huge clay jar, as big as his wizened scrawny self, with a chunky silver seal at its mouth. Well, alhamdulillah for something, he says to himself, and in case God is watching to see how he accepts this playful little bounty. It is never sensible to be petulant about bad luck, as the Great Giver of Justice might be sitting watching to see how much trust you have in His Mercy, and by your petulance you might learn a lesson in keeping faith in His Wisdom by getting even more rotten luck. So the fisherman says, alhamdulillah for something, and thinks the silver seal will bring a little, as will the jar itself if it's not too filthy inside. With that he struggles with the seal and eventually yanks it off. A huge spume of smoke immediately gushes out of the jar, black and yellow and red, and smelling of fire and dungeons and scaly flesh. The fisherman, who has of course been thrown to the ground in shock, scrambles to his feet and runs away as fast as he can. But before he has got very far, the great column of smoke, which is now so huge and low that it obscures the sun, begins to thicken and solidify into a jinn covered in silver scales and holding a shining, long curved knife in his hand. The fisherman inevitably stands rooted in terror and waits for the jinn to bend down out of the sky and breathe his ancient sulfurous breath on him. "For more than a thousand years I have been imprisoned in this jar," the jinn booms, "put in here by the great Solomon whom God in His Wisdom had given authority over jinns and animals. Solomon laid a great spell on the seal and despite all my efforts I could not remove it. For the first hundred years I swore to bestow kingdoms and riches and knowledge and wisdom and eternal life to the person who opened the seal. For the second hundred years I vowed to give my liberator just the kingdoms and riches. After the next hundred years, I swore to kill the person who opened the seal, for letting me remain penned for three centuries. And each hundred after that I devised filthier and filthier ways of making that person die. So here you are, you disgusting little nobody, you have won the prize. You are mine and you are about to die evilly."

So the fisherman, thinking he is about to die anyway, puts on a bit of swagger and nimbly comes up with a plan. "I don't believe you really came out of that jar or that the great King Solomon had really imprisoned you in it. Why, sir, you are so huge, so magnificent, so imperious, not even your big toe will fit into that jar." At which the jinn laughs delightedly and says, "I'll show you." He turns again into a great cloud of smoke and streams back into the jar, and the scrawny fisherman leaps forward and claps the seal back on, and carefully rolls the jar back into the sea. Alhamdulillah, he says, giving a little glance upward, thanks a lot.

I moved one of the jars near to the bed, and then, first stepping on the bed, I got into the jar. Standing, the jar reached to my nine-year-old shoulders, but I found that if I squatted into the belly of it, I disappeared. The jar was cool and gloomy, with a pleasing clamminess, like I imagine the bottom of a dry well would be on a hot afternoon. When I spoke, which I did experimentally, saying alhamdulillah, my voice reverberated down a long tunnel and had a flatness which was unrecognizable, as if the space itself was pressing my head down on my larynx. I tried other words, imagining other worlds, and in due course I fell asleep. (Of course I didn't, but Ali Baba did and woke up to find himself in the cave of the Forty Thieves.) Anyway, that was the room where Uncle Hussein came to eat with us that Friday, and which the following week he came to live in.

I want to look forward, but I always find myself looking back, poking about in times so long ago and so diminished by other events since then, tyrant events which loom large over me and dictate every ordinary action. Yet when I look back, I find some objects still gleam with a bright malevolence and every memory draws blood. It's a dour place, the land of memory, a dim gutted warehouse with rotting planks and rusted ladders where you sometimes spend time riffling through abandoned goods. Here it's a chilly, darkening afternoon, already bright with warming streetlamps and agitated with the deep low-key rumble of traffic and unresting crowds, an unceasing buzz like the nattering and nuzzling of an insect encampment. The other place that I live in is still and murmurous, where speech is soundless and hardly anybody moves, a silence after dark. That is where I always find him, my poor father. He was a small man, quiet and punctilious, walking to work every day in his clean white shirt, head slightly to one side, eyes lowered. At lunchtime he came home, stroked the faces of his two sons, showered and had a siesta. Later in the afternoon he went out and sometimes returned late at night, the worse for wear and shamed by drink. I sometimes imagined my father having a father, and wondered what he might have thought about him. Or what his father would have thought if he had seen what had become of him. I never once heard him mention his father or even his existence. I wondered if he walked with his head lowered because he knew that his father would not have esteemed him, or because he feared that we did not reverence him and would never think to mention him to our own children, or because he knew that he had lost my mother's love. It was later when I thought about such things, when so much else had happened that there was nothing it was impossible to think about, when nothing was sacred anymore. And by then I knew that my father's father was a disappointment, a wild man who drank and fornicated in brothels and died young.

When I was so young I would not have known to think of my father as a poor small man, or even to think of my mother as beautiful and capable of loving my father and withdrawing her love from him. But he was small, too small for Uncle Hussein for sure, who was too big for all of us. Uncle Hussein was a man of appetite and relish, a proper grinning blackamoor, who nevertheless brought my father happiness and vigor when he came to live with us. My father, on the other hand, was afraid of the dark.

I don't remember anything about how the arrangement was made, just that one afternoon all of us were cleaning the room, moving the clay pots into the courtyard, beating the rug as if it was Ramadhan and then rolling it out to make the room suddenly glow with deep amber colors. My father was smiling and joking, teasing Hassan about how his English would now improve since he would be able to practice on Uncle Hussein, and taking no umbrage at my mother's muttered reservations about the new arrangement. It would only be for a month, until the end of musim, he said. Then Uncle Hussein was there. Every morning I greeted my mother and my father before breakfast, and stopped by Uncle Hussein's open door to greet him on my way to school. And every morning he quietly gave me a shilling and Hassan two shillings, his finger across his lips so we should not tell about his generosity. In the afternoon, my father sometimes took his lunch with him, and then the two of them sat chatting for an hour or two before he retired for his indispensable siesta. Later they went out together to the café or for a stroll, and then came back to listen to English programs on the radio Uncle Hussein had acquired for himself. Sometimes people called to sit with them and listen and chat, people I didn't know were friendly with my father at all, and they all spoke in loud voices mixing English and Arabic and Kiswahili in polyglot good humor, and the laughter and noise from the room filled the whole house. Even the coffee seller started to include our house in his rounds, calling in every night to see if the gentlemen cared for a drink, then stopping for a while to admire their foh-foh-foh, which was his way of imitating their English. My father's visits to the grubby Goan bar in the shadow of the Catholic cathedral stopped then. I don't know if that was where he went, it was the only bar whose existence I knew of, so I assumed that was where he went. For a long time I thought bars always looked like that, with rusty wire grilles in the windows. When my mother came home in the evening, she greeted the men without looking into the room, calling out as she walked past and summoning us to follow upstairs if she knew we were sitting in there.

Uncle Hussein never came upstairs. There was no need to. There was a bathroom downstairs at the back of the courtyard. Well, there was a room with a flushing toilet, a standpipe, an aluminum bucket and a scoop made out of a Blue Band margarine tin, all perfectly respectable and clean, cleaner than you would find in many other people's homes. It was a little dark in there, and a terrifying prospect at night, only to be used if the upstairs bathroom was occupied and the need was at crisis point, but then Uncle Hussein had traveled hundreds of miles across the seas to be there, and would hardly notice the scurryings in the shadows as he saw to his ablutions. Anyway, he never came upstairs. If he needed anything, he stood at the bottom of the stairs and called out my father's name. If my mother answered, because my father was out or was having his siesta, she would not show herself but speak standing back. If it was Hassan or me, we would stand at the top of the stairs to show respect, or come hurrying down to collect whatever it was Uncle Hussein had brought. Whatever the response, he would state his business with his eyes lowered, in case my mother was standing at the top of the stairs and a careless glance upward might embarrass her. He generally brought something every day: some fish we would have for supper, fine fruit or vegetable which caught his eye, coffee beans and sweet dates, a pot of honey once which he bought from a Somali sailor, covered in a tight-fitting hessian sleeve, another time aromatic gum and myrrh, and sometimes whimsical objects which he handed over without comment, a Chinese phrase book for me, a rosary for Hassan.

He usually came home just before my father, after the noon prayers. He sat on the rug in his room with the door ajar, his reading glasses on, checking through his notebook or reading the Koran. The glasses always seemed like a bit of a frivolity, as if he did not really need them, or as if he was not really doing his sums or reading, but was just smilingly having a bit of fun. When we passed on the way in or out of the house we called a greeting. He would call us back if we passed by silently. It did not feel unpleasant to be demanded of in this way. If women visitors passed by and called a greeting, he replied without looking up, to show respect. When my father came home, he stopped at the door and they exchanged a few words, or more often than not a lot of words, yards of incomprehensible verbiage, speaking in English and laughing and joking so much that sometimes my father forgot to call for Hassan and me so he could stroke our faces with his particular sadness. At times he called for his lunch to be brought down along with Uncle Hussein's, and the two of them sat downstairs eating and talking for up to an hour.

It was Hassan's task to take Uncle Hussein's lunch tray down to him. My mother usually served his food first and then the rest of us ate our food together upstairs. After lunch, Hassan went downstairs to collect the tray, and then returned to Uncle Hussein for his English lesson. It was Uncle Hussein's idea, the English lesson. Hassan had recited his Brutus speech one afternoon, at my father's insistence, and Uncle Hussein had been impressed to such effect that he suggested the daily afternoon lessons. He said that Hassan had a talent for the language, so my father boasted to us. So then every afternoon Hassan hurried through his lunch and waited for Uncle Hussein to call for him. If my father was downstairs chatting, Hassan fidgeted and strode about, irritably waiting for his summons. I had to go to Koran school after lunch, every day, whether it was wet or dry or storming, so I never witnessed any of the lessons and Hassan for some reason was not interested in talking about them. All his stories now were Uncle Hussein this and Uncle Hussein that. Did you know he's done this or seen that or been there, and look what he gave me today? A wristwatch, a fountain pen, a notebook, expensive things. I was avid for the stories—though they did not seem as exciting as the ones about merchants and poor men, and enchanted princesses and enraged jinns which my mother told—and I was envious of the gifts—though not unbearably so because Hassan was generous with things—but most of all I wanted Uncle Hussein to like me too, as much as he liked Hassan. I wanted to have him call me into his room in the afternoon, and sit beside him while he told me stories and gave me his priceless gifts.

It must have been during that time that the agreement was made through which my parents lost the house. I was too young then to have noticed or understood a matter of such adult complexity, and I suspect it was never spoken in front of me in case I blurted it out inappropriately, the way children do. When I came to hear about the agreement my father made with Uncle Hussein, it had become a crisis and could only be spoken about as a grievance and an act of treachery. I remember how happy my father was in that month or so that Uncle Hussein stayed with us, how fulfilled he seemed in the discovery of a new friend and how he seemed more like a father then than he had seemed before: assured and opinionated, peremptory with his affection and his demands, busily brushing us aside to get on with his own consuming business, coming and going with male self-importance in the company of his worldly men friends. To hear him uttering obscenities and laughing in the raucous, callous way of the streets was a revelation, he who before walked with his head lowered and was sometimes silent for days. I imagine that it was out of that joy and that self-assurance that he found the temerity to go into business with Uncle Hussein. Perhaps that was what some of those conversations in lowered voices were about, the two of them sitting on the Bokharra, reclining on an elbow, one knee raised, leaning a little toward each other while the incense burner gently fumed by the side of the bed. They spoke in English, which was only foh-foh-foh to me, so there was no need to lower their voices, but that was how they were, murmuring in tones of seduction, afraid of being over-heard. The arrangement as I understood it later was that my father bought into Uncle Hussein's business with a loan which he secured with the value of the house. When the business failed, as Uncle Hussein said it did, my father had no money to pay back the loan and had to give up the house. In short. I only assume that that was how the agreement was made, Uncle Hussein tempting my father with secret arrangements that would yield importance in the world, and make him seem daring and know-ing, a proper man.

One afternoon I came home from Koran school a little earlier than usual, allowed out by the teacher because I was suffering from diarrhea. It must have been from something I had bought in the street. My discomfort was so unmistakable, writhing and groaning without shame, rushing to go to the toilet without wait-ing for permission, that when I returned the teacher told me to go home. I was ready for another bout by the time I arrived, only to find the bathroom occupied. I ran to the dark one downstairs but found that occupied as well. I went back upstairs and danced outside the door, calling out to whoever was in there to let me in. The shower was running in full spate, and I knew myself that the roar and volume of that water can sometimes be so enveloping that it's a wrench to turn it off. But I was desperate, and banged on the door and whined with all the pathetic piteousness of a nine-year-old about to explode. Hassan opened the door, stood there dripping and spangled with water, and then stepped past me with eyes lowered. I hurried in to do what was necessary, and only later, after the pain had subsided and I had washed myself, did I feel a little stab of fear.

When Hassan had first opened the door, his eyes were large and round with misery, or perhaps it was embarrassment or guilt. Then he had dropped his eyes without a word and walked past, deep in whatever it was that absorbed him. All that was unlike him. I had never known him to have a shower at that time of the afternoon. He had stood there gleaming in the nude, and then walked out of the bathroom like that when normally he was never undressed outside our bedroom. Had either of my parents been around, his nakedness would have seemed an intolerable indecency. Hassan was well-built and full, a youth, and recently he had been so conscious of his maturity that even when we were alone in our room he had taken to covering his genitals when before he would have lolled about without a care if the mood took him. And that look of catastrophe in his face, in someone whose eyes glared and stared or leaped with scorn and mischief and insurrection at any misuse. When I got to our room he had gone, and later I was too ill to care or remember about his strange behavior that afternoon. For it turned out that my diarrhea was something worse, and I passed into a delirium of fever and painful evacuations that lasted for days.

When I rejoined the world of the living, when I recovered consciousness, woke up and came to, it was to find myself sleeping alone in our room, and Hassan's bed stripped and bare. I had

been unconscious for three days—why is it always three days?—
and there were times when I had been given up hope for. It
sounds like the usual crap parents go in for about their children,
but evidently they really were scared for my priceless life. They
weren't sure what it was I had, and nor was the doctor, although
that was not anything unusual with him. Generally speaking,
he gave everyone an injection, because that swelled up the bill a
little, and some mixture or pills from his own pharmacy, because
that made the patients come back for more. His diagnosis was so
uncertain that they expelled Hassan from the room in case he
got it too, the firstborn and heir to the kingdom of air. He was to
sleep on a mat on the floor of the sitting room. But when he
heard about the arrangement, Uncle Hussein would not allow it.
The floor would be uncomfortable and he would get in everyone's way. If anything he, Uncle Hussein, should move out so
that Hassan could have the downstairs room. Now my father
would not hear of this. So they took the mattress off Hassan's
bed and carried it downstairs to Uncle Hussein's room. You can
have extra English lessons now, I can imagine my father said to
Hassan.

The night after I regained consciousness, Hassan was back in
our room, but he did not like it. He lay on the bed with his face
turned to the wall, paying the most desultory attention to the
invalid. I had heard him arguing with my mother when she had
first suggested it, and then had seen her becoming stern and insistent, almost frantic with anger. You're sleeping in your room
whether you like it or not, you child of sin, she said, speaking to
him with such unfamiliar rage that there was nothing more to
say. It made me wonder why she was so angry, and whether it was

Hassan she was angry with or Uncle Hussein. I had wondered
before then what she thought of Uncle Hussein living with us.
She had never said anything about him that I heard, but sometimes her silences were suspiciously eloquent. When my father
would be regaling us upstairs with stories of what Uncle Hussein
had said and done, and his tone would invite or even require our
joyful enjoyment and participation of them, my mother would sit
without a word, her face an impassive stare. I thought it was my
father she was treating with contempt for his embarrassing enthusiasm, as she often did for many other things, so it was not
clear if she found Uncle Hussein's stay with us irksome. At other
times, as she stood behind the top of the stairs to reply to his call,
or when the lunch tray was ready to be taken to him, she seemed
anxious that all should be well and that he should feel esteemed
by us.

Over the next few days I stayed home, too weak to go to
school, though no longer bedridden. Hassan was still angry with
me, or in any case he did not talk to me much. In the afternoon
he went for his English lessons with the same eagerness as before
and returned looking both excited and miserable at the same
time. I did not usually see him after his lessons with Uncle Hussein, because of having to go to lessons of my own, and I wondered if he looked like that because the lessons were hard. It was
then that I saw the look in my mother's eyes, and I knew that
Uncle Hussein frightened her. On the days I was home I followed my mother around the house all morning, and sat with her
in the kitchen while she did the cooking. I imagine she talked
and smiled, and cheered me and teased me in just the way a
mother would with her sick little boy. But there was one moment

I remember. We heard a key in the front door, and she sat quite still, only her eyes moving sideways and widening with attention. Then she swallowed and blinked, and for some reason it made me think that she was in danger or feeling unwell. Perhaps she glanced at me and smiled. Perhaps I imagine that she looked sideways in that dramatic way and swallowed and blinked. Perhaps I was elsewhere in the house when Uncle Hussein came home, and only later imagined how my mother would have looked when she heard the sound of the key in the door. And perhaps it was another day, not that same day at all, when I saw her talking to him and then following him into his room.

They must have thought I was out playing. I was well enough to be allowed out, and they must have thought I had gone round to one of the neighbors' houses. I had, but then had come back and crawled into one of the huge clay jars which had been moved out of the room and into the courtyard. I was curled up in the deep calm of the jar, looking up at the patch of sky above the upstairs terrace. When I heard her voice I chuckled to myself, thinking I would stand up in a moment and make her jump. Then I heard the insistent whisper in which she spoke and I hesitated. I peeped out slowly and I saw my mother and Uncle Hussein standing inches apart outside the open door of his room. Then I heard her say, "Unataka niingie ndani?" Do you want me to come in? She walked past him into the room, and he followed behind her and shut the door. That was what I saw, and I understood nothing but some unease, and a great deal of relief that I had not been discovered.

Uncle Hussein must have left soon after that on the return journey of the musim because I have no other memory of him that year. The men who came while Uncle Hussein was there continued for a while and then stopped. My father spoke about Uncle Hussein for a time, remembering one of his kindnesses or one of his exploits, but that too grew less frequent. In time the house fell silent again and my father returned to his quiet ways, although now there were bouts of unprecedented harshness in his manner, especially toward my mother. When before he had taken her contempt with averted face, seeming to cringe with distaste and hurt, now he growled and spat at her. At these moments his mouth turned down in a look of bitterness I had never seen before. But if for my father Uncle Hussein's departure was a kind of loss, for Hassan it was an abandonment, a bereavement. He hardly spoke to anyone, and when he was at home he lay on the bed with his face to the wall or he sat writing in the notebook Uncle Hussein gave him or writing letters on an airmail form. He went for long walks and marathon cycle rides alone, and seemed to have lost interest in the gang of boys he had been one of. The rumors started very quickly, and I was taunted about them by the boys at school. They said our guest had eaten Hassan, had eaten honey there. It was a way of saying something cruder, and they said it crudely too. One of Hassan's secondary school mates, who had been a former friend, chased after me in the street as I was walking to Koran school to ask me if it was true that I had a new father. When I passed a group of adults lounging at street corners, which they seemed forever to be doing, I thought they smirked behind me, I feared they did.

They never left Hassan alone after that, the plunderers of flesh. There was nothing gay in what they did or sought to do. They coveted his grace and his effortless, supple beauty, and muttered to him as he strolled by, offering him money and gifts and transparent predatory smiles. A man gave me a letter to take home to him, a page out of a school notebook, folded over roughly like a page of accounts or a shopping list. I tried to read it when I got home but it was written in English and I could make no sense of it. Hassan read it and then tore it into tiny shreds which he put in an old envelope that he put in his pocket to throw away somewhere far away. They never left him alone, the looks, the comments, the casual touch, all were suggestive, something between a cruel game and a calculated stalking exercise. And Hassan suffered. The brashness and the chatter disappeared as now he learned to avert his face from these callous acts of love, from seductive flourishes that promised only pain. I thought sooner or later they would wear him down.

Then one day an airmail letter came for Hassan. My father brought it home one lunchtime. He had stopped calling for us when he came home from work, and stroking our faces in that old way of his, after Hassan violently threw his arm off one day. My father stepped up and slapped the face he had been trying to stroke, and then never touched us after that. The day he brought the letter, he called for Hassan when he got upstairs and handed it to him. The airmail form had been slit open, and, as it was handed over, father and son exchanged long looks. It was from Uncle Hussein. Hassan told me that but said no more. He must have had his letters sent to another address because sometime later he told me that Uncle Hussein was coming back next musim, in a few months' time.

By the time he came back, our house was well set in its rumbling minor domestic tragedy. My parents barely tolerated each other, and Hassan had found new friends much older than himself. My mother went out most afternoons and did not return until the middle of the evening. My father came home later, smelling of drink. I don't know what Hassan was doing with his new friends, or if they had made him succumb to the torments they promised him. I never asked. When Uncle Hussein came back he did not stay with us, but he came to deliver the news that the business they had agreed together had not prospered, and the loan still had to be repaid. Until then, since Uncle Hussein had guaranteed the loan, he would hold on to the paper that offered the house as security, and perhaps the enterprise might prosper after all, in the long run. It could not have been as simple as that, but that was how it was told to me. Uncle Hussein had stolen the house from us, for there was no chance of my father finding the money to pay back the loan. The assassin. Almost incredibly, now when I think back to it, Uncle Hussein visited us sometimes, bringing gifts as he used to, fish and fruit and gum and ud and cloth, and once a gleaming ebony table for Hassan which my father threatened to destroy but which ended up in the downstairs room.

Hassan was hardly at home at this time, and when he was he seemed locked in endless arguments with my mother. When I asked him where he went he said to see friends or to see Uncle Hussein. He paid no attention to me now. He was never cruel but he lived in a faraway place that I did not know and where he did not want me. Then when the musim turned and Uncle Hussein left, Hassan disappeared. In short. He swaggered over the horizon with Uncle Hussein and we never heard from him again. Thirty-four years ago. It seemed an awesome thought at the time, and it seems even more awesome now, that he was able to collect himself like that and follow a man as if he were a young bride.

Hassan's departure was only the first act in a climax that was to bring our dreadful little story to closure. Uncle Hussein had sold the paper of the agreement, and with the money had repaid the loan. He had sold it to Saleh Omar, a furniture-maker who was a distant and estranged relative, and to whom the house now belonged. Two years later Saleh Omar won possession of the house and its contents and we were forced to move out. By that time my father, Rajab Shaaban Mahmud, had found sobriety and piety, so much so that people began to compare him to his re-vered grandfather Mahmud. He paid no attention to my mother, who in those years just before independence had found new in-volvements and a kind of delighted purpose in her life.

Then, thirty-two years after the loss of that house, a man called Rajab Shaaban arrives in England as an asylum seeker and needs an interpreter. It wasn't my father, he was long gone, and in any case I just cannot imagine him making that journey. It could be the man's own name, or it could be he had borrowed the name out of mischief or as part of a passport swindle or as a joke. Or perhaps I was dreaming it all up, in rancor and remorse and paranoia. Perhaps it was just foreboding. But I was con-vinced that someone was making a joke, that the man had bor-rowed my father's name as a kind of witticism. And I thought that that someone was Saleh Omar, who always had a miserable idea of what constitutes a joke, whose jokes sometimes ended up being funny only to him, as he sat smiling quietly to himself at some cleverness that was going on in his head. I had no real reason to think it was Saleh Omar, just a premonition, a miserable fear that that man had not finished with us yet. I wished I could ignore it all, shrug off the endless stories behind me, but I knew I would not be able to, would be fretted and frazzled by the possibilities and shamed by my cowardice and squeamishness. So I called the refugee office back and asked Rachel Howard to arrange for me to visit Mr. Rajab Shaaban sometime in the near future.

4.

I had visited Saleh Omar once before, many years ago. I was surprised by the way he received me. I expected him to be short and scornful, ready to expel me. That was what I anticipated as I stood by the open door of the house, face turned away from the gloom of the interior, and called out in a voice modulated to avoid giving offense. I expected that someone would emerge out of the gloom to stare coldly at me and scorn me silently for standing helplessly there, and then admit me because hospitality allowed no other choice. I have come to see Saleh Omar, I would say, the furniture merchant. I would then enter into the malevolent presence of the man and deliver the demand I had been sent to make and leave. Leave, leave, get away from all of them.

A tall fleshy man came to the door, emerging unhurriedly out the darkness of the house, and his face opened in a kind of pleased surprise when he saw me. He was Saleh Omar's *man*. He saw to things that needed seeing to, worked for him in his furniture shop, came to the door of his house when strangers or tradesmen called, swept the steps, went shopping, and did a great many other things besides, no doubt, that were only known and visible to the man he served. People called him Faru, rhinoceros, for reasons I've forgotten and no longer care about. I'd forgotten that it would be he who would come to the door. I had dressed carefully, expecting scrutiny, expecting to be looked over insolently, but the man's eyes did not leave my face. His eyes were interested and alert, as if my visit was anticipated and looked forward to. It seemed as if he would smile, but then his expression became politely bland and uneager.

"I've come to see him," I said.

"You're welcome," he said without any hesitation, and made a motion to invite me into the gloom of the house. "Everyone at home is well, I hope."

The smell struck me first in that obscurity—a deep and corpulent perfume had infused the walls and the rugs and made me heave for breath. After a few steps the man opened a door into an airy hallway flooded with light. It was a small interior courtyard, its walls tiled all the way round to the height of a grown man. The tiles were a delicate blue color which had been deepened by age, a familiar ceramic glaze from the bits of potsherd we sometimes found on the beach. Against one of the walls were two dwarf palms in large clay pots, made of the same ashy gray clay of the Ali Baba jar I used to play in years ago. Before I could stop myself, I glanced upward and saw that a latticed balcony ran all the way round the first floor and overlooked the hallway. I thought I heard muted women's voices in conversation.

"Tuna mgeni," the man who had welcomed me called out in a voice that was both gentle and intended to carry—a voice of such delicacy and cultivation, a trained voice, surprising in a man of his appearance and reputation. We have a visitor. The voices paused for a moment and then picked up again.

I was shown into the first room on the left. The man who had welcomed me stood beside the door, his posture inflected with an invitation to enter. His eyes were courteously lowered, but I thought I could see the smile in them again, and I wondered whether he was smiling because I was so ridiculous there beside him or whether he was laughing at himself for having to act like a rudderless eunuch in a story out of *A Thousand and One Nights*. I knew this man, had seen his eyes in the streets, had seen the way they looked at Hassan years ago, and had even taken a letter from him to deliver to my brother. And if it wasn't him I had taken the letter from, then it was a man very like him. And if those weren't his eyes from years ago, then they were very like them. That secret smile made me shudder.

The room I walked into was large and square, with two large gilt-edged mirrors on the walls. I could not miss the mirrors nor my reflection in them. They faced the door, side by side, and suddenly showed me to myself in a way that was bound to diminish and intimidate. Before you could even look away, they said to you, Here you are, then. This pathetic image is you. Saleh Omar sat in a chair by a window with a view of the sea. I think he was reading. When I entered he looked over the angle of his shoulder and turned back to the view for another moment, and then he rose to his feet and stood to await my approach.

So there I was, standing inches in front of the assassin, the man who after years of dispute and humiliation had dispossessed my father of our house and all its contents, and about whom I had heard endless stories of callous deceit and depravity and shameless greed. In the intense vicinity in which we all lived, I had had to learn never to look at Saleh Omar's face whenever I recognized his shape in the street, never to show that I had seen him. I was too young to know how to ignore someone. If I saw and recognized him I would be bound to greet him, because that was the courtesy we had been taught from the morning of our first ages. If I greeted him, that would be treachery to my father and mother. Standing there in front of him, I saw that his face was lean and resolute, and that his eyes looked steadily and sternly at me, as if he expected to find fault with me. As if, like a teacher or a parent, he expected me to disappoint him. As if he could hover over filth without soiling himself, and so could sneer and scorn at the rest of us who clumsily stumbled through it. As if he was the Master dai who had the Light and could tell evil from good. As if he wasn't a notorious licker of British arses, for whom he rifled through other people's belongings to find trinkets for them to take home as booty of their conquests. As if . . . as if he wasn't the man I had seen two years ago, lithe and elegantly dressed, standing over the debris of our lives and talking unhurriedly while his eyes moved with quick darting glances to take in everything around him.

The time I had seen him was when I followed the carts which delivered all our possessions to this beautiful house. My father had forbidden me, but I had followed the carts anyway. Everything was packed into three carts: the furniture, the rugs, including the Bokharra, the old wall clock with a silver face, my mother's sewing machine, the brass and stained glass goblets my father had inherited from someone, and even the framed tablets of verses from the Koran which hung on the walls. We were allowed to keep our clothes and our prayer mats, and the pots and pans for the kitchen. Even the mattresses were taken away, though they were inevitably soiled and smelling of bodies that would have twisted and turned on them for years. I suppose the stuffing could be taken out and left in the sun for a day or two to kill the bedbugs and leach away the smell of sweat and other involuntary dribbles, and it could then be packed into new mattress covers. I had stayed to watch the carts being unloaded, and that was when I saw Saleh Omar walking among the bits and pieces of our lives, picking out something and then ordering the rest to be auctioned there and then, as if the last thing he expected was that he would get anything but a pittance for them.

When he saw that I was not going to approach any nearer, he allowed his body to subside into a noncommittal posture, and then took a long time before indicating a nearby chair. I pretended I had not seen his perfunctory invitation and instead rudely looked round the expensively furnished room: the comfortable chairs, the rugs, a black almira with brass chasing, the gilt mirrors. All of them were objects which had beauty and purpose, but which stood like refugees in that room, standing still because pride and dignity demanded it but nonetheless as if they had a fuller life elsewhere. Looking like objects in a gallery or a museum, brightly lit and roped off, to celebrate someone's cleverness and wealth. Looking like plunder.

"Are your parents well?" he asked mildly. He was smiling now, amused by my silence and my rude surmise, but at least he had taken that look of stern disappointment off his face. In challenging him, I had worked myself up to such a pitch of indignation that I could feel my lips quivering. I was afraid to speak in case my voice had a tremor. (It was not through fear of pain that I felt my voice tremble.)

"Ismail," he said, prompting me to deliver what he assumed I was there to deliver. "Are your parents well? How may I be of use to them?" I had gone to his house, so it couldn't be business. He must have thought I was there for a handout, for alms, come to beg. And I suppose in a way that was what I was there for.

"My mother sent me," I said, and felt a little tremor in my voice. I had begged to be relieved from this miserable errand, but my mother had begged back, and I had no choice but to present myself to the shaykh al-jabal.

A pleased smile began to grow on his face, but he arrested it at once. "Then perhaps your message is for the Mistress," he said, beginning to move toward the door.

"She sent me to speak to you," I said, my voice firmer now that the work was at hand. "It is to do with a small ebony table."

He sat down in a nearby chair now, not the one he had been sitting in before which looked toward the sea. He leaned forward, right elbow on knee, chin in the palm of his hand. I remember, with an intensity that still sizzles through me after all these years, how I wanted to step forward and kick that elbow off his knee and then smash my fist into his face. A small fist, not used to punching, not even that used to being a fist. It would probably have hurt me more than him, which would have been doubly silly. I just remember that feeling of frustration as I watched him waiting so smugly to hear what ridiculous proposition I had to make about the ebony table. "She said to say that it did not belong to them. It belonged to Hassan. It was a gift to him. So she wants you to return it to her. She wants you to give the table back, for when Hassan comes back. She wants it back. It belongs to Hassan. It was a gift. She said to tell you it did not belong to them. So you shouldn't have taken it. It belongs to Hassan."

He let me go round and round like this until I ran out, then he gave me about twenty seconds of silence, so that I might hear the echoes of my rambling, before he replied. "I'm very sorry to say that I'm not trained in law, so I don't know how powerful an argument you are making. I took possession of the house and whatever contents were abandoned there. Those I had sold and sent what money came out of that to your father, who refused it. Then I had the money sent to your mother, who also refused it. So I gave it to the Juma'a mosque to be used as its caretakers saw fit. I kept a small table back, which is the one that your mother now wants, but I'm very sorry to say that I've sold it. Please tell your mother that, and give both your parents my warm good wishes."

The table was in his shop, up for sale. Someone who had seen it in our old house recognized it in the shop and told my mother. It was then that she remembered it was Hassan's and became concerned to get it back. Poor Hassan, we hardly spoke about him, and when she started to talk about the table, the misery and recriminations of his departure all came back. All of a sudden it became so important for my mother to get that table back. Not much chance of that, says I, but my mother begged me to try. For Hassan's sake, for her sake, for everything she had done for me. I tried, and stood like a fool in front of the man while he triumphed and smirked. After his little farewell speech, Saleh

Omar called Faru and I was escorted out. Left right, left right, and give my best to your parents. I was on my way out too, I was leaving, and as I think of it now, it's as if I went on from Saleh Omar's house and right out of the country, and through the years I have been finding my way to his other house by the sea. It was only a fancy, a momentary despondency that the heaving and straining had been pointless exertion, only to arrive at what was mapped out from the beginning.

L eaving. I've had years to think about that, leaving and arriving, until the moments acquire a crust and a gnarled disfigurement that gives them a kind of nobility. I left when I was seventeen to go to East Germany to study. If that seems far-fetched now, it is partly because East Germany has been transformed so furiously fast into a fantasy badlands of the imagination, a TV-land of obstinate crooked government and now disgruntled unemployed neofascists, their shaved heads silhouetted in the flames of the burning homes of migrants. It didn't seem like that all those years ago. To us it seemed like a gleaming new order, intimidating in its earnest and brutal self-assurance. The early years after independence brought changes too numerous to mention here, as we academics say when we are feeling lazy and don't feel like plodding through all the little steps that will allow us to arrive at our illuminations.

At first the United States of America and President John Kennedy took an interest in us, and invited our President to Washington for a state visit. The film of that visit, with our President standing smiling on the White House lawn next to the Emperor of Hollywood and rock 'n' roll, was shown for weeks as the opening item of any program in the cinemas. The United States Information Service opened an air-conditioned library and reading room as an annex to the embassy. Padded chairs, gleaming desks, reinforced glass in stern lines, squads of books and lines of magazines on angle-poise tables. In their sixty years of colonial rule the British never thought to do that. There was the English Club Library, strictly for members only, with wire grilles on the windows and a doorkeeper sitting at a desk by the entrance who granted or withheld admission. After independence and the departure of the Rulers of the Waves, the doors were shut and padlocked, and from the street the library looked like a disused warehouse or store. I don't know what happened to the books, abandoned, shipped out, sold. Some were pilfered and found their way out and into circulation, but I had left before the final fate of the bulk of the library became evident. The next best thing was our school library, which over the decades had been a favorite of departing administrators, who bequeathed their surplus books to it. Perhaps it was because most of the teachers at the school were European—English, Scottish, Rhodesian, South African—and so the departing conquerors could feel that they were leaving this fruit of Europe's intellect in responsible hands. We took random luck there, knowing the books were already screened for our consumption, and sometimes we did well. There was a section of the library which was out of bounds, but sneaky looks into those tomes revealed nothing to me—maps, Latin prose and an alienating tone of voice. I imagine they would have been the dodgy end of a gentleman's library, like Burton's translations of *The Arabian Nights* or something like that, whose particular learned naughtiness would have meant little to an adolescent native boy. And the books had a look and a smell, the spine faded or darkened by a well-preserved crust of usage, a history which was never separate from their former owners, whose names or dedications or marginal notes sometimes appeared to claim them back. Sometimes we did well, but sometimes we sat trembling through abuse and scorn that was all the more corrosive because we were hearing it for the first time.

The United States Information Service library was a different thing altogether. There you could read magazines and newspapers in air-conditioned comfort, and listen to records wearing padded earphones in a soundproofed booth (what is this thing they call jazz?), and borrow books. The books were beautiful: large and heavy, with thick gleaming paper, hardbound and edged with gilt and silver, their title and author embossed—emblazoned—on the spine, and with names our colonial education had never uttered. Ralph Waldo Emerson, Nathaniel Hawthorne, Herman Melville, Frederick Douglass, Edgar Allan Poe, names that excited a noble curiosity because they were not contaminated by a discourse of tutelage and hierarchy. It was incredible to be allowed to take such books home, to put them on the upturned crate which served as my table, and to see how they humbled the paltriness of everything else in my room.

Then the President became disenchanted with the Americans. Partly this was because of the swelling chorus of discontent with the United States across Africa at the time. They had shown their hand too openly in the murder of Patrice Lumumba in the Congo—boastful CIA officers could not resist making unattributable claims. They were murdering Black Americans at home, when they only wanted the vote and equal rights as citizens, aspirations familiar to all of us at the time, aspirations which chimed with our discontent over arrogant oppression of non-European people all over the world. Photographs of American police setting dogs on Black demonstrators appeared in the newspapers alongside pictures of the apartheid terror police doing the same thing. It seemed as if the Americans and their CIA wanted to interfere in everything, manipulating and controlling every small and big thing that caught their attention. The final straw was when, after long discussions, the United States government refused to finance some development projects which our President thought essential to national progress. The People's Republic of China agreed to provide finance. The Soviet Union offered arms credit. The German Democratic Republic offered training in management and scientific skills.

So halfway through the first decade of independence, we were jilted by the Americans for flirting with the enemy. In the meantime, our President had been converted to socialism and in due course was to become a theoretician and exemplar of a variant of socialism all his own. He made the speeches, he issued decrees, and then he wrote the books to explain how all this would end up with our humanity enhanced. Never mind. We now had the chance to read Mikhail Sholokhov (*Quiet Flows the Don*) and Anton Chekhov (*Selected Stories*), whose work appeared for sale in cheap editions, or browse through boxed sets of Schiller in the GDR Information Institute (copies not for loan). And of course we could have copies of *The Little Red Book* and lapel badges of Chairman Mao for the asking.

I was selected to go to East Germany to train as a dentist. The news was conveyed to me in person by an official of the Department of Education, where I and about a dozen others had been summoned to attend a meeting. Someone from the GDR embassy was also there, silver hair and pouting scornful red lips, scowling at first before the proceedings opened, looking a little impatient and even irritable, and then glowing with smiles once the meeting was underway. We had all asked to be considered for the scholarships to the GDR, and out of the hundreds of applicants, the official told us, the Minister had selected us. Some of us were to be doctors, some engineers, and I was to be a dentist, daktari wa meno. We all of us, including me, chuckled when that last one came up. The GDR official frowned momentarily and then gave me a firm, encouraging nod. There is nothing wrong with being a dentist. None of us were asked to state preferences, so we were anxious to find out what the Minister, or whoever he had delegated to the task, had chosen for us, never mind how. A dentist was a bit of a blow at first, but I got used to it as we began teasing each other by addressing ourselves by the titles of our future professions. Then the embassy official took over and explained the arrangements to us: documentation, travel, language school for a year, and then the professional course. He also threw in the fraternal greetings of the German people and their pride and pleasure in the friendship between our two countries.

My mother wasn't happy about me becoming a dentist. I could see that. She made an involuntary face of disgust when I told her. There is nothing wrong with being a dentist, I told her, but my reassurance was not enough. She smiled weakly and looked ludicrously unconvinced. A few days later I was called back to the Department of Education, this time on my own, and was informed by the same official who had spoken to us before that there had been a mysterious error. The Minister himself, Sheikh Abdalla Khalfan, had selected me to do a medical degree, but somehow someone had switched my name to dentistry. The official tried to look mystified as he said this, even a little suspicious, as if a malicious plot lay behind these confusing events. It was no mystery to either of us, and I was grateful to the official for his courteous playacting. My mother was the Minister's lover. For all I know she may have been one of two or three or perhaps more women at his service. He was a rising figure in the government, and would have been happy to demonstrate the authority of his pizzle in the numbers who display their availability at his bidding. No, I speak too harshly of her and I know so little of what took her that way. In any case, the Minister's official car came for her and waited at the end of the lane from the little house we moved to after my father lost our first house. Then my mother, unhurried and unafraid, almost fastidious in her refusal to be secretive, came strolling out, looking like a beautiful woman going to meet with her lover.

It was no doubt this connection that had got me on the scholarship list in the first place and now had me switched to a medical degree. I shrugged at the official and said that I wanted to do dentistry. He grinned and said the Minister had made his decision, and that I should not quibble at my good fortune. I said that I *really wanted* to do dentistry, and the official, who had been a teacher for many years and had only recently been moved to the Ministry, looked at me silently for a long moment and, I should think, just about prevented himself from saying, Your mother won't like that. She didn't, but she too just shrugged and said she thought being a body doctor was more honorable than being a teeth doctor, in her humble opinion, putting your fingers in all that saliva and those smelly mouths with their stained teeth, but if I wanted to be obstinate about it, that was my affair.

When I told my father that I was going to the GDR to train as a dentist, he nodded slowly and then returned to his reading. Nothing very much reached him where he was. Sometime during the struggle for the house, my father found God. He gave up the Goan bar completely, and gave up his time to repentance and prayer and study. Pious was not the word, not in a month of Sundays, nor does a single swallow a summer make. He became a shaykh: sometimes leading the congregation in prayers, reading the Koran all day after he came back from work, spending all evening at the mosque studying and reading from books of law and doctrine. The clean white shirts and the carefully ironed brown trousers were gone as well, kanzu and kofia and maqbadhi sandals now even when he went to work. When we finally lost the house and we were forced to rent a two-roomed house in another part of town, it seemed to make no difference to him. He walked all the way to the area where we used to live, to go to the mosque there among people he knew and people to whom his devotion to God was a matter of celebration. He hardly spent any time at our new home, and when he did he was immersed in his prayers and books. When he spoke to my mother it was with his eyes cast aside, and he never spoke to me unless I approached him. In that time when I was getting ready to leave for the GDR, he had become an imam, leading the obligatory prayers in a high-pitched singing voice, conducting funeral services with awesome fluency, pronouncing on the matters of religion and the law that were referred to him with incontestable assurance. It was as if the axis of his existence had shifted and he now occupied a different space from before, thrummed and vibrated there to resonances only he could hear. So when he nodded and returned to his book, I knew what he meant. Get lost, I couldn't care less, go and become a communist if you want. You'll know what's coming to you when my God and I get hold of you in due course.

On the afternoon of the day before I left, my father called me by name and asked me to accompany him as he set out for the mosque. We walked together in the blazing light of a beautiful late afternoon, along the retaining wall of the creek as the tide was coming in. He put his arm through mine, lightly, merely a flutter of intimacy. My father was a small man, and dressed in his kanzu and kofia, with his eyes downcast as usual, his arm linked in mine in that fluttery way, he seemed even smaller than usual. I wondered as I walked beside him, keeping my chin up so that we should not be seen strolling together with eyes cast down like a couple of fake philosophers, whether he still thought of Hassan, and whether it was Hassan's departure or the loss of the house that had made him give everything up and become the drone who buzzed for God. Or whether it was because of my mother that he had been the wounded, demanding man I had known all my life, and that now he had found salve and succor in the word of God and the chanting of His names. And I wondered what it was he would say to me when he found the strength to say it. People greeted him with reverence as we passed, and he replied humbly as fitted a servant and creature of God.

"Have you made all your preparations?" he asked.

"Yes," I said. "There isn't much to prepare."

He took me to the old house, and we stood in front of it for a while. It had been newly painted a creamy buttery color, the windows had been repaired and the front steps had been reconcreted. From where I stood I could see a glimpse of the sea down the lane that ran by the house, and knew from before that you would catch the sea breeze at this time of the day up on the terrace at the back. "This is our house," my father said. "It belongs to you and to me and to your mother."

"And Hassan," I said. He said nothing.

"It belonged to your aunt, my father's sister, and she left it to me," he said after the sound of Hassan's name had faded into the distance. "And those people stole it from us. This is all I can leave you when I'm gone. Your inheritance."

I could have laughed, I honestly could. Pull the other one, it's got bells on. Not in a month of Sundays. Over the moon, sweet prince. The pious old fart had brought me all this way to initiate me into a dynastic feud or something. "Do you mean you want me never to forget this house? Is that what you're trying to tell me, Ba? That you want me to come back one day and get it back?"

After a moment he put his arm into mine again and started to walk away, tugging at me a little to make sure I followed. I followed, though what I really wanted to do was remove that arm and walk away from him. Leave him to whatever story he wanted to tell himself, to his smallness and his defeats. I could not bear that they lost Hassan in the first place, and then that they could not show me how to grieve for his loss. He took me to the mosque, and made sure I sat beside him while we waited for the call to the evening prayer, which he then led. He stood facing the congregation until the first line had formed behind him across the width of the mosque, then he turned and walked into the qibla and began. After the prayer, he half turned, sitting cross-legged, and named in turn the benedictions he wanted us to recite in praise of the Prophet and his companions and his family. While the praises were still being sung by the congregation, he leaned out of the qibla and waved me nearer. "When you get to that godless place, don't forget to pray," he said. "Do you understand me? Whatever else you do, don't lose God, don't lose your way. There's darkness there."

That too was my inheritance. I think it was the last thing he said to me. For I left the mosque soon after that, and he had already gone to work when I woke up the next morning. In the afternoon I took the flight to Berlin. Her last words? I don't remember, nothing memorable. Probably she told me to check that I had my passport in a secure place, or warned me not to let them pull a fast one on me, not to let the Germans fuddle and gull me. She had already said that several times, and I imagine she said it all again in the taxi to the airport and in the terminal as we said goodbye before I went through for the mandatory search and security shakedown. She drew all eyes to her, her clothes fragrant with ud and her face beautiful and composed as she blew me a farewell kiss.

I don't know what my last words were before I left her. I don't even know if I really thought of her or of what she was thinking as she saw me leave. I remember that as I went through the barrier into the area restricted to passengers, I felt tremors of apprehension and anxiety. But that was because I was flying for the first time, and I did not want to do something embarrassing and childish. I did not think of her, and did not think what a long shadow that moment would cast over what was to come of my life. I did not think to myself that I should pay attention to everything around me so that later I would remember those last seconds before departure. I did not remind myself to secrete away the images and the sights and the smells of that moment for the sterile years ahead, when memory would strike out of silence and leave me quivering with helpless sorrow at the way I had parted from my beautiful mother.

It was October when we left, some two or three weeks after the beginning of the German school year. Since I was the only one doing dentistry, I was sent to a different town from the others. We were all to spend the first year learning German, but near the places we were to go on to study later. I suppose it makes sense, that you would grow familiar with the area, but I would have preferred to be with the others, especially on the train journey after we landed. The town I was sent to was called Neustadt, but I have no memory of that first journey there. Someone must have given me a ticket and put me on the train, and everything must have happened as it should have happened. I remember odd things: it was raining at some point and as the shower hit the glass, trails of mud appeared across the window. I remember how fast the train traveled, or so it seemed, how noisy it was. The landscape was dull and green and gray and muddy at different times, and orderly and regulated at other times, but the feeling of it was overcast and gloomy. A window was open somewhere down the carriage and a stiff, chill breeze blew through it. I am not even sure how I knew the station where I should get off. Someone was there to meet me, but I don't remember how we got to the college hostel, so we must have driven there. Later I realized that the man was the caretaker at the hostel, a middle-aged, unsmiling man who looked at the students as if they were an incomprehensible phenomenon and saw to the jobs he had to do as if they were unjust impositions. He was reassuring because, in that respect, he was like the caretaker at my old school, and whereas the other students gave fascist salutes behind his back and mocked his scowling looks, I was pleased that I had recognized a genre. Sometimes he drove a growling, smoky van, so it must have been in that vehicle that he met me at the station. I am sure we did not come back to the hostel in a bus, for I remember very clearly my first time on a GDR bus.

The hostel was a modern rectangular block, concrete and glass and asbestos, with tiny unheated rooms that were shared between two students. The corridors were narrow and sharply angled, so that although the building gave a monumental impression on the outside, inside it was cramped and suffocating. Until I got used to it, it felt as if I had to struggle to breathe, lying in bed in a silent panic, heaving to take in the bad air with its taste of vegetable decay. The windows were never opened because the whole block was so poorly heated. If a window was opened in the remotest corner of the building, a chill draft blasted through every crack and crevice, and led to an immediate hunt and punishment for the criminal. It made me think of the moment in *The Red and the Black* when Julien goes to stay with the Duchess in the almost certain knowledge of inheriting her fortune, and at night he leans out of his bedroom window for a smoke. What he doesn't know is that the Duchess abhors the smell of tobacco, and what he also doesn't know is that because his window is open, a chill draft blasted through every crack and crevice in the house and led to his discovery, expulsion and disinheritance. Or was that an incident in *Vanity Fair*? Whatever, but for sure no window could be opened in our monumental hostel without detection, so we lived and breathed and ate and evacuated in a fug perfumed with multitudinous corruptions.

I shared a room with a student from Guinea whose name was Ali. All the students in the hostel were from foreign places—that is, from dark foreign places. At first Ali took a sneering dislike to me. Only at first, for honor's sake, and perhaps to establish a hierarchy between us. He spoke English well, and before we became friends he used it to misdirect me whenever I asked him for assistance. He sat on his bed on that first evening and watched as I unpacked my paltry belongings, smiling and asking questions. Did you bring any chocolate? Or dollars? This is Eastern Europe. They don't have anything here. It's just as bad as Africa. When do you think you'll get to wear those stupid T-shirts? It's freezing here all the time. How old are you? Eighteen! (I lied.) Have you had a white girl yet? What are you waiting for? It's stew for dinner every evening here. They make it with pellets of dried meat, and no one knows anymore what the meat was originally or if it is meat at all or whether some of it is goat pellets or asbestos.

I got used to him quickly, and when I did not become irate or upset at his unkindnesses—indeed deferred to him and smiled ingratiatingly—he softened the cruelties and transformed them into a hard-edged banter. I had no choice. He looked strong and assured, and intimidated me with the crude potency of his every word of scorn and mockery and knowingness. I shared a room with him and wanted him to like me. Not like me as if I were a brother, but so that he did not persecute and stalk me and make me feel idiotic. I did not think about it at the time. And I had already seen that everyone had a friend, and that those who did not looked languishing and afraid. I don't know why I feel defensive about being ingratiating and deferential. It was a wise move, all the more so for being unreflected upon. Perhaps it was also instinct. Perhaps I sensed that there was a hint of exaggeration about Ali, that he was acting tougher and more cruel than he really was. In any case, after a few days he started to include me in his plans, and wanted to know about all my comings and goings. So perhaps I had no real choice in the matter of becoming his vassal.

All the students in the hostel were male, as well as being darkies of one hue or another, all from Africa: Egyptians, Ethiopians, Somali, Congolese, Algerians, South Africans. There must have been over a hundred of us crowded in that catacomb, with an order of precedence and exclusions and dislikes that was detailed and precise, despite the appearance of raucous, romping disorder. I had not lived amid so much noise and play and violence before, and at first I relished most of it cautiously, without questioning or wonder. In all my life until then I had not slept for a single night under a different roof from the one my parents slept under. Despite their eccentric comings and goings, they always spent the night in their own beds. It never occurred to me when I left that I would never share the same roof with them again. I wished it hungrily at the time, never to share the same roof with them again, never to see them again, to leave them to their indignant decline and their poisoned lives. It makes me feel guilty to think it now, but it was what I wished, and I wished it truly at the time.

I enjoyed the classes, I loved the classes. I woke up in the morning with a thrill of pleasure and anticipation, and then remembered why. I had classes. Our classrooms were in a smaller building next door, and they were very well-equipped: practice booths, comfortable desks, well-heated. We spent long hours of the day in there and were expected to do extra work in the evenings. Sometimes I stayed on until closing time because it was so much warmer there than in the hostel. My teacher told me I had an aptitude for German, and that my accent was already quite good. All the teachers were German, and the only other language they spoke was English, which many of the students did not speak, so there was plenty of room for confusion and misunderstanding and insolence and mischief. I didn't get the feeling that the teachers liked their students very much. Taken all together, I don't think we were good students. There was too much laughing and teasing. Strangest of all was the way the students acted superior to the teachers, as if we knew about things which the teachers had no inkling of—useful and complicated things, not just a couple of wedding songs or a sonorous prayer or how to play a harmonica. I wondered then, and still wonder now, who did we think we were? Perhaps we knew that we were beggar pawns in somebody else's plans, captured and delivered there. Held there. Perhaps the scorn was like the prisoner's sly refusal of the jailer's authority, stopping short of insurrection. Or perhaps most of us were reluctant students, and reluctant students are always like that with their teachers. Or perhaps still, something stern and unyielding and despising in our teachers' demeanor made us resistant to them. Or perhaps even further still, as one of the teachers told us, the heat in our countries and in our food had sapped our motivation and drive, and made us prisoners to instinct and self-indulgence. The only day we did not have classes was Sunday.

The routine and the strangeness were so exhausting that I did not leave the hostel except to go to class, and it must have been two weeks after my arrival before I went for a walk with Ali on the Sunday afternoon. Neustadt was a modern town, a new town, rows of gray and blue houses in a grid, with gloomy windswept lanes between them. Empty pavements and large open spaces, also empty. The houses had graveled walls with window frames painted gray or dark blue, and shallow-pitched roofs with here and there the spines of television aerials. There was one low brick building which had three separate signboards on it—post office, grocery store and a vegetable shop which had a low, dark entrance that looked as if it led underground. There were empty boxes beside the doorway. The other two doors were made of glass in metal frames, and they were locked with a padlock and chain. Still no sign of human life, except for glimpses of washing on the line in the gaps between rows of houses.

"It's Sunday. That's why it's so empty like this. People just sleep here and work in Dresden itself," Ali said, pointing to a bus stop. "It's not far. We'll go there one of these days, when we can find the fare. Spend the day there."

"Are we near Dresden?" I asked. "I have a friend near Dresden."

"From home?"

"A German friend," I said.

"What kind of German friend?" Ali asked, smiling, disbelieving. "You've only been here two weeks, and you've hardly left your room except to go to class or to the toilet."

"A pen friend," I said. "Elleke."

Ali whistled with derisive admiration. "You devil, we must go visit Elleke as soon as possible. Have you got a photo?"

"Not with me," I said.

I had felt treacherous enough after speaking her name, because the instant I said it I knew Ali's reaction would be to whistle in that way and start talking about having a German girl. I thought if I now showed him the photograph he would say mocking things about her in particular, her face or her clothes, or do some obscene play with the picture. But yes, I did have a photograph with me. I had brought that along with her address, not thinking that I would be near enough to meet her, but thinking I would write to her and surprise her. I had deliberately not mentioned that I would be coming to Germany, even though I thought of her as soon as the possibility arose. I had the first line of my surprise letter ready. Hey, guess what, I'm in the GDR.

Her name and address appeared in a notice at school, along with two or three other names, saying that these were students

in East Germany interested in finding pen friends. I wrote casually, to pass the time, and received a pleasant delighted letter in
reply. She had not expected to hear from anyone, she said, and
instead she had received news from thousands of miles away. So
for nearly two years we exchanged friendly, chatty letters, writing infrequently and immemorably. I don't think now, after all
these years, I can remember a single thing we wrote to each
other, and I don't think I would have been able to be any more
definite at the time I was with Ali. Books perhaps, or things we
did with our friends. The black-and-white photograph she sent
me was a group of six friends, all women, standing in a line and
wearing overcoats and smart shoes, as if they were on an outing.
"I am second from the left." She wore a leopard-skin coat, and
her light-colored hair was parted in the middle. Her left shoulder
was angled slightly toward the camera, and her left foot was half
a step ahead of her right foot. A calculated pose, but made jaunty
and knowing by a friendly satirical smile, as if she knew the
photographic genre she was parodying. The other five women in
the group were either looking slightly away from the camera or
looking straight at it, holding everything in and evading the
camera's scrutiny. When I wrote to her, I imagined her smiling
in the same way when she read what I had written.

I took more pleasure in her letters than I did in my other pen
friends. Yes, I had others: Adam in Kraków, Helen in Inverness
and Fadhil in Basra. Perhaps she was closest to me in age, or she
wrote well. Adam was inclined to give advice and debate the
merits of Byron over Keats (I preferred Keats), or send me photographs of himself taken on walking tours or rock-climbing trips.

I remember one photograph in particular, of Adam in shorts and boots and short-sleeved shirt, sitting on a rock by a frothing stream with a rucksack beside him. He was smiling with such wise self-assurance that I smiled back whenever I looked at it. I could hear the unhurried tone of his letters coming out of him, the elder brother manner he had adopted from the beginning because of the difference in our ages. To be truthful, I could not make the letters and the pictures he sent me come to life. Helen in Inverness told me about snow and the newest pop hits, and sent me cuttings from magazines and newspapers about her favorite stars. Her questions were about beaches and the sea and what it was like to live in a hot climate. Sometimes I had no idea what she was talking about, even after reading and rereading a passage in her letters. She wasn't interested in Keats. Nor was Fadhil, who nonetheless wrote lyrically beautiful letters about Basra and about Life. He thought there was something soft and false about the Romantics, he said. Fake idealism and fake radicalism. He preferred the uncompromising tones of Whitman and of Iqbal. I knew Whitman from the USIS library days, and probably pretended to have an opinion on the matter, though I had reeled from *Leaves of Grass* with fastidious disapproval. I preferred the Romantics then. Iqbal I had never heard of, sad to say, so typical of our colonized ignorance. I enjoyed Fadhil's letters, and tried hard to match them, but I know I failed. I could not get anywhere near the lucid, ceremonial beauty of his language, and wondered enviously how he had learned to write sentences of such completeness and balance. Then there was Elleke: no Keats there either, just talkative, entertaining letters with the merest hint of skepticism. They felt like letters from a friend, and I smiled when I read them.

I did not want Ali in that men's hostel mood to make fun of her and the pleasure I took in her. I don't think I imagined her as real, or as a woman, although when I looked at the photograph I thought of her as attractive. But I never imagined the letters as having behind them a hand you could touch or a body you could put an arm around. It was a voice I heard, with that friendly satirical smile hovering around it. I felt tender toward that memory. Ali looked at my silence and did not speak, especially as at that moment we saw a group of youths walking toward us, bouncing a football. I felt Ali tense, and when I glanced at him, I saw that his square face was glowering and his hands were beginning to flex and unflex in readiness. If I had been one of those youths, I would have taken one look at that powerful chunky body and crossed the street. But these were brave German boys, and as they got nearer their grins broadened, and as they passed us they could hardly contain their mirth. "Afrikanische," one of them said, and the others burst into uproarious laughter. Their swagger and their laughter made the word ugly. It was shocking, that casual mockery, but there would be time to get used to that and worse, time to learn to recover from such smug disregard.

Later, lying in bed in the dark, our beds only inches apart, Ali said: "That girl, your pen friend, is that why you came to GDR?" He said GDR the way our German teachers did, mocking them, deepening the G and rolling the R, making it sound grand.

"Oh no, it was nothing to do with that," I said, laughing with surprise. It was curiosity, to see places and things. I would have agreed to go almost anywhere, though it wasn't that I was driven to leave. I wanted to get away. But that wasn't what I said to Ali. To him I said: "I came to GDR to study, to learn a skill. As soon as I've done that, I'll go back home and do what I can to help my people."

Ali chuckled in the dark. "Is that why you came, you Young Pioneer? I did not want to come here. I wanted to go to France, but the only scholarships available were to fraternal socialist countries, either to come here or go to the Soviet Union to learn to drive a snowplow. I think all the students here would prefer to be somewhere else."

I had thought that too, and thought that that was why the students treated the classes and the teachers as if they were below them, because they did not want to be there. We all wanted to be in the land of Coca-Cola and blue jeans, even if it wasn't just for those refined pleasures that we wanted to be there. Why did I come? Because my mother talked me into it. It came up one morning after I had finished translating one of Elleke's letters to her, and she said: "Why don't you go there? I hear there are scholarships to study there, why don't you get one?" And after weeks of her nudging and shoving, I applied. I wanted to get away, to see the great world. She helped make it easy to go to GDR, though if I had a choice I would have preferred to go to Massachusetts. Such a beautiful name, Massachusetts.

"Why did you come, then?" I asked Ali.

"Because my mother wanted me to," he said.

"Me too," I said, once again laughing with surprise. "Why?

How?" Both of us laughing happily at the wiles of our resourceful mothers. No doubt both of us missing them badly and aching terribly as we laughed.

"Because she thought I'd be safer here," Ali said.

I can't remember how much he told me that night, but it was the first time he began to talk about such things with me. His father was in Sékou Touré's jail, he said, as were so many of the *intelligentsia*. I remember he used that word. His father had been a teacher of English in France for ten years, in Lyon. Ali was born there as was his elder brother Kabir. Then in 1960 Ahmed Sékou Touré, himself the great-grandson of Samory Touré who fought the French invaders for years in the nineteenth century, won an acrimonious independence for Guinea. Ali's father, in a burst of postcolonial shame, decided to go back. In due course, enthusiasm turned to bitterness, and who knows what indiscretion followed. But Sékou Touré was in no mood for even minor rebellion—there had been too many assassination attempts already. Like so many others of the intelligentsia who had returned, Ali's father eventually was arrested. That was three years before. They had word now and then from someone who was let out, or from a contact who worked in the jail, and whom they had to pay for the meager information that their father was still alive. Then two years after his father's arrest, his elder brother disappeared. He went out one evening to see a friend from work and did not come back. Someone started a rumor that he had run away, fled the country, as so many people were doing then to get away from the malice of the state. But it was only a Security attempt to discredit him and cover up the harm that had befallen him. Perhaps he was still alive in a jail, or perhaps he had already been disposed of. They could get no word of him. That was when Ali's mother persuaded him to leave, to go somewhere where he would be safe, because there in Conakry sooner or later he was bound to trip and stub his toe. There were relatives she could turn to if she was in desperate need, she said, and no one would harm a useless old woman like her. So he applied for a government scholarship to the GDR and here we all are.

Yes, there we all were, though there was great deal more of his story which has faded with time. There was a grandmother into whose house they moved after the father was arrested, who told stories that were cryptic and elusively wise, and which somehow managed to lift their spirits and make their anxieties into something noble. Ali talked about the school he attended in Lyon until the age of ten—his friends there, Karim, Patrice and Anton (their names have stuck for some reason), about a girl he was seeing in Conakry in the last months before he left. He talked about Conakry, the great port, and how hard and long the rain fell in that city. Such a great deal more. I don't really re-member how much I told him. I think I was very guarded, as much out of habit as anything. I don't recall that Ali was that concerned about me reciprocating, but I am sure I would have said things in the confiding intimacy in which we talked. It was not that there was anything important to hide, more that I feel embarrassed now to think that I might have told him stories of our ridiculous domestic melodramas in exchange for his terrible one of loss and oppression. I am sure I did not tell him how Has-san left, though when he described how his brother disappeared one evening, I told him that I too had an elder brother who was lost somewhere over the horizon.

I wrote to Elleke after I had been in Germany for about a month, but there was no reply. Ali laughed at me. She wanted you there, thousands of miles away, not at her doorstep, he said. After a few weeks I wrote again, and this time there was an almost immediate reply, a polite note of welcome and an invitation to visit her, as I had suggested, if I wished. Never mind. It was just a thought.

It was now deep in winter and bitterly cold. We had made our anticipated trip to Dresden in the new year to purchase warmer clothes for me and to have our day in the city. We did not have much money, and there was nothing much to buy, so we spent the day wandering around the beautiful city, trying not to notice how people were staring at us. I knew nothing about Dresden, even though for several months I had been living in what was practically one of its suburbs, a twenty-minute ride on the bus. I did not know about its medieval triumphs, its wealth and ingenuity, its great industries, its beautiful buildings. I did not know about the greatness of the Electors of Saxony. I had never heard of them. Nor did I know that Dresden was a huge port on the Elbe. I did not even know there was an Elbe. And I did not know about the devastation of May 1945. Or any of the other horrors that had been visited on it or that it had inflicted on its enemies and victims. I knew a little bit about the fishing banks of Newfoundland, and the Fire of London and Cromwell, and the Siege of Mafeking and the Abolition of the Slave Trade, because that was what my colonized education had required me to know, but I knew nothing about Dresden or a multitude of other Dresdens. They had been there for all these centuries despite me, ignorant of me, oblivious of my existence. It was a staggering thought, how little it had been possible to know and remain contented.

But Ali was not as ignorant as I was. He took me round the Altstadt, naming buildings and describing the bombing in May 1945 as if he had been there. We went to the Zwinger Palace and saw Raphael's *Sistine Madonna*. It was my first visit to an art museum, and I was happy to be a novice while Ali strolled slightly ahead of me. We passed the State Opera House but were not allowed inside. An armed guard turned us away, and did not yield to Ali's bantering pleas.

The next day brought a letter from Elleke. Please come and visit us, with instructions about which bus to take and where she would meet me. Ali never stopped badgering me all week, saying that I would get lost if I went on my own, or I might run into German thugs, and I might need help when I met up with Elleke. "You are so young," he said. "So inexperienced. Such a sad creature from the bush. You'll need some worldly advice when you meet up with the leopard-skin coat." I managed to hold him off, though by now, of course, I had shown him the photograph, and the leopard-skin coat had caught his attention. So on Sunday I took a bus to the city terminal, and waited by the ticket office as instructed. The idea was that Elleke would meet me there and we would then have a brief bus ride to her home, where her mother was eager to meet me too. I hoped she would not condescend to me when she came. So many Germans I had met seemed to find it impossible not to.

I had my eyes peeled for the leopard-skin coat, even though I knew that the photograph was at least two years old by then, and she might no longer possess it, or it might be frayed and faded and long since relegated to more menial tasks. So dedicated was I to spotting the leopard skin that I did not notice the man who spoke to me, standing barely a meter away. "I'm Elleke," he said.

No, I won't even try to describe how I took this ambush. My jaw dropped, I yelped with surprise, maybe.

"I'm Jan," he said, offering his hand. He was smiling broadly though there was a spark of anxiety in his eyes. If Ali had been there, he would have slapped the hand away and stormed off. What had happened to Elleke? Was this her boyfriend who had come to make fun of me? Her brother? I shook his hand and watched his smile turn into a relieved grin. "I can explain," he said.

So we walked a short distance from the bus terminal and sat on a bench in a small park. I was not getting on a bus with some Jan when I had been expecting Elleke, even if Jan had a round, smiling face and did not seem as if he was enjoying himself that much, either. This is his story, and for what it's worth I believed it and got on the bus with him to go and have tea with his mother. There was no Elleke, not as I had imagined her, anyway. A visiting speaker came to their college to talk about the work that the GDR was doing in Africa. He was a local man, an official in the city department of education, and he himself had just returned from a year as a volunteer adviser to an African state.

That was us. He spoke very optimistically about the important work that the GDR was doing and how it was keen for young Germans to get involved with fraternal African youth. He wrote the address of our school and encouraged the students to send their names to the principal, offering friendship. So Jan invented Elleke, on a whim, not expecting a reply, thinking that the visiting speaker was talking the usual campaigning rubbish about fraternal relations. When I wrote to Elleke at their home address in Dresden, he was delighted, overwhelmed. His mother read the letter and was thrilled by it too. After he wrote his reply to me, he got his mother to check over the tone, because he was so afraid that he would get the voice of Elleke wrong. Then the mother too became part of the conspiracy. She read Jan's letters before he posted them, and sometimes added something, and she read my letters to Elleke.

"It was just for fun," Jan said, smiling apologetically. "I hope you will not get angry." He was an inch or so taller than me, and perhaps a year older. Not much in it. He spoke more clumsily than the way I had imagined Elleke's voice.

"You sent a photograph," I said. "The leopard-skin coat."

I had asked for a photograph, and he did not know what to do. He had been thinking about it since he received my first letter. How deceitful should he be? Then one day a cousin in Czechoslovakia sent that group picture to his mother. They used to live in Czechoslovakia, his mother's family. The photograph seemed perfect. It was how he thought he would have liked to look if he was Elleke. I knew what he meant, it was how I wanted Elleke to look as well, I told him, so I suggested we go and catch the bus. I asked him why he did not reply when I wrote to him after arriving in GDR, and he shrugged ruefully, and I knew what he meant by that too. "I did not want to make you angry," he said. "Instead of Elleke you meet me. But then it seemed so rude, not to reply and to be so unfriendly. So we decided we would invite you to see us and explain everything. And now I am very happy to meet you."

We shook hands all over again, and spent the rest of journey talking about safer matters. What is the college like? What have you seen of Dresden? How many years do you have language classes for? I found out that he was a student at the Technical University, studying automobile design. "Perhaps you'll come there after language school." They lived in a first-floor flat in a tall old building. The stairwell was grubby and dusty, with electric wires hanging in loops from the ceiling. Jan knocked gently on the door, and after a moment an elderly white-haired woman opened the door. She was tall and slim, with a clean-edged face that would have been beautiful in its youth. Her eyes were brown, and large and calm, unperturbed, or perhaps past anxiety and strain. She smiled with her head slightly inclined, a gesture of gentle welcome. She beckoned me in and then extended her hand. I wiped my feet on the doormat, and as I did so I glanced down and saw there was blood on the mat. Jan's mother saw the blood too, because I heard her exclaim softly.

Something had cut through the sole of my shoe and gashed my foot, and I had not even noticed. They were the shoes I had brought with me, lightweight and thin-soled, loosely stitched across the front to let in air, altogether intended for strolling tropical streets and at the height of fashion when I left. They were no good for Germany, no good for the wet and the cold, and dangerous on slippery pavements. It was agony walking outside in them, as my feet became number and number until they went dead. Then it was agony when I got back inside and they started to warm up. My socks were thin too, well-worn tropical socks. I couldn't have got anything thick into those well-fitting little slippers. If it was raining, the water went right through, and I slid and squelched as I walked. The first time on snow, the very first step I laid on that peculiar stuff, I slid and landed on my arse. Every other step I made, I landed on my arse again. I learned to walk on snow like a novice ballet dancer, or better still, not to walk on it at all. Just stay in and look at it through the window. The trip Ali and I had made to Dresden a few days before had been an unsuccessful attempt to replace my shoes, because he thought I would get frostbite and would have to have my feet amputated, and also because he could not bear the smell when I took them off. "It may be too late already," he said. But we hadn't found shoes in Dresden, we hadn't even got round to looking for them. Instead we had walked through the streets while Ali showed me beautiful buildings and told me their stories. Wagner loved the State Opera House in Dresden, and Schiller lived down that street for a while. Schiller, our Schiller of the GDR Cultural Institute! It made him seem real, not just a figure out of legend and out of time. And all the while my feet became number and number and amputation loomed.

There I stood then, bleeding on the doormat outside Jan's mother's flat, my feet so numb that I had not noticed a gash on my foot. She stepped forward and took my hand and tugged at me to follow. Jan followed behind, making apologetic noises, and despite the drama of the moment, I noticed that he locked and bolted the door behind him. Jan's mother made me sit on the sofa, her face pinched in an agony of sympathy. She looked around for something to rest my foot on and then picked up an old newspaper from a small pile under the window. There were bookshelves on either side of the window, right up to the edge of the thick red curtains which framed the window. Two photographs on wooden frames stood on a shelf, one of a man in a sporty jersey with a view of mountains behind him and the other of a tall woman in a loose gown with a boy in shorts standing on a chair beside her, his chin resting on her right shoulder and his face half turned toward the camera. There was another bookshelf on the other side of the fireplace, with an old brown chair beside it. Behind it was a table with papers and a small stack of magazines piled up in a corner. On the wall above the mantelpiece was the shadow of a picture that had been removed, and as I looked around the room I saw that there were two other shadows where other pictures had been removed.

Jan came back into the room with a rag and a large ornate glass bowl of water which was engraved with a lacework of figures, its lip crenelated with half-parabolas. He put the bowl beside his mother, who was kneeling on the floor in front of me. "This is a terrible welcome we're offering you," Jan said. His mother said something under her breath and carefully undid the laces of my left shoe. When she lifted my foot up to remove the shoe, the sheet of newspaper came with it, stuck to the blood. Jan's mother tore it off, and then took the shoe off slowly. Then with Jan holding my leg off the floor, she peeled the sock off with both hands, tutting at the mess she found there. She tore the rag into three or four pieces, and put one of the pieces in the bowl of water and started to wash the sole of my foot. The water was cold, but the sensation was soothing. After a moment or two she said, "There's nothing in there, I don't think." Then she put a clean rag in the bowl and wiped the rest of my foot, between the toes, the instep, the back of the heel. She tore another rag into strips and dressed my wound, smiling and squatting on her heels when it was all done.

"I thought I would meet you, although I didn't know it would be you," she said.

I didn't understand what she meant, and must have frowned, but I did understand something, that she was expressing a desire which I fulfilled in some surprising way, something she had wished for and it turned out to be me. I thought I would meet you, although I didn't know it would be you. It sounds reasonable in a strange sort of way. If a doctor or a pilot of an airplane you're a passenger on said that to you, you would no doubt break into a cold sweat, but if an elderly German woman who looked as if she was once beautiful was squatting on the floor in front of you, after having washed your wound, and then said that, looking quite unperturbed and even comfortable as she said it, you would feel in the midst of significance. I believe so, you would feel at the beginning of a story. I did, anyway.

"Shall I . . . ?" Jan said, offering a hand to help her up, prompting her to rise.

"Yes," she said, taking his hand and raising herself to her feet, then smiling her thanks to him. Everything she did seemed considered, unhurried. I guessed that whatever event befell her, she would have that same unsurprised smile. "Do you remember when Odysseus comes home, after twenty years, and does not announce himself, and his wife Penelope does not recognize him. Do you remember? It is an old woman who recognizes him, Eureclita or something like that, because she washes his feet to welcome him to the house. As is the way with these stories, she was his nursemaid when he was a baby. Do you remember? Every great hero or prince was breastfed by a tired old woman who sits neglected by the ashes of the royal hearth. Eureclita recognizes the scar on Odysseus's foot, and she knows that the master of the house has come back. When you return to us in time to come, will we know you too?"

At that time I didn't know about Odysseus coming home, or anything very much about Homer or *The Iliad* or *The Odyssey*. What I knew came from movies like *Jason and the Argonauts*, *Hercules Unchained* or *Helen of Troy*. And what I knew about Odysseus from those movies I didn't like. Wasn't it his idea that the Greeks should build a wooden horse and trick their way into Troy, and once in there kill and maim and rape and set fire to the city? I was on the side of the Trojans in this matter. But she said all that with a growing smile, as if relishing the whimsy of it. And when I glanced at Jan, I saw that he too was smiling in the same way, half turned toward the bookshelf as if any minute he was going to reach out and read the passage aloud to us. Then in the next minute he did pull a book out, and ran his finger down the list of contents while his mother waited.

"Euryclea," Jan said at last, unhurried, and then read a sentence. "'As soon as Euryclea had got the scarred limb in her hands and had well hold of it, she recognized it and dropped the foot at once.'"

"Exactly her," she said. "Euryclea. The old woman crouched

in the shadows in Penelope's garden. Auerbach does such wonderful things with that passage. Do you know Auerbach's discussion of that incident? Oh, I will lend it to you. Can you read in German?" "Not yet," I said. "Not anything difficult." She made a sympathetic face. "Well, when you can I'll lend it to you," she said. She spoke English fluently but with an inflection that was unfamiliar to me. After they cleared away the rags and the bowl, and brought in some coffee, she asked: "What made you come here? What made you leave your beautiful country to come to this place? It made us so sad when your letter came. It made me feel happier to think of you living there by the sea, free and warm in bright sunlight, while we were here, apprehensive about small things. At least someone was safe. Look, Jan is worried already about what I am saying, in case you inform on us."

"No . . ." Jan protested, only half paying attention, busy measuring my bloodied shoe against a spare one of his. He did not look that worried to me, except perhaps by the size of my feet, which are exceptionally large. And I supposed they got the idea that I lived free and warm by the sea from all those charming letters I used to write, as I too would never have imagined that where they lived was as it was. I would not have imagined them at all, did not even know they existed—just a voice, speaking smilingly out of that leopard-skin coat.

"Were you very angry with Jan when you found out he was not Elleke?" she asked, leaning back in her chair and smiling, confident that I would not have been that at all. "Were you very disappointed?"

"At first," I said, sipping the bitter coffee and trying not to make a face. My foot was throbbing now as much from the pain as from the handling and its implication in stories of antique valor and cruelty. Should I not go to a hospital for an injection, in case of infection?

"Well, my name is Elleke," she said. "It's true. Jan was too lazy to think of another name. It's not the same thing, but in appearance you can say you met Elleke and it would be true."

"What is the real name of the woman in the leopard-skin coat?" I asked. "Your cousin in Czechoslovakia. Jan said your family came from there."

"Her name is Beatrice, the one who leads in the dark," she said. "Yes our family comes from there. They were big landowners near Most, not the town itself but near a village not far from there. Most is just over the border from here. You should go visit with Jan. He hasn't been there for years himself."

"They took my passport away when I arrived," I said. It had been worrying me. Why did they do that? Suppose I needed to leave? Or go visiting in Most? As soon as I arrived in the hostel, a woman in the office took my passport away and gave me an identity card. It made me nervous, to think that they mistrusted me on arrival, but I was too intimidated to put up a fight.

"Most was in Austria when I was a child," Elleke said. "A long time ago." She glanced at Jan, and gave him a rueful, apologetic smile. "He has heard these stories so many times, his heart has already sunk to hear me start."

"Tell him about that time, Mama," Jan said, nodding vigorously. "You always tell the story differently, so I never tire to hear about it. Please tell, Mama."

"Oh no, we don't want to bore our new friend on his very first visit," Elleke said, chuckling at what Jan had said. "But it is true what you say about stories. They are always slipping through our fingers, changing shape, wriggling to get away."

"I would love to hear about that time," I said, feeling that courtesy left me no option, and drawn by something in the intensity of their exchanges.

"Well, there was a great house with beautiful gardens," Elleke said. "More like a park than a garden, with a stream running through a wood, then emptying into a small lake. There were lawns and flower beds, always full and blooming, and beautiful orchards. An orchard is a truly satisfying sight, the blossom in the spring and then all that perfectly formed fruit later in the summer. There was a grove of dark purple rhododendrons, so purple, so very dark, as if the color was extracted from the plant's deepest viscera. There was a drive for the carriage, and a coachman and footmen, and stables and horses and grooms, and a legion of other servants and their families to do everything that was required. The drive was planted with trees of all kinds. An ancestor had started this love of trees generations before. There was a tree from Kashmir that was two hundred years old, a Kashmiri cypress, twisted and spread out like something straining to be released. It was the exotic tree of our childhood.

"These are memories of lost things," Elleke said after a silence that stretched for a long minute, while she looked from one to the other of us, and took a sip of her foul coffee without wincing. "It may be that I remember them more simply than they really were. I remember the beautiful flowers in every room, even in winter. When I think of those flowers now, it fills my soul with longing, and I don't know what for. Now I think also of all those servants, so many of them doing degraded work that we hardly gave a thought to, living without so many things. That was before the war. It was such a terrible war, so many disasters. And Austria lost the war and lost the next one, and then almost lost everything."

I saw that the memories were depressing her, and were depressing Jan too, but I wanted to hear more. How did they get from there to here? I glanced at the two photographs on the shelf. "Is that Jan?" I asked.

"No, no," she said, laughing. "Why would I have a picture of Jan on the shelf when I see him every day? That is my mother and my younger brother, and the one on the left is my father. The pictures were taken just before we left for Kenya, on a trip to the Carpathian Mountains that was our goodbye to what had been Austria."

"Kenya!" I exclaimed. So that explained the English. But I also wanted to say *the Carpathians*, such a beautiful word, not so supple and insinuating as Massachusetts, I didn't think, but in its own way snaky and secretive. "You were settlers?"

She winced. "Yes, settlers."

"Why Kenya?"

She paused for a moment before replying, then when she began to speak again, I saw that she frowned with concentration. "I don't think I've been asked that question in exactly that way before. You don't mean why Kenya rather than another place. Because in that way it did not matter whether it was Kenya or another place. We were European. We could go anywhere in the world we wanted. You mean why did you choose to go and take what belonged to other people, and call it your own and prosper on duplicity and force. Even fight and maim for what you had no right to. Isn't that what you mean? Well, because we lived at a time when it seemed we had a right to do all that, a right to places that were only occupied by people with dark skins and frizzy hair. That was the meaning of colonialism, and everything was done to persuade us not to notice the methods that made it possible for us to go where we wanted. My parents bought land in the Ngong Hills and became coffee farmers. The natives were pacified and labor was cheap. My parents didn't ask how that state of affairs had been achieved, and no one encouraged them to, although it was easy enough to see how when we lived there. Do you know the Ngong? Have you been to Nairobi?"

"No, I don't know anything," I said. "Or been anywhere."

"You've been to Dresden," Jan said, smiling.

"Yes, there is also an innocent form of that question, 'Why Kenya?'" Elleke said, ignoring us, pressing on with her story, instructing us. "To get away from Europe and its wars. My parents did not want to stay in Austria anymore, so they took what share came to them from the estate and bought that farm in the Ngong. That was 1919 and we lived there until 1938, doing what we thought were remarkable things, achieving so much. We traveled and we learned a great deal, though I know now we did not learn enough. As time passes it seems less and less remarkable what we did and felt there."

"My mother has written a memoir about the years in Kenya," Jan said. "In German. It's beautiful writing."

"It is only lying nostalgia," Elleke said, smiling and waving Jan away. "If I were writing it now, I would also tell the horrible stories and depress everyone, like a boring old woman. Do you know why we left to come to Germany just as war was about to start? Because the authorities warned us that once war started we would be interned, and somehow over the years my parents had found pride in being Austrian again. The Austria they knew no longer existed, of course. The part they lived in was called Czechoslovakia by then and the rest of Austria had become part of Germany. But still they came to that Germany of robber barons and arrogant triumphalists with their peaked caps and silver-braided uniforms rather than be interned by the British in Kenya. We all of us preferred to leave rather than be interned in indignity, and be mocked by the filthy natives in our misfortune. Forgive me, that was how we spoke. Or do not forgive me if you do not think we deserve it. But that was how we spoke, and I do not mean contempt now in speaking like that, merely to give you an idea of the self-pitying arrogance with which we regarded ourselves. My father was fond of saying that our superiority over the natives was only possible with their consent. All Europeans had to observe the thin line beyond which the mysterious moral authority over the native would vanish, and we would have to torture and murder to regain it. Poor Papa, he didn't think that it was the torture and murder that were committed in our name which gave us that authority in the first place. He thought it was something mysterious to do with justice and temperate conduct, something we acquired from reading Hegel and Schiller, and going to Mass. Never mind the exclusions and expulsions, and the summary judgments delivered with contemptuous assurance. Never mind the regiments and the jails. It was our moral superiority which made the natives afraid of us. Oh well, we would soon have our share of that, and come to understand that philosophy and poetry had only made the riddle grow greater, not smaller. But we could not stay in Kenya and have the natives laugh at us. So Europe and its wars caught up with my parents after all, and we came to live in Dresden. In this house. Not far from our old home. Oh dear, it gets worse from now on, and I don't think I want to tell you any more of my dreary tale. You only wanted to know about Beatrice, really, but once I start on these things, it seems harder and harder to stop talking. It's the egotism of age."

"I asked you about the photographs," I said. I meant to be reassuring, but the words came out in a feeble, sulking voice. I thought I was getting a fever from the wound, and the cold in the flat was biting now that it was dark.

"Asante," she said in Kiswahili, and then smiled. "I still remember a few words. My dear friend, how should we call you? Shall we call you Ismail? Is that what your friends call you?"

"Latif," I said. I had decided on the plane. I would not use the name I had been given, but would be Latif, for its gentleness and the softness of its modulations, God's name, which I would take with respect, meaning no outrage or blasphemy. My given name was Ismail Rajab Shaaban Mahmud. Those were the names on my documents: my name, my father's name, my grandfather's name, my great-grandfather's name. When I started on the journey the stewardess called me Mr. Mahmud, and that was what I was called by officials in GDR. There was no opportunity to contest that, and say that where I come from I would be called Ismail Rajab, my name and my father's name. I didn't want to contest it. And for good measure, I thought I would call myself Latif from then on, in yearning for a quality of gentleness. So that was that. From then on I was Ismail Mahmud, whose friends called him Latif. That was what Ali called me, and what everyone at the hostel called me, and what Jan and Elleke can come to call me. "Ismail is my formal name. My friends call me Latif," I said.

"See how everything turns out," Elleke said laughing, her eyes sparkling with a kind of joy. "Elleke becomes Jan, and Ismail turns out to be Latif, and they both probably smell as sweet." I got that reference to *Romeo and Juliet*, and gave a hearty chuckle to make sure that she knew. "Latif, I think you will not be able to go back to your hostel tonight with that bad foot, and not until we can clean and mend your very thin shoes. You must find better shoes than these, I think. Please stay with us tonight, and then Jan will accompany you to your hostel tomorrow. He will explain everything tomorrow. Now we'll have something to eat."

I saw the look of alarm on Jan's face, then he shook his head. "No, Mama, it will be better if Latif goes back to the hostel tonight. I'll go with him. There'll be too many questions for him if he is not there. They are very strict about foreign students reporting back. There will be questions for us too afterward. I'll go with him and make sure. Then perhaps he can come again another weekend."

Ali was disgusted when I told him that Elleke was a man. Or rather that Elleke was the name of the mother of the man who used to write to me and called himself Elleke. "These Germans have strange ways of getting their fun," he said. "Keep away from them. You don't know what they'll want from you."

But I didn't keep away, and the first time I arranged to go

back to Dresden to see them, Ali glared and sulked at me, as if I had betrayed him. My foot was now healed, but it was a miserably cold February day, and my feet were already numb and stiffening while I was indoors. Ali made me try on his spare pair of shoes, and frowned with disappointment when they fitted well enough for me to wear them. "Come with me," I said. "I'm sure they'd like to meet you too." But he grimaced and shook his head. "I don't want anything to do with their games," he said. "You make sure you don't get into any trouble with the authorities, either. They sound like troublemakers to me."

There was only one other passenger on the bus, a short, dark-complexioned man who leaned over the back of his seat and stared at me for about five minutes without interruption. He was wearing a dark, heavy workman's coat, its shoulders hunched up round his ears as his cocked arms spread out on the seat rail, settled down for a good long stare. I looked out of the window and was grateful for Ali's shoes, even though they were too tight and pinched my toes. It looked like it would snow. When I glanced back into the bus, it was to find the man's liquid eyes resting watchfully on me, unraveling a deep mystery. He had a big hairy mustache with bits of gray in it, and when I glanced his way it twitched slightly, nervously. I caught the driver's eye in the rearview mirror and I thought I saw amusement there. After his five minutes were up, the man made a snorting noise and turned to face the front again. In a moment he began to hum a tune and then to sing softly, his shoulders heaving in silent laughter. I caught the driver's eye again and saw that he was laughing too. I didn't know what they were laughing about. The sun came out as the bus crossed the river, a low-hanging sun that turned the water into a rippled sheet of lead and made the ships that lined the river throw a shadow of their nests of thickets and hawsers on the quays.

I remember that second visit to Jan and Elleke imperfectly. It is merged with subsequent visits, and they are all shaped in my mind by the pleasure they took in their hospitality, the ceremony they made over the modest meals, the elaborate and sometimes beautiful crockery, all of which had a kind of faded elegance. I remember the way they treated every question as if it tested their integrity, as if they had to guard against the duplicitous revision which alters the balance of a story and turns it into something heroic. I marveled at their assurance, and wondered whether what I saw was the self-pitying arrogance with which Elleke had said her parents regarded themselves in Kenya, or whether it was something else, something like an unstraining trust in the value of ideas that they thought beyond dispute. I would have understood it better now, that sustained passion for ideas that could not be destroyed completely, not even by living through the obscenities of colonialism, nor the inhumanities of the Nazi war and the Holocaust, nor by the authoritarian degradations of the GDR. I knew very little then, and saw their manner as an attractive eccentricity in the reduced reality of that flat in Dresden. "That's the way life takes us," Elleke once said. "It takes us like this, then it turns us over and takes us like that." What she didn't say was that through it all we manage to cling to something that makes sense.

More than anything else, the memories of my visits to them were merged and shaped by the stories Elleke and later Jan told. Elleke was twenty-eight when they came to live in Dresden, in the house they still lived in, only then they lived in all of it instead of the three rooms they were now allowed to occupy. Her parents came back wealthy. Elleke missed Kenya so much, and missed the man—she grinned at Jan—that she left behind there. His name was Daniel, and she would have stayed behind if he had asked her to. "But then I wouldn't have had Jan, and what would have been the point of that?" It was during that time of longing and disquiet that she began to write the memoir of their time in Kenya. Her parents encouraged her avidly. They too longed for Kenya, and were shaken by what they found in Germany.

There was hardly time to finish writing the memoir before German demands for the Sudeten reached a climax in August 1938 and crisis followed crisis until the approach of war. Elleke didn't talk about the war, just shook her head and looked away. Her brother Joseph was killed in North Africa, and her father died before the terrible bombing in 1945. He collapsed in the street and was helped home by strangers. Then came the GDR in 1949. That was the year her mother died, the year they took away the house, and the year she met Konrad, Jan's father.

"He got this flat back for us to live in. He's a big man in the administration now, but then he was a math teacher who was active in the Party," Elleke said. "He was a kind man, but impatient and restless. Eager for things I could not share. And perhaps he understood the time we lived in better."

"What happened to the family back in Czechoslovakia?" I asked.

"They were all expelled after the war," Elleke said. "Germans were expelled from everywhere, from the Sudeten, from Silesia, from East Prussia. Millions of them. Dresden was a pile

of rubble with thousands of refugees crawling over it. Everywhere and everything was ruined by our insatiable urge to de-
struction."

"But Beatrice," I said.

"Her grandfather was Czech," Elleke said, smiling, pleased
for her.

She said we should go and visit there, Jan and I. That was how
the plan for our trip started. We took a bus to Most and then
just kept going, to Prague, Bratislava, Budapest, an endless beautiful journey to Zagreb, and an anxious rail trip to Graz in Austria. I knew before we set out that Jan planned to escape, and I
joined him because he was my friend and because I was young
and did not know better, and did not care where I went or what
happened to me. We traveled on money he and Elleke had saved,
until we reached the German border when we announced ourselves as refugees from GDR. We were sent to Munich where we
lived in a secure hostel for three weeks, Jan aching with sadness
and guilt about Elleke. I told the immigration official who inter-
viewed me that I wanted to travel on to England, and he smiled
and arranged for me to receive a one-off subsistence payment
which paid for my rail ticket to Hamburg. Jan and I said goodbye
at Munich railway station, and never saw or spoke to each other
again. "I hope I have not ruined your life by forcing you into this
adventure," Jan said. I had not even said goodbye to Ali, afraid
that he would dissuade me, and sometimes I wonder where he is
and what he is doing. I thought of him in 1984, when Sékou
Touré died, and Conté's new government opened up the jails. I

wondered if his father was among the starved and the wounded who survived those dark dungeons, who staggered out, stunned, into the light of yet another gathering shambles. In those three months that summer, I had traveled all over Central Europe in a huge circle, and was sorry that I had missed Bulgaria.

I arrived in England at Plymouth, feeling as if I had circumnavigated the world's oceans. I disembarked with the crew and strolled through the gates with them. No one molested me or asked me to name myself. I walked for hours in the town, grateful at the luck beyond belief which had attended my wanderings so far. No one, it seemed, was that worried about me. No one was concerned to chase me away or to confine me against a later expulsion. No one desired my services or my allegiance. Late in the afternoon, a chilly summer rain began to fall, and I turned back toward the port, not sure what to do. Perhaps I should just get back on the boat and keep going, and see where I would end up. Live my life like that until I bumped into my fate. It was fear and shriveling will that made me think like that. Leave my life to someone else, to events. But when I got back to the harbor, the ship had gone and my journey was over. A guard at the gate asked me if I needed help, and when I told him the name of the ship I was looking for, he took me to the office of the Harbour Police. "I am a refugee," I told the stern policeman with close-cropped gray hair and clipped mustache. He sat up straighter and made his face even sterner, frowning at me with a flat suspicious look.

"Well, sir, those are big words," he said. "I understood you were a crewman who missed his ship. I'd better get the details of your registration and then we'll see the best way of making sure you get back with your mates."

"I am a refugee," I said. "From GDR."

"From where?" he asked, turning his grizzled head slightly to give me the full benefit of his left ear, as if to be sure to catch the elusive word I had uttered.

"From East Germany," I said.

He laughed with delighted incredulity, leaning back in his chair and savoring the delicious comic twist, and I imagined him constructing the narrative he would make later out of this unexpected morsel of life's little farces. I grinned with him, and saw his pleasure that I had seen the joke, or was agreeable to share in my ridiculousness. "Guten Tag," he said. I answered the questions he asked me, and after a few minutes I saw that something I said or did, or was, made him disposed toward me. Perhaps it was when he asked me how old I was and I said I was eighteen, for then he shook his head slightly and smiled, a brief tight smile, a mere token of the real lush thing, but a smile nonetheless. Like a brief handshake which nevertheless manages to convey amity. "Just the kind of idiot thing you do when you're eighteen," he said. I spent the night in the Harbour Police office, grateful for the share of the policeman's coffee and sandwiches. I hadn't eaten since I left the ship. He asked me to tell him the story of my time in GDR and the journey across Central Europe. It sounded grand to my ears as I told it, and I found that as I recalled the journey for him, I remembered sights and details that I had not noticed at the time. Or perhaps I was adding them in because that was what I would have seen had I been more alert. He interrupted me now and then to ask for elaborations but otherwise he let me talk, prompting me with leading questions while he leaned back in his huge swivel chair. "What was Hungary like? That's where Gypsies come from, isn't it? My old mum used to say there's Gypsy in us, but then every family says there's Gypsy in them somewhere along the line." At some point I must have fallen asleep, because I woke up at first light to find myself alone and covered with a blanket. I usually had difficulty falling asleep, but perhaps fear and tension had made me heavy.

His name was Walter. Before he was relieved by the morning shift, he gave me the name and address of a refugee organization and told me to clear off. "Go straight to these people and don't wander the streets. You'll find a public washroom on the main road just opposite the gates. Get yourself cleaned up," he said sternly. "And get a haircut. You young people are all the same."

5.

Silences

I stood by the open door of the flat, leaning on it with an outstretched left arm. It was a studied pose, a prepared position. I saw him as he took the final turning in the stair, pausing briefly with his right hand on the banister, the light of the huge landing window falling on him. In the morning, the sunlight that got through the passages between houses shone directly through that window, and held particles of dust and organic debris suspended in sinewy wisps. But by early afternoon, the light only trickled down the surrounding walls, and glowed thin and gray on the stairs. He stood in the watery radiance of that afternoon light, his face clean-shaven and lean, his body leaning slightly forward. His face was drawn and closed down, a guarded face. I would have looked twice at him in the streets, in the streets of England, and wondered if I knew him, and wondered if he was who I thought he was. So often I have walked by people in English streets, surprised by how strange and alien they looked there, and wondered guiltily if they were someone I knew, when I knew they couldn't be. I think I would have walked past him too, and thought how in some odd way he reminded me of someone I once knew, without perhaps worrying at the reminder long enough to give a name to the memory. Even, perhaps, hurrying away from the memory before it became solid enough to take a grip of me and summon other thoughts I had safely penned away. As time has passed, so many clean, sharp details have grown fuzzy and imprecise. Perhaps that is what it means to grow old, the effects of sun and squall wiping away line after line of the picture, turning the image into its furry shadow. Though even after all the fading and furring, so many lines still remain, now seeming like even sparser fragments of the whole: a warm look in the eye when the face is lost, a smell that recalls a music whose melody is out of range, the memory of a room when the house or its location is forgotten, a field of pasture by the side of the road in the middle of a void. So time dismembers the images of our time. Or to put it in an archeological way, it is as if the details of our lives have accumulated in layers, and now some layers have been displaced by the friction of other events, and bits of contingent pieces still remain, accidentally tumbled about.

I wish I could say that I remembered the eyes that looked at me as I stood at the door of my flat, eyes that tried to conceal everything behind blank equanimity and failed, but I think I would have walked past them if I had not known they were coming to meet me. I would have felt their resolute disinterest and suppressed mine. I moved my hand from the door when he began on the last few steps, squaring up to his approach. He was careful not to stumble but he was hurrying up now, so that he arrived in front of me smiling broadly and with his right hand outstretched.

"Salam alaikum," he said, smiling, playing safe, putting off the moment of recognition with this most inclusive of all greetings. I nodded and took his hand, not returning the greeting in the obligatory way. *Alaikum salam.* I saw that he noted the omission and suspected that he would now summon a little more caution. It seemed best to proceed with caution. He held on to my hand while he studied my face, my hand frail and bony and large in his, which was tremulously warm like the body of a small captive animal. "Latif Mahmud," he said.

I nodded again, then squeezed his hand and let it go. "Welcome," I said, and stepped aside to let him precede me. The kitchen was in front of us, the living room to the left, and the bedroom on the right as we stood by the open door, surveying the widening prospect of my home. I saw him take a quick look around, and saw his gaze pause over the small picture of an Andalusian courtyard I had taped to the cupboard just inside the kitchen door. I too had paused over that picture earlier in the day, and wondered whether it said anything more than I wished to give away, but then left it where it was with a sense of the futility of further secretiveness. I had burned lavender and fragrant gum in the morning, to give my home the smell of old age and approaching mortality, as if I had recently opened the trunk where my perfumed shroud lay waiting for its appointed day.

"I thought I would come to greet you, to pay my respects," he said, standing before me in the small living room, his fingers lightly gripped together by the tips. "The refugee organization got in touch with me a while back . . . months ago. I think they told you. They thought you needed a translator, but it turned out you didn't." He smiled, acknowledging my mischief.

"You are very kind," I said, smiling too at these gracious passes. "On this matter of English, I was advised not to speak it at first. 'Tell them nothing more than that you want asylum, nothing more.' That was what the man who sold me the ticket told me. He insisted on this."

"Why?" he asked, interested, though I would have liked to ask *him* if he knew the answer. "Without English you are even more a stranger, a refugee, I suppose, more convincing," he guessed. "You're just a condition, without even a story."

"Perhaps that way you can avoid answering difficult questions too," I said. "Or the man who sold me the ticket was making mischief. He was a mischievous man, he took pride in it. I don't think it did any harm in the end, and it brought about your kind visit."

"I should have come earlier," he said. "It must be nearly six months you've been here now."

Why hadn't he? I could imagine him stumbling against the wish to come, swerving away from it, curious and then raging about my arrival and my name. He wanted to come, he didn't want to come. Then in the end, life in general probably imposed its shambolic logic and dispersed the moment of desire.

"Nearly seven months now," I said, and sensed my voice sparking. "You waited a long time to come, Latif Mahmud. They only told me a few days ago that you wished to come. Rachel. She told me your name and said that you wished to visit. Though she told me about you more than six months ago, when she first spoke to you."

"I should've come earlier," he said, playing for time, perhaps thinking that I hadn't recognized him because he had changed his name, or his hair had thinned and turned peppery. Though I thought I saw in his eyes that he knew that I knew who he was. We were now sitting down in the living room, in chairs at right angles to each other, with a low rectangular table of no refinement between us. I poured two small cups of coffee out of the Thermos I had prepared earlier before speaking further.

"I'm surprised you didn't come sooner, out of curiosity, to see who had borrowed your father's name," I said.

There it was then, the moment of recognition. We sat silently regarding each other, and I wondered what he was thinking, what he thought I was thinking, sitting in front of him consoled and composed. I wondered what he thought he had come here to do.

"I thought it would be you," he said.

He waited for me to speak, a small resigned smile on his face, and I waited for him, not tense, not anxious, just surprised at how the stripping away of our fake aliases allowed sweet, cruel memories to come surging back. It was a relief to see that small smile and the resignation or calmness in it. He had not come to make war.

"What made you think that it would be me?" I asked, calmly, gently, suppressing any inflection in my voice, though I was surprised that he spoke so directly. "I find that hard to believe."

He shrugged. "I don't know. Some instinct made me suspect. The mischief of it sounded as if it might be you."

I could not help smiling with pleasure at that, that he would speak so openly. "It must be the instinct of the poet, the seer, that made you suspect so accurately," I said.

"How do you know about that?" he asked after a little pause, surprised that I knew that he was a poet, and thinking perhaps that I might know more than he thought I did. Oh, I so relished these pointless little exchanges, these little sallies and dances, a small feint here and the subtlest gesture there. Not satisfied with my pointless and valueless life, I still want to relish its gigantic pointlessness.

"Oh, we all know that you are a distinguished poet," I said, looking appropriately solemn and respectful. "We heard first of all about your scholastic achievements, and that you were a professor at a university in London. Then we heard that you had the poetic gift, which you practiced under a new name. To be able to write poetry of distinction in an adopted language! What an ear for music you must have. Someone even showed me one of your poems in a magazine that a relative had sent him. It made us feel very proud. When Rachel told me that Latif Mahmud wished to come and see me, I felt honored. I didn't know when you'd come, though I thought you would one day."

"I'm not a professor, and not a distinguished poet," he said, glowering sternly, looking away, looking displeased with my attempt at flattery. "I have a handful of pitiful poems in a little magazine which is too generous for its own good. I'm surprised anybody knew about any of them."

"Well, they did," I said, interested to see the way he punished himself for the achievement, which after all was real and his own, rather than accepting the meager applause lightly. Perhaps he took it for mockery. It made me think he was someone who could be cruel to himself.

"Why did you take my father's name?" he asked me, looking me in the eye, demanding a confession, refusing to be disarmed by courtesy. "After everything you did to him, why did you then take his name? Not that there is anything sacred about his name. Just why did you choose that one above all others? After everything you did to him."

I knew he would ask me this question, and that he would probably ask it with suppressed rage, yet when he did I found myself reluctant to speak. What everything? What did I do to him? I was wearied by what I had to say, tired beyond bearing by all the events that had led to this moment. But I also knew I had to answer him, otherwise he would think me a sinful and wicked old man, and he would leave my house thinking of me as he did before he came. And even if I was sinful and wicked before, it is a function of mature years to seek to explain and redeem the folly and malice of younger years, to give redress and receive understanding. I had an accounting to give, and I could not have wished for a more suitable shriver, for he too needed to know what I knew, to make complete the absences and to utter the silences in his life here in the middle of nowhere. I thought so.

"I took your father's name to save my life," I said. "There was sweet irony in that, after your father had so very nearly succeeded in destroying it."

I married in 1963. That was the same year I won the case against Rajab Shaaban Mahmud for possession of his house, and a year before the British departed in a huff and left us to the chaos and violence that attended the end of their empire. I fell in love with her, my wife, although I would have been too bashful to say in those words that that was how I felt about her. I knew the family, and at an earlier time would have known her as well. I would have seen her as a child running and playing in the streets like other children, running errands for her mother or her aunt, or strolling to school in her salmon-pink pinafore and cream shirt. But that is what used to happen to women. At a certain age they disappeared into the house, and then you forgot what they looked like, you forgot they existed, until they reappeared years later as brides and mothers. They came to the shop to have a sofa made, Salha and her mother, in a dark green velvet upholstery which they brought with them. A gift, Salha's mother said, from a relative in Mombasa, a beautiful piece of material, feel the softness of the fabric, and how the color ripples when you run your hand through it. They thought it would be perfect for upholstering a new sofa. Salha, I love the way you have to aspirate the end of the name, as if you're sucking it in or swallowing it. I fell in love with her there in the shop, though I would have been too calloused and naive to know that that was what had happened to me. I don't want to protest too much over this, but I would not have had the language then to describe what had happened to me. The only words I knew would have made me feel childish and bashful. I was thirty-two years old at the time, the same age as Nabi Isa the Nazarene when he was about to complete his ministry of compassion and love on earth, but I did not even know the syllables to imagine the uncomplicated affection between a man and a woman. Instead I asked the mother if she had a guest staying with her, meaning Salha. "No, no, this is my daughter Salha. Have you forgotten her already?" And Salha stood smiling beside her while I stuttered and tried to pick up my idle trader chatter. Perhaps she had been living away somewhere else, I suggested. No, she had been there all the time, Salha's mother said, and they had even passed by the shop here a few times, but perhaps I really only had eyes for business these days.

I have no doubt they passed the shop, but I would not have known who they were under the yards of black fabric women were required to wear to preserve their modesty. I always looked away when a woman preserved from head to toe in a buibui walked past. How could you know that it wasn't your sister or your brother's beloved that you were watching with disrespectful and embarrassing admiration? I had no sister and no brother, but the idea still remained. There were even stories of people who had watched their own daughters walk past, and audibly uttered their hungry pleasure, only to hear a moment later the voice of their own little girls wishing them a satirical good afternoon. So no, I had not seen Salha walk past, and despite her mother's suggestion that I was nothing more than a bloodless shopkeeper for having failed to do so, I was happy that I had seen her again in that dramatic way when she turned up at the shop and I fell in love with her.

They came to the shop twice after that, and once she spoke to me in the street, merely a greeting, nothing improper. "Hujambo, Bwana Saleh?" Are you well, Bwana Saleh? I did not even know it was her until she spoke behind the veil of her buibui as I was about to walk past her. Then I recognized her voice. A month later when the sofa was ready for delivery, I asked for her and was accepted. A month after that, in November of 1963, we married. That day was the happiest of my life. I have heard people say such things and cringed with embarrassment at the clumsiness and exaggeration, but it was true for me that day, and perhaps it was true for those others that I had thought insincere.

I only wanted a small wedding, the ceremony in private and then just a few guests and relatives for a celebration meal, but her parents would not hear of it. It was their expense as parents of the bride, Salha's father told me, and none of my affair. Salha was their youngest, and they did not want anyone saying that she was not loved. They would rejoice fully in their daughter's wedding, even if they became paupers as a result. So they put on a full three-day extravaganza, with music and song and dance, and a biryani banquet after the ceremony and a special halwa ordered for the occasion and a procession with music and song to convey her to my house. For the rest of the three days it was nonstop food, samosas and mahamri, curries and sesame bread, almond ice cream and jelabis, and there were crowds of guests, some of whom did not even bother going home during the days of the wedding, lofas and freeloaders to my way of thinking. It was a waste of thousands of shillings.

But also I had feared that a large wedding would embarrass me, since I had no family to speak of, or rather I had no family that spoke to me with any kindness. And I had no friends or intimates, since even those few that I had not neglected over the years had turned against me over the matter of Rajab Shaaban Mahmud's house. I had won my case only a few months before and feeling was still strong that I had not done right to persist with it when the only outcome would be the expulsion of Rajab Shaaban Mahmud and his family. At least this was the feeling conveyed to me in the words of those few who had addressed me on the matter. They were people who had an opinion on most things, and did not hesitate to deliver it, people puffed up with sagacity and pride, whose wisdom depended on their conviction of everyone else's idiocy. I was not concerned about their judgment, but I feared that it might be the view of all the others who were silent out of courtesy. It had even occurred to me when I asked for Salha, that I would be refused because of the feeling against me. But I was wrong about that, and I was wrong about the wedding. It was a time of rejoicing and happiness, a day better than any other because I had never felt so fortunate and fulfilled, so much part of the people among whom I lived.

She was nineteen, and I was thirty-two, not as big a difference in age as it might sound to some ears now. She had spent five or six of those few years in the dark, proving and ripening until a man came to ask for her. She had never been anywhere, hardly ever read anything and did not even listen to the radio. Her days in those years were the work and pleasures of the house, and decorating and preening herself to receive and visit other women in similar restraint to herself. While *I* had traveled, acquired a little, very little, learning, worked for the British and thereby understood something of the workings of our irredeemable world, set up a prospering business and owned two houses. We had hardly spoken, had never been alone together before our wedding, I had not even seen her standing without the black shroud around her. Yet we were fortunate and had few difficulties in the beginning of our life together. She loved the house as I did, and loved for us to sit in the upstairs room, the outer veranda door open to the sea a few feet away, and the other door open to the balcony over the inner courtyard, listening to the radio or playing cards. There we spoke and told each other things we had not said before. And I knew then what a desert my life had been before that, and learned the sweetness of silence between companions.

We weren't alone always, and people came and went as is our way, women visitors, requiring that Salha receive and entertain them on her own. The house had not received any women visitors in the few years before that, not since the death of my stepmother, and I felt their presence like an intrusion into intimate spaces in my life from which they excluded me when they came. I had to abandon the upstairs rooms, and listen to the rise and fall of their endless chatter from the downstairs room. Salha was used to their company, perhaps would have felt lost without it, would have felt cut off from all the other households she had grown up with, and from the friendly commerce of that circumscribed world. I do not mean mockery. Whereas I felt they were keeping her from me, taking her away from me. And I thought they hectored her because she would not fall pregnant.

She suffered because of that. Three times in two years she lost pregnancies, and she ached and wearied and became unhappy. In those two years I saw that her health was declining, that she was drawn and losing weight, and was so often listless and wordless, grieving. I pleaded with her that we should do whatever was necessary to keep her safe, never mind having a child. Beloved. The gynecologist she consulted at the hospital said that her womb was precariously angled, and the only chance she had to keep a pregnancy was to lie in for the period. I thought the women hectored her with their chatter, but perhaps they didn't. It was what she wanted too, could not imagine herself in any other way. Those were the years after independence and soon after that the time of austerity, years of cruelty and uncertainty, hardly a time for bringing a baby into a blighted world. But three years after our marriage she did fall pregnant and, as the doctor ordered, she was confined to her bed. We followed the doctor's advice in general, for the woman herself was not there to attend to the patient. She had fled the country by then, as did so many people who could earn a dignified living elsewhere, and so Salha's mother moved in with us to look after her.

Salha was blessed with a daughter. It had been a toil for her, the confinement, the pregnancy and the anxieties and shortages of the time we lived in. I feared for her, I feared that every small setback would be costly, without a doctor, without medicines, except those barks and powders that Salha's mother acquired and administered to her, and kept secret from me. But we were blessed. Salha chafed and fretted at the enforced inactivity, and her body became irritable in unexpected ways, but her health improved in the last months and she put on weight and acquired a new vigor. And she had plenty of company. It seemed that at any time of day or night there was a woman friend or her mother in the room with her, sometimes talking and laughing, at other times snoring contentedly on the floor beside her bed. When our daughter came, I wanted to call her Raiiya, a citizen, to make her life an utterance, a demand that our rulers should treat us with humanity, as indigenes and citizens of the land of our birth. It was a name with a pedigree, I told Salha, used for centuries to describe citizens of nations which had been overwhelmed by conquest. It was true that the conquerors in its use were Muslims and the conquered were not, and that to offer the vanquished rights after having taken away their freedom to conduct their affairs as they wished was hardly magnanimous, but the idea of a citizen's rights was a noble one, and we could use it for our own meaning. Salha said no, that would only be provocative, and no one would know about the other meaning, and the name would make the child into an object of mockery later on in her life. So we called her Ruqiya, after the Prophet's daughter with his first wife Khadija. The house then filled with cries and yells, but it also filled with joy and unexpected transformations. And women endlessly coming and going in a racket of chatter and laughter.

I visited your house once," Latif Mahmud said. "I don't know if you remember that. It was a very long time ago. And now a lifetime later I visit your other house here. It's as if a little length of string ties your claw to a post in the ground, and you scratch and scratch there all your time even as you imagine that you have flown worlds."

"I remember you did," I said. I waited for him to indicate where he wanted us to go next, but he wasn't ready.

"Now that you mention it, I heard women's voices then, when I came to your house. That was the year I left to go to Germany," he said, speaking gently, in that pensive mode we adopt when we contemplate our past selves in the light of later events, and see what it was we did then and what we were like. And then we ache at our naivety and long-lost conviction, which we like to remember as courage now departed. "In 1966. I came to your house just before I left, about twelve days before I left. It was a beautiful house, the tiled courtyard, I remember that, and the

latticed balcony overlooking it and light shining through the fret-
work. There were pots of palm and something growing against
one of the walls. Jasmine, I think. Is that right? Was it jasmine
growing on the walls? Yes. I don't think I'd seen that kind of
courtyard before, although I've seen it in pictures since, with a
caption saying something like: 'A typical traditional inner courtyard in a coastal house, showing the influence of Moorish Islamic
architecture.' I'd never seen the tiles and the latticed balcony before, not inside a small house like that, so I can't think it was that
typical. Maybe it was more typical in other parts of the coast.
Was it? I haven't visited other parts of the coast."

"Oh is that so? Rachel said you were an expert in *our area*," I
said, unable to disguise my surprise, though I recovered enough
wit to end my remark with a little twist of irony at Rachel's expense.

"I'm not an expert on anything," he said, sneering at himself.
"I teach English Literature. I never traveled anywhere while I
lived there, and I haven't been back since. Not once. That was
nearly thirty years ago. I see it now, as I sit in front of you I see
that house again. Now here I am at your other house, which is
perhaps not as beautiful as the one you left behind." He said this
with a smile, not meaning disrespect. "Maybe coming to see you
is like visiting a piece of the place I left behind. Does that sound
alarming?"

"Yes," I said, and he nodded, but I saw he had more to say.

"There was a man who came to the door. He worked for you,
some kind of hard man and factotum. I don't know if I'm using
that word right. People used to call him Faru. When he came
to the door he was like one of those scowling bawabs you read

about in the stories of *A Thousand and One Nights*, a big fleshy Black man guarding his master's doorway."

"Faru, yes. His real name was Nuhu."

"I don't know what you're smiling about," Latif Mahmud said sharply, frowning at me, on the point of discourtesy. He waited for me to wipe the smile off my face, and I did as he wished. "You remember him with fondness, perhaps. The bawabs in those *A Thousand and One Nights* stories were neutered as boys, so they could guard the master's valuables without temptation. That was why they became fleshy and docile, because they produced none of those restless urges down below. How did they do that in the stories, do you suppose? Neutered them. How do you suppose they did that? With a scalpel or by crushing the testicles with a rock? Not a rock, that would have caused complications, dangerous wounds. So a scalpel then, a science of neutering. All the stories about Faru were that he was a sexual menace, so perhaps you should have seen to that in his case too. Whatever happened to him?"

"Nuhu wasn't my slave for me to restrain or neuter," I said.

"Why restrain him when you could use his ugliness to intimidate?" he asked, fierce in his anger now. It never occurred to me to stop him, to say that now he had gone too far. And I didn't think he would go too far, or he would not have come in the first place. "It was an ugly business after all, wasn't it? Picking through other people's misfortunes to see if there were valuables there to sell, and Faru was just the man to do it, wasn't he? He could go about his ugly business and leave the master to behave with dignity."

Then, as if he *had* gone too far, he retreated and sat silently for a minute, gazing out of the window. That window too had a view of the sea, a distant view, a mere smear of ocean if you stood on tiptoe, but on a sunny day you could catch a glimpse of the light glinting off the metallic water. It was sunny that day he came, and I wanted to tell him that. That if he stood up on tiptoe and looked over the roofs of the houses he would catch a glimpse of the sea. "I haven't come here after all these years to quarrel with you," he said, smiling ruefully, looking disappointed with himself. The smile was small in magnitude, but it spread in contrition all over his face and into his eyes. "I came to see you, to see who you were. To see if you were who I thought you were. Not to quarrel, or be discourteous in your own house, or to pass judgment. Although it isn't always possible to withhold judgment, even if you wish to. It's just that I was thinking about him today, as I was coming here, your Faru. I was thinking about that time I visited you before, and I remembered him and how that name so perfectly suited his ugliness. And how there always are people like him, bawabs and eunuchs, spiritless in themselves but eager in their meanness, and how there always are people ready to use them."

I heard the judgment, and had heard such judgments before, and had no answer except that I too had judged badly before. But I also did not want him to storm off in a rage, and he had given me that mollifying smile, so I spoke placatingly. I offered him some coffee, which he declined. I offered to make some tea, though I did not want to rise from my seat. I felt weary and dispirited, and did not know if I had the strength for all the cruelty we seemed bent on revisiting after all these millions of years. Also, in recent times I sometimes had a feeling like hollowness in my arms and legs, as if there was nothing there but sticks of bone. At such times I found the idea of moving impossible. But he declined the tea too.

"His name was Nuhu, and it was my father who gave him that name Faru. Many years ago," I said, shifting and lightening the weight of my voice. "When my father used to sell halwa, it was he and Nuhu who made it. Nuhu did everything, really, all the drudgery. He chopped the wood for the furnace. It had to be clove wood, my father insisted on that, of a certain dryness so that the cooking temperature would be right and the halwa would be enveloped in that unique aroma of blazing clove wood. Nuhu weighed the ghee, the starch, the sugar, all of which had to be of different qualities and amounts depending on the kind of halwa they were cooking that day. He peeled the nuts, cleaned and pounded the spices. It took a whole day of preparation before they even began. Then after that Nuhu cleaned and greased the huge brass halwa pan, five feet in diameter, and then lit the fire in the furnace below the platform where my father would sit to stir the halwa in view of the street. When my father was ready, Nuhu would bring the ingredients and pour them into the pan while my father stirred. Both of them would be pouring with sweat by now, working so near the heat of that great fire. Sometimes, often, people would stop in the street to watch. It's a gloriously skilled thing, stirring the halwa with the long ladle while standing or sitting on that platform with a roaring furnace underneath you. And the halwa had to be stirred all the time to get the consistency right, otherwise the starch and ghee turned into lumps in seconds. Nuhu was so strong that my father would chant and sing his praises as he stirred. 'Look at him, like a rhinoceros.' That was how he got the name. 'Look at the faru there.' And Nuhu would swell himself up and play the clown.

"He was only a boy when he started to work for my father, a little older than me. Perhaps about nine or ten years old. I should have been doing that job, helping my father to make halwa and then sitting in the shop in a greasy singlet to sell it in little saucers, or in half-pound straw baskets to take away. But I had different talents, or at least my mother thought so, may God have mercy on her soul, and she insisted I go to school instead. So Nuhu made halwa for all the years, and sat in the shop to sell it or whatever else was required, and in time he liked to think himself part of the family. If any other work was needed in the house, he did that too. If he thought anyone was being abusive or threatening to me, he dealt with them. That was how he saw his place among us.

"Then, suddenly, my father died. I should think you were too young to remember that, and even if you weren't too young, it's not something you would remember after all these years. Just suddenly, early one morning, he sat up in bed and vomited violently, unstoppably, and then died. He wasn't young, but he hadn't been unwell, so it was a surprise. He had even remarried some ten years before, many years after my mother's death, may God have mercy on her soul. That was when we moved into that house where you came before. I was away studying then, and I came back to find that we had moved house and I had a stepmother. Anyway, after my father died, I stopped the halwa business. I don't know if Nuhu ever thought that would happen one day, but when it did there was nothing for him to do. I realized then I did not even know where he lived, or if he had family. It

---

turned out that he lived in a rented room in a house in Mbuyuni and that his family lived in Pemba. All the years of his life he had worked for my father and now he was going to work for me, whatever I wanted him to do. I could not just tell him to go. He cleaned up in the shop, he ran errands, he transported furniture to customers or to the storehouse. Every morning he turned up for work and he found himself something to do, whether I asked him to or not. If he was a bawab to his master's valuables, it was a post he appointed himself to."

"You make him sound so completely a victim," Latif Mahmud said, with a face that made me feel a fabricator, a teller of self-rewarding stories. "Almost noble in his oppression. And you even cast yourself as someone who benefited from his tragedy. Yet you must have seen his bluster and bullying, you must have heard his loudmouthed banter with other bullies as they swaggered in the streets. You must have known that he was a notorious predator on young boys, tormenting them week after week with offers of coins and packets of halwa until they succumbed, or until his interest forced someone else to make them succumb, after which in their shame they submitted to others. Him and others like him, who thought themselves strong and manly because they could stalk and torment and intimidate young boys until they forced them to submit in shame. You must have known that. When I came to your house all those years ago, that was what I saw. Not the victim who was denied his childhood and made to work in your father's furnace, while you strolled to school. I saw a cannibal who swaggered in his cruelty, a tormentor of the flesh of the young and the poor. Oh God, I'm quarreling with you again."

"Perhaps it's inevitable that you should wish to quarrel with me," I said.

"I would prefer not to," he said, and smiled.

I stared at him for a moment to make sure. "Bartleby," I said. I had not meant it to, but my voice came out in a hushed whisper.

"'Bartleby the Scrivener,'" he said, grinning all over his face, the skin round his eyes creased in lines of surprised pleasure, suddenly happy. "You know the story! It's a beautiful story. Do you like it? You like it too, I can tell. I love the impassive authority of that man's defeat, the noble futility of his life. Tell me how you came to know it. Did you study it? I used to teach that story years ago, when I first started working."

"I just read it. A long time ago. I used to get a surprising number of books when I bought the contents of a house, especially when the British were packing up to go. My time in that business coincided with their departure, so in many ways they were my best customers and I learned a great deal from them."

"Yes, people said you were very fond of the British," he said, his smile suppressed in the corners to suggest that there was more to it than that.

"I know," I said.

"Actually, they said worse than that," he said, grinning now, unable to resist repeating the wisdom he had learned from his own father. "They said you licked British arses, that you were a colonial stooge."

"Yes, I know," I said, but I did not say that it was his father, Rajab Shaaban Mahmud, who had started those stories, and that in addition he had said that I procured women for the British, and spied for them and did whatever else for them. "I sold them furniture and bought their house contents when they were ready to depart. But yes, I know there were other stories. Anyway, sometimes I bought books from them. I don't mean I bought hundreds of books from them, but a dozen here, a few more there. I think some of them were just handed on from one official to another, like part of the furniture. They couldn't have left them behind if they thought they were items of any value. They loved books, you could see that from the number and variety of them that they possessed and carefully packed away. Perhaps they had tired of these particular ones they sold to me, or they already had copies at home. I kept all the books, thinking that one day when I had time I would read them all, or at least try to."

"What kind of books were they?" he asked, still smiling, still thinking of those fevered accusations.

"They were mostly what you'd expect: poetry anthologies and colonial adventures and children's books, some of them already familiar from our colonized education. Rudyard Kipling and Rider Haggard and G. A. Henty. Lots of Kipling, as if they were books they had tired of. And *Origin of Species*, some copies of that, and information books from a more assured time, *The History of the World*, that kind of thing, and some old atlases. They were very interesting, the atlases, so competitive. Not only about how much of the world is colored red and that kind of thing, but pages of illustrations arranged like a ranking order: the tallest mountain in the world is in the British Empire, and then a page of other mountains and whose empire they belonged to, the highest waterfalls in the world, the longest river, the deepest sea, the driest desert. And also illustrations of the denizens of all those mountains and rivers and deserts, grizzled faces with eyes narrowed against the mountain light, spindly potbellied waifs in the savanna, all but naked and holding a bundle of sticks, turbaned peasants at a riverbank, working a waterwheel. But among these books I found the short stories of Herman Melville. I had never heard of him, and I never got to finish the stories at that time, though I did finish them later. I read 'Bartleby the Scrivener' then and thought it very moving. For some reason I was reminded of it when I arrived here, and I have been unable to get it out of my mind completely since then. It comes back to me now and then."

Were there any books among our possessions? I think I saw the thought flicker through his eyes. I don't remember if there were. He dropped his eyes and sat across from me with his chin in his hand, a gesture of quite incredible composure and delicacy.

"Did people ever come to demand their things back as I did that time?" he asked, ready at last. "Do you remember?"

"No, never," I said. "People sold because they needed to sell, or wanted to get rid of furniture they no longer liked. It was a business."

"The little ebony table that belonged to Hassan, my brother. Do you remember it? I came to ask for it back. Do you remember?" he said, still sitting with his chin in his hand. Then after a moment he sat up straighter and looked at me, forcing himself into brazenness. "The one that your friend Hussein gave him before he stole him away. Thirty-four years ago. It's such a long time ago, and to be still scratching away at these things. I haven't heard anything about him since then. He never sent word, not while I was there. Why didn't you just give that table back to her? My mother. Why didn't you just give it back? You had the house, the bits of furniture, all the rubbish. You had a beautiful house of your own, a wife, a daughter Ruqiya, whom you named after the daughter of the Prophet with Khadija. Why did you also have to have the table?"

"I don't know," I said. "Greed. Meanness. It was a business. I wish I had given it back." And what I saw in his eyes made me suspect that he knew less than I thought. His eyes were hurting for himself, for the embarrassment he had to suffer on that errand. And they were hurting for his brother, who ran away after his Persian lover. They were not hurting for my meanness over the table, a meanness for which I was to pay dearly. His eyes were hurting for himself, and for his own failure to care more about what he had left behind. I thought so.

"Thirty-four years ago. Did he ever come back? Hassan. I never heard anything from anybody. I don't even know if there has been any news of him," he said.

I waited for a long moment and when he said no more, I asked, "Will you have some coffee?"

He noticed that I had not responded, and I saw a small sigh escape him, as if he did not really want to know what had happened to his brother, after all. "No, no, I won't have any more coffee. Thank you, but I really should not stay long," he said. "Your daughter Ruqiya, how old would she be now? Thirty or so?"

"She died before her second birthday," I said. "It seems absurd to call her mine. She didn't live long. She died while I was not there, and so did her mother Salha." Beloved.

Ruqiya was born on January 24, 1967. So Salha would have been in confinement when he came to the house to ask for the table, and the voices he would have heard would have been her talking with her mother or one of her many visitors. I knew her for such a short time, and now it seems always with a knowledge of losing her, that sometimes I fear that I imagined her or dreamed her. There were so many unrealities after those four years with her that I lose my certainty of what it was that really happened and what it was I dreaded in my nightmares. She seems more real when other people speak of her and mention something she did, some moment they remember of her in those years when I knew her.

Now, after such a long time, it seems a peevish thing to have done, to have refused to hand over that table. It would have been courteous, generous, even civilized to give it back without a quibble. I did what I did in pique, even though at the time I thought I was being above it all, refusing to take part in the malicious bickering that had preceded that moment.

I think when Hussein asked me for that loan I was flattered. Here was a man who had stories to tell of those distant beautiful places that were only marks on a map for me, those places that were beautiful because they were so distant and fabled. Even if he had not been to all these places himself, the stories involved him and made him seem part of the great world. Also, he told me his stories with such intimate fellowship, and told them in English, intensifying our sense of mutual difference from the place where we were—the puny, ragged, small place where we were. I thought we had become friends through that difference. I was seduced. Asking me for a loan was like anointing me as a man of the world too, an offer of his trust, an embrace. Then also, I had the money. I had done well, and when he asked I could not resist putting on a bit of swagger. But despite being seduced, I don't think I would have agreed to the loan if I had not believed that Hussein would return the following year. I believed that, at least for a while, even though I knew the rumors about his pursuit of the young man. I had no interest in Rajab Shaaban Mahmud's house or in what it contained. I had no idea of the disruption Hussein would cause in that house, that he would spirit that young man away and force the mother into such humiliation, and then speak about his doings to men who thought such escapades amusing, and who would speak to others in mockery. All of that came out after he left, and after the young man had disappeared without a word to anyone. Perhaps Hussein had sworn his admirers to secrecy until he was safely away, or perhaps in the manner of scandals, the details take a little time to be whispered around, or perhaps some of them are only inventions.

I inched forward, speaking as much in gesture as in words and silence. He knew some of what I had to say, and I did not speak to him in exactly the form that I have here, but still I inched forward. It is unbearable to hear some things aloud. So I waited, moved slowly, until I could guess how he was taking my words. He nodded to me and I continued.

This is the story, repeated in convivial exchanges over cups of coffee, and retailed with righteousness and relish: that Hussein was pursuing the young man to great effect when he was staying with the family, and because the mother suspected something like this, she offered herself to him if he would leave her son alone. There were already rumors about her so this shamelessness on her part had a kind of plausibility. Hussein agreed to her offer. There were even details of what he made her do, and any details in such matters can only dishonor. It was at this time that he made the business arrangement with Rajab Shaaban Mahmud, making him a partner in some enterprise he suggested, on the strength of a loan he would negotiate and which would be secured by the house. When he returned the following year, it was to announce that the venture had not prospered but there was no need for panic. In the meantime he continued his seduction of the young man successfully, and secretly arranged for him to follow him to Bahrain. At the end of the musim he returned to Bahrain and the young man disappeared. That was the story.

That was the musim of 1960, the year I met him and he befriended me, and the year he came to me for a loan, and in return gave me the agreement with Rajab Shaaban Mahmud as security. I should have known better, but I didn't. I thought it would be an arrangement, drawn up and witnessed according to the law, and that the following year he would return with the money and collect his security.

By the time the story of his seductions was known and spoken about, I knew that Hussein would not return, and that I too had been duped and seduced. In all likelihood there was no enterprise, and the agreement with Rajab Shaaban Mahmud was an ugly piece of malice and mischief, a fiction to mock the cuckold by getting him to sign his house away. Hussein was probably telling the truth when he said that he had no intention of enforcing the penalty on Rajab Shaaban Mahmud. It was probably just a speculation, a foolishness, humiliating the man as he made free with his loved ones. Then he got to know me, new in business and without any connections or prestige, and something in his fertile brain started to grow, and he waved the paper under my nose and took thousands of shillings from me, promising to return.

I had made a good start in business, but my luck did not stay good, and the loss of that money was irksome. The elections of March 1961, with which the British were preparing us for a kind of minimal self-rule, ended in riots and killings, and the declaration of a state of emergency. Proper troops, British troops, had to be brought in to restore order and assist the King's African Rifles flown in from Kenya. It was all too much for our rulers, and once they had got their charges back into their cages, they began negotiations for independence. In that atmosphere of departure, no one was interested in buying expensive exquisites, and of course the cruise liners no longer made a day stop. That was more or less the end of the business as I was running it. I thought now my best move would be to expand the furniture-making, or at least improve the quality of the furniture I was making for my local custom. To do that I would need a little

more investment in machinery, in expertise and in new premises. My carpenters worked by hand. They sawed and planed by
hand, and painted and varnished laboriously and sometimes
clumsily. Styles were changing, and to get the shapes and quality
of smoothness that was becoming fashionable I needed new machines. I went to Dar es Salaam to see what the big manufactur-
ers were doing there. They were all Indian and all bursting with
complaints about business and politics. Their lives and their enterprises were apparently in a permanent state of impending
collapse. To me they seemed flourishing, and close-lipped as always, telling me half-truths compulsively out of habitual secretiveness. I learned enough, though, to draw up a kind of plan
and to guess at how much money I would need.

After the elections of 1961, when Hussein had not sent any
word by anyone about his affairs, I wrote to him in Bahrain. I
thanked him for the gift of the map and told him how happy it
had made me. Then I asked him when he thought he could repay
the loan I had made to him, and explained why I needed it. He
did not reply to me nor to the letter I asked a solicitor to write to
him. I was in a quandary. In July or so of that year, I sent word to
Rajab Shaaban Mahmud, asking that we should meet to discuss
some business. This was the idea I had in mind, and even now it
seems to me a reasonable and honorable one. I would explain to
him how I came to own the agreement he made with Hussein. I
didn't think he would be aware that I had, in a sense, bought it
from him. I would explain further that I had no desire to possess
his house or its contents, but that I needed the money to reinvest
in my business, to anticipate the changes that would come with
independence. The proposition I would make to him was that he

agree to let me arrange a bank loan on the security of his house. The bank would not know that the house was already mortgaged to me, and as soon as the loan was agreed I would tear up the agreement he had made with Hussein, and the one Hussein had made with me and write off that loan as a business loss. Instead I would make a new agreement with him, Rajab Shaaban Mahmud, promising to repay the bank loan he had taken in my name in agreed installments over so many years, with my business as security. In that way he would regain possession of his house, albeit mortgaged to the bank, and I would be able to invest in my business and repay his bank loan for him. He would lose nothing and regain his house at no cost. There was no accounting wizardry or underhand trickery in what I proposed.

I sent word with Nuhu, to his house, to say simply that there was a matter I wished to discuss with him, and I would be grateful if he would call on me at his convenience. Nuhu brought back no word, just that Rajab Shaaban Mahmud had listened and then thanked him and shut his door. I was unhappy about having to do business with him, as he was not a man I had any fondness or respect for. Before the disaster that befell his household, he walked about with an appearance of humility, but there was a look of grievance on his face, as if he thought life had wronged him. During the day he walked about as if a sudden noise would make him jump, and then in the evenings he went prowling the streets, looking for women who would come to him for money, and then he went drinking. To drink alcohol in that place, after God's edict against its consumption, was simply to have no fear of indignity, to be foolish beyond recklessness because of the mockery and persecution it invited. Everyone has a reckoning to make with God, sooner or later, and that is a matter for them and their creator, but to go drinking in that place was like giving up the right to respect.

His father, Shaaban, had been like that too, but people said that he was as he was because the grandfather Mahmud had been such a holy man, and sometimes things worked out like that, that the children of the pious turn out to be wickedness itself, as if Satan had personally selected them for corruption and sin, so as to expose the thinness of human resolve and demonstrate the power of evil. And Shaaban Mahmud did his sinfulness without any appearance of shame, rolling around drunk in the streets, singing at the top of his voice during all hours of the night, visiting brothels, more or less living in one, and during the day strolling about with the self-important air of someone who saw himself kindly. He even died in his forties, a year before his holy father, making an early exit to save everyone trouble. Rajab Shaaban Mahmud must have been about seven or eight when his father died, about a year or so older than me. I remember that for some reason I used to be terrified of Shaaban Mahmud. If I saw him in the street I ran in the opposite direction without hesitation or dignity, and anyway at six or so I would have had little to do with dignity. He knew that I was scared of him, and once crept up on me when I was playing with other children under the neem tree opposite the police station and put his hands on my shoulders just to hear me squeal and see me run. Then he joined in the laughter of everyone in the street at my ridiculous escape.

Why Rajab Shaaban Mahmud took to the same ways I don't know. It must have happened slowly, secretively. And it was clear to everyone that his weaknesses made him ashamed. Then when the rumors started about his wife, everyone said it served him right. She had lost respect for him and lost respect for herself. It was just as well that his grandfather wasn't alive to see such wickedness. I don't know how true all these stories were. I never saw him whoring and I never saw him drinking, but this was what was said of him, and somehow I thought it was his own foolishness that such stories were told about him, whatever their truthfulness. Then when disaster did strike his household, he turned to religion with such zeal that it made me look away in embarrassment. His humble airs deepened, his voice turned into a whine, and he walked about with his head lowered and turned to one side, like a sacrificial victim. As if everything that had happened was his fault and his punishment, such a display, such arrogance. He was in the mosque all hours after work, reading and praying, acting as if he was already in purgatory, living his life like a slow suicide. I have wondered since then if perhaps the misery and the humiliation and dishonor he suffered at the hands of Hussein took away his mind, took away his sense of the balance between things.

Nevertheless, he had been wronged, and what I had to propose to him was not palatable, even if it was reasonable. In addition, he thought himself wronged by me in other ways, though at that time I was not sure how much of that still stayed with him. So after several days had passed and there had been no further word from him, I spoke to him at the mosque one evening after the maghrib prayers. I went to the mosque when I could, and trusted to God's understanding for the times when I failed to fulfill his demand of me on time. I carried, in this way, an enormous loan to my creator. On this occasion I expected that I would meet Rajab Shaaban Mahmud at his usual place, a pace or two from the mihrab. I asked if I could call on him to discuss a matter there was between us, or if he had time to call on me at the shop sometime in the early afternoon the next day, a time of day when he would have come back from work and when I usually shut the shop for a couple of hours because everyone was sleeping off the heat of the afternoon. Haya, he said. He'd be there.

I left one of the folding doors of the shop slightly ajar, so no passerby should think that we were whispering something disreputable between us, and so that we would get a little air from the street. He sat on the small wooden bench where I usually seated my visitors, a delicate slatted folding bench, curved very slightly to accommodate the bend of the back and the bulge of the buttocks, so that when you sat on the bench it felt as if the slats moved marginally to fit you. There were lacy brass chasings on the top bar across the back, and the folding frame was made of light cast iron painted black. The bench once belonged to a Gujarati banker who was powerful in the years before the war in 1939, but whose fortunes declined after that. His name was still engraved on the brass plate fixed to the center of the backrest, with the date 1926, which perhaps coincided with the time of his greatness. It came to me when one of his descendants, now a travel agent, decided to modernize his office furniture, and sold me that and one or two other items as part-payment for the refitting my carpenters would do in his premises. Rajab Shaaban Mahmud sat on this beautiful relic with his eyes lowered and his head turned slightly away. I sat near him, on a chair in front of my desk. I did not feel encouraged by his demeanor.

It was a hot afternoon just about the beginning of Kaskazi, when the seas roughen and the winds begin to change to north-easterlies that will eventually steady into the monsoons. From a clay ewer I poured each of us a glass of water which had been steeped in aromatic gum to give it fragrance. I loved water like this, with the special coolness of clay and the zest and perfume of gum. I began by explaining how I had come by the agreement he had made with Hussein. As I suspected, he did not know that it was in my possession. He stared at me with surprise and perhaps a little terror, and for a moment I thought he would weep or let out a cry and flee. When I began on my proposition, he frowned slightly and then dropped his eyes again. I had decided that I would state my proposal plainly, and make no attempt to persuade or embellish until he had made a response. I suppose I expected that he would be resistant, but to be honest I did not think he would have much choice but to agree in the end. He refused, of course.

He sat in silence for a minute or two after I had finished, his eyes still downcast, and it was so hard to resist saying more. Then he looked into my face and said that he could not believe that he had really heard me say the things I had said. How could I sit there beside him and say such things after all that had happened to him and his people. I must have planned it from the beginning, with that wicked liar, that dog, that evil. He did not say his name. We must have arranged it all between us, from the beginning. More and more like that. "I can't believe you really said that to me, I really can't believe. You must have planned all this from the beginning." Every time I tried to speak, he shot out an index finger in warning. *Be quiet.* Sweat was standing in little bubbles on his brow and streaming down his cheeks. His eyes were bulging with affront and rage, and between indignant remarks he muttered prayers to calm himself. When eventually he paused, I tried to explain that I could not have planned to lose such a large amount of money, and that what I was suggesting involved only nominal risk to him, since by the agreement between us, my business would secure the loan he would obtain from the bank. I don't think he listened to a word I said.

When I finished speaking, he rose to his feet and flung out an outstretched arm like a melodramatic prince in a movie, a rigid index finger pointing at me in accusation. "You're a thief," he said. "You stole my aunt's house from her, and now you want to steal this one from me. What have we done to you and yours that you should be so vengeful to us? Or is it simply that you think we are weak and foolish? You're a thief." He was shouting at the top of his voice by now, pointing and spitting at me, walking backward toward the doorway as if he feared I might rise and attack him. He kicked the door fully open and stood fuming there for another moment or two. "Thieving dog," he said in final benediction. "You stole that house from us and now you want to steal what little we have left. Oh, I really can't believe that God could have made someone as wicked as you." And with that he slid into the bright sunlight and disappeared.

Our conversation had not taken very long, perhaps ten minutes or so. He had not touched the glass of water, so I picked it up and went to the door to throw it out into the street. There was not a soul in sight, but somehow I felt as if there had been an audience in the street, listening to Rajab Shaaban Mahmud's accusations. It must have been the paranoia of living habitually cheek by jowl with people. There was no one there, although an audience wasn't necessary on such occasions. I felt sure that in his indignation Rajab Shaaban Mahmud would pour his story out without delay. I had been to the bank myself, of course, to try and arrange a loan. I tried all three banks in the town, and they all refused. British bank managers always refused us loans, and all three bank managers were British, I think. They were European, anyway. When I say *us*, I mean any merchants or businessmen who were not Indian. I merely state this here. It was their own money, and they could appoint whoever they wished to manage it, and give it to whoever they thought most likely to safeguard it and increase it. I merely state here that European bank managers did not think us trustworthy or talented in business, so they always refused loans, to my knowledge. So I was still in a quandary. There was no possibility now of any arrangement with Rajab Shaaban Mahmud, not after all the accusations of historical crimes. I found the accusations shocking, although I was not surprised to hear them. Nobody had ever said that to my face before although I had intimations from the rumors which had been reported to me by the gossiping sages.

So it was really pride that made you go ahead with the repossession," Latif Mahmud said, sneering at me, enjoying the discomfiture I had described. I had feared that he would not be able to bear listening to what I had to say, that he would rage at me for my lies and fabrications and then leave. I did not tell him everything I have described here, but nearly, very nearly. More or less.

"Yes, perhaps it was pride," I said. "And the injustice of the accusations. Also, I needed the money, as I have said. I felt I had no choice."

He nodded. I thought he would be getting hungry and would be wanting to go away now before I said any more, but he made no move to leave, only saying that he should go. I did not offer him food. I had very little to offer, and perhaps not the kind of thing he would consider food. In the evening I boiled a banana, or a piece of marrow or a slice of pumpkin and ate that sprinkled with sugar. Then I drank a glass of warm water and that was enough to see me through the night. I wanted him to go with what he had and come back later, but I also did not want him to go yet. I wanted to find a place to stop and say to him, That will do for now, I'm tired. Go now and come back another day.

"I remember when he came home that day," Latif Mahmud said quietly, looking away from me, looking back. "Well, I remember the story about how you had stolen the house from his aunt and now you wanted to steal our house. I don't even know if I remember that day, but I remember the story. It was the story of my youth. When I read 'Bartleby' for the first time I realized that that was how I thought of my father, resigned in his futility and you his persecutor. I learned to read the story differently later, to see that it was not all about resignation and futility, but the first time I saw him in it. You found the story moving. I remember you said that. Moving. Why didn't you find him moving? My father. Did you find him moving? Do you mind me describing you as his persecutor? I mean of course you must mind, but do you find it annoying, improper, discourteous beyond bearing?"

I shook my head, feeling tired now, wanting him to go, thinking that I would open a tin of sweet red beans after he had gone and eat them cold. I did not know if I had the strength of mind to speak under challenge about all those miseries again.

"Just a moment ago I was thinking that I can't really believe that this is happening," Latif Mahmud said, angry and perhaps getting tired too. "The unlikeliness of it. I thought it would be you. I don't know why. I would have no reason to think it would be you, just a guess, an intuition. Then even when I thought that, I did not want to come here. There didn't seem any good reason to do so apart from to speak angrily to you, and after such a long time I didn't want to do that. Now I think it was that I was not really angry but felt I would have to be. If I was angry with anyone it was with myself, although I think it is more feeling guilty and defensive about my ignorance, about the distance I have managed to create between my life and those times. Do you mind me talking to you like this? Now I've come and you're talking to me so openly, I can't believe this is really happening. I can't believe the luck of it. I don't want to hear what you are saying. I didn't know I wanted this kind of luck, but I must have done because I came. There you are, in addition to everything else I want to grant myself the luxury of having acted as I have because I know what I'm doing. As if that is how I conduct myself, instead of stumbling from one constraint to another, hiding and risking nothing. Then we have been open and courteous when I had not imagined it would be like that when I came. I think I imagined you as a kind of relic, a metaphor of my nativity, and that I would come and examine you while you sat still and dissembling, fuming ineffectually like a jinn raised from infernal depths. Do you mind me talking to you like this?"

"If you have to," I said. "Which jinn do you have in mind? Which jinn sitting still and dissembling, fuming ineffectually?"

"Do you mean which story?" he asked, smiling, frowning, trying to tease out a memory. "I can't remember. I have an image."

"Horned? Does the jinn in the image have a horn? One horn in the middle of a huge forehead?" I asked.

"Yes," he said triumphantly, grinning all over his face, and for a second he looked like his mother rather than the brooding self-punishing man he had been all afternoon. He had something of her suicidal gaiety. "You are a clever old one, aren't you? All right then, tell me which one, which story."

"'Qamar Zaman,'" I said. "That story has the stillest, shiftiest jinn in the whole *A Thousand and One Nights*. With a horn in the middle of his forehead. My favorite jinn, an utter grotesque, which is how you imagined me."

"No, no, definitely not 'Qamar Zaman,'" he said. "I know that story very well."

"Well, which, then? You're the expert. Which story has a jinn raised from infernal depths who is sitting still and dissembling, and fuming ineffectually? That fits the jinn in 'Qamar Zaman' perfectly."

"No, it wasn't that one. I don't remember which yet, but I'll find it. I'll tell you next time I come."

It was turning into a gloomy evening outside, still light but with that heavy watery grayness that so leadens the heart. I looked out of the window, ostentatiously, to persuade him to remark on the lateness of the hour. If he was coming back another time perhaps he could go away now and let me rest and collect my thoughts. Let me restore order in my catacomb.

"Am I tiring you? I must go soon," he said. "Tell me one thing. You said that you pressed on with the case because of the injustice in my father's accusations. What injustice? Will you untangle that for me?"

I shook my head. "That's a long story, and perhaps it will be a difficult one to listen to. Hasn't enough been said for today?"

"I can listen if you feel able to continue," he said, looking shamefaced because he knew he was insisting, but a little superior too because he was demanding to be told, challenging me to make good my claim.

I knew I would tell him. I needed to be shriven. Not to be forgiven or to be cleansed of my sins, which were ones of pettiness and vanity rather than wickedness, and whose consequences had already been steep for me and for others. Little could be done to lighten those sins, I needed to be shriven of the burden of events and stories which I have never been able to tell, and which by telling would fulfill the craving I feel to be listened to with understanding. He was my shriver, and I knew I would tell him what he had asked of me. Then after telling him, I would have found a good place to stop and tell him that even Shahrazad managed to get some rest every sunrise. I was just pressing home my advantage, pretending greater reluctance than I really felt, to make sure he would go after I answered him. And he had spoken well about himself, and I did not wish to seem ungiving in return. So I made a pot of sweet black tea and resumed.

The first I knew about the complications surrounding the ownership of the house was when I returned from Makerere College in 1950. I had been away for more than three years, not hurrying back when my course was completed. I had made two very good friends in my time in Kampala, Sefu Ali who was from Malindi in Kenya and was studying Fine Art, and Jamal Hussein who lived in Bukoba on the Tanganyika shore of Lake Victoria, who was studying Business Administration. Sefu was passionate about everything and spoke as if he only had himself and his conscience to satisfy, a proper artist. Jamal was studying business because his family wanted him to, and was more likely to champion responsibility and useful skills when Sefu launched one of his diatribes against custom and duty. I was studying Civil Administration, and at the time seemed doomed to be a clerk in the colonial government. Our rooms in the hall of residence were in the same corridor, right next to each other. We may have been doing different courses, but otherwise we did everything together. We studied for our various tests and examinations together. We went to the refectory as a group. At that time we were only allowed to enter the refectory with our red student gowns on, as if we were Oxford on the Equator. We strolled to the town together, played football, loafed under the enormous fig trees, broke fast at the end of each day of Ramadhan, celebrated Idd together. Everything.

It was adolescent, I suppose, and some of the other students teased us, saying we even went to the toilet together and what else. But it was a wonderful time, and we had a kind of fellowship which we expected to last a lifetime. I don't remember us ever saying such a thing, but with hindsight I know that that is what I expected, the kind of fellowship you had with a brother, unexamined and permanent. Pardon, I never had a brother. By making that comparison I am speaking of another of my optimistic expectations perhaps, wishing I did and imagining what it would be like to have one. Anyway, after our studies were over, we were reluctant to separate. I felt sadder about separating from these good friends than I had felt about anything else, except for the death of my beloved mother, may God have mercy on her soul, and her death when I was eleven felt more like a natural disaster than a separation, a convulsion, a tidal wave, an eclipse of light.

So, to delay the moment of rupture somewhat, we decided that we would visit each other's homes for a few months, staying for a month or two or for as long as parents, or the various government offices to which Sefu and I were bound to be deployed, allowed us to. For a start, we stayed on at the campus after everyone left, sleeping late, playing cards, learning tennis, or whatever, secure in the unassailable sense of frivolity which comes with such assurance when you are young and away from home. In the end the bursar, who was a kind and understanding man as a rule, ran out of patience with us and chased us away. Then we went to Bukoba, to stay with Jamal Hussein's family. We took a lake ferry from Entebbe for the crossing, and I remember it rained all the way, forcing down the endless papyrus on the shores and turning the lake surface into dark quicksilver. Lightning sheeted across the low-hanging sky and the wind howled like a creature terrified. That was the only time I made the crossing, and it saddens me that all I saw was this gothic extravaganza, not to mention the rising panic of all the passengers as the ship staggered about in that downpour.

Jamal Hussein's family ran a hardware business, pots and pans, and hammers and nails, and flowery enamel-coated bowls and trays spilling onto the curb out of a large gloomy shop in the main street. They also ran another business which sold bicycles and farming equipment in an airy warehouse on the edge of town. With the beginning of postwar prosperity, the family firm had opened a car showroom and a one-pump service station next to the farm equipment warehouse, specializing in Austin cars. It was either that or Morris cars. This was British Tanganyika, where it was not so easy to become a dealer in *foreign* cars like Ford or Peugeot. In short, it was a prosperous family business, perhaps on the verge of becoming very wealthy. I never quite worked out the personnel, and how they were all related to each other, but there were various uncles and cousins working tirelessly about their affairs, striding about with dramatic airs at times, and at other times congregated in raucous huddles to share gossip and news or enjoy some respite from their endless anxieties. There were aunts and more cousins equally restless at home, cooking, washing, coming and going, apparently shouting at each other. I say apparently because I couldn't understand what they were saying since they spoke to each other in Gujarati, and so I could not tell if the shouting was sustained low-level bickering, or whether it was an exchange on ordinary practicalities like whose turn it was to sweep the yard or something similar. Their ill-tempered gestures, though, often suggested the former.

The whole extended family lived in two large houses along-side each other, with a shared backyard that was fenced off all round with chicken wire and a pigeon-pea hedge. In the yard, which Jamal called the garden, there were some banana trees, jasmine bushes, a guava tree, a small bed of herbs by the back door and a chicken run. There was a concreted area in a corner with an outside tap where the washing was done by a dhobi who came in every day except Sunday, and lengths of washing line crisscrossed the yard in every direction. Sefu and I were given a room in an outbuilding in the yard. The outbuilding had two rooms with their own outside doors, and a toilet in between. The other room, which was kept locked, was used as a store, and sometimes we saw a cousin come to fetch household supplies from there.

I had sensed the tension when we arrived. Jamal had not warned his family about our arrival, and had assumed from the stories he told them about us that they would be happy to have his friends stay with them. It was probably part of that same sense of well-being which made us so happy in those last months in Kampala. Jamal was the only one of the three of us who lived near enough to Kampala to go home regularly during vacations, just a ferry trip across the lake, although Sefu also made the journey to the coast once at the end of his first year to attend to a family bereavement. I know Jamal told his family about his friends in Kampala, because some of the cousins repeated to us tales of our sillier escapades. From all this Jamal thought that we would all sleep in his room, or the room he shared with which-ever of his brothers and cousins. Seeing the close-knit and pur-poseful way they lived, instantly on seeing that, and seeing the young female cousins of the house, I knew that we could not possibly be made welcome in the household. But it distressed Jamal that we were housed in one of the stores, and he was sensitive to the possibility that we might see this as disregard.

They were not really stores, the toilet in between them made that obvious, but rooms intended for the servant or the gardener. It was just that the family did not employ such personages and so could put the rooms to other uses. We tried to make a joke of it to Jamal, saying how nice it was to step out of the door and into the garden in the morning, how we could stay up late playing cards without disturbing the family, how private we were. But there were other tensions. We ate separately, called to fetch our dishes by one of Jamal's sisters, always the same flowery enamel bowls as if they had been set aside for us. And Jamal himself was often required to attend to various obligations which he did not always explain to us. Above all, it distressed Sefu that the aunts and cousins spoke about us to our faces, in Gujarati, staring at us with undisguised impatience when we appeared in the yard. After a few days, Jamal explained that he was required to attend daily at one or other of the family business premises, and so we would not be able to make those trips to interesting places nearby as he had promised us. Though we would be able to join the family the following Sunday when they went for a picnic some miles up the lake road.

We were only able to last there for about two weeks or so in the end. One afternoon, Sefu and I were walking along the back of the houses, heading for the passage that led to the road and then to our intended stroll by the lakeshore. Jamal was nowhere in sight, although he had said that if he could get away he would join us for a walk. Suddenly a gush of warm water hit us from above, and we both looked up just in time to see a woman's face at an upstairs window grinning at us before disappearing inside. Then we heard excited laughter, and a moment later three other faces appeared at the window to admire the spectacle. There was nothing more to be done after that, especially since we were both convinced it was used soapy water they had thrown at us. We had cleaned ourselves and changed and packed our few belongings by the time Jamal came hurrying down from the house, shouting over his shoulder. As soon as he appeared, full of explanations and apologies, Sefu picked up his large clumsy case and struggled out of the room. I followed right behind him, of course. When we were almost on the road, he turned to Jamal and said, "You're arrogant stupid shits, all of you." I said to Jamal, "Write to him, you have his address. Don't leave things like this." But he never wrote. It was so sad. Perhaps he was too ashamed to, or perhaps he decided that there was nothing to write about. I remember the sweet plums they grew there in Bukoba and the violet light off the lake in late afternoon.

Sefu and I took a bus to Mwanza and then another one to Kisumu and from there caught the train to Nairobi and finally Mombasa. It took four days of travel, sleeping at the bus depot one night and then on the train. We spent the night in Mombasa with one of Sefu's relatives and then took a bus to Malindi the following morning. Being back on the coast was like being at home, or more than that, like recognizing that here I had a place in the scheme of things. So much of what I had learned in Kampala was crushing, glimpses of the extent of my ignorance, and the self-assured puniness we lived with. Back on the coast, I felt

part of something generous and noble after all, a way of living
that had a part for me and which I had been too hasty in seeing as futile raggedness. I spent three months with Sefu and his
various relatives, traveling everywhere along the coast as far north
as Pate and Lamu, stopping for a few days where Sefu knew
someone or had been given the name of someone who would welcome us, then getting on the bus or on a boat to go somewhere
else. Everywhere we went we were treated like sons of the family,
and shared whatever hospitality was available. Everywhere we
went, it seemed, someone knew who Sefu was, even when it was
someone he had never met before. It was an incredible time, and
everywhere people opened their arms to me too. Sefu tried to
persuade me to stay and find work in Kenya, but he knew I
couldn't, since the terms of my scholarship were that I would return to work for the colonial administration for a period of at
least three years.

Some weeks after first arriving on the coast, I had written to
my father to tell him where I was and to explain I was on my slow
way home. I had written not expecting a reply. After all, he had
not replied to a single one of my few and desultory communica-
tions over the previous three or so years. This had not seemed to
me unkind, I did not think of him as unkind. I sent him news
now and then because I was obliged to, whereas fathers did not
write letters unless they had something they wanted to commu-
nicate, some instruction or prohibition. He wrote to me in Malindi, saying that it was now time I was back, as a government
official had been to see him to inquire of my whereabouts. I was
required to report to my new posting as soon as possible, as this
was my duty, and one which I seemed to have forgotten. In any

case it was time I was back as there were other matters to see to, and would I be sure to let him know which ship I would be arriving by as he intended to meet it. That last instruction was the oblique announcement of his remarriage, although I was not to understand its meaning until I got back.

My father had married two years before. When he first told me, I thought it a futile act. We were walking home from the docks, and I was in the euphoria of returning after so long, exchanging greetings with people I had not seen for years, so I could not have been very attentive. But I know that between grinning and waving to the people we passed, I thought to myself: Why would an old man like you wish to marry? I did not say anything like that to him, of course. He would have swatted me across the road without a second's hesitation, for my insolence. In any case, I'm glad I didn't because I know different now. I know that you never stop wishing to live, or wishing for companionship and purpose. He must have been concerned that I might take the news badly, because of the way my mother had been so loved by both us. But that never troubled me, not then, not ever. When we arrived at the house, the house he had moved to since his remarriage, I remembered the people who used to live there before. "This is your mother," my father said, and his wife and I kissed politely and made courteous conversation. I should have said "my stepmother" instead of "his wife," but I never thought of her like that. She was my father's wife. I remembered her from before as Bi Maryam, and that was what I called her always, without disrespect.

I said I remembered the people who used to live in the house before, and that may give the impression that they were distant from me. Perhaps I should have said that I knew very well who they were. Bi Maryam's former husband had been a nahodha, a dhow captain and a man of business. Everyone knew who he was. A nahodha cut a figure in the streets, a man of the sea striding about, attending to merchandise and technicalities, calling and urging porters and crew before the tide turned or the wind dropped. When he walked past, going about his affairs, people greeted him and called out to him, sometimes by name and sometimes by his calling. I did not remember his death, so it must have happened while I was away in Kampala, and my father must have snapped up Bi Maryam as soon as she was out of mourning. I have no idea how that came about or what made him do it, or for that matter what made her do it. All I can say is that in the years I lived with them they seemed untroubled in their ways, and as self-righteous and opinionated as you might expect. If I had not known otherwise, I would have thought they had been living together for decades rather than the few years since their remarriage. One always seemed to know the other's opinion, and I never saw them contradict each other when it mattered. When my father was on the attack about something, Bi Maryam would be sure to have a little pebble or a small dart that she could hurl as well. Her methods generally were more subtle than my father's, who was inclined to insist and take offense when he did not get his way. When my father desired a particular delicacy or Bi Maryam was unhappy about an arrangement, their wishes never seemed irksome to each other, at least not in front of me. In brief, though I do not wish to appear casual or unimpressed in saying this, they seemed content.

What I do know is this, because my father told me a few

weeks after my return, so that I would know what was going on
when the gossip reached me, as it was bound to in the end. I repeat here what I understood and believed. I honor my father to
this extent, even though in many ways he was ignorant and hardheaded, and as greedy as any man raised in the hardship and
acquisitiveness of their time. I believe that he too spoke to me as
he understood things to be, that he told me what it was possible
for him to tell me. I did not ask him if he had married Bi Maryam
in haste, if he had leaped at the widow because of her wealth. I
could not ask him that. He would have thought it disrespectful.
And he probably thought of himself as lucky and resourceful to
have acquired the rich widow before anyone else could. I don't
know if that was how it was, or if for years he had been fond of
Bi Maryam, and then moved swiftly when the opportunity came.

What I do know is this. Bi Maryam's first husband, Nassor
the nahodha, whom everyone liked and who was greeted with
smiles and greetings in the streets, had his own everyday story of
family squabbles over inheritance. First of all, his relatives denied him his inheritance from his father. They took everything
even before he was born, shared it all out between them while he
was still contentedly rocking in his amnesiac broth, wrapped
tight in his amniotic caul. He was born after his father's death,
an orphan, and his male relatives took what there was and shared
it between them while he was still pending, leaving nothing for
him. Not even a length of cloth for a shroud, as older people
used to say. This had happened in Oman, in the town of Muscat.
His mother also received nothing from her husband. Instead she
was offered marriage by one of her husband's brothers as soon
as she was out of mourning. The brother already had two other

wives and a crowd of children by them, but he offered Nassor's mother marriage as a way of giving her protection and respectability, he said. She thought she had no choice but to accept, as she saw no other way to clothe her shame and abandonment. His mother's new husband also took Nassor, and brought him up as a dependent relative in his house.

When Nassor was old enough to understand such things, his mother told him how his birthright had been stolen. Treachery had been committed on both of them, she told him, while she was probably huddled up in a dark place and weeping for her poor husband. What the relatives had done was against God's law, she told him, which stipulated the laws of inheritance with precision. Here they are. When a person died, his property was disposed of in this manner: (1) the debts of the deceased had to be repaid, as well as any other business or public obligations; (2) half of the remaining inheritance was to be divided equally between surviving male children; (3) a third was to be divided between surviving wives; (4) the rest was to be divided between the daughters. Since Nassor was the only male offspring of his father, or any kind of offspring come to that, he should have inherited at least half of what his father owned. This was two houses in Muscat and a piece of land with some date palms in their home village. And she, his only wife, should have received a third of what he had left. The relatives knew that she was with child at the time of Nassor's father's death, and hurried with the distribution of the inheritance so the child would have no claim. And she, Nassor's mother, was required to marry one of the relatives and so forfeited her own third. What they had done to them was treachery and sin. The law was clear on this matter, set out in detail in the Book, although she could not name sura and line. The Prophet himself had been born an orphan, and he too had inherited nothing from his father. His birthright was divided up among his uncles, while he became a poor ward of his grandfather's and was raised by Bedouin in the desert. That was why God's Book specified the portion of inheritance each relative was to have, to avoid the injustices of the time of ignorance.

At an early age, perhaps twelve or thirteen, Nassor made the musim journey to our part of the world for the first time, as some kind of shipboy, and after that he came back every year. That was also when he discovered his talent for the sea, and when he returned to Muscat he became a sailor, indentured by his uncle to various nahodhas from whom he received Nassor's wages. Matters went on like this for years, and would have gone on like that until his death, for his uncle's sons would have seen no reason to treat him any differently when it came their turn to be heads of the family. His mother was safe, for she had produced children in her marriage to his uncle, but Nassor was only a dependent relative and had to make himself useful as best he could. His mother hectored him and harangued him, prodding him to make a claim for his father's inheritance, but Nassor knew that if he did so, if he even dared so much as to utter the possibility of such a notion, his cousins would beat him and expel him from the family, and soon after that his life would end mysteriously. So one musim he did not return, sending a letter to his mother saying that he would go back when he could, meaning that he would go back if he had to, if all else failed or if she found herself in difficulty because of his absence. He must have been seventeen or eighteen then, and he found work as a sailor on ships trading all along the coast. He was hardworking, sharp-witted and frugal, and by the time he was thirty or so, he was a partner in several small enterprises and was part owner of the dhow he was nahodha to.

In all the years Nassor had not gone back to Muscat once. One musim he received a letter from his uncle, delivered by the hand of one of the merchants. It congratulated him on the prosperity he had achieved, word of which had reached them in Muscat. His uncle now required him to return so he could marry while his mother was still alive and able to share in the celebrations. They had already selected a wife for him, one of his cousins, and would expect him to arrive with the return musim. Nassor wrote back gleefully to announce that he was already married and did not require another wife, and that he would endeavor to visit when business and health allowed him to. Which was never. But he understood now that his relatives knew about his affairs, and began to fear for his new family should an accident befall him. Therefore when he came to buy a house, he put it in the name of Bi Maryam, so it would be safe from his grasping relatives should he die unexpectedly, as those working at sea were always in danger of doing. He planned that when the children came, he would put the business in their names, so that they too would be safe. But no children came, sadly. This too was reported to his relatives, who renewed the offer of a wife, and sent pleas by his mother that he should remember his duty to ensure that his father's name did not die out.

Nassor had lived a contented life with Bi Maryam until his family discovered him, and these new approaches decided him. He resolved to put everything he owned solely in her name, the entire business, because there was no law to prevent him from disposing of his property as he wished while he lived. That way, if anything happened to him, the relatives could get up to whatever they pleased but his wife would be safe. But because he wanted to keep the arrangement secret, so that it would not cause anxiety among his partners and associates, he delayed doing so for far too long. In the end, God in his mercy took him away before he could do so, not at sea as he feared but from a stroke which felled him as he rose early at the start of a new day. While Bi Maryam was still in mourning and therefore unable to receive male visitors or conduct business, a cousin came from Muscat to represent the claims of the family. Since there were no male children, according to the law the relatives were able to obtain most of Nassor's property after his debts had been paid off. Except the house. That was safe. And Bi Maryam did receive a third share of what was left, as the law required, though the bulk of the property went to the relatives. Everyone who knew of the outcome rejoiced in Bi Maryam's good fortune and applauded the resourcefulness and care of Nassor the nahodha, who was even better liked in his death than he had been while living. No one muttered a word against God's law.

Now I should explain who Bi Maryam was and who she was related to. I have held this back in order to tell Nassor's story without complications. Maryam was the youngest daughter of the pious Mahmud. There were three of them: the eldest was Sara, who was followed by Shaaban and then came Maryam. Shaaban was the same carousing mad dog who was the father of Rajab Shaaban Mahmud. In short, my father's wife Bi Maryam was the aunt of Rajab Shaaban Mahmud.

When Bi Maryam married Nassor, her father was still alive, and it was seen by many as a blessing on the nahodha that the pious old man agreed to this union, despite the terrible suspicions people had of men who worked the sea. What suspicions? Men who worked the sea spent so long away from decent scrutiny that there was no knowing what perversities they indulged in. And then the sea and all its unruly emptiness had a way of turning minds, making people intense and eccentric, or even strangely violent. But the pious Mahmud had no hesitations about Nassor the nahodha, and nor did Bi Maryam.

Her brother, Shaaban, was also still alive, reeling and singing through the streets most evenings and bringing shame and misery on his father, but he was happy with the man Bi Maryam had chosen for a husband, a man known for his generosity and for his good nature, and rarely to be seen in a mosque on account of his dedication to business. Shaaban preferred to avoid people who frequented mosques unduly.

The eldest, her sister Sara, was on her third marriage as Bi Maryam was starting on her first, having seen her first two husbands die on her without very much delay. Her third husband was a short plump man with quiet manners and an addiction to snuff, a most effaceable man. Bi Sara was only four years older than Bi Maryam but was something of an invalid and gloomy in outlook, always expecting the worst, which made her a little overfond of adding a cataclysmic edge to the mildest bit of gossip or scandal. She had had no children, and did not seem likely to have any, if her many ailments were taken into account. But her previous widowhood had not been unprofitable, and after the death of her second husband, she had inherited the small house she lived in. It would be unkind to suggest that it was the house which brought her her third husband, but despite her piety she had very few other charms that would have appealed to one, and her expectation of gloom would have discouraged many. It was this same little house, which Bi Sara inherited from her second husband, that was later to become the object of contention between Rajab Shaaban Mahmud and me.

By the time Nassor the nahodha died so suddenly, a decade or so later, Shaaban was already dead, expiring quickly after a short, uncertain illness. His father, Mahmud, followed a few months later. Bi Sara's third husband had also succumbed, and she had not bothered to acquire another one, or perhaps her reputation for disposing of husbands was now so terrifying that she had not managed to persuade anyone to risk an early departure by marrying her. She invited Rajab Shaaban Mahmud, his beautiful wife Asha and their two children to live with her. She would have asked them to move in sooner but she had to wait until after the death of Rajab Shaaban Mahmud's mother. She would not have been able to abide that woman in her house, she said, because of what she described as her disgusting, unhygienic habits, releasing foul-smelling farts without any appearance of restraint, and then laughing as her potent gases made people grumble and scatter. I had no experience of her performances myself, but her behavior was legendary. She must have had an illness in her bowels, and it was said that she was not completely well in her head.

So by the time Nassor the nahodha died, worrying until the last moment, no doubt, about securing his property to his dear wife, the only adult male relative Bi Maryam had in the whole world was Rajab Shaaban Mahmud. In such matters a male relative is essential, to be present at negotiations and to agree to arrangements, and just generally to ensure that courtesies are observed. Rajab Shaaban Mahmud was in his late twenties at that time, married and a father of two children, but he was mild of manner and demeanor, and probably intimidated by Nassor's greedy relative. It was Bi Sara who instructed him to consult my father, who if nothing else was a solvent businessman and known to be reliable in matters of delicacy.

Bi Sara had been a friend of my mother years ago, and until the end insisted that I called her aunt, or when her emotions were high, that I called her mother. After my mother's death, she consulted my father on various matters to which I was not privy because of my youth. Perhaps she might even have considered him as one of her replacement husbands at some stage or another, to be kept warm until the moment of need arrived. Perhaps. There is no end to the variety of ways we maneuver and outmaneuver each other and ourselves. In any case, now Bi Sara sent Rajab Shaaban Mahmud to my father for advice, and he probably did what he could to be wise and worldly, but none of it was enough to prevent the relatives walking away with most of Nassor's property. Maybe that was how my father came to be there at the head of the list of suitors when Bi Maryam's period of mourning was over, or perhaps she was grateful to him for whatever he did to help, or perhaps Bi Sara did some urgent matchmaking. I never asked my father or Bi Maryam to tell me about how their marriage came about. Perhaps they just simply chose each other. He was fifty and she was nearly forty when they married, childless after more than a decade as a wife to a man that everyone held to be worthy and kind. There was no desperation about her when I first knew her. She was forty years old, a woman of property and maturity, not a child whose life was hostage to her parents, and her choice was made with some knowledge of the world. When I saw them together after returning from Kampala, they seemed content, and lived their lives that way for the eight years together that remained to them. I never asked how they came to marry in the first place, for to see the way they shuffled themselves for each other's convenience was to imagine that this was something they wanted.

The house we lived in before I went to Kampala was the one I was born in and where my mother died so painfully in 1941. As a child I was not told what she died of, but I remember the suddenness of it and the agony in her face and the unbearable sounds she made. Later, after I returned from Kampala, I asked my father what she had died of and he said it was a burst appendix. In his ignorance he had not known about such things, and thought it was something in her bowels, some blockage or constriction, so he had given her a laxative. People at that time had great faith in laxatives. He wanted to fetch a taxi and take her to the hospital, but she said no, let the laxative work. She tried to be brave, until then it was too late and the poison spread inside her and made her die in such torment. He took her to the hospital in the end, and the doctor there, an Englishman, shouted at him in words he could not understand but he knew they referred to his ignorance and his negligence. The nurse did not translate to save his feelings, just made sympathetic noises, but he knew the doctor was angry with him for having let her die so painfully. That was what your mother died of, he said, gulping his sobs. May God have mercy on her soul.

We rented two upstairs rooms with our own front door and an outside staircase. It was not uncommon to build like that at the time. I lived there all my life until I went to Kampala. While my mother was alive, the front door was open all day, and women visitors came and went, or sent their children on neighborly errands. After she died, my father kept the front door padlocked or bolted on the inside, and when I came home I had to go and find him or knock on the door to have him let me in. My father had the front room overlooking the main road, and I had the back room with a view of the muddy creek where fishermen dug for bait. When the moon was full, the tide came all the way up the creek and transformed that stinking inlet into a glittering lagoon.

After his marriage to Bi Maryam, my father gave up our old rented house and moved into his wife's, taking all our things with him. So in a sense he moved me as well even before I knew about my dislocation. They spent a large sum of money improving the house over the years, and a lot of it must have been his, for aside from the house itself, Bi Maryam had not inherited much money from her husband. It was a new passion for my father. He had not shown any interest in decorating or improving his surroundings in the years I lived with him, and I don't ever remember the rooms being painted or anything being replaced unless it had stopped functioning, and even then, not always or not with any great urgency. When I returned from Kampala, my father had become meticulous and demanding about the house he shared with Bi Maryam. Her former husband, the nahodha, had been esteemed for his generosity to others, but he had not been too generous to himself or his wife. The house had no electricity. Its bathroom was gloomy and stuffy, ventilated by two narrow slits high up on the wall, a dungeon, a place of shameful necessities. Some of the ceiling beams in the house were worm-ridden and the decoration was in need of refreshing. Bi Maryam and my father made many small alterations while they were modernizing the house, adding windows and latticed shutters and potted plants, which made it lighter and more airy, and beautiful.

I think all the anxieties about property that Bi Maryam had lived with during her years with Nassor the nahodha must have been with her in her time with my father. Or perhaps they had found something more than contentment in their marriage, and she wanted to commemorate it in an act of trust and love. She had the house that Nassor the nahodha had so resourcefully saved for her, made out jointly in my father's and her name. I did not know about this until after his death, when Bi Maryam, overwhelmed by grief and shock at this second deprivation, told me about what she had done. She did this while they were both alive, so that neither of them should be tormented by relatives, whichever of them was forced to go first. Only she never really thought it would be so soon, so sudden, so without warning.

On the night of his death I heard her shouting and calling, and I knew even before I got upstairs that it was him and he was dying. His face was still moving when I got there, while Bi Maryam knelt beside the bed, her hands moving frantically over him, as if looking for something to pull or turn or switch off. His face was still moving but he was not breathing. His bedclothes were spattered with vomit. I knelt down beside my father too, and took his hand. His face was still moving but he was dead, and I was moved by the strangeness of what had happened to him, that he had just stopped living, passed on, departed. I made the necessary arrangements for his burial, and neighbors came to our assistance in that abandoned way which only death elicits. Nuhu and I helped wash the body, and I marveled at its leanness and spareness. Even in death my father looked firm and full of vigor. I did not know then that death often looked like that. Nuhu sobbed without restraint. In the afternoon of the following day we carried the body in a bier to the mosque and there said our prayers for the dead. We recited our prayers silently, scores of people standing in rows in front of the bier, making a takbir four times, *Allahu Akbar*, neither kneeling nor prostrating. Then we carried the bier out of the mosque, chanting God's name, and people in the streets rose as we passed and joined the procession for a while, so that the crowd had swelled to a hundred or more by the time we arrived at the cemetery. In the meantime, Bi Maryam once again went into the seclusion and abstentions of mourning for the next four months and ten days, as God's law required.

He had not been a particularly good father to me and I had not been a good son to him, neglectful and caring for each other by rote, but in Bi Maryam he had touched something that now swelled into an unassuageable grief. A widow in mourning is allowed only women visitors and the nearest and closest male relatives, so I have no one to compare Bi Maryam's grief to, but when her visitors left they too were often in tears, and when she was by herself she sat quietly in her widow's shawl, her eyes turned inward. Her sister Bi Sara, ailing as always with mysterious maladies, dragged herself to our house every day during the months of mourning, but even she, with her greater experience of such tragedies, could not persuade Bi Maryam out of grieving. She left her affairs entirely to me. I was now part owner of the house Nassor the nahodha had saved for her, and she was part owner of the halwa shop which Nuhu continued to run in our names. My father also left some money in savings, and this was divided between us as the law required, although neither of us chose to touch the money yet. It was at this time that I began on the plan to close the halwa shop and refit it as a furniture store, but she showed no interest in such matters, telling me to do what I thought best.

For the first three months of her mourning, Rajab Shaaban Mahmud, her nephew, did not visit her once, although he was her only male relative in the world. Some days, his wife Asha came with Bi Sara and once or twice with the younger son, but there was no sign of Rajab Shaaban Mahmud himself. Perhaps he thought his aunt would be exercised by his call, or perhaps since he received daily bulletins of Bi Maryam's condition from Bi Sara, in whose house he lived with his family, he did not think he needed to inquire of her personally. Then one evening, while I was sitting downstairs listening to the radio, Bi Maryam got into something of a panic. Since my father's death, she did not like to be left on her own upstairs at night, and so after listening to the news on the radio, I went up to the spare room and slept there. On this occasion I may have stayed down longer, or she may have been feeling more delicate than usual. In any case, I heard her calling for me in a voice of desperation, and ran up as fast as I could. She was sitting on a mat in the reception room, leaning against the wall, looking drained and condemned. "I'm going," she said. "I have no more strength."

I knelt down before her and remonstrated with her, telling her that she should not speak like that, as it only saddened her and saddened me. I would fetch a doctor, I said, reminding myself of how my father had waited too long with my mother, and making a note in my mind to put in an application for a telephone. But I could not reassure her. She was convinced she was dying, and she wanted me to go and tell her sister Bi Sara at once, should she wish to or feel able to come and say goodbye before she was taken away. I did as she wished, and hurried round to Bi Sara's house, there to find the house in an uproar. Rajab Shaaban Mahmud had come home the worse for wear from drink. Normally he avoided these encounters, apparently, but on this occasion Bi Sara had somehow intercepted him. When I arrived with my message, it was to find Bi Sara, who opened the door to me herself, in full spate about the wickedness of her nephew. He was nothing but a sinful waster, as bad as his father had been, a drunk. What would his grandfather say if he were alive to see this? Rajab Shaaban Mahmud was nowhere in sight, somewhere upstairs, and Bi Sara walked about in the dark courtyard, sometimes leaning against the open stairs, delivering her lamentations and disgust. She stopped at once when I told her about Bi Maryam, and hurried upstairs to fetch her buibui. Before descending, she delivered another blast on the landing, finishing with the news that her sister was dying, and at least she was going to be spared living with this new shame.

Bi Maryam didn't die, not just then, perhaps tugged back by Bi Sara's indignation at what had happened, which she seemed unable to check even though she was supposed to be attending her sister's deathbed, habitually a place of solemnity and reconciliation. Perhaps having toyed with the idea of death herself for so many seasons, she did not really think that Bi Maryam would get to go at her first try, just like that. Bi Sara stayed that night, and I could hear her talking for hours, pouring out her indignant humors. The following day I went to Dr. Balboa's surgery on the way to work, and asked him to call on Bi Maryam as soon as he could, as she had had something of an attack the previous night. When I got home from work it was to find that the doctor had been and had prescribed some sedation and given her an injection as usual, and that Bi Sara was only waiting for my return before setting off for her house which now was tainted with iniquity, as she put it. Dr. Balboa, in his stern and worldly way, had managed to calm Bi Maryam down, and after her panic she seemed clear-eyed and thoughtful rather than abandoned to grief.

A few days later, while I was at the halwa shop one afternoon, something I had taken to doing to give Nuhu some relief, Rajab Shaaban Mahmud came to the house in my absence, at the specific request of Bi Maryam herself. She told me later that she had asked him to come because Bi Sara had told her things she wanted to put before him. In her indignation Bi Sara had said that Rajab Shaaban Mahmud was not only wicked and dissolute and a drunk, but was speaking scandal, saying that my father had fooled, had tricked Bi Maryam into signing her house over to him. As a result of this cleverness on my father's part, I had inherited the house, and would inherit everything else that belonged to Bi Maryam when she died. He, Rajab Shaaban Mahmud, as her nephew and her lawful inheritor, was going to take me to court when his aunt died and claim back everything my father and I had stolen from her. This Bi Maryam put to Rajab Shaaban Mahmud, reporting that it was her sister who had told her, and asking him to confirm or deny. According to Bi Maryam, Rajab Shaaban Mahmud stuttered and protested, saying he was only thinking of her and the good of the family, but he did not deny.

When Bi Maryam told me this it was some weeks later, when she had had time to be appalled at the prospect of a repeat of the quarrels with relatives that she and Nassor the nahodha had had to go through. When she told me, she had had time to think about what she wanted to do. She was then just out of mourning, and her intention was to have a solicitor draw up papers putting the house and the business entirely in my name, as soon as possible. That way there would be no squabbling at her death. Her nephew had become a drinker, she said, like his father. And she feared that in any case if she allowed him to share in her property, he would only waste it in drink. In her view I had a full right to the share of the house I now owned. And since I had been everything a son should be since I returned to live with them, she had no other wish but that I should have her share too when she was gone. The only way to ensure that, since God's law so clearly required the division of property between relatives, was to put it all in my name while she was still alive. Her nephew's scandals against my father were unbearable and those against me were unjust, and she did not think it right that I should suffer indignities after her death which I had done nothing to deserve.

All this was a complete surprise to me. I had no idea that Rajab Shaaban Mahmud was whispering about me, although now that I knew this I heard again some things people had said to me, hints and probing to see if I had anything to add, anything to make the scandal thicker and tastier. My first reaction to Bi Maryam was to pull back, to advise caution. I did not want a feud lasting into generations on my hands. But as I thought some more I became less fastidious. My vanity and greed were flattered by what was proposed, and I found a way of making it palatable to me despite my initial qualms. Bi Maryam and my father had made what arrangements they did between themselves for their own reasons, out of trust and affection. And my father had paid his share in improving the house and making it beautiful. Now if Bi Maryam wished *me* rather than her nephew to have her share of it, that was her choice to make. Why should I try to be wiser when luck comes my way so unexpectedly? As a compromise we agreed that she would have the papers drawn up but would not have them implemented until she had had time to think some more about all this.

But she didn't do that, as I discovered later. She had the papers filed within days of completion, the day after Bi Sara stayed the night with us again. This time it was Bi Sara who came to us, distraught at the sight of Rajab Shaaban Mahmud, who had come home drunk and tearful, accusing and blaming, calling for his sons to come to him, so they could leave this house of whores and liars and intriguers and live somewhere clean together. Asha had bolted the door to her sons' bedroom from the outside so they could not come out and see their father as he was. Bi Sara stood at the top of the stairs, small and brittle, barring him from approaching his wife while he paced inches from her face, shouting and howling and spitting with rage and tearful accusations. In the end Bi Sara could not bear the terror she felt at the sight of her distraught nephew, could not bear the futility and misery that she saw lying in wait for them. So she abandoned Asha to her husband and came to lament with her sister and put her in a panic once again. A few days after that, Bi Maryam arranged for her solicitor to implement her new wishes.

Neither of them lasted very much longer after that. One morning, three months later, Bi Sara fell down some steps on the waterfront and broke her hip. Who knows what she was doing down there, perhaps looking to buy fish from the fresh catches being delivered there by the fishermen, or perhaps she went down on a whim, or perhaps she was remembering an earlier moment in her life when she had done such things, or she went down out of curiosity, not realizing how slimy and slippery those steps were. She never regained consciousness and died a few hours after the operation. The surgeon said the trauma on her feeble and wasted body was too great. Crowds came to her funeral, as if she were someone beloved, someone holy. It made you wonder what Bi Sara was up to when she was out of sight. Bi Maryam died of typhoid a month later, swiftly and silently, after buying a contaminated fruit drink in the street beside Dr. Balboa's surgery. She had just been to see to him that morning and he had prescribed a repeat dose of the sedation and given her an injection as usual. The mourners at her funeral thought there was something fitting about her death so soon after her sister's and her husband's—not wishing her ill and it was all in God's hands anyway, but they thought it right that she did not linger after her loved ones had so suddenly been called away. To me it seemed like a small tragedy, when she was so very nearly over the worst of her depressions, and she had not had time to think again about all the arrangements she had made. I buried her with propriety and respect, and grieved for her and the sadness she had suffered in her last few months.

Rajab Shaaban Mahmud inherited Bi Sara's property, which was the house he lived in with his family, and some gold jewelry, which was very likely her dowry from her marriages. When it became known that Bi Maryam had put everything in my name before her death, the rumor and the malice intensified, so much so that people reported it to me. They said that my father and I had fooled her, tricked her into signing everything away, that we had disinherited the family of the pious Mahmud through the foolishness of an unworldly woman. But I went on with refitting my new furniture shop, and had the courtyard in the house decorated with beautiful blue tiles like the ones I had seen in my travels with Sefu all those years ago in northern Kenya.

Latif Mahmud sat leaning back, his gaunt face tight in a grimace of fortitude, his lips pressed together and widened into the beginning of a grotesque smile. He did not know, I suppose, whether to snarl at me for my story of his father's inadequacy or to smile like a worldly man who could not fail to find our domestic squabbles paltry, and could not find my efforts to exculpate myself anything but contemptible. The room was now in the lingering dusk of an English summer evening, a light which at first made me anxious and irresolute but which I was learning to tolerate. I was learning to resist drawing the curtains and flooding the room with light, just so as to expel the gloom of that slow leaden onset of night. I thought I should rise and make some more tea, put the light on in the kitchen, break the grip of the silence in which we had been sitting then for a few minutes. But as soon as I stirred, Latif Mahmud uncrossed his legs and leaned forward. I waited for him to speak, but he said nothing, and after a moment he sighed and leaned back again. I rose carefully, so that I should not stumble in my weariness and let him think me feeble, and went to the kitchen. I put the light on and avoided glancing at the cadaverous shadow of a man reflected in the windowpanes, avoided the hard-edged sourness which lingered on that face all the time, which lingered there like a deep failing that subterfuge could not disguise. I drew the curtains with my face turned away, and then stood staring into the sink, trembling uncontrollably, feeble after all, overcome by memories which never seem to dim, overcome with pity for myself and for so many others who had been too feeble after all to resist the puniness and raggedness of our souls. So many deaths, and then so many more deaths and mutilations to come, memories I have no power to resist and which come and go to a pattern I cannot anticipate. I don't know how long I stood there, perhaps a moment too long. Perhaps I made a noise. In any case I heard Latif Mahmud stir in the other room, and stirred myself to fill the kettle and rinse the cups for our tea. I heard him appear in the kitchen, felt him in that small space, and when I turned to him I saw that his eyes were large and luminous, glistening with hurt. He looked straight at me and I dropped my eyes, afraid of what he was now going to say, weary of the bitter recriminations that had worn down my life.

"I have tired you," he said gently. I struggled not to weep at the respite he offered me, even if only for the moment. Feeble, after all. When I looked up it was to see him wearing a strained smile on his face, and I thought he was in need of some respite too.

"It must have tried you to have to listen to me say some of those things," I said. "It must have been very unpleasant."

"I'd forgotten so much," he said, frowning, unfrowning, brightening up, trying. "Willfully, I suspect. I mean that I willfully forgot so much. I was listening to you and thinking, Lord, that's what it was like. That is precisely how it was. All that bickering and pettiness. All that insulting. Old people with their unending grudges and their malice. That was what it felt like as a child, whispers and accusations, and complicated indignations that stretched further and further back all the time. That sense came back to me as you were talking. And Bibi, I haven't thought about Bibi for years, Bi Sara as you call her. We called her Bibi at home, Grandmother. I'd forgotten her. No, that can't be possible, can it? I must have made myself forget her. She didn't like us very much, even though she invited us to go and live with her in those last years. But yes, I remember that night, the one you were talking about. Well, I remember now that you remind me, now that you force me to remember, now that you make me think back to it. I hated to hear you speak about it. I thought of it as something that had happened in the family and no one else knew about it. Yet you knew about it all the time, and who else, and what else. I must have been about seven or eight. I haven't the slightest memory of the night Bibi intercepted Ba, nothing at all. I must have been asleep. I don't feel the slightest tug on a nerve or anything like that, as you do with a memory you have suppressed, just amazed interest. But yes, I remember the night my father screamed for us to come downstairs, and Ma bolted the door from outside and shouted for us to go to sleep. I remember that, my father shouting abuse and sobbing. He never shouted, you see. The sobbing was unimaginable, your own father sobbing in that heartbroken way, and if you had not said it I probably would not have been able to bring it to mind. But the shouting abuse was shocking, and Ma shouting back, calling him a drunk, and Bibi crying and telling him to be quiet, to leave, go away, you child of sin. Yes I remember that now. Such a fuss about drinking, such a great fuss about nothing. I'd forgotten about Bibi leaving the house, her own house, but I remember the shouting. She never stopped, Bibi, finding fault, giving instructions, complaining about every little neglect. I felt we were a disappointment to her. I felt she disliked us."

The kettle had come to the boil so I turned round to see to the tea. I did it the English way because there was no time to let the milk boil and put the tea in it to brew.

"Perhaps it'll be better not to start on that now," he said behind me. "I've been here too long already today. I'd better go now."

I turned back and grinned at him. "I don't think you'll ever go," I said.

"You grinning blackamoor," he said after a moment, smiling slightly. "I'll have my tea and go. But then I'll be back. If I may. After all, we're related it seems."

"Only by marriage," I said, in the same bantering tone. "And there was no issue."

"Yes, but then you took my father's name. Doesn't that combination make us related? And we are in a strange land. That would more or less naturally make us related, or so people tell me when they ring to ask me for a favor. You still haven't told me about that, why you took his name. It's all history, anyway. None of it matters, really. I'm not saying that *history* does not matter, knowing about what happened so we understand what we are about, and how we came to be as we are, and what stories we tell about it all. I mean I don't want recriminations, all this family business, all this muttering that stretches further back all the time. Have you noticed how the history of Islam is so tied up with family squabbles? Let me put that another way lest I offend you. I know what a sensitive lot we Muslims are. Have you noticed the incredible consequences of family squabbles in the history of Islamic societies? The Ummayyads displace the Prophet's grandson Hassan and lord it for a hundred years in Damascus. Then the family of Abbas Abdulmutallib, the Prophet's uncle, go to war to remove the Ummayyads in the name of the holy family and rule from Baghdad for five hundred years. Well, they don't quite *rule* for five hundred years, it's true—the generals and the Turkish mercenaries do that after the first couple of hundred—but they do so in the name of the family of Abbas. In the meantime, in North Africa, we have the Fatimids, after the descendants of the Prophet's daughter Fatma, and her sons Hassan and Hussein. Then come the Ottomans, descendants of Uthman, who for a brief few seconds ruled half the world and managed to cling to large bits of it into the twentieth century.

And in our own time we have the children of Abdulaziz ibn Saud, sitting on a sea of black gold, on a territory they call Saudi Arabia, after their family name. I hate families."

I handed him a cup of tea, and he sipped at it at once, as if he was too desperate to wait for it to cool down. He grimaced and cringed and turned away from me for a moment. I thought perhaps he wanted to give himself a breather after his outburst and went ahead of him back to the sitting room.

"What happened to your friend Sefu?" he asked. "The fine artist. Did he become one?"

"He became a teacher," I said, and I saw him grin, as if he had known all along that that would be the answer. "At first, anyway. We wrote to each other for a while, and he came to visit us and stayed with us. I never got to go to Kenya again. Then some years later, just after independence, he got a scholarship to go and study in the United States, and I never heard from him again. I suppose he's living there now. I don't know if he's an artist there or whether he returned. Not many people returned."

6.

She came unexpectedly, late on Saturday afternoon. Rachel. Unannounced. Such a strange way of thinking, such a meaningless idea, taken on its own. That you should have to wait until you are announced before you may politely visit. To do that, to call unannounced, you would have to push past the footmen and under-saddlers and deputy chamber pots, or whatever their proper titles are, as well as the butler, and barge into the drawing room in foaming haste, brushing aside discourtesy and rejection. As if they were people mimicking themselves mimicking an idea of how they should act. Rachel pressed on the buzzer and announced herself. On occasions she warns me to expect her and then does not turn up. On this occasion she turns up without warning. Yet her willfulness, which is meant to charm, I think, is always courteous and therefore is almost bearable.

"You should get a telephone," she said, defending herself against my involuntary frown of irritation.

"I almost did once," I said. "In my earlier life."

She waited to see if I was going to say more, weighing in her mind whether she should prod me. I was, of course, referring to the time I applied for a telephone after Bi Maryam got into a bit of a panic. On that long-ago occasion, I was put on a waiting list and heard no more about the matter. Rachel was leaning against the doorway of the living room, rather than sitting in the chair I offered, perhaps to indicate that she was only stopping for a minute, or possibly because she had come to attempt to drag me off to somewhere. She did this now and then, the latter. And that Saturday afternoon it turned out to be the latter. That was probably why she did not pursue my reply to her habitual grumble about my resistance to a telephone. Her eyes, brown with a kind of transparency that was almost amber, were alive with plans, when at other times they were subdued and still, watchful in their stillness. She was a good listener when she wanted to be. "My mother is staying with me for the weekend, and we'd both very much like it if you came and had dinner with us. She is cooking, so the food is bound to be delicious," she said, frowning as she finished, because she could already see me shaking my head. She raised her eyebrows slightly, inviting me to explain.

"I'd prefer not to," I said.

"Oh you're doing your Bartleby act again," she said, sighing with exaggerated resignation. "Oh dear. I hope it doesn't last as long as it did last time. Please tell me why not. It doesn't seem a courteous reply to my quite genuine and generous invitation to come and meet my mother and eat her delicious food. I would really like you to. You've never met my mother and I think you'll like meeting her."

I had mentioned the story of Bartleby to her and she had read it, and told me that she had her doubts about its greatness. Too much gloom and resignation in it, she thought, and the symbolism was oppressive, the walls and the Tombs and the pyramids and the thin grass growing in the shadowy prison yard. Too much self-pity for her liking, all that nineteenth-century melodrama. Perhaps she was afraid that I saw myself as a kind of Bartleby, as someone with a secret and burdensome history who sought to expiate it with silence.

I anticipated her by asking if she did not recognize something of him, if she did not respond to something in him. Was there not something familiar about him, something wished for, something heroic?

"Not a bit," she said. "He made me think of someone dangerous, someone capable of small, sustained cruelties on himself and others weaker than himself, an abuser."

I had never thought of Bartleby like that although he was cruel to himself, that was true. "Perhaps in these times you have come to see people who choose humility and withdrawal as duplicitous," I said. "To see them as damaged beyond redemption and therefore only capable of deranged cruelties. Perhaps you have lost tolerance for that desire for isolation which faith in a spirit's ambition made heroic. So the kind of self-mortifying retreat Bartleby undertakes only has meaning as a dangerous unpredictability. Especially since the story does not allow us to know what has brought Bartleby to this condition, does not allow us to have sympathy for him. It does not allow us to say, yes, yes, in this case we understand the meaning of such behavior and we forgive it. The story only gives us this man, who says nothing about himself or about his past, appears to make no judgment or analysis, desires no reprieve or forgiveness from us, and only wishes to be left alone."

"An existential hero," she said, smiling, a little condescendingly. "He seems to me like someone consumed with self-pity, relishing his defeat."

After a brief silence, when both of us, no doubt, thought back to this earlier conversation, she said: "Why not come and have dinner with us tonight?" She sat down at last, and leaned forward to begin her attempt at conversion. "My mother would love to meet you. I know. I'd told her about you before, and when she came this afternoon she asked about you. So I thought why not get you to come round? She loved that idea, and when I left to come here she had already started on preparing the fish. She's a celebrated cook, and she hardly ever comes to visit me, so this is an occasion. They lead such busy lives up there in faraway London. My father *never* comes to visit, and he doesn't even answer the phone, let alone make a call. Never mind . . . Anyway, she's here now. She's got lots of stories to tell and she's brilliantly well-read. I told her some of your stories, I hope you don't mind. You'll love her. *Don't* shake your head like that before I've finished. You'll get on . . . I know it. And you need to get out, not just lock yourself in here. Come on, get your trainers on and let's go."

She had bought me a pair of trainers as a gift, which I have managed to persuade myself to wear once but I felt gaudy and clownish as I walked on the waterfront with them, and so have not worn them again, yet. The way she bought the trainers was not unlike the manner she springs kindnesses on me. She persuaded me to go out for a walk with her one afternoon, and steered me with prior intent into one of the large department stores. It was not one I had been in before, although I was gradually and pleasurably visiting several of them during my wanderings. I always walk through the perfume sections for the astringent scents in the air, and to marvel at the hard-edged lights and the chiseled faces of the young women who serve there. Anyway, while we were in the department store she had taken me to, she made me try on a pair of trainers, making it seem like a joke. I did as she wished, and said polite things about the shoes, to be helpful, not to seem incapable of a little bit of fun, and then she told me they were a present to me from her. I protested at first, and then as I saw the beginning of embarrassment on her face, I felt I was being ungracious and unkind after her gesture of care and regard, and accepted the present with thanks.

"I don't know why you say I lock myself in. I go out every day," I said.

"To the furniture stores," she said.

I told her that once, in an unguarded moment, when she was attempting to persuade me to go out for a snack lunch or something. An excellent Lebanese snack bar just down the road, you'll love it. "I go out every day," I told her. "I visit the furniture stores in Middle Square Park every morning." To her it must have sounded like the kind of thing a lonely old man at his wit's end would do. Perhaps that is how it would sound to anybody.

"This morning I walked along the promenade for fifteen minutes," I said, smiling now at the way she was harrying me. "From the Avalon Sports Center all the way to the pier. There was a congregation of nuns in brown-and-white habits outside the Hampton Hotel, standing on the pavement in a crowd, waiting for the arrival of a dignitary, it looked like. Beside them were two large, resplendent bawabs, dressed in braided uniforms and peaked caps, waiting to open the doors of the limousine when it arrived. And the flags of the Hampton tugging and snapping above their heads. These two large men, standing broad and solid on the curb, and the crowd of small anonymous-looking women flutter-ing beside them, their headgear blown about them like the dowdy plumage of a flock of peahens. There was something eternal about the sight, those men unable to resist the impulse to strut."

"What did you call the two men? The commissionaires. What was that word?" she asked.

"Bawabs," I said. "Doorkeepers, an indispensable article in any civilized and prosperous culture. When at the end of his first journey Sindbad returned to Basra with a fortune, he bought himself a house and then a bawab before he purchased concu-bines and memluks with which to entertain his friends."

"They are called commissionaires in these quieter times," she said. "People expect them to strut and fuss like that. Was that before or after the furniture stores?" she asked.

"Yes, after, certainly. The stores are always best early in the morning, before the artificial fibers are disturbed by the day's business. They have brought in a new range of tables in the one I went to today, quite out of character with their usual style. Thick pale wood and brutal straight lines," I said. "I have a fond-ness for little curls and filigrees, and delicate decorative borders. I can see the quality of the wood in these tables, but I am re-pelled by their bold utilitarian hubris, their celebration of their ugliness."

"Is that what brought on the Bartleby mood? So you thought

a walk along the waterfront would calm your nerves. Come, get your trainers on and I'll take you for a drive to the cliffs. We'll catch the sun sparkling off the water, and then I can talk you into coming to dinner tonight."

I was too tired, I explained. I saw that she had given in, and as always with Rachel when this moment arrived, I felt I had been ungrateful when she had been offering kindness. I resisted the impulse to say yes, I'll come. I really did feel tired, or at least too tired to begin making conversation from scratch with someone I had never met before. Or perhaps I was only becalmed in spirit, and was looking forward to sitting with the book of travels in central Asia that I had bought earlier in the day at the secondhand bookshop next to the florist. There was another secondhand bookshop across the road, but the man in there looked as if he hated his books, standing over them in his grubby suit and tie with his arms folded across his chest, glowering as if he was standing guard over a troop of rebellious baboons. He kept the books in boxes, piled up and tumbled over each other like hastily acquired merchandise that he was selling on the cheap. *Herat* by G. B. Malleson, 1880. I had opened it and read this sentence, and so I bought it: "From the carpets issued vapours of amber." It made me nostalgic for my ud-al-qamari and for the incense of perfumed gum.

I have come to love Rachel, though I wouldn't dare tell her that. She visits me when she does, sometimes without warning, and more often than not with a plan to go and do something. Not all the plans are inspired, and I have to put up spirited resistance to prevent myself being dragged off to something unwelcome. But often the plans are surprising, forcing me to reconsider my inclination to refuse, to stay in and read a book or a map. She disapproves of my inclination to maps, I think, although I don't know why, because she will never quite say that she does and even brought me a book about medieval Portuguese mapmaking recently. Maybe it makes me seem eccentric, or too sedentary, when she would prefer me to have more energetic interests, as a demonstration that some youthfulness clings on in me despite appearances.

And her visits have done me good, have shown me more than I would ever have been able to see had I been left to my own devices, have made me remember courtesies and care, have brought me affection and allowed me the opportunity to be affectionate in return. Not such paltry gifts, not in the least, though I fear to dwell on them too long, even when I am on my own, in case I have misunderstood, and foolishly return a love that was not first offered. Yet I know her visits have done me good. I don't know why she visits me, or why she cares that I should go out and see this valley or that cliff or walk along a stony beach that has no attractions to the naked eye. I have never asked her, and she has never volunteered a discussion on the subject. She just comes and bustles or sits in the chair and we talk for a while over bitter coffee or sweet black tea, and if she is inclined and I am in the mood, we stroll by the sea or she drives me wherever she chooses, and she speaks to me in that hectic, disarming way of hers. Her visits have done me good, and have made me love her like the daughter she reminded me of the first time I met her. Sometimes when I see her take her unruly hair in her hands and wring it as if in distraction, which she has a habit of doing for no obvious reason, then I think of that first meeting with her at the detention center, and for no accountable reason I think about my daughter Raiiya, my daughter Ruqiya, whom I knew only so briefly before I lost her. Every time she does that I think of my daughter Raiiya, my daughter Ruqiya, though she never had hair like that and never pulled it like that. I wouldn't dare tell her all that, and I don't know why she takes the trouble to come and see me, to descend on me, as she puts it. She complains that I don't have a telephone, and so she can't ring me beforehand, and instead she is forced to come all the way to ask me if I'd like to do something which I turn out not to want to do, and she then has no choice but to wheel away like a busy tornado and head in another pointless direction. Like now. But I did not want a telephone. I would hate to have the noise of it, and the intrusion of unwanted callers at any hour they chose, talking to you whether you want to hear or not, from here or anywhere, talking to you when you haven't even seen them coming and taken time to prepare a courtesy or an excuse, leaping into your house with that grinding, growling, buzzing clarion and then requiring answers and politeness from you. I preferred Rachel's erratic visits, which in any case I feared and expected would soon diminish and end. And as I thought that, I wondered if my behavior in refusing to go and have dinner with her and her mother would only hasten that day, and then I almost gave in and said yes, I'll come.

"Tomorrow, lunch," she said, smiling, coaxing. "Come and have lunch tomorrow. You must come. If you don't come, she'll say I invented you. She loves saying that, that I'm a dreamer and I live in a fantasy world. Or at least she used to say that. Until I started to do this asylum work, then she thought I'd woken up to the real world. 'Now that's something worth doing,' she said. She likes to think she knows about the real world, my mother. I must say when I hear her tell the story of her family, my family, I think *she's* living in some historical fantasy that she's making up as she goes along. Apparently centuries ago we lived in Haifa and then became Sephardic in Spain from where centuries later we were expelled to Trieste and then moved to Geneva, and then her grandfather moved to London at the end of the last century. Far-fetched, in a manner of speaking."

"She knows stories about those journeys?" I said, or rather asked, always avid for stories about odysseys and impossible journeys. "Spain at the time of the expulsion of Muslims and Jews from Andalus?"

"I expect so," Rachel said. "Why don't you come and ask her? I can see the two of you chatting away until the early hours about, the walled gardens of Córdoba. She collects books about Jews in Spain. She showed me a book once about religious songs from Andalusia, Muslim songs. What do you call them?"

"Qasida," I said.

"Yes, a small beaten-up book."

"I would like to hear her stories of Andalus, but I have a guest of my own tomorrow," I said, feeling as if I had been secretive. "Latif Mahmud. Do you remember? The man you once arranged to—"

"Yes, I know. I've spoken to him on the phone. He rang me during the week," she said, smiling with secret knowledge, almost smirking.

"Oh," I observed. Now what?

"He told me you were related. You never mentioned that. I think he's quite excited about having met you. All sorts of things that he hadn't thought of for years, he said, and some he didn't even know. It made me envious, in a way. He was so excited. Imagine being like that, I mean finding out things about your life that you didn't even know had happened. It made me think about what we do, at work. So often we're trying to get people to remember, to make a case for themselves. And if they can't remember we have to make it up between us. Imagine someone else completing those stories that are missing. It would be like being a child or something, when your parents tell you what you did and said, and you have no memory of it."

"Some things are not worth knowing," I said.

Rachel considered that for a moment, head to one side, looking stern. "No, I think that's a one-way street to lying and chaos. I think it's better to know, on the whole. Is he coming to see you about terrible things? I mean are you having to tell him sad things that he's forgotten or didn't know about?"

"Yes," I said.

"And sad for you, too? I'm sorry. He's not bothering you, is he?"

"No, I want him to come," I said.

"He was so pleased to have met you, he said so several times, so it can't be all sad, what you have to talk about. Anyway, he sounds all right. What do I mean? . . . Oh, I don't know, calm and thoughtful and interesting. I'd love to meet him. Next time he comes we'll do something together, maybe. Drive to Water Valley and have lunch there, and take a long walk along the lakeshore or something. Or would you rather I stayed away?"

"No, no," I said. "Next time."

The buzzer rang on the dot of the agreed time, which made me wonder if he had been waiting downstairs before ringing. I had prepared a meager lunch of rice and some fish poached with vegetables, and as soon as he arrived, smiling and eager, I led us to the kitchen to partake of this sumptuous repast. I had no idea in what state he would be when he arrived, despite what Rachel had said. I did not know whether he would have come to do acrimonious battle, to accuse me of mendacities and distortions, or whether he would be embarrassed and uncertain about what to say. I was also ready to be surprised by how he might look. Although I had spent a whole afternoon and part of the evening with him only a few days before, I found it hard to remember fluid details of his face. Perhaps I avoided looking at him while I talked, and avoided his eyes when he did, but I realized as I thought of him during the week that I would not be able to describe his face in motion or his eyes as they took in the stories I told him. I don't mean that I would not have recognized him, simply that I could not be sure what I remembered of the subtler movements of his face. That's why I thought lunch as soon as he arrives, to give us time to find a place from where we can begin talking to each other again.

Well, he was smiling when he arrived, and he shook my hand with vigor. So that was fine, he probably wasn't here to rant at me. We then moved on to courtesies. How have you been? How was your work? How is the family? "I have no family," he said. The way I asked this question was: "Is everyone at home well?"

And his reply: "There is no one at home." I did not say any more, and saw him notice my silence and smile.

"There was someone I was with for a long time," he said as I placed our lunch on the table and invited him to help himself. "Six years, but it was always going to end sooner or later. We were not happy together. Her name was Margaret. We lived together and got by, and shared our pleasures but we were not happy. There were many irritations and I know that sometimes I quite disliked her, hated her. We had met as students and just clung together. We were a cliché, despite the happy moments and the caring, and we became bored with each other long before we dared admit it. Then I was with someone for two and a half years. Not such a long time ago, about a year or so. Now and then we would talk about finding a place to live together, but it never happened. Weeks would go past and I wouldn't even think about it, and then something would happen and I would think no, never. Not again. I'm not living with anybody ever again. It was easier, safer to stay the way we were. She had a maisonette in Clapham and I had a flat in Battersea. Do you know London?"

"I've never been there," I said. "What was her name? The one you have just parted from."

"Angela," he said, smiling at the omission. And after naming her, he began to think about her, and his face tightened momentarily. "She worked as a freelance translator, textbooks, scientific articles, that sort of thing. Italian was her language. Anyway, she got tired of our arrangement sooner than I did, and she wanted me to make a decision. I just couldn't. I mean I didn't want to. Families. And I could not forget something she told me in the early days when I knew her. She and her brother had to go home to Dorset one weekend to speak to their mother because she would not have sex with their father anymore. It was so unfair of her, she said about her mother. And she and her brother went home to have a talk with her, to tell her off about her selfishness—and the father encouraged them to do so. I couldn't forget that story, especially when talk of living together became intense. I imagined my children coming home in an expedition one day to lecture me about not having sex with Angela—while she sat nearby, grumblingly encouraging them. I couldn't bear the thought of that. Oh really I think I didn't want to, but I just couldn't forget the messiness of that story either. So in time she refused to see me in the casual way I preferred and we stopped. I haven't bothered much since then. It's very kind of you, the food."

"It's nothing, just something meager to keep hunger away."

"It's very good of you to let me come again," he said. "I thought I tired you last week, and made you talk about difficult things, and I was unpleasant and rude."

"No, I wanted you to come. You're welcome," I said.

"Anyway, all week I've been thinking about the things you spoke about last time, trying to make them agree with what I remember and what I thought I knew. I know something in me resisted what you were saying, even though I was gripped by it. So I've been thinking about that and putting the stories along-side each other, and seeing the gaps that I will never fill, and the ones we managed to avoid last time. I feel worn out after all this time, after all these years of thinking about that time and that place. And living here with all the comings and goings, and the trooping of my life through hostilities and contempt and superciliousness. I feel worn out and raw, livid with sores. Do you know what I mean? You must know that feeling. I was thinking about that this week, how worn out I am after all these years of knowing and not knowing, of doing nothing about it and how it can't be helped. So I was looking forward to coming here, to hear you talk, for both of us to find relief."

"Yes, to find relief," I said.

"Please tell me what happened to Faru? I asked you that before."

"Nuhu. His name is Nuhu. He became an officer in the Harbor Police. You know, those people who stand at the harbor gates and search all the vehicles, and keep unauthorized people out, and require a bribe for everything. You didn't need to be able to read and write for that kind of job, a lowly job in most people's eyes, which I suppose is how Nuhu got it. I didn't know he was attracted to that kind of work, uniforms and those heavy boots. He went there after my arrest, I found out later, because at first he worked for me in the store, of course."

"I didn't know you were arrested," he said, a spoonful of rice frozen halfway toward his mouth. I would not have doubted it, from the shock on his face as he said that, but I pressed on.

"Many people were arrested," I said. "Thousands. Anyway, after a few years Nuhu found a way of leaving, of escaping to God knows where. He was in a good position to do that, you might think, but in those early years the Harbor Police were very vigilant, the ones with guns and powerful motorboats not the slouching bawabs of whom Nuhu was one. The penalties for attempting to escape were severe then. He must have stowed away in one of the cargo ships, and to judge by the destination of the ships that used to call on us then, he is now living somewhere in Russia or China or the former GDR. If he survived undetected, or if the crew did not throw him overboard, or if he did not find a way of jumping ship earlier in Aden or Mogadishu or Port Said."

"I was in GDR," he said, shaking his head at the petty complications of our lives. "In Dresden. Well, near Dresden."

"Yes, you told me," I said.

"Did I tell you about a pen friend I had who turned out to be living in Dresden? I was writing to him from home, and then when I went to GDR he turned out to be living just down the road. His mother taught me how to read Homer. Well, she did not teach me directly, but she made me want to read it. I'm sorry, you were talking about Faru."

"Yes, you told me how you came to see me just before you left for the former GDR. There was one thing you left out of that account. You didn't mention that Salha came down to speak to you while you were there. Perhaps you've forgotten. Nuhu told her that you'd come, and she came down. Your mother used to visit her when she was confined, and she must've thought you'd come with a message. She shouldn't have come down. Salha. She was required to rest and avoid the stairs, but she came down because your mother used to visit, despite all the bad feeling between your father and me. The women had a stronger sense of mercy, of the balance between things. They looked after each other, they cared that things should not go so far that we would not be able to find our way back. Salha spoke to you, she asked after you and after your mother, and you refused even to look in her direction. Then you left without answering her greeting. I suppose you've forgotten that. It was a long time ago."

"No, I haven't forgotten. I didn't remember, but it didn't seem such a big thing not to remember. I'm sorry I was so rude to her."

"It was a long time ago. And I should've given that table back. Such a small thing. Salha told me to return it, but I was too angry. She was appalled that I had taken the contents of your father's house, though there was hardly anything to take. She thought it was vindictive and unforgivable, and perhaps if she had been with me then, if we were married, she would have talked me out of it. Then I had no one to talk to me, and only frustration and grievance to guide me. I was angered by the slanders, and felt that I had right on my side. By the time it came to the table, slanders had been compounded by your father's impossible holiness, and his boasts that God would make me see my sin and that I would one day return everything to its rightful owners in shame. I could not return the table when you came to ask for it, though it would have been better if I had. It turned your mother against us, finally."

I offered a compromise even after Rajab Shaaban Mahmud turned down my first plan, even while the case was going through the British colonial courts. I explained that I did not want the house. I just wanted to be able to raise a loan because my business needed capital and I was just about to get married. The money was rightfully mine, but I did not want the house, nor did I want them to move out or pay any rent. Let me have the nominal ownership of the house so I can raise a loan, and when my business was on a sure footing I would return the legal ownership of the house to him. But he refused utterly, and when the case was won, he took himself and his family to a tiny house he had rented somewhere. Things had gone too far by then, and I had lost track of the meaning of what I had done. I rented the house and negotiated a loan, which turned out to be much smaller than I required. Banks were getting nervous soon after independence, and they were right to be, as it turned out. The austerity and chaos of the government was to culminate two years later in the nationalization and plundering of all the banks. It was done in the name of the people and self-reliance, but it was really just plunder, as was the sequestering of anything that earned a profit. Our rulers built very little, mostly they took away from those who did and then they stuffed their guilty bodies full.

That was yet to reach its climax at the time I acquired Rajab Shaaban Mahmud's house and tried to raise a loan, but the banks had already scented danger and were cautious. The small loan I was able to raise did not enable me to realize the plans I had drawn up, did not enable me to do very much at all. It didn't matter that much in the end. Within a year or so, the country was in chaos and everyone who could was looking for ways to get money out of the country. All I could do was carry on as before, although now there was no market for exquisites. When I got the ebony table back, I put it in my shop not because I thought I would be able to sell it, but because it was beautiful and it brought back to me daily the futility of friendship and ambition.

Rajab Shaaban Mahmud came to pray in the local mosque even though he had moved to another area, and every day he walked past my shop with head bowed, the defeated and humiliated man of God. And people looked as he walked past and lamented the tragedy that had befallen him and his family, and looked at me as the maker of evil. By this time his wife Asha was the mistress of Abdalla Khalfan, the Minister of Development and Resources, or some other title like that, some hideous fiction or another. His government car collected her from her house and took her to wherever the Minister appointed, and drove her back later. They had been lovers for years, rumor had it, and now that Abdalla Khalfan was somebody, they saw no reason to go on hiding. I suppose it did the Minister credit that he did not, at this moment of his ascendancy, abandon his lover and choose a younger woman. For Asha was no longer young, although she still was beautiful. The Minister was no longer young either, but that had never prevented men in his circumstances from acting as if they were. All the more tragedy on Rajab Shaaban Mahmud's pious shoulders.

Then I refused to return the table, after Asha had visited my wife in her confinement, and had been conciliatory during and after the court case, and had sent her son Ismail to come to ask for this small favor. My pettiness must have disgusted her, for it turned her completely against me. After that, she began her own campaign, one which in time she saw to complete victory. She had the help of the Minister, of course, though it took a while for his intervention to begin to tell. Whatever it was she had in mind for me, matters were out of everyone's hands once the machinery of terror began to grind. Over the next two years the following series of persecutions befell me. I set them out here in the order in which they occurred. Before I do so I should mention that it was also in the early stages of this series of events that Salha ended her confinement and gave us our daughter Ruqiya. May God have mercy on their souls.

He interrupted, not for the first time. I have not mentioned the other times because I did not want to clutter up my account, and because mostly it was to express surprise or ask me to give more details. But this time he stood up from the table and walked away, out of the kitchen where we were still sitting after our lunch. He returned immediately, looking furious, enraged.

"Now you're going to start on her," he said, frowning, his face darkened with dislike and anger. "You've finished with him, I guess. He's just a vindictive, inadequate man who refused to see sense. His impossible holiness. So that's all settled. Now it's her turn. Yes, I knew about the Minister, everyone knew about that. She was a good woman. I remember her like that. I used to panic when I used to see her in the afternoons, dressed up to go out to him. I used to be terrified, I don't know of what. I don't know why she had to become like that. I've been listening to you all this time and thinking, He's lying, he's lying. He's just obsessed with his narrative. He wants to make it work. But now you're going to improve on it, to make it into a real drama. Now it's the turn of her and her filthy Minister to persecute you."

I avoided looking at him. It was not such a great piece of wisdom, but in prison I learned to avoid making eye contact with someone who was angry. I learned to sit near him and look in the same direction as him. So I looked away and waited while he stood in the doorway and spoke his rage.

"I don't want to hear any more," he said, and walked out of the kitchen again. I waited for a few moments and then rose to clear the clutter of plates and dishes and wash them in the sink. Then I put on the kettle and began to prepare a pot of sweet ginger tea. When I went into the sitting room with the tray, he was standing at the window, looking out toward my strip of sea. I poured out the tea and waited until he came to sit down opposite me.

So then these are the events that befell. Many of them are difficult to speak of without drama, and some of them fill me with anguish, but I crave to utter them, to display them as judgments of my time and of the puniness of our duplicitous lives. I will tell them briefly, for many of them are events I have tried hard not to dwell on, for fear of diminishing what little I have left with bitterness and helplessness. I have had many years to think about them and to weigh them in the scale of things, and in that respect I have learned that it is as well to live quietly with my grazes and sprains when others have to bear intolerable cruelties.

After the nationalization of the banks in 1967, which event was announced to us on the radio in ringing tones by the President of the Republic himself, I received a summons from the manager of what had been the Standard Bank and was now the People's Bank, requesting a full settlement of the loan I had taken out with them. I went to the bank to plead, for even though right was on my side and I had made an agreement to repay over five years and only just over two years had passed since the start of the repayment period, this was not a time for citation of rights and legalities. I went to the bank to plead for mercy from the manager. The nationalization meant that all the senior personnel had to change overnight, for fear of sabotage by the previous crowd who were mostly foreigners. The new manager refused to see me, and an assistant explained to me that the request for settlement was nonnegotiable. They were acting on instructions from the relevant government office. The foreigners had cut off credit, and there had been heavy withdrawals from customers over the previous few months, so all loans were being called in. Why had I not heard of this from any other businessman? I asked. Well, the assistant explained, the loans are being called in in stages, and I was the first stage. I did not have the money to make a full settlement, I said. In that case the bank would have to take possession of the house I had put up as security.

Four weeks later, the house I had fought Rajab Shaban Mahmud through the courts for was gazetted as the property of the bank, and the tenants I had installed in it were given notice to quit with immediate effect. Rajab Shaaban Mahmud and his wife Asha moved back in as soon as the house was empty. He walked past my furniture store every day on his way to the PWD after that, where he had now risen in the administration. And when before he paraded his humiliation, walking by with eyes downcast and neck angled to one side, now he looked in my direction with blazing eyes. He had come back into his rightful property and I was paying for my sins. Even when I did not look up, which I learned not to do as soon as I saw him approaching, I could feel his eyes clinging on me as he walked past. I hardly ever caught sight of Asha in the streets now, even though she had come back to live in the old house, now that she had a car at her disposal, but when I did, it seemed to me that she added languor to her step as she passed by without a word.

Then five months after this, I was summoned to the Party headquarters. The instructions were delivered by the chairman of the local branch, who came to the store on a Wednesday morning and took a glass of water with me before he told me that I was required to attend the following afternoon. He explained that Rajab Shaaban Mahmud had filed a complaint against me. In his submission he charged that I had falsified the will of his aunt Bi Maryam, and after her death had fraudulently acquired the house I now occupied, even though I was no relation to her. I told the chairman that that was not true, but he shrugged and said it was not for him to say anything. I could tell them all that at Party headquarters and see what they said. When I told Salha about the summons, she despaired. She had been waiting for another blow to fall on me but after all the months she had begun to believe that the worst was over. I had feared worse than the summons to headquarters. I had feared indefinable humiliation and injury, a mutilation. Sometimes, in that dreamworld between sleeping and waking, I caught glimpses of a figure who had been around in my childhood, a man whose nose had been sliced off completely, so that in the space between his eyes and mouth were two flesh-colored holes which led directly into his head. He had been mutilated like that as punishment for rape, and walked the streets in rags, with no option but to bear the mockery and ridicule of the puniest among us, too cowed even to contemplate retaliation or defense. I had feared worse than the Party headquarters, and yet I also trembled at the thought of what they had in store for me there.

We knew about the hearings at the Party headquarters, which were really summary courts that made laws as they wished. They were chaired by the Party Secretary-General and were constituted with whoever had time on his or her hands, sometimes the President of the Republic himself, if he was in the mood to play among his subjects, sometimes it was his driver or the Chief of Police. When I appeared before the Party committee, it was made up of the following people. I name them here because I wish that their names should be known, so that the things that befell us should not seem to have happened of their own accord. (1) The chairman was the Secretary-General of the Party, whose name is known to everyone; (2) the Minister of Development and Resources, Sheikh Abdalla Khalfan, who was the lover of Asha, the wife of Rajab Shaaban Mahmud; (3) the Chief Immigration Officer, Abdulkarim Haji; (4) Lieutenant Ahmed Abdalla of the People's Army; (5) Bibi Aziza Salmin, schoolteacher. They sat in a long line behind a table, and I sat on a chair facing them, in a large gloomy room with a veranda in the rear of the Party headquarters building. The gloom was welcome at that dazzling hour in the early afternoon, but the air had the dank decomposing smell of an underground room. The local branch Chairman had accompanied me inside and sat on one side, witnessing and preparing a report for the gossip mill back in our area.

The committee took it in turns to harangue me for my crime, which was taking advantage of a gullible woman to defraud the family of a good pious man of its rightful property. The Minister of Development and Resources said very little, but he seemed pleased with the progress of affairs. I suffered most at the hands of the Chief Immigration Officer, Abdulkarim Haji, and the schoolteacher Bibi Aziza Salmin, who were inclined to see me as a representative of men who made a profession of preying on women. I had not met any of the personages on this committee before, though I had heard of all of them.

I was asked to reply to a handful of self-incriminating questions. "Do you admit that you planned to rob Bi Maryam from the moment your father married her?" I attempted one reply before being silenced. I explained that the house became mine while Bi Maryam was still alive, not through inheritance. Her will said nothing about the house because she had already arranged for it to be legally mine while she was alive, to avoid accusations and recriminations. I was not able to say much more than this before Bibi Aziza Salmin expressed astonishment at my barefaced nerve, and the Chief Immigration Officer suggested that the committee should consider adding another charge to the one I was already facing—that of taking the committee for fools. Otherwise nothing more was required of me but to listen to the abuse, which I did for about an hour and more. Their judgment was delivered to me while I sat there in front of them: Bibi Aziza Salmin spoke first, and the others followed with increasing rancor, until finally the chairman of the committee, the Secretary General himself, gave a summary of the verdict. I was to deliver the papers concerning the house to the Secretary General's office the next day, after which the legal title would revert to the family of Bi Maryam.

I walked home with the chairman of the local branch, who

assured me that it could have been a lot worse, and that I had done well to say nothing more after that one ill-judged outburst. I still had my business, so I wouldn't starve, and who knew what else God would bring? We packed what we could that night, and with Nuhu's help transported barrowfuls to Salha's parents' home and to the store. Nuhu was no longer working for me, but he came when I called for him to help. Neighbors watched from behind slightly open windows but said nothing to make us feel worse, and some of them softly uttered pious words to lament the times we lived in. We avoided the main road in our comings and goings, pulling and pushing the barrow over the rutted paths which ran behind the backs of the houses. I insisted that we all spend the night with Salha's parents, in case there was an attempt to remove us forcibly from the house. Early the next morning I took the deeds to the Secretary General's office, where I had to wait some hours before the personage himself arrived, some short while before noon. I was admitted to his office where he sat behind his desk, smiling in his kindly way. He accepted the papers and put them on his desk without glancing at them. Then he offered me a cup of coffee and allowed me to take two careful sips of it before he gestured to the military officer who was in the room with us. The officer stepped toward me, hands on hips, and indicated with a curt swivel of his fleshy head that I should leave the office ahead of him. He took me to a small room with a high barred window and then left. I heard him bolt and padlock the door from outside. The room smelled of urine and was streaked with faintly dark patches that looked like marks of pain.

They came for me a long time later, late in the afternoon, two young soldiers armed with machine guns. I was desperate for the toilet by then, and I was afraid that in my terror I would be unable to hold on and would soil myself, and compound my indignity with shame. They searched me and took what little I had on me, shouting and handling me and slapping me for the sheer pleasure of their work. Then they pushed and shoved me down the corridors toward the covered jeep that was waiting outside the Party headquarters, there in front of everybody, in the mild afternoon sun. There were witnesses, and I am not sure who is worse in such moments, the criminal or the innocents who stand by and watch and act as if nothing evil is taking place. There were witnesses outside, people walking by as if nothing was happening, strolling to their favorite cafés for a chat or to call on family or friends.

I only spent a few weeks in the prison, crowded with more than a dozen others in a small cell, which was nonetheless airy and light. All the cells had a barred half-wall that looked into a central yard, or perhaps it would be more correct to say that the central yard looked into all the cells, so that even at night you could not be sure that there wasn't someone in the yard keeping an eye on what you were doing or dreaming of doing. At least it meant that we had some air and could see the prisoners in the other cells, and so in some small way it seemed less like a prison than I had expected it to be. Our cell was in one of the corners and did not receive as much breeze as some of the others, which meant that at night we were badly troubled by mosquitoes. There was neither a leaf nor a blade of grass in the concreted yard, nor even a weed clinging to a crack in the wall.

I knew so many people in there, for the government had been

filling the prison up from the day after independence. All of them looked more drawn and weary than they used to do, their clothes faded and well-washed. Despite the squalor and the deprivations, a kind of courtesy ruled. We spoke politely to each other, made room if possible, looked away and said nothing while the necessary had to be done, asked after each other's aches and pains, and talked endlessly. I had very little to say, and a great deal to learn from these men who, though jailed in some cases for two or three years, seemed so well informed about the outside. I listened to the avid conversations with politeness and some eagerness. Some of it was very entertaining, the kind of impossible humor that people in difficulties sometimes manage despite their circumstances. Twice a day we were allowed out of our cells to clean up and exercise in the yard, and twice a week the doctor visited. Every afternoon, relatives brought a basket of food for their loved ones, who would otherwise have only the meager rations of the prison: cassava, beans and tea. Not impossible rations, but the basket of food brought the home closer, made the people there seem near, made the bread we broke seem blessed by affection and care. Once a week the basket contained a change of clothes, a T-shirt and a saruni.

The baskets were handed over to the guards at the gates. The relatives were not allowed to see the prisoners, and the guards searched the baskets to make sure there were no messages or weapons. Labels were attached and they were then all put in the yard for the prisoners to collect. On occasions the guards pilfered the baskets, and made this seem a joke. I received a basket on my third day there, which filled me with stupid relief. At least she knew where I was, as if that would bring comfort to her.

Sometimes there were punishments, beatings and abuse, and I heard from the others about the terrible things they had witnessed in their time there. Beatings with rubber hoses, truncheon whippings, being made to walk barefoot on broken glass. The prisoners spoke about these incidents in detail and discussed the consequences on their victims with lowered voices, as if that would spare them knowledge of their cowed humiliations. The punishments were administered in the open yard by people who still walk the streets of that town today, as do some of their victims. In my time there all I saw were shouting and abuse, and floggings with a bamboo cane.

In my third week, the President of the Republic dropped in. He did this now and then for the sheer pleasure of seeing his enemies all safely locked up, all abject and terrified, and to hear them beg for mercy and release. He didn't linger in front of our cell, strolling past in beastly good health, while his entourage of the doctor, the prison governor and his bodyguard followed almost stealthily behind. He didn't linger in front of our cell because he had favorites that he always called upon, particular enemies that he gazed on with satisfaction and exchanged jocular banter with. He asked the doctor to examine them regularly, to make sure that they were well, and if not to arrange for them to be offered treatment immediately, so that they could go on enjoying being in prison for a long time to come.

In front of one cell, he paused for a long minute to stare at one of the prisoners, as if he was seeing him for the first time and found something intriguing or troubling about him. The prisoner was a primary schoolteacher who had offended by giving way to outbursts on political rights in Nature Study classes. Even after several friendly warnings from parents, it appeared that he could not control himself, and in the end a group of parents reported him to the relevant authorities. The tall, gangly man was so thin and feeble-looking that the President of the Republic must have wondered who the specimen was and where he had found the spark to do whatever reckless thing it was that had brought him there. Or perhaps he knew well enough who the man was, and was only reflecting on the unpredictability of the children of Adam. Who can guess at the workings of the mind of the President? He paused there for a few moments longer, and delivered an impromptu speech on the need for unity and hard work, the motto inscribed under the national arms. If we all lived by that humane motto, he told us, turning now to include all of us in the prison yard, the nation would grow stronger and progress. Then, the tour over, he stopped at the gateway out of the central yard and surveyed us with satisfaction, his body rippling with low rumbling laughter.

At the end of my third week, I was called out of my cell in the early evening, after we had all been locked in for the night. The guard warned me not to make a noise, even though he knew that everyone in their cells would be watching in the light of the yard. I was taken through the gate out of the central yard into another smaller yard beyond. I knew that was where the punishment cells were, and where the solitary prisoner was kept, although no one knew who he was. The guards said he had been in there for thirty years, locked up by the British for a crime he had committed in another country, something political probably. After so long he was completely deranged and unable to make any sense. In any case, no one any longer understood the language he spoke, and there was no option but to leave him where he was. I was put in one of the punishment cells and locked in the dark, smelling the damp distemper of chalk and lime on the walls. I saw a glimpse of the stars through the narrow barred slit high in the wall. I sat on the bare floor and stretched my legs out, feeling for the bucket that I expected to be there but which was not. For a while I felt comfortable and at ease in my solitariness. I tried, as I had been trying since my first arrival in prison, not to think about the meaning of what was happening, or what had befallen the loved ones I had been taken away from. I tried and did not succeed, and tried again and failed again, and went on like that as long as my energy held out, keeping thoughts of my anxieties at bay by trying and failing and trying again. When I was exhausted, misery swamped me and I lay curled up on the floor and sobbed. Mosquitoes crowded around me.

In the darkest hour of the night, I heard voices outside the cell and my heart leaped. I had fallen asleep, and the voices woke me, and for a moment I forgot where I was. I must have thought I was at home, and the voices were intruders who meant me harm. Torches shone into the cell, and I heard someone laugh. Someone shouted for me to get up, shining the torch in my face so I could not see where I was going. I heard someone else laugh—two of them, or perhaps more, laughing together. I thought one of them sounded familiar, and I was afraid. I was made to climb into the back of a covered jeep, and made to lie facedown on the floor. The voices stood talking and bantering in the yard for some time, while someone sat with me in the jeep, his boot on the back of my neck. I suppose it was to keep me from leaping out and running off into the night. The pressure of the boot made the blood rush to my head, and in the roar I could no longer catch the familiarity of the laughter I thought I had recognized before.

When the courtesies were over, someone else got into the back of the jeep, and my tormentor at last took his boot off my neck. The new voice was excited, flattered by the attentions of the superior it had been conversing with. "Do you know what he said? He said, 'I won't forget this, young man.' He's going to be a big man one day. He's already more or less the deputy . . ." The one with the boot interrupted him and made him stop. I guessed then that they were talking about the Minister of Development and Resources himself, who was spoken of as a big man with a dazzling future, already more or less the deputy to the President. That must have been the laughter that was familiar, for even though I did not know Abdalla Khalfan that well, I had heard him give speeches and knew his voice well enough for it to be familiar in the dark. I could not believe that he would be reckless enough and petty enough to come and arrange my little trip personally, when he could have left it to so many eager hands. Perhaps I underestimated my vileness to him and to Asha, and had not anticipated that he would want to administer what had been decreed for me with his own hand. I could not suppress a catch of terror, gulping and coughing as I choked on the smell of petrol and sweat at the bottom of the jeep. I knew then that I was to be taken to a beach in the country to be disposed of, as rumor had it so many others had been. But I was not to be shot. When the jeep stopped, dawn was rising and we were in the harbor. I turned away from the soldiers who transported me there, and in an uncontrollable spasm of relief I urinated at length on the harbor cobblestones.

I was escorted on board a motor launch which was tied up alongside, and taken below. There were two other men down there, chained by the ankles to a low rail that ran along the side of the boat. I too was made to sit on the floor and was chained by anklets to the same rail. I did not recognize the two other men, and it turned out they were from another island altogether, en route to our common jail. In time I was to discover that they were brothers who had been accused of poisoning an uncle who was their benefactor, and who were accused of doing it through witchcraft in a part of the country where people still believed in such things. They were innocent, of course, so they said. The boat set off immediately, and after a journey that lasted for some hours, we arrived at our destination in early afternoon. My companions had been cheerful most of the way, chatting with some animation about the comical eccentricities of people they knew, filling me in with the necessary background when they thought I needed it, inviting my opinion on the strangeness of actions which they thought remarkable, as if we were lazing under the village mango tree on a long, eventless day, or passing time outside a café over coffee and conversation. When we arrived, our chains were taken off and we went up on deck, and saw that we had stopped at a small island. I had guessed this would be our destination when they brought me to the wharf.

The government had been using the island as a detention center since independence. They rounded up whole families of people of Omani descent, especially those who lived in the country or wore beards and turbans or were related to the ousted sultan, and transported them to the small island some distance offshore. There they were detained under guard, until eventually, several months later, ships chartered by the Omani government took them away in their thousands. There were so many of them that it was weeks before the ships stopped coming. It was known that there were still some people detained there. The whole island was out of bounds to visitors, so what was known about what happened there relied on rumor and a photograph snapped by someone unknown and printed in a newspaper in Kenya. It showed a scene which was not unfamiliar from press photographs of other disasters—a crowd of people squatting on the ground, some of them with heads bent, some looking toward the camera with tired melting eyes, some with cautious interest, bearded men capless and worn out, women with heads shawled and eyes cast down, children staring.

The officer in charge of the island came down to the jetty himself to meet us off the boat. He was a bloated, laughing man, and as he shouted his welcome to us he took off his forage cap and waved it at us. It was as if we were longed-for guests that he was happy to see at last. This was his manner all the time, laughing and shouting his enjoyment of everything, glistening with joy at the unexpected complexities that life was full of, until he became irritated or cross. Then he became foulmouthed and violent. It was not always easy to predict what would irritate or cross him, and as it turned out, he had his favorite victims that he loved to torment. He escorted the three of us along a rising path, talking cheerfully about the wonderful, pleasant place we had come to and even putting an arm around each of our shoulders in turn. At the top of the rise, where the ground leveled, was a building with an under-house. That was the guardhouse and he took us there to record our arrival. His office opened onto a large veranda which had a beautiful view of the island and the sea, and in the far distance the shore of the main island. He sat in a cane chair on the veranda, leaning back and slowly stroking his belly as he smilingly studied us, while we sat in the sun, cross-legged at his feet. After a few moments of this kindly re-gard, the smile faded from his face and then he leaned forward and lectured us about our crimes and about the rules of his kingdom.

Apparently my crime was to be found in possession of state papers, which fortunately were of only minor economic interest, intended to enable me to commit fraud, whereas if I had been found with anything that endangered national security, he, the commanding officer of the Island Detention Site, would have shot me personally and fed me to the sharks. "Yes, there are sharks in these waters," he said, turning now to the two brothers. He could see, I suppose, that I was not likely to make a dash for freedom by swimming off the island, but the brothers looked strong and hardy, capable of that kind of impetuosity. "What," he said, "is all this nonsense about witchcraft? You embarrass us with these ridiculous crimes. You want everybody to think we are backward people who do witchcraft? If I catch you doing any of that stupidity with goat stomachs and frog testicles, I will whip you with my own personal hand. In this country now people have certificates and degrees, and you people in swamps and bushes still think you can get your own way with poison and bat's blood. Are you hearing me? I will whip you until only your eyes are left if I catch you doing that nonsense here." He told us that we had been brought to the island because we were dangerous and stupid, and that we would be kept there until we had learned better.

There was a prison building on the island, constructed by the British at the turn of the century as a secure location for any difficult natives that might arise, rise up, but very few did and it was not used for long. A prison in town, the same one I had been a guest in for a few weeks, had at first been thought vulnerable to acts of rescue and insurrection, but had after all proved convenient and safe. There were no acts of rescue or insurrection. Then, in an act so characteristic of the magnanimity of British colonial rule—which, once it had secured its supremacy, never failed to remind itself of the high moral purpose behind the whole enterprise—the island was turned into a sanatorium for convalescent tuberculosis victims. The new quarters were themselves little more than cells, but they faced the sea and each had an unbarred door that opened on a clearing shaded by casuarina trees. Even though the prison was not in use, a caretaker was appointed to keep it in good order, and to clean and tend the graves of the three British naval officers buried on the island after a disaster at the end of the nineteenth century. The headstones said they all three died on the island after an accident at sea. The caretaker was one of the convalescent patients, and he stayed on after the island sanatorium was closed and a new one opened in town. The decision to close the sanatorium was made as a result of the increasing confidence of the British medical authorities (two doctors) that TB was under control in the territory. The caretaker was still there when I was taken to the island,

and his prison was still standing, though walls had collapsed here and there. And the sanatorium cells were still usable, kept under lock and key and regularly aired. And the three graves were still carefully weeded, and the headstones kept clear of climbers, as their relatives would like to know, if they still remembered them or remembered where they had died or why. The caretaker was a shrunken, sprightly old man with scheming eyes, living a secret life of imperial duties and hoarded stores, tending the monuments of an empire which had retreated to the safety of its own ramparts and forgotten him.

I suffered no hardship on the island. The commanding officer, as he liked to call himself, took no interest in me, nor did the other five soldiers under his command. I offered no resistance to any instructions and obeyed all the rules. The two brothers settled in cheerfully, sitting talking with the soldiers like old friends, willing butts of their teasing, helping out, pilfering from them when they had the chance, climbing trees, swimming, like two scallywags on a romp. The eyes of the commanding officer twinkled with pleasure at their mischief, and sometimes when he had not seen them for a few hours, he demanded that they be fetched before him, to keep an eye on them, he said, but really because he liked to have them tumbling nearby. Somehow I did not think they would spend very long in jail. There were eleven other detainees on the island, all men, and all awaiting deportation. They had missed the relief ships that took so many to Oman, and were still en route to the island from other detention sites when the boats stopped coming. Now they were being held on the island until word reached the Omani authorities of their plight, and some means of transporting them *home* could be arranged. In truth, they were no more Omani than I was, except that they had an ancestor who was born there. They did not even look any different from the rest of us, perhaps slightly paler or slightly darker, perhaps their hair was slightly straighter or slightly curlier. Their crime was the ignoble history of Oman in these parts, and that was not a connection they were allowed to give up. In other respects they were indigenes, citizens, raiiya, and they were sons of indigenes, but after their treatment at the hands of various commanding officers, they were eager to leave, and spoke as despisingly of their persecutors as their persecutors did of them. It was to these detainees that the commanding officer and his troops devoted their attention, tormenting them, ordering them to do endless menial tasks, abusing them, and at times beating them. One of the detainees kept a diary of all the persecutions that befell them, hiding the torn scraps of his futile indictment between the pages of his copy of the Koran.

It was in contemplation of these miscreants that the commanding officer arrived at his inspired attempt at mercy one morning. "Why not go with them when the ship comes?" he suggested. "We haven't yet received any information about the arrival of the ships, but why not just go with these others when they do arrive? No one here will stop you." I wondered if this was the arrangement all along, that I would be kept on the island until the ship came for the remaining detainees and then I would be deported. "No," I said to the commanding officer. "You are very kind, but I can't even contemplate such a course of action. I can't even think such a thought. My wife and my child are waiting for my release, and I must act with fortitude and accept what punishment has been decreed for my crime, so that in time I can return to them and live with them. They will depend on that and will expect that. I have no desire for any other place or any other way of life." I saw him weighing me up, turning over what I had said in his mind, wondering, no doubt, whether he should bother getting cross with my sanctimonious rejection of his generosity. Then he laughed, his big belly leaping with mockery, but not unkindly. "Women," he said. "Well, I hope she's still waiting when they let you out."

I suffered no hardship on the island. The prison building was arranged around a yard like three sides of a rectangle. The open side faced the sea, and had a platform built over the water as an outdoor latrine. It was safe enough to use, and could at times be pleasant, squatting over the opening with your back to the sea and your saruni draped over your knees, so there was no indecency in the sight. The prison building had an upstairs, though none of the cells up there were in use. Five of the down-stairs cells were in use, and I had one completely to myself. The brothers shared one and the other detainees shared the re-maining three. They preferred to be kept together like that. The cells were locked only after dark, otherwise we were free to wander around the island during the day or swim. It was a very small island, and it was necessary to find a space that you liked and claim it, so others would know that was where you preferred to be and would leave you to it. Every day I sought out the old caretaker and sat with him for a little while, listening to his sto-ries of the British and the duties they had left him with. The troops slept in the under-house and the commanding officer on a camp bed in his office. Why did they not use the sanatorium houses? I asked the caretaker. The old man grinned in toothless

mischief and said that he had told them the cells were still infected with TB, and if they slept in there they would get it too.

"Why do you want them kept empty?" I asked. "They'll get
the damp and collapse with all this sea air."

He said: "No they won't, I air them every day, and I sweep
them and repair the plaster when it shows any sign of corruption."

"Why?" I asked him.

"Who knows when the doctors will come back," he said.

"Babu, they won't be coming back," I said.

His eyes danced with secret knowledge but he did not reply.

Months passed this way. In the morning we did whatever
chores we were required to do—cleaning, washing clothes, weed-
ing and digging the small field that provided the guards as well
as the detainees with vegetables. Then the prisoners took turns
to cook or bartered one chore for another, and then we ate together, guards and prisoners. Late in the afternoon, I sat on the
beach below the guardhouse and watched the outriggers setting out singly from the town, leaning a little to one side as the
breeze bellied out the sail, beautiful fragile crafts in that red-
dening sun. They would be fishermen setting out for a night's
work, and they were under instructions to avoid the island, but
often they came near enough to see us and return our waves. At
any time the guards could explode with irritation and blows, and
once it was dark we were locked in. We smelled the food they
cooked for themselves in the evening. Every fortnight or so, the
motor launch called with provisions: cassava, bananas, rice, even
meat, which was intended for the troops and had to be cooked
and eaten the same day, as they had no way of keeping it for longer. Our food was rice or vegetables, and we ate once a day.

One day we saw the launch come as usual, but it brought no supplies. It had come for the men awaiting deportation. The commanding officer sent his troops to gather the detainees and then gave them one minute to collect what they wished to take and then line up by the jetty. It was another of his persecutions, even at this late moment. When they were not quick enough for his liking, he fumed and raved at them, laughing as they ducked his blows and tried to evade his kicks. When they were lined up by the jetty and waiting to board, he looked for me and asked me to approach him. "Go with them," he said, frowning, still breathing heavily and running with sweat from his exertions with the Omani detainees. I was afraid that he would be irritated if I refused his generosity again, but I shook my head and retreated from him. I was then thirty-seven years old, midway through my life as I thought of it. I had no desire to abandon Salha, the woman I had come to love so unexpectedly and now could only think of alone and in the dark, for fear of sobbing with longing for her. Nor did I have any desire to abandon the daughter I wished to love more fully for what would be left of my life after my release. If I left and they refused to let her follow me, I would be lost, more lost than I was or could ever become. If they thought that I had abandoned them to whatever was to follow in order to save my puny life, I would have lost the only affection I had been able to cherish, and my life would be devastated. I would accept what befell me with what fortitude I could, and suffer as she had to suffer on her own, so that one day when the oppression ended I would be able to return to her with myself intact, and listen to her tales of suffering with a sense of having borne what we did for something, after all. The commanding officer shook his head sadly at me as I retreated. Briefly, in a moment of terror, I wondered if he knew something I didn't know, if he knew of something proposed for me that he was trying to save me from. But then he grinned and made a gesture of despair as he waved me away.

In a few moments the boat began to pull away, and we watched as it made a large loop and then built up speed toward the main shore. The detainees did not look back, or at least they did not return my wave. I stood watching for a long time, until they disappeared over the curve of the world. For the next few days, the troops left our cell doors unlocked at night, and we even sat with them on the veranda in the evening and shared their food and played cards with them. The commanding officer sat nearby, listening to a transistor radio, and I heard the date and marveled. I had been detained for seven months, and had not heard a radio in that time. My hair had grown big and my clothes were worn out. My body was drawn and aching.

"You should've gone with your brothers," the commanding officer said.

"They're your brothers too," I said, though I said it mildly for fear of offending our ruler, so mildly that I had to repeat it before he heard me.

"Yes," he said, laughing. "The Omanis fucked all our mothers."

"And this is as much their home as it is mine, as it is yours," I said.

"Sote wananchi," he said satirically, booming with his knowing laughter. *All of us are children of the land.*

ABDULRAZAK GURNAH

Every night, the commanding officer's radio broadcast
speeches by one personage or another, haranguing and hector-
ing, rewriting history and offering homespun moralities that
justified oppression and torture. The radio service never tired of
this raucous sermon, though for variety it provided a news bul-
letin now and then, twisted and angled and squeezed news, but
welcome nonetheless for the way it brought the possibility of life
nearer. The news was all about Nigeria on the brink of war, and
how we were the only country in Africa, perhaps the only country
in the whole world to recognize the existence of Biafra. The an-
nouncer loved saying the name of the Biafran leader, Colonel
Ojukwu, and every time it came up in his commentary there was
a tiny pause as he swelled his mouth for the beloved words.
Kanal Ojukwu. Behind and all around us was the pounding of
the sea. Sometimes we felt the lightest touch of spray. We sat by
the light of a small kerosene lamp, placed in the middle of the
board on which we played cards. On the moonless nights of
those few days, the commanding officer was barely visible on his
side of the veranda, just a slight thickening of the night where he
sat, and a glowing eye of rage when he smoked. From the veranda, the view was all sea and the stars. At night it was as if
there was no sky, just a dense mass of stars bearing down. The
sea frothed and turned endlessly, catching the light of the stars
in filigreed crests, sighing and snapping and rushing at the rocks
on our lee. Low on the horizon, the glow of the town was visible
as an aurora on the far edge of the sea.

Some nights, after returning to my cell in the prison building, I heard singing coming over the crown of trees, hovering
there like something light and unreal, a whisper in the air. I

thought it was the old man singing to himself, for the sanatorium buildings were on the other shore of the island through the copse of trees, but when I asked him he said it wasn't him. A snake lived on the island, he said, near the pond in the hollow, and it came out at night to feed on the frogs. Now and then it wandered away from the pond, and perhaps I had heard the disturbance in the air that it made as it slid by. Once, he said, he saw a column of spray race across the surface of the sea and stop on the island. When he went nearer to investigate he found a large Black figure, a jinn, sleeping under a tree with a large casket open beside his head. In the large casket was a woman, stroking her hair and singing to herself, and then licking her jeweled fingers one by one, as if something sweet still remained on them. Perhaps it was her I had heard, he said. Some poor creature stolen by a Black jinn and kept in a casket for his pleasure. Did I know why she was licking her jeweled fingers like that? he asked me. Because while the jinn slept, she seduced any man that was nearby and took a ring as a token of her pleasure. So when she licked her fingers like that she was living again the feeling of all the men she had taken. Then I saw that for the old man the island was crowded with enchanted life, with British naval officers and British doctors and convalescing patients, and serpents and imprisoned women singing in the night air, and dark jinns that raced across the sea to rest from their immortal questing for mischief.

One morning, a few days after the dispatch of the deported detainees, the boat came for us. We were being taken off the island, all of us. The troops were in no hurry to leave, and by the time the boat was loaded it was early afternoon. I tried to find the old man, to say goodbye to him, but he had disappeared like

one of his enchanted creatures. On that small island it was difficult to imagine where he could be hiding, and after making a
circuit twice, I gave up in case my searching should cause him
anxiety. Perhaps he feared that we would take him with us, and
had turned himself into a column of spray and slid out to sea to
await our departure. It was dark when we arrived in town, and
the harbor was deserted and silent. It looked as it always had,
and it was a pang to loiter in that way on the threshold of home.
I had not even dared contemplate the possibility of release, and
so it turned out to be. I was ordered into a jeep and driven for a
few minutes and asked to get off again. It was not until I was
aboard the ferry ship with about thirty other prisoners being
transported to the mainland that I realized that I had not had
time to say goodbye to the two good brothers, either.

The ship left in the dark, and arrived on the mainland later in
the day, but we were not disembarked until it was night. Then
we were loaded in two trucks, our names called out to go in one
truck or another. I recognized some of the names. When we set
off, the two trucks went in different directions, and our guards
told us that we were heading for the south. I have taught myself
not to speak of the years which followed, although I have forgotten little of them. The years were written in the language of
the body, and it is not a language I can speak with words. Sometimes I see photographs of people in distress, and the image of
their misery and pain echoes in my body and makes me ache
with them. And the same image teaches me to suppress the
memory of my oppression, because, after all, I am here and well
while only God knows where some of them are. Just recently I
saw a photograph like that, an old photograph. It showed three

Jewish men on their hands and knees—one dressed in a dark suit and tie, the other two in their shirt-sleeves, one with sleeves rolled up. They were scrubbing the pavements of Vienna with hand brushes. All around them, close up to them, on the pavement behind them and in front of them, stood crowds of the Viennese, grinning and looking on. People of all ages, mothers and fathers and grandfathers and children, some leaning on bicycles, others carrying shopping bags, standing smiling in their ordinary respectability while those three men were degraded in front of them. Not a swastika in sight, just ordinary people laughing at the humiliation of three Jews. God knows what happened to those three men.

Altogether I was kept in three different detention camps, supervised by soldiers and only occasionally suffering punishment or brutality. The soldiers subdued us with terror and violent, unpredictable outbursts. Everything about the condition we lived in was bleak and uncomfortable. We grew our own food, cleaned and built latrines, washed the soldiers' clothes, wove baskets, and we became weak and worn out from malnutrition and disease and tedium. Insect bites turned into sores that turned putrid and refused to heal. Our bowels tormented us all the time, with hunger, with constipation and wind from the unvarying diet of starch and beans, with diarrhea from the bad water and from infections. My bowels tormented me so much that often my self seemed contracted into them. We did whatever the day required until it slid into the relief of an arid night. Sometimes we had news from outside, whispers and rumors of assassinations and arrests, an approaching amnesty which never materialized, wars and coups. We were not allowed a radio or books. At times I felt such hatred that I have no words to describe it. I shook with it, could have destroyed myself with the rage of it, thrown myself into a fire, or off a ledge of a cliff or on to the gleaming blade of a saber or the point of a bayonet.

Instead we prayed: every day, five times a day, as God commanded. He had caught up with all of us, the worst and the best. We prayed at the precise times specified by the tradition, not a little later or the next day or not at all, as was often the case in the pointless frivolity of our ordinary lives. At dawn: the time for prayer was between the appearance of the first line of light and the first sight of the sun, a briefer moment than might be imagined. At noon: the specified time was the moment after a vertical stick planted in the ground had lost its shadow, the very instant after the sun had passed directly overhead. In the afternoon: we rose to the silent prayer at that time of day when the shadow of the stick had grown to be equal to the length of the stick. At sunset: we prayed between the setting of the sun under the horizon and the disappearance of the sun's glow. At night: we waited until the descent of deep darkness before we prayed and then afterward stretched out on our mats to sleep. The prayers filled out the days, as did recitations of the Koran from memory, which we retrieved according to our degrees. They brought order and purpose to our chores, and a stoicism that would otherwise have been inconceivable. And we told stories, some remembered, some invented, laughing as if we were once again the same age as when we first heard them.

I was moved twice, once because my malaria became critical and I started to pass blood. When the blood began to turn dark, my fellow prisoners read Ya Latif over me, fearing the worst. I had passed out by then, but I know that my fellows did all they could think of from the lore of the treatment of malaria, and I recovered. I was feeble and unable to move for days, but I had survived. I can't describe how sweet that knowledge was. After recovery, I was moved to Arusha under doctor's instructions. The doctor and his two assistants turned up unexpectedly in their white jeep. He was a Swedish man in brown shorts and white shirt, his face red and his fair hair burnished a deep gold from the sun. His fleshy lips were turned down in a look of weary disgust as we were lined up for a medical. What was he doing there? Who had sent for him? I don't know why he ordered I should be moved, and to somewhere so far away. Perhaps it was a protest against the inhumanity of our conditions, an attempt to do something for at least one of us. Or perhaps he could not resist exercising the authority a European doctor possesses in countries such as ours. In any case, they took me away in their white jeep, covering my threadbare rags with a red blanket that smelled of disinfectant and decency. They delivered me to an army camp some miles away, whose existence we had not even known about. From there I was transported in an army jeep all the way to Arusha.

I was moved alone, and the time I spent there among complete strangers was lonely at first but became unexpectedly fulfilling as I learned more about growing vegetables and fruit. While I was there I was treated with a passionless brutality that gave purpose to every day and every minute. I was sent away from there when two inmates died from an outbreak of cholera, and we were all sent to a camp in the northwest, to die perhaps without inconveniencing others. That was the third detention center I was sent to. But no one else died, so in time we were dispersed to other detention sites, and I was returned to the one in the south where I had spent three years before and was to spend another four before my release. Most of us fell ill in that time, and two of our fellows died, but little else changed. The guards came and went and that sometimes made a difference, but it did not alter the magnitude of our circumstances. A medical team visited every few months, perhaps as a result of the Swedish man, and sometimes people living nearby came to watch us from a distance, and at night raided our vegetable fields. When we complained the guards told us it must have been animals.

I was released under amnesty in 1979, eleven years after my arrest in the Party headquarters. The amnesty was extended to prisoners who had served more than half their term, and whose crimes did not include treason or murder. In the case of those who had committed treason, they would be expelled from the country. It was to celebrate the victory of the nation's armed forces over the brutal dictatorship of Idi Amin in Uganda. All of the prisoners who had been brought from the ship in that one truck that dark night were released—all of the ones who had survived, which was eleven of us. The majority were released on condition of accepting immediate exit visas which would expel them from the country. In other words, most of my fellows were in detention for treason, it would appear, though it would be hard to imagine a less likely-looking group of traitors. It would have been funny had it not been tragic to be detained for so long only to be turned into a refugee from the memories you had clung to over the years. And since no one had expected to be released and so had not negotiated entry into any other country, all those about to be released under this condition had to wait until they could show that they had received an entry visa to somewhere. They could not do that in prison but they could not be allowed out until they could, or could get their relatives to do so. So it was no release at all, and three of us who had not been served expulsion orders chose to stay in detention until the ones who had been expelled were also released. At least we knew that we had served half the sentence even if we did not know what the full length of the sentence would have been.

There was no difficulty once the United Nations Refugees officials became involved, and the released detainees were all offered asylum by the United Arab Emirates. So one day in January 1980, we were issued with release papers and taken by truck back to the capital where we were separated, the refugees into the hands of UN officials, two of my fellows to their relatives in the capital, while I made my way to the harbor. I was at last able to imagine how changed Salha would be and how tall my daughter Ruqiya would have grown. I took ship back, and walked from the harbor as I had done with my father a lifetime ago. No one spoke to me, no one recognized me, and I kept my eyes lowered when anyone approached. Houses had collapsed, shops were empty. As I walked nearer my old store I saw familiar faces, but I did not want to be delayed and still no one seemed to recognize me. I stopped in front of my old store, boarded up and padlocked, and stared in amazement at how familiar it looked, as if I had only last seen it a month or two ago. I felt an arm on my elbow, and turned to find the coffee seller, whose business opposite I had assassinated years before, standing old and infirm beside me. It was he who told me that Salha had died, passed away, may God have mercy on her soul, and my daughter Ruqiya, my daughter Raiiya, had preceded her by a few days, may God have mercy on her soul. That they had both died in the first year of my imprisonment. Her parents with whom she had been staying after my arrest left the country. The coffee seller did not know to go where, although someone would know. I will say no more about that, except that both mother and daughter died after a brief illness, typhoid it was thought.

The old coffee seller, who was no longer working, took me to the chairman of the local Party branch, a different man from the one who had accompanied me to the Party headquarters the day before my arrest. With his permission we broke the lock to my store. Everything was as Nuhu and I had left it, except for the dust and cobwebs and some fallen plaster. Neighbors came to gaze and exult over my return, and many offered me food and kindness. I cannot describe the kindnesses I received in those weeks after my release. I lived in the store, and in time cleaned one of the back rooms and moved in there so I could start trading again, though in a different way now. I sold what items I had that were of value, and bought fruit and vegetables for sale, and gradually added other small items of a similar kind, matches, soap and some tinned fish. Nobody asked me to speak of my imprisonment.

So many people had left or been expelled or died. So many evils and hardships had befallen and were still befalling those who remained, and no one had a monopoly of suffering and loss. So I opened my store and devoted myself to a quiet life, speaking without rancor about what it was necessary to say, listening with fortitude to the anguished stories of the life that had become our lot. People treated me as a man destroyed by prison and personal tragedy, and they spoke to me kindly and forbearingly, and I responded with grateful and witless goodwill. And later, when I was on my own in the darkness of my crumbling store, I lamented the loss of my loved ones and grieved for them, and when that grief palled I was saddened by the wasted life I had lived.

Yes, Rajab Shaaban Mahmud now lived in the house I had used to live in. I avoided passing that way, and when he walked past the shop, which he did every day, I dropped my eyes and let him stare with his undiminishing hatred. He was much changed, ascetic and demented-looking, his clothes threadbare and unclean. Sometimes I had a fancy that it was he who had been in prison and not me, for despite appearances I was resolute inside to avoid further indignities if I could, to live the wasted life that was my lot with what composure I could manage, as a mute recognition of what little bits of decency had come my way. I fear that I sound pious and holy, but I had time in prison to reflect and learn gratitude. I ceased to care about the house and about Rajab Shaaban Mahmud in those years in detention, and when he walked past the shop, glaring with hatred, I offered no resistance or acknowledgment of his claim on me.

His wife Asha had died. Her lover, the Minister of Development and Resources, had fallen in 1972, in a bloodletting among the beasts, which we had heard about when we were in prison. The President and the Secretary General of the Party were assassinated while they sat at one of the very sessions that I had attended so long ago, and in the reprisals that followed, the former Minister was arrested. He managed to save his life and flee, and was now said to be in Scandinavia somewhere, organizing our liberation. Rajab Shaaban Mahmud had walked through the streets exulting over the humbling of Abdalla Khalfan, I was told, making a clown of himself as he spoke fierce words about his cuckolding for all those years, when it had seemed in all that time that he had no thoughts on the matter. By then, Asha and Rajab Shaaban Mahmud were living in our old house. It was while still living there several years later that she died, a year or so before my release, although no one volunteered to me what she died of, just that she died.

For years I lived like that, poor and frightened like everyone else, ears cocked for the latest malice and vindictiveness by our rulers, although our condition eased a little over the last ten years. No, I never thought of leaving. To go where? To do what? I did enough business to feed and clothe myself, and as time passed I was able to live in reasonable safety and comfort. I still had several of the books I had acquired all those decades ago from departing colonial officials, some of them chewed and holed by cockroaches now, and I worked my way slowly through them. Some people began to persuade me to make a claim for the old house. So many people had got their property back by doing just that. I had never been convicted in a court of law, and those who had tried me were all in disgrace or dead, so they would not be able to bring influence to bear on my plea. The deeds of the house named me and were still available in the Registry office, no doubt, to confirm my rightful ownership. But I had no interest in the house, and neither strength nor desire for a fight, and I smiled my gratitude to these well-wishers and let the matter pass.

Rajab Shaaban Mahmud passed away in 1994. Living alone in that house which was always shuttered and locked, he was not discovered until two or three days after his death, when he failed to appear at the mosque. In the end neighbors forced open a window and found him decomposing in his bed. May God have mercy on his soul. I went to the reading after the funeral, as did many others in the neighborhood, but I stayed in the courtyard of the mosque for fear of offending anyone.

A few months later, sometime last year, out of nowhere, Hassan returned. Yes, Hassan returned. One of the customers told me, exclaiming that even the passing away of those God loved brought some good with it. For the death of the pious father has resulted in the return of his beloved son. Yes, Hassan returned to claim the house that belonged to his father. Yes, he came back after thirty-four years to lay claim to that wretched pile of rubble and misery, when he had not thought to announce himself to his father even once in that time. He was a man of means now, a man of the world, you could see that, tall, bearded, well-dressed, nothing of the youthful wayward lover left in him. In the first days after he arrived, he dressed in the style of the Gulf, a long baggy kanzu of heavy bafta, the pockets bulging with a wallet and a Filofax, a small cap on his head and his face wrapped in reflecting sunglasses. He was received with amazement, and strolled through the streets like a prodigal, Sindbad back from his first voyage, smiling broadly at his joyful return and handing out gifts and alms to the needy.

We were taking a walk on the seafront when I said this, and Latif Mahmud stopped to listen, his eyes looking away from me in attention. "So he's back at home," he said, smiling sadly and frowning irritably at the same time. "I asked you if you had any news of him, and you said no. You just had to have your moment of drama, I suppose."

"No, not for drama. I wanted you to see the moment he came back. I wanted you to see what that moment meant," I said.

"Where has he been all this time? Do you know?"

I shrugged. "I don't know. In the Gulf, I think, from the way he was dressed, in Saudi Arabia, in China for all I know. He didn't speak to me, not about that, and people who spoke to me avoided mentioning him because of all the meanness with your father. He looked a well-traveled man, Hassan, a man who had traveled well, and returned after a generation blessed with prosperity and honor and knowledge. When he walked he swung his arms freely, like someone ready to embrace the world. He was quite transformed from the secretive youth who had slid away with Hussein at the end of that musim."

"Yes, what happened to *him*?" Latif Mahmud asked, and I thought he asked with an edge of apprehension or anxiety, though I couldn't imagine what he feared.

"I don't know," I said.

"Tell me," he said, frowning, restraining himself from reaching for me, demanding of me. "You do know, don't you? Tell me."

"I don't know," I said. "Only that your brother Hassan inherited from him, though there were other inheritors as well, relatives and offspring. Hassan even looked a little bit like Hussein. Your father would have been proud to see him so triumphant."

"My father, yes, how terrible. I didn't know he only died last year. I thought they had both died years ago. Perhaps I dreamed it, fantasized it. Perhaps I wished it and thought it had happened as I desired. It sounds impossible, unnatural to say it like that. Sometimes I thought I had done it, that I had killed them by wishing them dead. But they weren't dead at all, they were there all the time. I never wrote to them, you see," Latif Mahmud said. We were walking on the promenade again by this time, and he stopped and turned round fully toward me, a look of scorn on his gaunt face. "When I escaped from GDR, I never wrote to them, and I guessed that they would not know where I was so they would never be able to write to me. I wanted nothing to do with them, and their hatreds and demands. Their hatreds of each other, the hatreds that made him rage and mumble and fall into that corrosive silence of his. I know you're not supposed to be able to say that about your parents, but it was a bit of luck, being able to escape from the GDR into a kind of anonymity, even to be able to change my name, to escape from them. To be able to start again. You know that fantasy?"

"But people knew where you were," I said carefully, not wishing to add to his pain. "We heard about you."

"So it seems," he said, smiling despite his gloom. "So Hassan's back . . . to claim his inheritance."

I marveled at Latif Mahmud's sternness about his parents, not because it was inconceivable from so far away, where the insistent demands of intimacy can be deflected with silence, but because I wondered about the price he would have had to pay for his perverse triumph, and how much those looks of pain owed to the inevitable distress and guilt he would feel. I marveled less at the gaunt unhappiness in his face after the misery he had inflicted on himself with his daring.

"If it is his inheritance, then half of it is yours too," I said, and saw him wince, which encouraged me into a little more mischief. "Your father did not leave a will, and the law requires that his property is divided between his male offspring in equal shares."

"Are you suggesting I should go back too? To claim my share?" he asked, a broad derisive grin on his face.

I shrugged. "I only mention that if Hassan inherits, then half of the house is yours. There are complications, though. It turns out that the Registry office still has an entry recording the deeds to the house in my name. I delivered the papers themselves to the Secretary General's office and they've disappeared, so your father never had legal title to the house. When Hassan came back, he lived in the house, and he treated me as an obstacle to his full rights to the property. So he sought to make legal the ruling made at Party headquarters all those years ago, that I was guilty of fraud and so on. He cultivated powerful people after his return, and because he was treated as a kind of returning hero by everyone, there was every likelihood that popular feeling would be on his side. He came to the shop one day, my little corner shop that sold vegetables and sugar and razor blades, not the carefully lit emporium where I sold expensive furniture. I say that so you can imagine it as it was. He asked for a glass of water, and after sipping from the glass, and after the obligatory courtesies, he asked me for any papers to do with the house. I told him I had none, that I had handed them over to the Secretary General of the Party as I was required all those years ago, though that personage was now gone, assassinated in the bloodletting in 1972, as I was sure he knew. Then he told me that the law would take its course, and that he would also bring a case against me for the money I owed his uncle Hussein. No no, I told him, it was

Hussein who owed me money. I had the papers to prove that. He asked for those papers, but I refused to give them to him. He told me that he had inherited from his uncle Hussein, and part of his inheritance was the money I owed to him. He too had the papers to prove that I owed the money, an affidavit that Hussein swore in Bahrain some years ago, with witnesses who would testify that they had witnessed the transaction here during the musim of 1960. I have no idea why both of them, Hussein and Hassan, should have undertaken such malice against me, and I said that to your brother. He laughed, the big-man laugh with which he announced his prosperity in the streets but which only thinly disguised the hatred and determination in his face. I looked around my shop, drawing his attention to its paltriness, and told him I had no money to pay him, even had he right and the law on his side. "We shall see," he said, his jaw clenched, his lip trembling with rage. Then he stepped into the doorway of the shop, in sight of passersby in the street, and abused me in public, the same way your father used to do now and again. He repeated the accusations, and then threatened me with imprisonment or worse when his case was won. I sat behind the shop counter like a whipped creature while he leaped and swooped and raged all around me, and a crowd gathered with broadening smiles to watch the spectacle. I thought he would beat me, until in the end someone approached him with solicitations of honor and propriety, and led him away to save further embarrassment to his self-respect. I had no trust in our legal system, and no strength for more hurly-burly in my life, so I packed my casket of ud-al-qamari and left."

The wind off the sea was beating strongly now, and perhaps

I staggered a little, because Latif Mahmud took me by the elbow and turned me away from the seafront toward one of the side streets that led back into the center of the town. "Why did you take his name when you decided to leave?" he asked, after a while of waiting for the traffic and negotiating crowded pavements. I felt so tired now, and wished he would take me by the elbow again and lead me to a table at one of the cafés we passed, and insist that we pause for a while and drink a cup of coffee. But he walked a half step ahead, dragging me on with his eyes and his body, pulling me, it seemed, against my will. "I asked you that question last time I came. It seems an age ago. I didn't ask it kindly, because I feared that it was done in a kind of mockery, gloating over him . . . because you had defeated him over the house. I didn't know about your arrest, about your wife Bi Salha and about your daughter Ruqiya, your daughter Raiiya. But now I know, it seems even stranger that you should have chosen his name."

"It is a ridiculous story, but it has a sweetness about it. One of the conditions of my amnesty was that I would not be allowed a passport," I said. "I suppose so that I would not go somewhere abroad and cause mischief, although I suspect it was just vindictiveness. Among the bits and pieces of furniture your father insisted on leaving behind when he gave up the house you all lived in—I did not want you to leave, I just wanted the title to the house. Anyway, I don't have the language to put that right, and the more I protest the more I will seem like another guilt-ridden old man seeking forgiveness. Which I do, of you and of all the others I have harmed because of my thoughtless vanity. Among the things he left behind was a box with some papers, and among those papers was his birth certificate. There was nothing else of value, old bills, old letters, some pamphlets and instruction leaflets. I noticed the birth certificate at the time and kept it out of mischief, thinking that its loss would cause him some inconvenience. I gave away everything else. I wanted nothing to do with the things you all left behind. Just the birth certificate, and the ebony table, I kept that as you know. I just kept that beautiful little table, which in later years was a scourge to remind me daily of my vanity and my loss. When Hassan came to the shop, I thought he would see the table, because Hussein had bought it for him all those years ago, but his eyes never lit on it."

Latif Mahmud hesitated for a moment, almost coming to a standstill. "I have a memory of you picking out some of the pieces and then sending the rest for auction. I have a picture of that," he said. "I followed the cart from our house, and I have a memory of you walking among the pieces and selecting things which you wanted."

I stared at him in astonishment. "No, it's not possible," I said, my voice trembling at this new accusation. As we stood there I thought I would collapse with exhaustion from age and blame. I pointed to a café a few paces away and we went to sit down. "After you left the house and I heard that some furniture was left behind, I sent word to your father that he should come and collect it, but he replied that we could keep it for all he cared. So I instructed Nuhu to remove everything and sell it, and send the money to your father. Neither your father nor your mother wanted the money, so I told Nuhu to give it away, that I did not want to see it or have anything to do with it. After disposing of the furniture, Nuhu brought back the box of papers, and the table because he remembered it from the shop. He told me the rest of what he removed was not worth much, and I did not care to inquire into it."

"The Bokharra, a big beautiful rug. How can you say that was worthless?"

"I'm sorry," I said.

"I have a memory of it, of you walking round that pile of furniture," he said wonderingly, stubbornly. He ordered coffee and cakes, and while we waited he looked away from me and I thought he would be ransacking the picture of that time, and wondering if I was lying to him or if it was possible that I had secreted away the memory in guilt. "Perhaps I wished that too," he said in the end, still wondering, still doubtful. "One of my self-gratifying fantasies, wishing you into the man of malice we knew you as in our house of hatreds. Perhaps it was Faru I saw walking among the things. Let's say for the moment that I imagined it . . . But it seems so strange to have a picture. Anyway, you talk too much about words like honor and courtesy and forgiveness. They mean nothing, just words. The most we can expect is a little kindness, I think, if we are in luck. I mean, *that* is what I think. Those big words are just part of a language of duplicity to disguise the nothingness of our lives. Go on, tell me about the birth certificate, although I think I can guess the rest."

"When I returned from prison it was still there, the birth certificate, and I kept it without thought. When I began to think of leaving, I gave it to a man who does such things. He acquires birth certificates of people who have died, often of dead children, and when someone needs a passport he finds a certificate that is of a reasonably similar age, of the age the child would have been had it lived, and applies for a passport in that name. I thanked God for that birth certificate, and so I became your father and obtained a passport in his name. After that I took out some of the money that was left in the bank, and gave it to someone else to arrange my ticket, and then I presented myself here for asylum."

He stayed with me so late that Sunday that in the end I offered him the sitting room, and he arranged some cushions on the floor and slept there. It was strange, after so many years, to have someone sleeping nearby. It made me feel younger. In that small space, I could hear his movements in the next room and it reminded me of living in our old house, and a little bit of being in prison, although there sleep was always hard to come by, and that night I slept without a second thought.

In the morning, I was up before him, which disappointed him, I think. (I mean, *that* is what I think. Such precision, a man of words.) Perhaps he did not want me to think him self-indulgent and self-pleasing, the kind of man who would lie in bed late when he is an unexpected guest in a house. I could have told him that it is hard to sleep late when you grow old, and I had risen so early because lying in bed tires me. He drank some coffee and made ready to leave, drinking it black and bitter and hot the way I had made it for myself but did not expect him to share. It made me smile to see him wince as he sipped.

"You must get a telephone," he said, as he stood by the door, one arm leaning on the doorframe.

"I have no urge to do so," I said, and saw him smile. I thought

I knew what he was thinking. He would have preferred me to say, *I prefer not to*. But I had been thinking of what Rachel said, and thought I would read "Bartleby" again before speaking his words as the utterings of an admired desperado.

"Then I'll just have to descend on you without warning next weekend," he said.

Which he did, and Rachel took us for a drive to somewhere called Water Valley where people swam in the lakes, and played with a kind of water cart, and others floated on nylon wings from the high steep slope of the valley toward the Downs. Then Rachel took us back to her house for a meal, and the next day Latif waited for me while I packed a few clothes to go and spend two days with him in London. He insisted, saying it was a crime that I had been in England for nine months (only seven but he swooped on regardless) and had never been to London, even though I only lived an hour away. So I was to go and stay with him for a few days. He would show me the city, and show me all those places every visitor wanted to see, and show me other places I did not know existed but which I might enjoy seeing even more than those stops on the Monopoly board. Although the Monopoly sites too were buildings and monuments of great presence and power. Then when I had seen enough, he would put me on the train and Rachel would meet me at the other end, as if I was a decrepit old father that they shared between them.

When I went into the apartment he lived in, it made me think of the room in my store where I had spent every night on my own for fifteen years. That room too had reeked of loneliness and futility, of long silent occupation. The living room light was too bright. The walls were bare, no pictures or decoration or even a clock. The furniture was cheap and sparse, except for a large chair in front of the television. On the television was an ashtray full of stubbed filters in a bed of ash. Beside it was a wineglass smeared with dregs of red wine. "I should've cleaned up," he said, picking up the glass and the ashtray and taking them to the kitchen. He returned and gathered up unread newspapers, books, a crumpled cardigan, a dressing gown which smelled as if it needed a wash, and put them down in a pile in a corner of the room. Then he stood over the pile with his hands on his hips, pleased that he had done something about all that mess. Then he gathered up cups and a dirty plate and took them to the kitchen, and opened a window and lit a cigarette. Then he looked into the fridge and recoiled, and said he would go to the corner shop and get us something to eat, or did I prefer a takeaway. I shrugged to say I was in his hands. Despite my months in England I had not tasted a takeaway of any kind, so I hoped that would be his choice. By such forced means I could then get a surreptitious taste of this famed dish. Before this matter could be resolved, the phone rang, and it was Rachel to ask if all had gone well, and the two of them stayed on the phone for twenty minutes, laughing too hard like the way I imagined people do at the beginning of a friendship. I wandered around the flat, looking into nooks and crannies, opening cupboards and doors, trying out the windows to see if they opened, locating the place where he worked and wrote, looking to see if I could recognize the place where I would sleep, and while I was about it, researching the possibility of clean sheets and warm bedding. Latif was still on the phone when I finished my little tour. My subtle and courteous investigations had failed to raise even a sniff of clean sheets. The place just did not smell as if there were clean sheets anywhere. I wondered whether in his pleasure and excitement—I could hear it in his voice—he would remember about going round the corner to get a takeaway. I only ever had a light supper, anyway, and I had Alfonso's towel with me if worse came to worst.